THROWING SHADE

MAGIC AFTER MIDLIFE

DEBORAH WILDE

te da media
vancouver

1

It's a truth universally acknowledged that angry women get shit done. On the Richter Scale of Midlife Simmering, I was a solid eight, meaning I'd already crossed twelve items off of my to-do list and it wasn't even 10:30AM.

As the librarian here at Chan Wilkins Shechtman LLP, I was researching some tedious historical legislation for one of the senior partners when my mojo was disrupted by Blake Cunningham, a husky blond Associate. He loomed over me like an inflatable tube man hawking discount cars, unleashing spittle and vitriol all over my desk as he informed me of a deadline I'd missed.

I'd fulfilled his last request three days ago, so if he'd stop speaking over me every time I asked for clarification, we could get to the bottom of this.

While I kept my expression neutral, ever the consummate professional, I eyed the fat law dictionary that sat out of reach on my desk, next to the *Book Wizard* mug that Sadie had given me last year for Mother's Day. Had I been an actual book wizard, I'd have telekinetically brained Blake with the heavy tome.

Murder hadn't been on my list for the day, but I'd been

extraordinarily productive this morning, so I was willing to pencil it in.

Alas, it was also a truth universally acknowledged that single moms wanting to keep their jobs didn't engage in such acts, no matter how justified. The chances of getting an all-female jury who'd acquit the defendant with high-fives while singing Aretha Franklin's "Think" were pretty much nonexistent.

Blake jabbed a finger in my face and I jerked my chair back, clenching my fists to keep from breaking the offending digit. My performance review was coming up and unlike some, I couldn't shit on people and still expect a raise. My track record needed to be stellar and it was, but Blake was higher in the firm's pecking order and matching his boorish behavior would cost me.

He finally took a breath and I jumped in.

"I'm unaware of any new assignment that you gave me. What are you referring to?"

"The email I sent you yesterday," he said, wiping spit from his face. "I need that Law on Remoteness for the Santos trial. I won't look bad because you can't be bothered to do your job."

I twisted my monitor around to show him my inbox. "I didn't receive any email from you. Please don't disparage my ability or work ethic."

He snorted. "You must have deleted it."

I pried my fingers off the screen. "Excuse me?"

"You think that because Cecilia Chan hired you, you get a free pass? There isn't a quota system for women here."

No, but there was one for assholes. To be fair, most of our lawyers were great, but every now and again, a toxic jackass showed up.

Someone knocked on my office door, and Blake opened it before I could to reveal an unfamiliar young woman.

Her cheerful smile indicated that her soul had yet to be

2

sucked out by this industry, while her bright eyes denoted that she hadn't yet started pulling longer hours than her male counterparts to prove herself.

"You're new, aren't you?" I said.

"Is it that obvious? Articling Student in the house." She held up a stack of periodicals. "I wasn't sure where you wanted these."

"Put them on the cart out there, please," I said, pointing into the library outside my office.

Blake ran a hand through his hair. "Hey, Addison. You know you can dump that on a paralegal, right?"

"It's good to familiarize myself with all aspects of the firm," she said. "Oh, Tamara was also wondering if the books she requested were in?"

My left eye twitched. I'd explained to the lawyer that the law volumes were on back order, but she persisted in asking constantly, like someone repeatedly hitting an elevator button to make it arrive faster. "Not yet. Still coming in on the same date."

"Okay, I'll drop these off then," she said, backing out, her high ponytail bobbing.

"Thanks," I said. "The procedures around here can take a while to get the hang of, but if you have any questions about the library, I'm happy to answer them."

"I appreciate that," she said.

Blake kept his sleazy smile on full wattage until Addison left, at which point it dropped like a power outage. "Look, I can let the secondary sources slide until tomorrow if you need to take your extended coffee breaks or play solitaire or whatever you do when no one's watching here, but get me that case law by end of day, Mara."

Wait. What?

Mara was the sixty-something administrative assistant who worked directly for Daniel Shechtman, and as the senior partner always joked, the real power around this place. Blake

3

had been at this firm for six months. Were all women over a certain age an interchangeable blob to this douchenozzle?

My skin was hot and itchy, my throat tight with a torrent of curses.

"I'm Miriam," I said, evenly.

"Yeah, so?"

"You called me Mara. You sent the email to the wrong person." I *could* just shove the law dictionary so far up his ass he tasted paper for a week. Or better still, follow the ancient Chinese practice of Lingchi, death by a thousand cuts. The classic tortures were the best.

Blake turned red and puffed out his chest like a blustering bagpipe. "Whatever. Get it done or I'll take this to HR," he said.

Chanting "performance review" like a mantra, I pasted a pleasant smile on my face. "You got it."

I'd have to stay late to get everything accomplished, so I fired off a quick text to my kid, grateful she was sixteen and self-sufficient, and pulled relevant law books off the walnut bookcases. I wanted to throw something or stomp between the stacks, but the idea of damaging a book in my collection was anathema and my heels sank into the thick carpet that absorbed sound.

Days like today, I felt like *I* was being absorbed, especially when, hours later, I had yet to see another person.

By three o'clock, my eyes swam from reading small print, so I grabbed the *Book Wizard* mug and headed into the staff kitchen for a much-needed caffeine jolt.

"Miriam!" Fahim, a bright-eyed and eager recent hire, flagged me down. "I just sent you an email requesting you pull work safe standards on containing cast-in-place concrete on construction sites."

"You mean, safety procedures for watching cement dry?"

He frowned. "Concrete and cement aren't the same thing."

Sighing, I cut him off before he could launch into an explanation. "I was kidding," I said gently.

"Oh. Good one." He sounded dubious.

I refrained from shaking my head. Law school had destroyed any sense of humor in our current batch of Associates. "I'll get what you need."

"Thank you."

The staff kitchen was fairly quiet, with only one person ahead of me for the cappuccino machine: Mara.

The machine clicked twice and burst into a loud hum, firing two thin streams of espresso into the mug.

"A double?" I raised my eyebrows. "That kind of day?"

"Every day is that kind of day around here." Mara patted a strand of gray hair back into her bun, watching the frothed milk dispense. "I blame my husband. If he hadn't been so supportive of me going back to work after our sons were born, I'd have enjoyed a long and leisured career as a trophy wife."

"Please. If you didn't have all the lawyers to boss around on a regular basis, life wouldn't have that same sparkle."

She rolled her eyes, then grinned. "How's my favorite librarian?"

"Eh." I took Mara's place at the machine, setting my cup under the nozzle and hitting the selection for an Americano. "Did you hear? Poor Blake suffers from acute myopia. Except with age not distance. He chewed me out for failing to follow instructions in an email that he'd sent to you."

"Ah. I wondered about that. Well, fair's fair, I guess. All those youngsters look alike to my feeble old brain," she said, with calculating shrewdness. "I hope I don't confuse him with someone else the next time he needs to see Daniel."

"That would be a pity." I grabbed my coffee.

"Wouldn't it, just?" Mara patted me on the shoulder. "Nolite te bastardes carborundorum."

I laughed. "Fake phrase, but good sentiment. To you as well."

The caffeine put a spring in my step as I returned to the library, and my work smile reached my eyes when I saw the visitor in my office.

"I bring you glad tidings. And food crack." My best friend, Judith Rachefsky, rubbed Vaseline on her red dry potter's hands, avoiding the wrist brace she wore for her carpal tunnel. It was the major downside of working with clay, along with constant smudges of dust across her black T-shirts and jeans.

A familiar brown bakery bag sat on my desk.

I inhaled the heavenly scent of my favorite zucchini chocolate chip muffin. My stomach growled and I shoved a piece in my mouth, sighing blissfully. "Thank you, o dealer mine."

She squirted out more petroleum jelly with a farting noise. "If I'd have known you'd be this grateful, I'd have insisted on house cleaning in payment."

"Always have a contract in place." I tore off some more of the muffin. "Today has not been fun. One of our junior lawyers accused me of being incompetent, discharged a half gallon of spit on my sweater, and topped it off by calling me Mara."

"Ouch." Judith got comfortable in my desk chair, tucking the small tube of cream into the pocket of her jean jacket. Balancing one cowboy boot heel on the ground, she pawed through my drawer until she triumphantly waved a letter opener. "Here's the plan. We lure him in to the men's room before he leaves and..." She made stabbing motions. "Then we prop him in a stall. No one will look for him till tomorrow. We'll have plenty of time to come back after hours to dispose of the body." She tapped her wrist brace. "No one will suspect me and I'll cover for you."

I picked up the scarf that had slid from the chair onto the

floor for the third time this afternoon. The rose print was beautiful, but the silk was a pain in the ass. "Not unless you've upped your lying game. Ten seconds of scowl from that border guard and you were confessing your two pairs of smuggled socks."

Jude scrunched up the back of her curly red hair with her hand. "To be fair, those guys are pros."

"Body disposal isn't necessary. I snitched to Mara."

Jude crossed herself, then stopped halfway through. "Oh, wait. I'm Jewish. So what's your resident blowhard got you doing?"

"Researching the Law on Remoteness."

She shuddered. "This is why you couldn't pay me to work a corporate job anymore."

"Yes, but you envy my cornucopia of medical and dental benefits." I pulled a paper napkin out of the bag and wiped my fingers.

"True." She poked one of her teeth. "I swear this one is being held together by crazy glue and a prayer. In penance for that depressing reminder, you can be my mid-afternoon entertainment break. Hmm. Since I doubt you have pasties on under that wrap dress, you'll have to amuse me some other way." She snapped her fingers. "I know. Let's check your dating profile."

"Let's not."

"Come on, Miri. I could use a laugh." She winked at me.

I twisted my shoulder-length dark hair up into a bun, and jammed a pen through it. "I deleted it, okay?"

"I'm sorry. I shouldn't have made fun of you. It's hard putting yourself out there. Believe me, I know."

"The emotional vulnerability of online dating in general is bad enough." I shuddered and sat on the edge of my desk. "But this was a nightmare."

"How so?"

"Two words for you, my friend: septuagenarian balls."

"Ewww." Judith shook her head. "That's so wrong on so many levels. You're attractive, you have all your own teeth, you're gainfully employed."

"Intelligent, funny…"

She snorted. "The two most prized qualities on dating sites."

I pushed up my boobs. "Great rack."

"True. We'll list that before the teeth."

"It won't help. The boob game out there is too strong. Plus, I'm forty-two and I have a kid. Thanks for playing." I beheld my little kingdom of books, covering such heart-pounding topics as construction law and application fraud. "I was so excited to turn forty. Finally, I could give zero fucks, free of all the BS that dragged me down in my youth. And that's true to an extent, but mostly I feel like I missed some Kafkaesque ceremony where I was presented with a pair of mom jeans, the number for the easy listening station on my FM dial, and the admonishment to 'go gentle into that good night.'"

"Where's the rage and rock 'n' roll when you need it?" Jude said.

"Oh, there's rage."

One of the paralegals waved at me from the library and I held up a finger, grabbing a memo off my printer to give to her.

"This should fix the login issues," I said, "but let me know if you're still having problems."

The woman thanked me and left.

"Don't give up. Forty is the new twenty," Jude said from my office, once more rooting through my desk drawer.

I reshelved some more law books. "Tell that to the men on the dating site. And why the hell would I want to be twenty again?"

"No aches or sags."

"True, but I earned my body. I *like* my body. Though the

one thing I do miss from that age? That life was in front of me and I could be anyone." I tilted my head, lost in contemplation, the book in my hand momentarily forgotten. "Forty isn't the new twenty, it's a fast track to invisibility and irrelevancy."

"You need a new game plan, honey. Quit your job and move to Spain." Jude shook the bakery bag with the rest of my muffin at me.

"Packing and downsizing would be so much extra work," I groused, putting the rest of the books away. "Honestly, it's not so bad here. Most of the time no one micromanages me, plus I wouldn't have that sweet, sweet health insurance to cover all the therapy my daughter would require for pulling her out of school. My little Hermione Granger does love her structured academic life."

"Sadie's adaptable and this job was only supposed to be temporary while you got on your feet after your divorce ten years ago. Go sling sangria." She held up my tube of lip gloss with a questioning look.

Walking back into my office, I nodded for her to go ahead and use it. "You're ludicrous. Maybe I just need a purpose. Oh. I could start volunteering."

She uncapped the tube. "Volunteering is good, but I'm not sure it would fulfill you. You need something that makes you feel powerful."

I ate the last piece of muffin, talking while chewing. "You mean empowered, and slinging sangria hardly fits the bill."

"It's a blurred line. You can't take control of your life, whether it's slinging sangria or running for Prime Minister, if you don't feel like you have the power to do so."

"That's free will. Choice." I peered hopefully into the empty muffin bag, then threw it into the trash.

"And your choices are limited when you don't think you have power. Thus limiting what you do and any further power you gain." Judith sniffed the lip gloss and recoiled. "Bubble gum? What are you, twelve?"

"It's Sadie's." I made a new to-do item on my phone to look into volunteering opportunities.

"Like that girl would use any scent other than grape with undertones of smash the patriarchy," Jude said.

I licked my lips. "Mmmm. Coffee and male tears."

"Bubble gum lip gloss will not get you laid, my friend."

"The lip gloss isn't the cause. It's been so long that my vagina took early retirement."

Judith tossed the gloss back in the drawer. "Did she get a nice severance package?"

"Not really. I forgot to buy batteries."

"That's it. We're going for drinks tonight. My treat. You can get loaded and I'll be your designated." Jude never drank if we went to the bar on Fridays, since it messed with her ability to wake up early on Saturday morning and get in some pottery time on her successful line of dishware, mugs, and teapots.

"Can't," I said. "I've got to finish up this research for Blake, then I should go home and spend quality time with my daughter."

"Your sixteen-year-old won't begrudge you a night out. Fun, Miri. Remember that?"

I pushed her out of my chair. "I have fun."

"Is that what we're calling putting everyone else in your life first and then ending up on the couch in your pjs exhausted from all your emotional labor?"

"Ah, but I chase it down with a lovely vintage."

Jude scraped at some clay under her nails. "Fun isn't a trendy abbreviation for functioning alcoholism."

"Another time. I promise."

Jude bit her lip, eyes troubled and downcast.

"What?"

She sighed. "I wasn't going to say anything but I've been

having some health problems and I could use someone to talk to."

I squeezed her hand. "What? Is it serious? Of course, I'll go out with you and..." At her smirk, I brandished the law dictionary menacingly. "You lying cow."

"A lying cow who is dead on in her assessment of you. Come on. Live a little."

"Live a little, Adele." My dad gave a lopsided grin and exaggerated hip wriggle as he beckoned Mom to come dance with him to Sinatra singing "Come Fly With Me." Mom threw her bright yellow dish glove at his chest, laughing and saying the last time he used that line she lost a really nice bra. I shuddered and rolled my eyes with the heavy disdain that only a fifteen-year-old could. It would be the last time I ever did.

I blotted my forehead with the back of my hand, the buzz of the air conditioning drilling into my temples.

"Mir?"

Blinking away the specter of the past, I smiled at Jude. "A drink sounds good."

My friend stood up, refastening her wrist brace. "I have pieces to glaze at the studio so once you've finished your overtime, meet me at Chambers."

With something to look forward to, my task went a lot easier. Blake got his case law and even thanked me stiffly. I replied with equal enthusiasm and headed out for that drink.

The nearby bar on the waterfront that all the lawyers went to on Fridays after work wasn't somewhere I'd frequent in my free time, but Chambers had one big plus: Jackie, the bartender, was generous in her pours. She said that I deserved the top up after dealing with some of my co-workers.

Sadly, Jackie wasn't there tonight and Jude had yet to arrive. I politely waited my turn, fiddling with my sapphire engagement ring that I now wore on my right hand, but after ten minutes of being ignored by the new guy tending bar I got more forceful, waving and saying "excuse me" every time he got into my orbit.

Nothing.

I wrote my name in a spill of water from the pitcher on the bar, watching the letters dissipate, beyond done.

Life was like a night sky where every decision was a star winking into existence, some a faint pulse, others so beautifully luminous that we continually oriented ourselves by them even years later. Trying to order a drink was an ordinary action that I didn't think twice about, barely visible in my personal constellation. Too bad I'd forgotten that even the most seemingly inconsequential choice could suddenly explode like a supernova, leaving you desperate to survive the blast.

2

"Is this place always so crowded?" A handsome man around my age with short blond hair and an easygoing smile, who I'd never seen before, pushed in next to me.

"Well, it's Friday, which means the law crowd requires booze to help them molt out of their human skin." I grabbed a napkin and wiped off my fingers.

"Unfair. I'm a lawyer," he said.

"Then you know the drill."

He gave a shocked laugh. "Don't hold back or anything."

"I'm off the clock, as is my filter."

The bartender spun in front of us to grab some sliced lemons and my new acquaintance flagged him down.

"What can I get you?" the bartender said.

"Whiskey, neat." The blond man turned to me. "And you?"

"Gin and tonic."

"Right away." The bartender pulled out two glasses.

"Thank you." My pleasure at finally getting some booze was short-lived. I'd been standing here for ages, but this guy waltzed up and got served in seconds? I stabbed a swizzle stick into my napkin.

It wasn't his fault though, so I made amiable small talk with him until we got our beverages, at which point he invited me to continue our chat.

Alex was a divorced property lawyer with no kids who'd moved to Vancouver from Alberta. We joked about a couple judges that were notoriously hard-assed, and he praised a keynote speech that one of the partners at my firm had given at a conference here in town.

"Yeah, I heard it was really well received." I squinted at his shirt, not sure what I was seeing.

Alex sighed. "Okay, go on and ask. You've been staring at it this entire time."

"What exactly is on your tie?" I squinted again. "I can make out men's boxers, but I can't see what's printed on them."

He pulled the tie out for me to inspect.

Frowning, I shook my head. "Scales of justice? I don't get it."

"They're legal briefs."

I snorted gin and tonic out my nose. "That is the nerdiest thing I've ever seen. You should be held in contempt."

"My paralegal assured me it was business casual appropriate."

"Your paralegal is a smart person who wants a nice year-end bonus."

"You think?" He frowned at the tie, then winked at me.

Alex was fun, but my head was pounding from all the competing scents of aftershave in a packed space, and really, I was only here for my no-show friend.

Fifty bucks said Jude was still at her studio. Her heart was in the right place, but she was prone to losing track of time when she worked on her art. It still kind of bugged me, especially since tonight had been her idea, but it was part of the package of who my best friend was and I'd mostly learned to live with it. Maybe if I had something I was passionate about, I'd be the same way. Nah, I'd still consider being on time late.

I grabbed my purse from under my chair and thanked Alex for his important role in procuring my booze.

He tapped my empty glass. "You're sure I can't convince you, stay for another?"

"I'm sure, but it was great meeting you."

I paused outside the bar to text Judith and tell her not to bother coming. *Glaze away without guilt. I'm leaving. xo*

The bar noise had fallen away to a dull murmur, leaving me alone under a streetlight with the water and the dark press of trees in the distance at Stanley Park for company.

I headed away from the Convention Center, a stunning sustainable building with a living roof composed of local plants. Our office tower was only a couple blocks away, so I cut across Jack Poole Plaza toward the fountain containing the Olympic Cauldron, a five-piece glass and steel structure resting in a shallow pool.

When Vancouver had hosted the games, the flames on top were lit with the Olympic torch by hockey legend Wayne Gretzky. Nowadays the Cauldron boasted fire only on special occasions. Usually, like tonight, the steel beams glowed a deep blue.

I stuffed my cardigan in my leather bag, enjoying walking in the fresh air on this warm June night and dreaming of slipping off my heels after a long day.

The occasional tail light streamed past up ahead on West Hastings Street, the rose gold glass tower where the firm was located, a mere block and a half away.

Footsteps behind me cut through the silence.

I sped up, rummaging through my purse for my keys to lace through my knuckles. This was a good part of town. Mostly. But it was well past dark and there was no one else around. My shoulders tensed as my follower sped up and my other hand went for my phone.

"Miriam, wait," Alex called, twenty feet away.

I turned, pausing. He'd seemed nice. Surely he wouldn't—?

He held up my silk scarf. "You left this at the bar."

I relaxed. Not all men were dickheads. We knew mutual people in our industry and besides, serial killers would think twice about wearing that tie. I walked over and retrieved the scarf, tying it around my purse strap. "Thanks."

He stuffed his hands in his pockets. "How about you let me buy you dinner in thanks for my gallantry?"

"I think I'd get the better end of the deal there."

"Doubt it. You're the first woman I've really connected with since my divorce. I'd like to see where this could lead." His voice lowered when he said that. He didn't make my pulse race, but it was nice having someone attracted to me who didn't qualify for the senior's special at Denny's.

I bit my lip, rolling on to the outside of one heel. Eating warmed up leftovers at home wasn't an exciting prospect and while things wouldn't go past dinner tonight, maybe this was the start of my new game plan? He had made me laugh, which was a plus.

A trio of young women passed us, arms linked. The one in the middle animatedly recounted a story, her friends helpless with laughter, and all three radiating easy, inescapable joy.

Alex blatantly checked them out, a smile playing at the edges of his lips.

I. Was. Standing. Right. Here. So much for this guy. "Am I the low-hanging fruit of getting laid?"

Alex blinked and opened his mouth like he was going to protest, but with a shrug, his entire demeanor changed. "Aren't you? A middle-aged woman drinking alone on a Friday night and happy for attention?"

I rubbed the heel of my palm against the sting in my chest. "Not happy any longer. You can leave now."

He grabbed my arm. "I don't think so."

I froze, every self-defense move deleting itself from my brain.

Alex twisted my arm up behind my body, the violence of the action knocking the air from my lungs. Fear sliced through me like a knife, shackling me in place, and my assailant tightened his grip on me, escape impossible.

I screamed, but my throat had closed up and I only managed a strangled *eep*.

The world froze for an instant and the image of a closed door manifested in my mind. No. I panicked, scrambling at the ground. I couldn't go there. I'd sworn I wouldn't.

Alex dragged me into the alley at the end of the block. I tried to fight back and escape, but I felt disassociated from my body, watching myself be helplessly carried off as if by the tide.

I kicked him in the shin, but he barely flinched.

The knob on that door in my mind glowed, tempting me with promises of safety which I did my best to ignore. Siren calls always sounded beautiful before they crashed you against the rocks.

"I thought we'd have time for some fun first," he said, "but I'm bored of this game."

I was a game and a not-even-entertaining one at that?

My ears filled with a loud whooshing sound and the hard black ball of rage that had been tamped down under years of pleasant smiles, shrugging off slights, and losing myself bit by bit, shattered. A churning, thrashing wave surged up from my depths, rushing out to fill every inch of me. It crackled the air, charging it with a dangerous sharpness.

This was my chance to take up space. Make a fuss.

Reclaim myself or risk disappearing altogether.

I stomped on Alex's instep and yanked free. Grabbing the

small aerosol can of maximum strength hair spray in my purse, I blasted him with the sharp citrus-smelling spray. Pity mace was illegal in Canada.

"Take thaaa—"

Alex swore. He made a circle with his index finger and thumb, then shot them out in pistol formation.

An unseen force pried my hand open and I dropped the bottle, which rolled into the shadows and under a dumpster that had been pushed away from the wall.

He—what—fuuuuuck....

Eyes red and watery, Alex caught me by the throat, slowly crushing my windpipe.

I gasped, losing precious breath, and frantically scrabbled for purchase on tiptoe while his shadow asphyxiated mine in a gross parody of the real thing, the bare bulb above a back door spotlighting this deadly pantomime.

My scream was barely a whisper.

Images rushed through my mind: Eli's sweet smile the first time he asked me out, me holding a newborn Sadie against my chest... even work earlier took on a nostalgic air. A wave of dizziness rushed through me, my lungs straining for oxygen, while black dots danced at the edge of my vision.

Dying was not the new game plan.

I closed my eyes and returned to the door in my head. I'd run out of options. Gritting my teeth, I threw it wide open, a weight I'd carried for years lifting off my chest. The door slammed shut behind me with a startling finality, but for better or for worse, I'd stepped through to the other side.

My shadow rose up, independent of any contact with me. Suddenly, I was in two places at once: paralyzed in my physical body and inside my shadow, a bouncy, fluid entity that had weight and substance.

Seen through the shadow, the world took on a green overlay like some type of night vision, but all looked normal through my real eyes. It was vertiginous seeing two versions of the world simultaneously.

Alex froze, craning his head up to look at my shadow, which hovered above him. In his shock, he slackened his grip. "You're not a sap."

That was an oddly old-fashioned insult.

"Nope." I made a weak fist, feeling my shadow do the same. Giddy, I hopped from one foot to the other. *Punch him in his fat trouty mouth.*

My shadow had a hell of a left cross.

Alex's head snapped back. His faint stubble rasped *my* knuckles as if I'd hit him myself, and my physical hand stung.

Frowning, I flexed my fingers, gingerly touching a scraped knuckle.

My shadow skittered up a wall.

With another specific hand gesture, Alex pinned my arms against my sides, magically glued my feet to the dirty concrete, and sealed my mouth shut.

I thrashed against my invisible bindings, my heart thundering against my ribs.

The night vision flared stronger for a moment. My shadow. Right. A hysterical laugh burbled up.

It dropped down on Alex like a net. He punched his way out, every blow knocking me double, and the shadow jumped off him, spinning mid-air to land in a boxer's crouch and launch a flurry of hits.

The magic binding on my feet disappeared, ratcheting down my panic a notch. If I got the upper hand, I could free myself.

Each meaty thwack shuddered through me, my actual knuckles split and aching. I was a bookworm, not a boxer, but my shadow was a warrior and through it, I hungered to make Alex pay.

This *thing* had picked me out as prey and he'd intended to

leave me broken or dead because he thought I was weak. Irrelevant.

Plot twist. I was no longer a shadow of my former self.

I was the shadow master.

Alex made another hand gesture, but my shadow kicked, sweeping low, and he tripped forward, breaking the magic paralysis on me.

"The game has changed, asshole," I said, scooting behind the crooked dumpster. It smelled like Eli's hockey bag: baked-in sweat and stinky feet dipped in Satan's farts. "Having fun? Because I'm enjoying myself immensely."

"Not for much longer, bitch." Alex fired more magic, but I pressed tight behind the dumpster, unhurt, because he required a line of sight to attack me directly, though my shadow was still vulnerable.

I swallowed against the nausea creeping up my esophagus from maintaining both sets of perceptions and screwed my eyes shut so that only the night vision remained.

A few feet away, Alex and my shadow circled each other warily. Behind his blue eyes lurked a deep malevolence and my skin crawled in revulsion. He feinted left, faked me out, and hit me with his magic, forcing my shadow to throw itself against the broken edge of a mirror sticking out of the trash container.

I screamed and clapped a hand against my shoulder, warm blood oozing through my fingers and onto my torn shirt.

A thin gap of moonlight streamed through the shadow's shoulder.

With a snap, I was expelled from that inky form onto my ass, narrowly avoiding a questionable puddle, a hand still pressed against the wound. Exhausted and in pain, I couldn't even stagger to my feet to save myself.

Jaw tight, Alex stalked toward me, a deadly glint in his eyes.

A black mesh swam up from the ground and enveloped me. I no longer cast a shadow. Instead, it cloaked me, its edges blurring into the rest of the darkness.

"Where'd you go?" Alex cautiously felt out with a foot.

I rolled sideways onto my back, narrowly missing coming in contact with him. I brushed my finger against the mesh's velvety softness and a tingle rippled through me.

Alex peered behind the dumpster. "Where are you?" he growled.

I hugged my knees to my chest with one arm, the other applying pressure to the injury, certain either my raspy breaths or the pounding of my heart would give me away, clinging to this magic invisibility by my fingertips.

My brain screamed at me to finish this, because letting Alex escape would be more dangerous than the actual attack, but the idea of killing him made me shudder.

It's him or you, Feldman.

Swallowing a sour disgust, I tried to stand up, still cloaked, but only got as far as my hands and knees before sighing in defeat, my arms wobbling. I couldn't even if I'd wanted to. I had nothing left.

Casting one final worried glance around, Alex swore and hurried away, periodically glancing back until he left the alley.

Tapped out, I had no choice but to let him leave. The black mesh flickered, holes punched in both my shield and the life I'd so carefully built. This wasn't over. The past had taught me that much.

I took a ragged breath. Forty wasn't the new twenty, because if it was, I would have run home and hidden behind locked doors, denying what had happened. However, I was older and wouldn't shy away from the truth.

The magic that I'd kept hidden for almost thirty years had been unleashed once more.

Shaking, I sat up, caught on a knife's edge between fear

and exhilaration. For most of my life, I'd been convinced that using this power would be signing my own death warrant, but tonight I'd go home and hug my daughter, breathing in her coconut shampoo and laughing when she made her inevitable crack about being taller than me. All because of…

Shadows littered the ground, mine as ordinary as the others. For now, at least.

The bottom dropped out of my stomach. I'd made a choice in order to survive, but I had no doubt that the shock-waves from this supernova would hit hard, fast, and deadly.

Behind me, my shadow kissed both its biceps, then held a fist up in victory.

3

I HAD QUESTIONS ABOUT THE SUDDEN RESURGENCE of my powers and about letting Alex go. Many, many questions, starting with, "How the fuck?" followed by, "Why the fuck?" and topped off with, "Am I fucked?"

I hit the wrong button on the fob twice before I unlocked my car and got inside.

How could I have let my powers out? I'd been so careful for so long, lived under the radar, staying far from the magic community despite the slow and methodical shriveling of my soul. It was the price of a peaceful life.

Nervously, I jerked the car into gear and hit the gas.

Had Alex known that I was one of the Banim Shovavim, the "rebellious children" born to Lilith and Adam? Our kind was rare, but our magic was infamous.

Was word already getting around?

I wove in and out of the lanes, cursing every vehicle on the road going at a snail's pace.

Was Sadie safe? Had I made the worst mistake of my life by choosing to walk through that door and unleash these abilities? I didn't just have myself to think about. It wasn't like I could run like I had the last time. Much as I hated to admit it, the past cast a much longer shadow than I could escape.

I closed my eyes at a stop sign. Shadow master, what a joke.

Blowing through a red light in my dash back to East Vancouver, I finally pulled crookedly up to the curb in front of home and unclipped the seatbelt that had been pressing against my shoulder wound.

"Sades?" I shut the front door behind me and kicked off my heels, relieved that my voice sounded normal.

My daughter's bedroom door creaked opened upstairs. "Yeah?"

"I'm home and—" I started for the stairs to get a hug, but at the sight of my banged-up and bloody reflection, stopped. Yikes, I was lucky no one had stopped me on the way to or from my car.

"What, Mom?"

"Nothing, sweetheart."

"Okay. I'm going to bed. 'Night. Love you."

"Love you, too." I tossed my keys into a red glazed ceramic bowl in the foyer that Judith had made me, and dumped my purse on the ground, hissing as I pulled my shirt free of the bloody glue plastering it to my skin. The gash on my shoulder throbbed and my movements were stiff, but it was scabbing over.

Still, I liberally doused it in a topical antibiotic, slathering the stuff over the bruises on my neck as well, which hurt more than my side. Under the crappy bathroom light, they were a sickly shade of yellow, interrupted by five purple fingerprints.

When puberty finally kicked in at fourteen and my magic manifested, I'd named my shadow Delilah, after the woman who brought down Samson, the strongest Israeli warrior. Oh, to have the invincible conviction of youth. Mine had been shattered years before because of magic, but I'd rebuilt my life, fighting to regain some sense of security, which now lay in shredded tatters.

While Delilah had no senses or ability to feel pain, I did. If she took a punch, it was my body the injury translated to, and she'd been thrown about pretty roughly tonight. My poor shoulder was really tender. I shook my head, wincing, and headed for the kitchen, where I swallowed a couple painkillers, grabbed an ice pack from the freezer, and slapped it on my shoulder.

Delilah shot double middle fingers at the beige void I lived in, but I ignored her, my brain doom-scrolling through all the ways that having released my magic could go wrong.

All my fears notwithstanding, I danced through the rooms, punch drunk. It was as if my entire body had been cramped up and I'd finally stretched out those muscles, leaving a delicious ache and a deep sense of satisfaction.

The house hadn't undergone the same radical shift as the rest of my universe. Each room was still painted in a sensible light taupe, Sadie's laptop and homework dominated half of the dining room table, and a jumble of pillows were thrown on the plush sofa next to a folded knit blanket. Nothing too messy, but not anal retentive in its tidiness. Nice and average.

Sinking onto the couch, I pushed aside a few pieces of the Broadway posters jigsaw puzzle that I'd been beating my head against. A blobby red and blue piece that I'd picked up and discarded about a dozen times fell off the coffee table, and from my weird angle when I retrieved it, I suddenly knew where it fit. I popped it in to the middle; then, convinced I had this section solved, tried three more pieces.

None of them worked. I swept them onto my puzzle mat with a sigh. Slow and methodical was the only way to succeed.

If the universe cut me a break and my actions tonight went unnoticed, then I'd tuck away the memory of how good it had felt, and never use magic again. How could I? Magic was dangerous, full stop. I cared too much about my kid, my job, and myself to risk it.

My fingers drifted up to the bruises on my neck. However, I couldn't in good conscience allow Alex to remain free and prey on any other woman. He'd picked me out because Chambers was frequented by Sapiens—powerless humans who had no idea that magic existed—and he thought I couldn't fight back.

He was a predator who had to be stopped, but how could I do so and keep my magic under wraps? If I went to the Vancouver Police Department to lodge a complaint, I'd be putting them in jeopardy.

With an ex-husband on the force, I'd heard a lot about his various colleagues. Hell, we'd had a bunch over for BBQs when we were still married, so I could easily reach out to one. And as a cop's wife, I'd accepted the danger that Eli faced every day on the job, but I couldn't knowingly send some unwitting officer up against someone like Alex.

I tossed the ice pack next to the jigsaw puzzle. The ideal solution would be to report Alex to an Ohrist on the force, but how would I find one? Most if not all of the cops were Sapiens, because Sapiens made up most of humanity.

Breaking the global population down by size, Ohrists, those whose magic involved light and life energy, would be a tennis ball to Sapiens' basketball, with Banim Shovavim a marble in the dusty corner of the gym.

There was no handy way for me to differentiate the three types. People were people and unless they busted out their magic, I couldn't categorize them further.

Shoving a pillow under my head, I stretched out and stared up at the ceiling. Would it be better to open Eli's eyes to the existence of magic? Had I inadvertently denied him an important tool that could keep him safe or would the truth be too unbelievable, explained away as Sapiens always did? And when was the last time I'd dusted my overhead light?

Even if I was successful, would Eli see me as an abomination? I scrubbed my hand over my face, none the wiser as to what I should do, and wishing there weren't gaps in my magic knowledge. My parents hadn't taught me much beyond the basics, my childhood had been spent in a remote part of northern British Columbia with very few Ohrists, and once I'd moved to Vancouver, I'd kept my distance from all that for my own safety.

When it came to magic crimes, Ohrists policed themselves. These Lonestars followed a Wild West mentality, taking the law into their own hands, where their prime directive wasn't justice, but ensuring that magic remained hidden. I laughed bitterly. Serve and protect only applied to their own interests.

Could I find the Lonestars here in town and anonymously report Alex? I'd have to poke around at least briefly in the hidden magic places around the city, but Vancouver had a large enough Ohrist population that it wasn't as if everyone was on familiar terms.

That was one of the reasons I'd felt safe moving here to live with my mom's Sapien cousin, Goldie Feldman, as a teen.

I made a new to-do list in my head, my anal retentive heart happy to have actionable bullet points: find a magic establishment, get the contact information for the Lonestars, turn them on to Alex, and then close the door once more on all magic. Any interaction with the Lonestars would be anonymous and limited.

I evaluated all the risks, then nodded. This was a smart and sensible plan.

A weight settled in the middle of my chest and I hugged a cushion, finding my errant shade crouching in the corner of the ceiling. When animated, she had a very limited sentience, fueled and controlled by our psychic bond.

The nausea of the double vision slowly subsiding, I hooked Delilah's fingers over the picture rail, hanging off like a rock climber before dropping her to the ground. She turned insubstantial, her re-engagement a soft purr against my back, and I closed my eyes, committing the sensation to a cherished memory.

Tonight would forever be memorialized as my magic re-awakening. Magic re-deflowering? It was a lot more memorable than the five-minute wonder of my sexual deflowering, where I'd stared at the guy's digital alarm clock for the entire thing, while Marvin the Martian's voice in my head insisted that there was supposed to be an earth-shattering ka-boom.

I wasn't going to use my powers in the long term, but until I'd dealt with the Alex problem, it was good to have all the available tools in my toolbox—and know how to use them, since a lot of details about my magic use were fuzzy.

After I put on pj's, I bundled under my covers, at ease for the first time tonight. My bedroom was the one place I'd allowed myself to indulge in whimsy—the closest I came to magic. A mural of wildflowers covered one wall, courtesy of one of Jude's artist friends, while the other three were kissed with a lilac blush. My cream tufted headboard edged in silver complemented the cream curtains and matching tufted bench at the foot of the bed.

I readjusted the duvet cover with its dizzying lush blue and purple swirls and reached for my phone off the bedside table. Damn, I'd missed an earlier message from Jude, saying she'd been held up but was still coming.

Me: *You up?*

She didn't respond. Oh well. I'd see her at brunch tomorrow.

I reached out to turn off the light, then froze when a garbage can clattered to the pavement in the back lane. All at once, the old chill crept up my spine. Had they come at last for me?

Don't be stupid. I breathed in and out, calming myself down, then peered out between a crack in the curtains. Nothing was amiss.

"Argh!" Punching my pillow flat, I tried to sleep. When that proved elusive, I opened our latest book club pick, a Work of Great Literary Importance that was so far up its own ass, no less than three old white male reviewers had called it "transcendental."

I would have rather read a good mystery but that was far too low-brow for the women in my club. I'd have to resort to my normal M.O. before the meeting this Thursday: google the most obscure academic article vaguely related to the book's theme, and drop it in during our discussion while I rage drank shitty rosé because I kept going back and acting like I had something to prove.

It was one thing to behave responsibly, but did it have to extend to investing emotional energy in this type of a situation? I wasn't even friends anymore with the person who'd first invited me, because she'd moved and we'd drifted apart. So what if my fellow book clubbers were unhappy with my decision? I'd never see them again and I didn't have to be Miss Congeniality for everyone. I tossed the book onto the bedside table.

If one positive thing came out of tonight's shit show, it was my resolve to quit book club and be rid of the totalitarian regime of Military Marsha, the de facto head of the group. Maybe it wasn't the ultimate in empowerment, but baby steps were still steps.

At some point I crashed, but when I woke up my brain felt like sludge and I lay there wondering how soon I could go back to sleep. Groaning, I kicked off the covers and dragged my butt into the bathroom, slathering on the concealer and foundation to hide the bags under my eyes.

My neck still looked like it had gotten in a fight with a meat tenderizer and lost, so I basted it in arnica cream and gingerly slid on a soft mock turtleneck T-shirt in a deep blue, gritting my teeth against the stiff burn in my shoulders. A vise gripped my chest, the memories of the attack sucking all the air from the room, and I gripped the bathroom sink, breathing slowly and reminding myself that I wasn't a victim. I'd survived Alex and I'd survive letting my magic loose. Once he was off the streets, my powers would be right back where they belonged, safely behind closed doors again.

I gave a confidence boosting chin nod at my reflection in the mirror. "How you doin', you supernatural siren?" Ew. I flung my hair back with a sultry pout. "Meet the Queen of the Night." I wrinkled my nose. Ah. I jumped into a crouch, fingers extended like they were a gun. "Magic mother-fuckahhhhh!"

Wow, no, that was… I blew my bangs out of my eyes, glancing around to make sure Sadie hadn't caught me.

With that out of my system, I pulled out a pair of capris, narrowing my eyes at my closet. Before I could overthink it, I stepped in and shut the door. Due to the lack of light, I didn't cast a shadow and I couldn't do shit. I'd been curious if that had changed, but I still required a point source of light to animate Delilah.

Still, this experiment had a better outcome than the last time I shut myself in a closet. I shuddered at the memory of the wet kiss I'd gotten from Dan Simon's fish lips when I was twelve. Seven Minutes in Heaven had been a disappointing lesson in false advertising.

Stepping out into my bedroom, I fished an elastic from my pocket, pulled my hair into a low ponytail, and headed downstairs to find a crazy ringmaster complete with a purple velvet coat, top hat, wide-legged striped pants, and thick black eyeliner circles around her eyes, eating cereal at the kitchen counter.

I removed an empty carton of milk from the fridge and held it up. "You know, we got rid of your sister for lesser infractions."

"Yeah, but she was one crazy bitch," Sadie joked back through a mouthful of Shreddies.

"This from the kid who looks like an escapee from Ringling Brothers Asylum." I squashed the carton and unlocked the kitchen door to toss it into the recycling container on the back porch, doing my best to move normally so Sadie wouldn't wonder what had happened to me.

My sixteen-year-old heaved a sigh that carried all the weight of the world. "Ringling Brothers? Geez, Mother. This insane mannequin only performs in the finest of netherworld circuses. Give my cosplays more credit."

"The milk." I tugged on the short blonde wig hiding her black straight hair.

She pushed my hand away and adjusted the wig. "Fine. I'll go buy more, but you need to give me money."

I grimaced. "You're going to go dressed like that, aren't you?"

She shot me an angelic smile and I pushed the knife block out of her reach.

"Ha. Ha." Sadie rinsed out the bowl and put it in the dishwasher. "Tell Aunt Jude to play her next Scrabble move already. I've been waiting three days."

"I will. Take five bucks from my purse." I swallowed a couple of painkillers, flinching from the movement of putting the bottle back in the cupboard.

"You okay?"

"Yup." Banim Shovavim manifested their magic in puberty. I'd been watching Sadie closely for years, but to my relief she didn't show any signs, and since she was now sixteen, we'd probably dodged that bullet. The magic often skipped generations.

"Mom, you're spacing."

31

I poured myself a coffee, dumping in a ton of sugar to compensate for the lack of milk. "Sorry, Sades. What?"

She held up my wallet. "I said, could I have twenty instead? Nessa wants to go for dim sum later."

"Is Ah Ma going?"

My daughter busied herself searching through my wallet. "Perhaps."

Busted. If her grandmother was taking her and her cousin to eat, she'd be treating the kids.

"Five bucks," I said. "You want cash, go work in the coal mines."

"Like my poor sister?"

"Yes, she got paid double time as a canary." I swatted Sadie's butt. "No more extortion today and please wear Ah Ma appropriate clothing because you know she'll phone me about it."

"Of course, Dad's her prince. Ooh, how about I extort him?"

"Totally acceptable." I hugged her tightly, wrinkling my nose at the sickly sweet stench of baby powder from her off-gassing wig. "Be safe. Be smart. No headphones if you're walking alone." I kissed the top of her head. "You're my joy and my delight, kid. Love you."

"Blech. Your perimenopause is making you emotion vomit again." She squirmed free. "Go away now, but be sure to give Jude my message."

I would have, except Judith never showed.

4

At first, I thought that I'd missed her because I'd gotten held up in construction on the way to our brunch place on the beach, but our regular hostess assured me that my friend hadn't arrived.

I nursed my coffee, holding off on ordering until Jude got there, but after forty-five minutes of her not returning any texts or calls, my appetite was gone. Yes, Jude often got lost in her work, but our brunches were sacrosanct. She'd never been late to one.

After checking in with a mutual friend of ours who hadn't spoken to Jude in a couple of weeks and had no idea where she was, I paid up and drove over to her workshop, every single rut in the road sending a fresh wave of hell through my neck and shoulder.

The iconic four-story warehouse at 1000 Parker Street was crowded with studios of varying sizes. Smaller ones housed painters, jewelers, and photographers, while the larger rooms were rented by furniture makers and re-uphol-sterers.

Every November it was the main hub of the East Side Culture Crawl, a massive event where all the artists threw open their galleries in hopes of making holiday sales. Food trucks would set up outside and the place took on a carnival air, people packed elbow to elbow, but today it was quiet.

As I headed to the entrance, my phone rang, but it was just a recorded message from Sadie's school about the final PAC meeting of the year, so I dismissed the call. I'd been an active member of the Parent Advisory Council when my daughter was in elementary school, much like I'd volunteered for endless bake sales and to chaperone field trips. High school was a whole other ball game. Let some other poor schmuck step up, I'd served my time. I'd even performed a mock ceremony in which I'd passed the torch of making her own lunches over to Sadie at the start of grade eight. Eli declared it was hilarious, Sadie, not so much.

Weaving through the maze of empty halls on the first floor, though, my amusement at the memory quickly faded under my worry for Jude.

Rows of narrow windows lit the high-ceilinged corridor in the arts collective, bathing the space in a flat light that diffused all shadows. I couldn't raise Delilah, but I did pull my cloaking over me, the world once more viewed through a black mesh.

All right. My animated shadow required a hard edge, but the cloaking worked under various lighting conditions. I added this knowledge to my stockpile, my librarian side delighted with each fact that I re-confirmed, even if this was all temporary.

An artist stepped out of a studio, pushed up her welder's mask, and wandered toward the water fountain, scrolling on her phone.

I resisted the urge to get out of her way and held my ground until she knocked into me, and looked up startled. I dropped the invisibility after she'd blinked once in confusion.

"I'm sorry," I said.

"No, that was me. I really didn't see you." She held up her phone. "Damn addictions."

We exchanged a couple more very Canadian apologies and continued on our separate ways. The cloaking didn't prevent anyone from bumping into me, though she'd rationalized it as her being zoned out.

All Sapiens had a natural perception filter that glossed over magical things, even people literally appearing out of nowhere.

I jogged up the stairs and poked my head into Judith's neighbor's door. Harley was a painter specializing in Van Gogh-esque acrylics, his studio floor stained in an explosion of color.

He stood next to a large canvas on an easel, mixing white paint into a bright yellow blob with a metal palette knife, a slash of blue tangled in his beard, and death metal audible through his headphones.

I waved my hands and he pulled out an earbud, a paintbrush between his teeth.

"Hi, Harley. Have you seen Judith this morning?" I said.

He shook his head.

"Do you know what time she left last night?"

He removed the paintbrush, accidentally flicking a drop onto his cheek. "She wasn't here."

"Are you sure?"

"Positive. Another potter on the fourth floor came down looking for her."

I frowned. Jude had lied to me? Why? She'd been my best friend since university and my shoulder to cry on through my divorce, while I'd supported her through her mother's dementia.

You misjudged Alex, a dark voice in the back of my head whispered. I shook it off. No, this wasn't the same thing, but lie or not, where was she?

My car keys were already in my hand, but randomly

driving around in a panic wouldn't help. Thanking Harley, I ran through the most logical possibilities. What if she was in her studio but something had happened to her?

Jude had keys to my place, and I had ones for her townhouse but not for her workspace. I tried the knob, which was locked, but the lights on either side of her door gave me a magical idea.

I rubbed my earlobe. Using my magic for this couldn't hurt, could it? Especially if it helped find Jude. I decided it was safe enough. However, breaking in to Jude's studio would be a gross invasion of privacy. What if there was a perfectly innocent explanation for her disappearance, and I pissed her off by nosing around in her business?

On the other hand, how would she find out? One peek and I'd go. If she was inside lying in a coma, then I'd lie about how I found her and be grateful that I'd gotten to her in time.

Situational ethics were a necessary evil.

Glancing around to ensure no one was watching, I let Delilah slip free to slide through the crack.

The bottom of the door scraped against my actual back as the shadow wriggled under. I laughed, incredulous, and as if punishing me for my second of doubt, the shadow got stuck like Winnie the Pooh in Rabbit's doorway. Oh, bother. I willed her to move, but nothing happened. Scowling, I sucked my hips and butt in, feeling Delilah tighten in response.

She popped out on the other side and I gasped.

The studio had been trashed.

Tools spilled off metal shelving, sealed containers holding glazes were dumped on their sides in half-congealed puddles, plastic-wrapped packages of clay had been torn open, and Jude's electric kiln was knocked off its base onto the floor. All of it was clearly viewed through that green night vision, but there was no sign of my friend.

Delilah trailed her fingers over the long table running the length of the long narrow room, anchored at one end by an industrial sink. Nestled amongst broken pieces of unglazed pottery was a crudely-made featureless head and a few misshapen arms.

The window at the far end was intact and the door was locked. This wasn't Jude having a tantrum and destroying her art, someone had broken in and targeted her. It felt like a message, but from who, and what did they want?

I ran back to my car, cutting through downtown to get across town to Jude's townhouse in Kitsilano. Years ago, this west side neighborhood had been hippie central, but you'd never know it from all the boutiques and restaurants lining Fourth Avenue now. Jude and I spent a lot of time here, but right now every passing block amped the sharp edge of fear inside me.

I tried every key on my keyring, growing more frantic until I found the one for her front door and let myself in to her dim foyer. "Jude? You home?"

A quick search proved that she wasn't. I didn't see the purse she'd had yesterday, her keys or her phone, nor did I find the clothes she'd been wearing. I flicked off the light, throwing her unmade bed and explosion of laundry spilling out from the hamper onto the floor into darkness. This wasn't another attack, just the way her bedroom always looked.

Spinning around, I sprinted into her tiny office, smiling wistfully at the three colorful ceramic mugs stained with tea dregs sitting on her desk. Judith was meticulous in crafting her pottery, but equally as insistent that the pieces then be well-used and loved. I grabbed the laptop shelved with her books, its gray "spine" barely noticeable, which she always hid there when she left the house. Unfortunately, the computer was password protected and the calendar on the back of the office door was a bust.

Photos of Jude with various family and friends crowded the bookcases. I traced a finger over the one of her with Sadie and me on the ferry to Ellis Island last year, then stilled. What if she hadn't gotten my message, so she'd shown up at the bar and run into Alex? If he was preying on women of a certain age, she'd have been an attractive target. I slammed my hand against the shelf. I should have phoned her last night and made sure she had gotten home.

Distracted and unsure of what to do next, I left the office and collided with a body coming out of the guest bedroom.

A five-foot-ten male with an Elvis pompadour and a stocky torso stood there, his leopard-print robe open revealing tighty-whities. Talk about chiseled features. His skin was smooth as silk, the unnatural color of a red cartoon heart and free from any pores or blemishes.

I blinked in disbelief. No way. He could not be made of clay. And yet, that's exactly what he was.

He brandished a bottle of bourbon menacingly. "Who are you?"

"You're a golem." The ground felt like quicksand under my feet and I wasn't sure it would ever be solid again. Jude had magic?

"What gave it away, Sherlock?" He snapped chunky fingers at me. "Name, toots."

"Miri," I replied, too stunned not to. "And you?"

"Emmett." He studied me with a lascivious look from over the rim of the bottle. "You're Jude's friend. The oldie with the not-bad rack."

I covered my girls. Ew. And fuck him, my youthful rack was top notch.

I'd trained myself to ignore magic to the point that I no longer reacted if I saw small examples of it in the street, but even I couldn't have ignored a golem at my friend's house if I'd seen one before. "Where's Jude?"

"I was about to ask you the same question."

"Someone destroyed her studio," I said. "What's going on? Is she in danger?"

"I don't know." Emmett took a swig from a bottle of bourbon.

"Is she your..." I swallowed. "Lover?"

He spat out what I could only assume to be Jude's most expensive alcohol. "What is wrong with you?"

Well, that was a relief. "Mother?" I tried.

This time, the golem laughed so hard he sprayed out another swig of booze. "Call her that when I'm around to hear it. I'll pay you five bucks."

I wiped off my cheek. "But she made you?"

He fired a finger gun at me. "Her own little minion."

I made it to the sofa on rubbery legs, unsure of what to freak out over first, the half-naked clay man, or that Jude was an Ohrist. Was anything in my life what I'd thought it was? "What do you do for her?"

He patted down his pompadour. "Get answers."

"More specifically?"

He tied his bathrobe closed. "Client confidentiality. You want to know more, ask her."

"If I could ask her, I wouldn't need you to find her."

"It's a conundrum."

"She could be in trouble," I ground out.

"She knows the risks."

"The risks of what?" I dug my fingers into the cushion.

Emmett took another belt of booze.

Awesome. The one magical entity I'd found who wasn't trying to actively kill me was an unhelpful numbskull. "You're a dick."

"Yup," he replied cheerfully. "That's why the ladies love me." He held up the bottle in a mocking salute.

"Mazel tov," I said, sarcastically. This was a dead end. I headed for the front door, intending to go back to my car and come up with a new plan.

"No tov. Just mazel."

I spun around at Emmett's dreamy tone and gasped. The entirety of his eyes had been replaced by cosmic swirls and starlight.

My shoulder blades prickled and I reached for my magic, braced to animate Delilah. "Mazel?"

"There is a ripple. The mazel changed, the first domino played."

"Mazel? As in luck? Is this relevant to what's happened to Jude?"

"It's relevant to everyone." An asteroid streaked across one eye.

I crossed my arms. If you were going to make some big pronouncement accompanied by a supernatural light show, have the courtesy to be specific. Seriously. Of all the cryptic bullshit … "I'll bite. What's this domino?"

Stars winked into existence in his eyes, growing and bursting into supernovas in seconds, until like a roulette wheel slowing, the starbursts stopped.

"You," he said.

5

———

EMMETT PASSED OUT AFTER DROPPING THIS bombshell, snoring softly on the carpet, his clay limbs splayed and his bathrobe bunched under one hip. I'd caught the bottle, which now sat on the desk, and had crouched down next to the golem as if staring at him long enough would make sense of all this.

Golems, while rare, were useful because of their "no task left uncompleted" work ethic. This made them great flunkeys, but they didn't have natural divination powers, so what the hell had happened?

The drive home was a blur, punctuated by me screaming in frustration two or six times. This was ridiculous. Some kind of practical joke that Emmett had played. I was a divorced single mom who worked as a librarian in a very dry law firm. Magic didn't come with some contract stating, "By accepting these powers you agree to any and all vague prophecies about your person."

I always read the fine print and I'd have demanded an exclusionary clause to that wording big time, because I had a plan. Short-term magic use for greater good and then done.

Once home, miraculously in one piece, given how

distracted I'd been, I found the contraband bag of Doritos that I'd hidden for emergency PMS salt cravings, thrilled that Sadie hadn't rooted the chips out. If my vacuum cleaner of a child saw them, there'd be none for me, but Sadie was still out with her cousin.

I tore the bag open with my teeth. Screw you, universe with your dominoes. I'd always hated that game because it was dependent on the luck of the draw. And I wasn't going to be the opening gambit in anything, especially when golems couldn't predict shit.

Delilah nuzzled against me and I dropped my head into my hands.

Emmett hadn't looked or sounded like he was messing with me. If getting my magic was the first move, then whatever this was had already been set in motion, but one play wasn't the entire game, and I wasn't some inanimate object. I had free will.

But to do what? Yesterday morning, I'd passed as just another Sapien, off any magic radar. Last night had changed that, but I'd determined the least dangerous way to report Alex. Now, my best friend was missing, some golem was making pronouncements about my existence, and every minute risked something else sucking me back into that world.

Fuck that.

I shoveled nachos into my mouth like the fate of the universe depended on me amping my salt intake to comically elevated levels, then sighed.

Did Jude have a clay army poised to take over the world? What was she up to? Any lingering self-righteous anger that she'd never confided in me about her powers or this side of her life drained away, because I'd done the same. She would have assumed I was unable to see it anyway.

The only salient point was that Jude was out there somewhere and I had to find her.

I muscled down a cheesy lump. It was plausible Alex could be stopped based on an anonymous tip, but Jude's disappearance warranted questions I'd have to answer since I might have been the last person to see her. I mangled the chips in my hand into an orange mess that rained onto my shirt. Swearing, I brushed them into the bag, which I tipped into my mouth. Waste not, want not.

I couldn't chance getting up close and personal with the Lonestars for Jude's case, which left me with the VPD. There was no waiting period here in British Columbia to report a missing person, but if I went to police headquarters saying an adult friend stood me up a couple times and that the only factor in her disappearance might be due to a golem side hustle, they'd ask me what I was on and call Social Services. I gnawed on my bottom lip.

I'd have to bring Eli into this if I were to go the VPD route, except I didn't know if it was even possible to tell a Sapien about magic. Sure, he'd be safer knowing of its existence and he'd be a better resource for finding Jude, but would I be able to break through the perception filter?

Okay, I'd keep my magic for a while longer to convince Eli. Also, feeding him couldn't hurt. My rule-happy baby daddy was always more amenable to my ideas after food.

I checked in with Sadie about what time she was coming home and then went grocery shopping, soldiering bravely through the packed store to the produce, which had been thoroughly picked over. I was sorting through containers of bruised and shriveled strawberries, trying to find one that was halfway decent, when an elderly man joined me.

He grabbed a package and the berries inside plumped up to fat, juicy pieces of fruit.

Ordinarily, I'd have kept my expression neutral, but Eli really liked berries and whipped cream, and the fruit on offer was crap.

I caught the shopper's eye. "Help a compatriot out?" I said quietly.

"Happy to." The man revitalized another bunch and handed them to me.

Ohrists took their name from "ohr," the Hebrew word for light, and the Kabbalah concept of a supernatural life force that existed organically in the universe. While Sapiens couldn't sense or tap into the "ohr," Ohrists were gifted. Their ability to manipulate light and life energy manifested in a ton of different ways: from healing, to animating objects, manipulating organic material like Alex had done with my body parts, to screwing with emotions, and a slew of abilities involving light.

My mother had said magic was analogous to singing. Some people had raw talent, some had to unlock it with training, and others, even with the magic gene, were tone deaf. Regardless of their power levels, most only had an affinity for one form of manipulation. A magical disposition, as it were, so if you were a shifter—a common Ohrist ability —you couldn't also shoot lasers.

Before I could ask the man how to contact the Lonestars in order to deal with Alex, a boisterous family showed up. He wished me a good day and headed for the check-out counter.

I sniffed the container, my mouth watering at the ripe scent that flowed off the fruit.

The mother nodded at my stash. "Lucky. You got the last good one."

"It's my day."

An hour later, I was surrounded by the wreckage of my dinner making. Flour was spilled on the butcher block countertop and down the front of the red maple shaker cabinets, while oil heating in the cast iron pan splattered on the gas stovetop. Messes could be cleaned up; rooms were made to be lived in.

I closed the vintage white curtains with their cherry print, the soft spotlights bouncing off the cream walls imbuing the space with a snugness. I'd already made it through half a bottle of a robust Malbec, and was a bit fuzzy on which of us required the booze more tonight, me or my ex. As I dredged chicken breasts for the chicken piccata to get Eli in a receptive mood, I sorted through various approaches to ease him into this strange new world. Forty-five minutes later, it was all systems go on the dinner front, not so much on my brainstorming.

The sauce was thickening, the final handful of parmesan had gone into the zucchini risotto, and I was shaking my hips to "Disco Inferno," because disco made everything better, when Detective Eli Chu of the Vancouver Police Department let himself into my side of the duplex. We'd bought it when we'd decided that co-parenting Sadie was our priority while we worked through the wreckage of our marriage.

"It smells amazing in here." Eli gyrated into the kitchen and placed a bottle of Riesling in the fridge to chill. He must have stopped at home first because he was no longer wearing his badge, gun, tie, or suit jacket.

"I aim to please."

Twerking across the room, he pretended to spank me to the beat. His biceps shifted under his button-down shirt, his thigh muscles rippling in his suit trousers. He'd bulked up since our marriage, not really my type anymore. That shy boy who'd fallen in love with me had been relegated to a bittersweet memory, made easier to bear because it no longer fit this version of him.

No use pining for things I could no longer have, though I missed having a romantic partner, someone to curl up with at the end of the day, or those heated looks and quick brushes against my lower back that were a promise of more to come. It felt like forever since I'd had that anticipatory flutter because someone desired me.

I shook off my musings and poured the sauce over the chicken on the platter, the two of us still grooving to the music.

Sadie arrived a few minutes later. She'd changed into a cute cat top complete with ears on a hood and skinny jeans, looking young and fresh-faced, until she rolled her eyes. "Why can't you two hate each other like normal divorced people?"

Eli grabbed her hand and spun her in a double turn. "Because we live to traumatize you in new and interesting ways. Now wash up and set the table, spawn."

"Be nice or I'll get Ah Ma to beat you." Sadie nudged me away from the sink and squirted dish soap into her hands.

Eli said something to her in Cantonese and she laughed. His parents had immigrated to Canada almost fifty years ago from Hong Kong, and like a lot of first generation kids, Eli hadn't learned English until he went to kindergarten. Sadie couldn't speak it, but since her grandmother talked to her and her cousin in a mix of Cantonese and English, she understood enough.

I was a firm proponent of Sadie knowing another language, especially one connected to her heritage, but sometimes, like today when my nerves were raw, I felt like the outsider on the playground watching the cool kids make their inside jokes. They'd explain it to me if I asked, but with all my other preoccupations right now, I didn't have the energy to request that they fill me in.

Eli dropped an arm over my shoulder. "How was your day?"

"Fine." With a meaningful glance at our daughter, I shook my head and mouthed, "later."

Eli held out his arms. "Come here." He wrapped me up in a huge hug and I tried not to flinch because of my sore neck and shoulder, my cheek resting against his staggeringly well-defined pecs. It had taken *a lot* of therapy and time, but while

I'd lost Eli as a husband, I'd kept him as a friend. Our relationship was unconventional, but it worked.

Would it be the same after tonight? I broke out of his embrace. "Wine?"

Dinner was a light-hearted affair. Sadie shared her grandmother and friends' recent trip to Vegas—or as my kid called it, "the mahjong cabal's visit to Sin City"—and Eli told us about a recent homicide case that he and his partner had solved.

I smiled in all the right places and kept our glasses filled, because the alcohol took the edge off my pain as I mulled over how best to broach my topic. We polished off the berries with whipped cream, which tasted as good as they looked, but I still hadn't found the best opening line.

Once we were stuffed to our eyeballs, Eli offered to scrub the pots.

Sadie dumped the food scraps into the countertop composter, then stacked the dirty dishes in the dishwasher. "Did you tell Jude to play her Scrabble hand?"

Blessed as I was to have an astute daughter, it also reinforced the fact that I wasn't the only one to notice Jude's radio silence.

"Sorry, I forgot," I lied-without-really-lying. I'd find Jude before Sadie had to be told anything.

"To make up for it, you should let me sleep at Nessa's," Sadie said.

I dried off the saucepot that Eli handed me. "You have a chem test to study for."

"She's in my class and we can study together. Please?"

It might be better to have Sadie out of the way, depending on how badly Eli lost his shit after our talk. I fit the pan into the cupboard with great precision because one wrong move and the pots and lids would tumble out like a Jenga game. "Fine."

"I'm going to grab my stuff and tell Nessa to pick me up."

She shoved a pod in the dishwasher, hit start, and raced upstairs.

Once the kitchen was clean, I shook the last drops of Malbec into my glass, swirling them around like I had a fortune telling technique that would reveal the best way to go about this.

"You have on your serious face." Eli rinsed out the sink. "What's up?"

"Remember how you blew up our marriage because you like men and taking it up the ass?"

A startled laugh burst out of him. "How hammered are you, Mir?"

"Fairly?" I hadn't intended for it to come out that blunt, but so it had. Oh well. I'd always been a more direct person than he was. "Sorry. Let me rephrase that."

"No need. That's basically what happened." Eli shut off the tap and dried his hands on a tea towel. "I just can't imagine what you're going to equate it to."

"Bear with me. All will be made clear."

He retrieved the Riesling from the fridge and rummaged through a drawer for the corkscrew. "In that case, I also recall that I wasn't the only one who enjoyed anal."

"True. Though you were never as excited giving as taking."

"You'd think that was a clue," he said, dryly.

"You'd think."

Eli yanked the cork out and frowned. "Do you have regrets about our sex life?"

"Non, je ne regrette rien." I finished my wine and held out the glass, which Eli obediently refilled. "Little known fact. Edith Piaf was actually singing about butt sex."

He rubbed a hand over his bald head. "That explains a lot about the French."

I screwed up my face, trying to remember my original point. "Okay, back to what I was saying. When you first brought up the truth of your sexuality, it was hard to accept, but with a lot of work we got to a good place. Together. Right?"

Eli eyed me warily, raising his glass to his lips. "Right."

I disengaged my shadow, making Delilah shadow box around him.

My ex didn't react. He continued to stare at me, waiting for me to say something.

Delilah punched him in the shoulder and Eli shivered.

"Someone walked over my grave," he said. "So, what's up?"

The perception filter, that was what was up. Eli wasn't picking up on Delilah doing anything, even when I made it painstakingly obvious. I pursed my lips. Maybe hoping he'd see something his brain was used to writing off, like the shifting movements of a shadow, was too much.

He knew I was here, though. Perhaps I could use that.

"Hang on." Grabbing the empty wine bottle, I threw it in the recycling bin on the back porch, calling up my cloaking power when I stepped inside the room and not dropping it until I'd sat back down.

Eli started, sloshing the wine in his glass. "Damn." He shook his head and yawned. "I'm more tired than I thought. I totally spaced out and didn't see you come back."

I made Delilah jump up and catch the light fixture. She hung upside down, swinging back and forth in front of him. "Weird. You don't see anything new about me?"

He grimaced. "Is this a trick question? Did you get a haircut?"

Delilah sank to the floor, a normal shadow. I might be able to literally hammer him over the head, but I didn't want to hurt him. I sighed. Sure, I could say it to him in words: "Hey, by the way, I have magical powers!" but without anything he could see to back it up, he'd think it was the wine. Or perimenopause. Or a million other tiny excuses Sapiens made up for this stuff.

The perception filter was, unfortunately, too strong.

"Ness is here," Sadie called out. "Bye!" The front door slammed shut behind her.

"Now that the kid's gone..." Eli gave me an inquisitive look and I scrambled to come up with something suitable to tell him. "Are you also going through an identity crisis?"

"Of sorts," I said.

"You know you can always talk to me," he said.

I toed at my shadow. I can talk, you just won't always hear me. "I know. We can discuss that another time. I'm more worried because Jude was supposed to meet me last night for a drink after work and she never showed. She didn't come to brunch either, she's not at her place, and the artist next door to her studio hadn't seen her."

"Did you report it?"

"Not yet. I wasn't sure if I was overreacting. Do you think they'd write me off as paranoid if I called Missing Persons with nothing more concrete than a gut feeling?" I couldn't mention her trashed workspace as I had no way of explaining how I'd seen inside.

Eli squeezed my hand. "I'm sure there's a simple explanation for it, but it's best to get an investigation started as soon as possible. Let me talk to a friend of mine." He asked me some questions, including whether Jude had any problematic exes or was suffering from money trouble.

I answered both in the negative.

"Are you going to tell Sadie?" he said.

"Not unless I have to. I really hope I'm wrong and something innocuous came up, but she's never done this before." I paused. "I know it's not a lot of information to go on."

"The first seventy-two hours are the most critical, but the majority of cases are solved in that time period and Terence is tops in his unit. He'll be able to work with this." He used the voice he took with his mom when he didn't want her to worry, versus the one where he was certain of an outcome.

I slugged back the rest of my wine.

Eli fired off the information in a text, then he yawned again. "Early shift tomorrow. I'm going to hit the sack. Let me know if you want to start your midlife crisis."

"Asshole," I said affectionately.

He scrawled the name and number of his Missing Persons contact in his chicken-scratch handwriting. "Yeah, but I'm your asshole."

"Please no. I leave that to Chris"—Eli's on-again, off-again lover.

"He'll be delighted at the sole custody."

I stuck the paper on the fridge. "Thanks for helping me with Jude."

"Anytime, babe, and don't worry. We'll find her." Throwing a wave over his shoulder, Eli headed home.

I wouldn't hold my breath that I lucked out and Eli's officer friend had magic and could be confided in. Since stopping Alex meant a quick foray into the Ohrist community anyway, I'd ask around about Jude, and then back to my original plan of putting all magic behind me.

My shadow lifted her head and turned it in my direction, but I walked briskly out of the room and snapped off the light.

6

WHAT EXACTLY WAS MAZEL? I'D BEEN SO FOCUSED on the domino part, I'd ignored the rest of Emmett's message. Librarian skills to the rescue. The literal translation was "a drip from above." It had a lot of different connotations, depending on its context, but they were all connected to this basic idea of something trickling down to us from the stars.

Had I known that and it had subconsciously colored how I framed decisions as stars in the constellation of life?

Feeling totally bloated from all the risotto expanding in my belly, I browsed some more websites, taking notes. When we Jews said "mazel tov," we were really saying "may your stars align favorably." The belief went as follows: everything has mazel, a specific pattern of blessings for health, wealth, etc., set out by God. A Torah at the front of the ark where the scrolls are housed in the synagogue had great mazel because it was used often, while the scrolls at the back didn't.

In my haste to learn more, I jostled my laptop, grabbing it to keep it from listing sideways off the sofa cushions. While a person's whole future was mapped out in the stars by God, a Jew couldn't go to a fortune teller and find out what would happen tomorrow, because that was a form of idolatry and forbidden in the Jewish faith.

However, Jews were able to either harness their mazel or overcome it entirely. If I was born under the influence of Mars, for example, my mazel predicted I'd be a bloodletter. So that might mean a murderer, but if I harnessed that mazel for good, then I might be a doctor.

Thus, we were given mazel (destiny) and the ability to rise above mazel (free will).

Is that what had happened last night? Putting my computer aside, I sifted through puzzle pieces for green ones to complete the *Into The Woods* poster in the middle of the jigsaw. Had my destiny, my mazel, been to hide my abilities for the rest of my life, and by reclaiming my magic, I'd somehow changed it? Jude's ideas about power and empowerment came to mind. In keeping my magic suppressed all these years, had I limited my choices, my free will? Is that why I'd struggled in part with feelings of marginalization?

I turned a puzzle piece between my fingers.

Was exercising my free will in this manner even a good thing? Delilah's reemergence was like the best cocktail I'd ever had, but I was drinking it in a club surrounded by strangers who would either make my night or kill me.

Hiding my magic had kept me safe, and that had been my choice. It still was. End of story.

My perseverance with the jigsaw paid off and I filled in Red's cloak with a satisfied nod.

This was why it was better to not know the future, because having heard Emmett's domino crap, I was now second-guessing everything, trying to base future decisions on the meaning of his vague pronouncement, and tying myself into knots wondering how it fit into mazel and free will. So long as I followed my plan, all would be well.

Since I was too tipsy to drive, I called an Uber to take me

back to Chambers. Assuming Jude had gone to meet me last night, maybe someone had seen her. It was my only lead.

It was a few minutes after 8PM and the place was only half-full. I headed for the bar, where the same guy was working, and showed him a photo of Jude, but he hadn't seen her, nor had one of the servers who'd been on duty last night.

On my way out, I saw Alex sitting in a back booth.

I grabbed a table that would keep him in my sights, nursing a cranberry juice and soda as I spied on him. He didn't speak to anyone, putting away shots like he was celebrating. I left when he did, throwing down some cash and keeping a safe distance between us.

There was still a good half-hour until sunset, with a lot of people milling about Jack Poole Plaza, but Alex headed for the seawall, a less populated path that wound around the waterfront. Was he on the hunt for someone else to attack?

I couldn't risk some other woman being assaulted. With the sun so low in the sky, I cast a long shadow, and if the worst came to pass, I could cloak myself, and possibly someone else.

As I followed Alex, I estimated his height and weight, as well as noting what he was wearing in case I had to describe him. Nothing about his appearance was off, nothing indicated that this was indeed the kind of dude who would try to rape you in a back alley if he got the chance. Just slicked-down hair and brown shoes, one more tired lawyer making his way somewhere, but something set off alarm bells.

It wasn't until he passed under a newly switched-on streetlight that it hit me: Alex's shadow was a sickly gray flecked with crimson.

I blinked rapidly, willing my brain to turn this impossibility into a trick of the moonlight, but it didn't resolve itself. Was this a function of his magic or something more nefarious at play? It hadn't been that way yesterday because I'd have noticed.

In my shock, I'd stopped, and Alex disappeared around the back of the restaurant that anchored the west edge of the plaza. I hurried after him, but when I came around the far side of the building, which was closed for renovations, he was nowhere to be seen.

This well-lit side of the restaurant featured a narrow patio section adjacent to its own tiny plaza just off Jack Poole. Smack dab in the middle of the smaller plaza stood a glass elevator tower that was connected by a walkway to the restaurant's roof. Also accessible by stairs, the walkway allowed people to stroll onto the grass roof of the building. Why this was a selling feature, I had no idea.

I strode across the smaller plaza, coming to a dead stop when Alex stepped out from behind the elevator tower.

"We meet again." He turned cold eyes level with mine, and flexed his fingers. "You surprised me yesterday. That won't happen now."

The wrongness of his shadow made the back of my neck prickle. I had no idea what he'd done for it to get like that, but the urge to destroy that abomination came from the very marrow of my bones. This was more than a gut instinct; it was a magically heightened sensitivity spurring me on.

Delilah disengaged, and the world split into two versions: one in night vision and one in Miri vision, but I didn't immediately attack because the plan had been to gather information, not go for round two, especially when I had no idea what his diseased shadow signified.

Any damage that my shadow took, I suffered, and I was still injured from our encounter last night. I curled my toes under inside my runners, steeling myself to wing it as best I could, but I glanced around for something to hide behind, since I couldn't let him paralyze me again.

"Sparing me all your yammering tonight?" he said. "Thank fuck. Though your attempts to flirt yesterday were impressive."

I bounced on my toes. "Did you just neg me? I bet you're a hit with the incels. Who brings the Bud Light to your basement circle jerks?"

Alex fired at me, but I'd caught the telltale motion of his fingers and flung myself sideways.

Before he could attack again, Delilah grabbed him in a chokehold.

Alex turned beet red.

"Did you go after Jude last night?" I demanded.

"Who?" He tugged ineffectually on Delilah's arm, his words raspy.

"Red-haired woman, the same age as me. She went missing last night and I'm not a big fan of coincidences." When he didn't answer, Delilah choked him harder.

Alex made a gurgled sound, struggling to pry her arm off him.

I fixated on his diseased shadow. Its very existence was repellent to mine, and yet, I was drawn to it like a moth to a putrid evil flame. Before I'd reconnected to Delilah, I hadn't paid attention to people's shadows, but now that I was attuned to her, I sensed the wrongness of Alex's shade even more.

Thrusting my hand over top of his shadow, I caught hold of it like it had substance.

A soundless scream tore from Alex's throat, his tendons straining, but he was unable to move.

Whoa, that was new. Feeling my way instinctively to the next step, I crumpled his shadow in my fist. Darkness oozed through my fingers, hot to the touch and viciously seething.

HATENEEDFEEL

The world swung sideways in a vertiginous blur along with the strongest sensation that I'd jumped feet-first into a pool of rot. I stumbled drunkenly and lost my grip.

He cracked his neck, regrouping with a mean little smirk

that faltered when a giant body soared off the restaurant's rooftop.

Alex and I froze.

The massive white wolf was easily over six feet long and two hundred pounds, made bigger by bristling hackles and erect ears. It had to be a male, because boys and their size issues. His head, large and heavy with a wide forehead, boasted a long, blunt muzzle, and jaws that could make short work of anything.

Green eyes stared unblinkingly at Alex and me, the kind that glowed cold and hungry out of the darkness while puny mortals built fires they prayed would keep them safe.

I clenched my bladder, goosebumps breaking out all over my body, telling myself this wasn't a real wolf, merely an Ohrist shapeshifter, and thus, human, somewhere in there.

That didn't lessen my terror. Especially since we were less than fifty feet from tourists in Jack Poole Plaza, and yet not one of them seemed to notice a wolf. In downtown Vancouver.

"This isn't your fight." Alex sounded kind of pitchy, and yet not surprised.

The muscled killing machine prowled slowly toward us.

Sweating so hard I had boob soup, I let out a strangled yelp.

The wolf blinked.

Alex brought his thumbs and index fingers together in a "W" formation, but a split second before his magic blazed, the wolf bit off the man's finger and threw it aside.

I screamed almost as loudly as Alex did, blood burbling out of his stump.

Two crows swooped down on the finger, breaking into a squabble over their prize.

The beast seized Alex by the scruff of his neck and flung him into the glass tower like he weighed nothing.

"Stop!" I cried.

Cracks spiderwebbed in the glass, but Alex staggered to his feet and bolted, zigzagging towards the seawall, leaving bloody drips in his wake.

The sky turned luminous, lit up in an orange, pink, and gold sunset, its beauty undermined by one of the crows muscling the finger down.

I gagged.

The white wolf took off in an easy lope and intercepted the man, lazily batting him to the ground.

Alex bounced twice, then rolled to a stop, pinned in place under the enormous paw that the animal rested on his neck. He began babbling, begging for his life.

Shaking, I hid under my black mesh.

The wolf grabbed Alex's belt in his teeth and bounded up the stairs onto the walkway with his prey.

Was the wolf going to kill Alex?

For a second, my feet refused to move. There were a million reasons to walk away, including the extremely important one of self-preservation in the face of the Big Bad Wolf made flesh, but I couldn't let Alex be murdered.

We had a moral imperative as humans to do something.

That argument wasn't as compelling when applied to a psycho who preyed on women, but if I could get him to confess and be locked up, then the victims he'd harmed in the past would have justice. He was also my only lead to find Jude.

The flaw with this was that I also had a moral imperative to stay alive for my daughter and the only way to save Alex was with magic.

Exhaling hard, I swore under my breath and kicked into gear, but those precious seconds had cost me. I'd lost sight of them, so I dropped my cloaking and sent Delilah ahead of me.

The wolf was on the roof of the restaurant with Alex at his feet. He snarled, saliva flecking off his sharp canines.

Delilah jumped onto the shifter's back, pulling out her best grappling hold. His fur was dense and wiry, covering a body of pure muscle.

Alex belly crawled away.

The white wolf's growl vibrated through my shadow and into me.

I slowed to a stop at the edge of the grassy roof, but kept Delilah choking him.

The beast caught my shadow in his mouth, but when he flung her away, he was oddly gentle, because my sweater didn't tear and no teeth marks broke my skin, nor did he simply rip Delilah's arm off entirely.

He snagged Alex by the pant leg, and dragged him back, giving the man a grass and dirt facial. Alex's shadow vibrated so hard it was palpable.

My stomach somewhere in the vicinity of my toes, I stepped forward with my hands up. "Don't kill him."

The wolf bared his lips, leaning onto his prey's back with one paw.

Was the wolf enemy of my enemy, my friend?

"He tried to force himself on me the other night," I said, "and he may be responsible for my missing friend. Please. Help me get answers."

No matter how much Alex struggled, the animal didn't budge. Under his unnerving primal stare, I was about to get the hell out of Dodge when the wolf barked, sounding a tad impatient. He flicked his tail at my combat-ready shadow.

The Ohrist shifter understood me, but that didn't mean he'd cooperate. I was a goldfish trying to reason with a shark.

"You don't like that? No problem." I returned Delilah to a neutral position.

The clear peal of a trumpet sounded.

I jerked my head around, searching for the source. "Did you hear—"

The wolf's claws extended, glowing like they were made

of pure light, and he tore into Alex's chest, ripping out his heart and dropping it back into the body cavity with a wet splat. Alex went limp, his head twisted to face me, and a swirling phantom of crimson and gray exploded out of his corpse.

I shrieked and ducked, meeting Alex's lifeless stare. His shadow once again looked normal, the putrescence now freed and dive-bombing the wolf, who leapt, growling and attempting to catch hold of the mass.

Why the fuck was the sick bloody ghost thing still going like the Energizer Bunny? And why did Alex have to die?

I didn't mourn the piece of shit, but this wasn't right. He should have faced justice, except that thought warred with my desire to push the wolf aside and rid the world of the phantom thing myself.

The pulsing entity whipped close to my face, anger roiling off it, and I flung my hands up. Never mind, let the wolf handle it, because unless I could vanquish this thing with the power of sarcasm, I had no clue how to fight it.

As the dying sunlight slipped away, the angry ghost mass attacked the wolf faster and faster, but the Ohrist shifter fought it off in a blur of motion.

A car alarm in the distance beeped insistently.

The wolf sank his front claws into the crimson and gray specter that had burst out of Alex's corpse, holding it aloft like meat on a spit.

Rays of golden light sprouted up from the wolf's back paws, blooming across his legs and torso with a hypnotic fluidity. It turned his white fur into a blinding snowscape that forced me to shield my eyes.

His emerald eyes turned black, and a pained howl burst out of the animal, a desolate sound that shivered up my spine.

Keeping the crimson mass speared on one front paw, the

wolf flexed his other one, slashing his glowing claws through the air and opening a portal into a yawning chasm.

I clasped my hands over my ears, the half-humming half-vibrating noise emanating from it hitting me at a painful frequency. And yet, I crept closer, awed at the maelstrom of storm clouds on the other side. A plume of fog rolled in with jagged movements that reminded me of teeth. Goosebumps prickled my skin, but I was unable to turn away. Even the stench of rotting onions that belched from the gap did little to dissuade me.

Had the wolf really torn a hole to another dimension or was this an illusion?

The wolf flung the writhing mass into the chasm, and the wind on that side picked up with a furious howl. Cars, people, cell phones, all sound on my side narrowed down like it was far away, reality suspended until the light drained from the wolf, and with a quiet whoosh, he was released from his torment.

The portal winked shut, the crimson mass gone.

The world snapped back into a cacophony of sound and motion and I released the breath I'd been holding.

The animal's claws returned to their normal color, and he bowed his head, his flanks heaving.

I sagged against the railing on the walkway in horrified fascination. My relief that the blight from Alex's shadow was no longer around froze into icy spears stabbing into me with the certainty that the wolf would turn his focus to me now. I tried to grab his shadow as I'd done with Alex's but I couldn't. It remained on the ground like all the others.

The wolf's fur rippled.

"Oh," I whispered, having never seen a werewolf change before. A stripe of skin appeared over the ridges of his spine and his claws morphed into fingers. It was almost like watching a sunrise on a foreign moon, an alien light cascading through darkness in little peeks, and then a more steady glow, illuminating a rugged, foreign landscape. Unfamiliar, but beautiful in its own way.

But maybe I made a noise or something, or my "oh" was too loud because the wolf growled and shifted fully back into his animal form with a crazed glint in his once-more emerald eyes.

I jumped backwards, smacking my tailbone on the railing. Beautiful? Was I crazy? He was a wolf shifter with lethal instincts, a canny intelligence, and if that failed, claws and teeth made for snacking on me.

He lunged, his jaws barely missing my side.

I bolted, a scream caught in my throat, running blindly across the smaller plaza until I stopped, winded and gulping down air with my arms over my head to get rid of the stitch in my side.

I blew a strand of hair off my flushed face. Who did that wolf think he was, anyway? My magic was out of the bag and I wasn't leaving without answers, even if it was nothing more than Alex's driver's license with a last name and address to follow up.

I stormed back to the stairs, making no effort to hide my approach.

A man kneeled next to Alex's body. He seemed a few years younger than me, probably in his late thirties, and was about six inches taller, putting the shifter at about six-foot-two. His hair was a riot of dark curls.

The man's jaw was firm, his lips full, but right now, they were set in a severe line. Moonlight kissed the olive skin of his broad shoulders and leanly muscled torso, a trail of hair leading down to—

Jeans. I gusted out a breath.

The man huffed softly. "You came back," he said dryly, with a slight accent I couldn't place. "You've got balls, I'll give you that."

I gave a weak laugh and he locked his brilliant emerald

gaze onto mine. Thickly lashed, his eyes were what I would have called beautiful in his human form, but there was a hardness to them—like he'd seen too much and all innocence was long gone.

Eli had looked that way after his first year in homicide. Fuuuuck! This guy had to be a Lonestar. Okay, looking on the bright side, he could help me find Jude—if he didn't destroy me. I'd been so bent on getting answers from Alex that I'd thrown away every single safety procedure that I'd lived by and shown a stranger my magic. I could have left when the shifter took off with Alex but no, I had to play detective.

I reached behind me, clutching the railing to bolster my rubbery legs.

The Ohrist reached into a duffel bag, revealing a nasty silver jagged scar that ran halfway up the left side of his back, and pulled on a faded blue T-shirt that said, "Bite Me." This wasn't a gym rat with a six-pack for show; he was a warrior and his body was his well-honed weapon, in or out of wolf form.

Ohrist magic was based in light and life, while Banim Shovavim powers were rooted in death and darkness. Historically, they'd taken that as clear-cut signs of good and evil. They pitied Sapiens but had hunted my kind into near extinction.

There was even a skipping game sung by Ohrist kids: "Clap for the light, 'cause light is right. All other magic is a blight. How many shadow freaks will we smite?" At which point they'd jump as fast as they could while counting.

I eyed the wolf shifter with a sinking feeling that he'd probably counted pretty damn high.

Maybe he didn't remember the exact details of his time in his wolf form? Could I bluff my way out of here?

"Did you want something?" he said, impatiently.

My brain short-circuited. "I'm guessing that light magic

allowed you to cut through his breastbone and rib cage only using your claws," I said, "but why isn't there blood all over the place?"

I could have smacked myself. This was not the time for curiosity or further questions like "How do you have more than one magic ability?" It was the time for well-crafted lies.

"The magic cauterized the blood vessels." The man rolled his "r's." He grabbed a box of table salt from the duffel bag.

"Regular sodium," I said thickly. "How bland. I prefer Pink Himalayan to balance the delicate flavor of human flesh."

"I'm not eating him." He dumped the salt over the corpse. "It interferes with the scent so animals don't show up before Ohrists get here to retrieve the body."

"That's good, because cannibalism can make you sick. You get this brain disease called kuru and—"

"Like mad cow?" He tapped the last of the salt onto the body with a contemplative expression.

I blinked. People didn't generally come back with follow-up questions to my random facts. "Not quite. People can't get mad cow disease, but in rare cases they get a form called..." I shook my head because cows, mad or otherwise, were not the issue. "Was Alex human?"

Or was he some other species entirely and did that make a difference to the answer? He had looked human, even if what was inside of him wasn't.

My moral compass was having trouble finding true north.

"Not anymore," the wolfman said.

I knelt down beside Alex to close his lids because his life-less stare felt accusatory, but the shifter batted my arm away.

He lay a hand on the deceased's forehead and stared into his eyes as if committing him to memory. There was both a gravitas and a resignation in the shifter's expression, and I couldn't tell if he did this to honor the dead or torment himself with a parade of his kills. Maybe it was one and the same.

When he was done, I checked Alex's back pockets for his wallet.

"The man's body isn't even cold and you're robbing him?" Wolf Dude said.

"I'm looking for identification," I said through ground teeth. There was a cracked phone but no wallet. It must have fallen out at some point during the fight. A vise tightened around my chest and I shoved the Ohrist, banking on the fact that if he'd intended to hurt me, he'd have done it already. "You ruined my chance to get information about—"

"I saved you." The man stuffed his bare feet into motor-cycle boots, which also came out of the duffel bag. "I don't know what interrogation skills you think you have, but I can assure you that dybbuk wouldn't have given up shit."

"Dybbuk?"

"Merde," he said in perfect French. Ah. "You went after him without knowing what you were dealing with?" His full lips twisted. "Fucking BS."

He remembered.

I took two wobbly steps back, Delilah by my side, but he didn't come after me.

He laced up his boots. Okay, he was a derisive son of a bitch, but he lacked the horror others of his ilk displayed upon meeting my kind, nor did he seem inclined to kill me.

I'd take the win.

"Alex had attacked me once already," I said, "and if he did something to my friend—"

The shifter pulled out a beaten-up brown leather jacket and shrugged into it, his shoulders bunching. "Then she's gone. Sorry for your loss."

My eyebrows shot up. Yes, this guy was an ass, but surely he was connected to an infrastructure that could help me find Jude. "Sorry for your loss? How about you help me find her? Aren't you a Lonestar?"

He laughed without an ounce of humor. "Hardly."

Then what was he? He'd already killed one person, and yes, that dybbuk thing seemed to justify Alex's death, but I was alone out here. If he was working on his own vigilante moral code, how safe was I?

I eyed the stairs. How many were there? Thirty? Then perhaps another fifty feet to lose myself in the crowds? He'd be faster than me, even as a human. I bit my lip. If I screamed for help, would anyone come?

Screw that. I had magic and could cloak and get away at any point, but his rudeness was grating. I threw my hands up. "That's all you have to say?"

"No." The man raked a shrewd glance over me. "Should we ever have the misfortune to meet again, get out of my way."

"Or what? You'll huff and you'll puff and you'll blow my house down?"

He bared his lips, briefly shifting his canines to wolf form. *My, what big teeth you have.* A strangled laugh burbled out of me. My epistemological crisis involved a hell of a Freudian undertone.

"I'll do whatever the fuck is necessary," he said.

"Is that your action hero catchphrase or something? Because it's a little on the nose."

He zipped up the duffel bag. "My reputation doesn't precede me? Shocking." His voice was laced with bitterness.

"Wow. Someone is full of themselves. I've got no idea who you are."

He peered at me suspiciously. "Are you new in town?"

"No."

He shrugged. "Then you know who I am."

"Hate to disappoint you, but you're just some rando who crashed my party and ruined my plan—"

"To get answers from someone who wouldn't tell you anything you actually wanted to know. Brilliant strategy. You've the mind of a tactician. Even if you did get something out of him, did you think he'd let you walk away after?" His accent thickened when he got annoyed.

"I had my shadow."

"I wouldn't brag about that if I were you."

"For your information, I'm doing an admirable job. Before yesterday, the only monsters I had to worry about were of the human variety." I shot him a pointed look.

"There's no way you didn't know about dybbuks. You're too—" He snapped his mouth shut.

Delilah puffed up behind me. "Oh, no," I said. "Finish that sentence."

The man crossed his arms, rustling the leather. "Old," he said levelly.

My shadow bopped Wolfman in the nose with a swift jab. Ha!

The man pinched his nostrils together to staunch the bleeding, his emerald eyes glinting dangerously.

My amusement drained away, my magic swirling around my feet, ready to cloak me, but I'd hit the wall and I was out of fucks to give.

"Should we ever have the misfortune to meet again, get out of my way," I said.

"Vraiment? Why?"

"I'm a woman in my forties who's remembered how powerful she can be. Don't fuck with me, Huff 'n' Puff." Head held high, Delilah and I sailed past him into the night.

7

SUNDAY MORNING, WEARING MY FAVORITE POPPY-print sundress and a scarf to hide the bruises since I wasn't flush in mock turtlenecks, I made a new plan over heavily buttered toast, a latte made on my stovetop Moka pot, and my jigsaw puzzle.

After painstakingly sorting through the remaining pieces to find the final gold one for the *A Chorus Line* poster, I conceded defeat. Hopefully, I'd have better luck elsewhere.

Emmett hadn't known where Jude was, but he knew what she was up to. I should have pressed harder for an answer yesterday, but I'd been thrown by his pronouncement and then he'd passed out. So, he'd be my first stop.

Before I went golem hunting, I checked in with Eli's cop friend, Terence, a nice man who didn't have much to give me. There'd been no movement on either Jude's bank accounts or credit cards. Her car had been found at an impound lot, having been towed near her studio yesterday morning. The officer gently asked me if Jude was suicidal, and when I replied emphatically not, he said that Eli had given them her home and studio addresses, and both had been checked out. There was no evidence of foul play.

"Nothing was… stolen or disturbed in either place?" I dumped the dregs of my cold coffee down the drain.

"The lock on her studio was busted, but nothing was out of place. We asked the artist next door"—there was the sound of rustling paper—"Harley, to take a look. He said that Judith kept the studio fairly orderly, and he couldn't see anything missing. The building's had some problems with theft so the broken lock wasn't indicative of anything other than someone poking around for something to sell."

I frowned, squirting dish soap on the sponge. Terence was wrong. Someone had broken in to clean the studio up, but who, and why? Covering their tracks?

"If nothing comes to light to indicate foul play," Terence said, "you should brace yourself for the possibility that she walked away from her life to start over, a not-uncommon occurrence. In which case, you'd need to respect her wishes."

Jude could be impulsive. I snorted softly, rinsing suds off my breakfast dishes. She'd once gone out to buy runners and bought a townhouse instead, because she'd liked the sunlight on the patio when she'd driven by. She constantly trolled the web for last-minute, sell-off travel deals, and she had told me to blow up my life and move to Spain. Was that advice actually a clue as to her own intentions?

I could have almost bought it except even if Jude was making a massive personal shift, she'd tell me, and if not me, Sadie. Jude never wanted kids, but she took her role as aunt very seriously, and was as important to my daughter as her dad and me. Jude's father had started over with a new family, and having gone through that, she would never abandon her niece.

"Jude would never pull a *Sap* move like that," I said, to suss out whether or not Terence was an Ohrist.

"Huh?"

"Nothing." I sighed and turned off the tap.

The cop assured me that they'd keep searching because

the critical first seventy-two hours weren't up yet, but I didn't hold out hope. There'd be no assistance from this quarter, no matter how well-intentioned. Whoever had caused Jude's disappearance was tied to the break-in at her studio, the golem, and those risks Emmett had mentioned, and I was on my own to get answers.

Grabbing my purse, I texted Sadie on the way to my car to let her know I was going out and to call me before she came home from her cousin's place. The kids wouldn't be up for at least another couple hours, leaving me free to interrogate the golem.

Damn it. The laundry. I ran back inside and grabbed the hamper with the colors from our bathroom, hurriedly shoving everything into the washer in the hall closet. There was too much for one load, so I did what any self-respecting woman who despised housekeeping would do: I crammed it all in as hard as I could and flipped the setting to extra-large. What was the point of that option if not to use the washing machine as my own personal TARDIS?

The bubble of hope lodged in my chest burst when I swept through Jude's condo to find that nothing had been disturbed since my last visit and the golem was gone. My search this time focused on finding anything that would lead me into the magic community. There was no handy directory for that, but I did find a few matchbooks on the kitchen windowsill with "Stay in Your Lane" written on the front, with no address or further information listed. Jude didn't smoke and wasn't big on candles so there wasn't a practical reason for her to have multiples of these.

I turned the matchbook over in my fingers. This might be a perfectly normal matchbook with a humorous tagline, but the same instincts that had led me down many a research trail said otherwise. I struck a match, waving it under the matchbook cover, but no hidden name or address appeared, nor did anything happen when I held it up to a light bulb.

If this was a magic artifact, there was another way to activate it, though that could horribly backfire. Before I could second-guess myself, I nicked my index finger with a steak knife and rubbed the edge of the matchbook against the red droplet.

Nothing.

Feeling slightly foolish, I headed for the sink to wash off the knife and return the matches to the drawer where I'd found them.

The matchbook tugged against my palm to go in the opposite direction, towards Jude's front door. I stepped closer to the sink to make sure my mind wasn't playing tricks on me, and received another tug.

I tossed the knife in the sink and ran out the door.

Matchbook GPS was stupidly inefficient and almost caused me to crash three times when it gave me last-minute directions to turn, but at last I hit Yaletown, an old warehouse district downtown that was now home to condo towers, upscale restaurants, cocktail lounges, and local designer and homeware boutiques. The matchbook fell dormant, its cover mangled from being gripped in my hand for the past fifteen minutes.

I stood at one end of the block and relaxed my vision, as if I was staring at one of those stupid hidden 3D stereograms, half of which I was never able to see. If I was successful, the secret magic place would emerge in the same way as the hidden 3D picture. I willed the concealed physical reality to reveal itself, but mostly, I looked like an idiot and more than one person asked if I was unwell. Blinking rapidly to clear my vision, I took a deep breath and tried again. Given enough practice, this reveal would become instantaneous, even possible while driving.

After another minute with my face screwed up, a beat-up brown door with "Stay in Your Lane" written in silver metallic letters across the front popped out partway down the block.

I hurried toward it, my head pounding with the strain of keeping it in my sight, but inevitably, when I got close enough to grab the handle, the image fell apart.

There was a sucking noise and the door began to fall back into obscurity.

I tucked in my elbows and threw myself through, landing in one piece with all my limbs intact. This time.

The traffic noise and smells of exhaust and baking from outside was replaced by a seductive musky perfume and the clatter of pins being knocked down.

"Hold my balls, sug." Two small bowling balls, the kind used for five pin, were thrust into my arms. A lithe Black woman about my age, with an afro shaved close to her head and brown eyes magnified by funky cat-eye glasses with bling in the corners, carried a cardboard box with bowling shoes sticking out of them.

"Buy a lady dinner first." I traced a crack in one of the balls with my thumb.

She propped the box on her hip. "What'll a bag of M&Ms get me?"

"Peanut?"

She frowned. "Like any other kind is viable. Don't insult me."

"In that case, I'll not only hold them, I'll handle them any way you want."

She grinned. "I'm Ava."

"Miriam. Miri."

"Love the dress. Well m'lady, follow me," she said. "Oral delights await."

"At long last." I followed her out of the foyer and into a large bowling alley, where she dumped the box on a counter, ducking under the bar flap into a small area with dozens of cubby holes for shoes.

Ava motioned for me to put the balls in the box, adjusting the hip belt on her low-slung capris. Grabbing a couple of packages of candy from the rack on the back counter, she tossed one to me.

"Thanks." I tore open the package and popped a handful in.

While Ava unpacked shoes, inspecting the laces and soles on each, I leaned back against the counter to survey the room.

One woman knocked down a single pin, followed by a blur of speed and the rest tipping over. In the blink of an eye she'd returned to her starting position, yelling "strike" with her arms thrown up in victory. Another patron rolled a gutter ball. His friend laughed, shit-talking him, and the bowler's neck puffed out like a cobra's about to strike.

"Hey, Willie!" Ava said. "Shift in here at your peril." She waved a broken shoe at him.

He hissed at her with a forked tongue, but when she planted her hands on her hips, her eyebrows raised, he ducked his head and changed back to human features.

The alley was only about a quarter full, but being around this many Ohrists set my teeth on edge, even if they couldn't tell what I was unless I showed them. I doubted there were any other Banim Shovavim here, since our kind was so rare.

I'd asked my dad once why Ohrists disliked us so much. I mean, we all had magic. He'd replied that Banim Shovavim and Ohrists were like two magnets with the same poles touching—we repelled each other. I'd pointed out that if you reversed the poles, the magnets would stick together. He'd patted my head and said maybe one day I could make Ohrists understand that.

Hands sweaty, I babbled, "Did you know that evidence of bowling was found as far back as ancient Egypt?"

"Uh, no." Ava gave me the "why do you know this" look that I was all too familiar with.

"I'm a Librarian?"

"You're not sure?" She whisked off a tattered lace and set the shoe in a separate pile.

"No, I am. I've worked in different libraries and you pick up random facts. Like hey." I pointed over at a rack containing packages of chips, pretzels, and peanuts. "The oil in peanuts contains glycerol which can be processed to produce nitroglycerine, one of the key components of dynamite. So if you're ever under siege, go for the snack food and kabam!"

She looked at me like perhaps I should be escorted outside.

Abort! "This place is fun," I said, like a normal human being.

Ava surveyed her territory with an amused smile. "It has a certain charm. So what brings you to my establishment?"

I pulled up a photo of Jude and showed it to her. "Do you know this woman?"

She tore a broken rubber heel off a shoe. "Why?"

"She's a friend of mine and she's missing. I found your matchbooks at her place and was hoping someone here might know where she is."

Ava nodded. "Yeah, I know Jude. She's bowled here off and on over the years."

Her grim tone turned the candy in my mouth to cardboard. I twisted up the bag and stuffed it in my pocket. "I sense a 'but.'"

Ava fished a loose shoelace out of the box, frowned, and tossed it in a drawer.

I leaned forward. "Please. I'm really worried about her and I don't know where to look. Anything you can tell me might help."

Ava sorted through a few more pairs of shoes, then sighed. "I heard she's gotten involved with the Blood Alley crowd."

Located in the heart of touristy Gastown, Blood Alley was only about two blocks long, a cobblestoned wide alleyway housing a variety of restaurants. Supposedly, its name came from the abattoirs and public hangings that had taken place there, but neither were true. It was merely a rebranding campaign back in the 1970's to give the area more allure.

"Like with some of the restaurant staff?" I said. "Any place in particular?"

Ava shot me a weird look. "No, the vamps. That's their territory. How do you not know that?"

"I had a sheltered upbringing." I sat down heavily on the bench provided for customers to put on their bowling shoes. I'd been a researcher in one guise or another for over twenty years. When I'd started out, it was in the film and television industry working on a reality show about serial killers. Humans were plenty monstrous on their own, but vampires?

I fisted my hands in the fabric of my silky dress. My magical education certainly left a lot to be desired. However, stories of evil creatures were as old as humanity itself. Was it so implausible that some of those were anecdotal and not allegorical?

That's it. I'd have to find a way to induct Eli and Sadie into all things magic because it was either that or make sure neither of them ever left the house after sundown again. Hell, I didn't want to leave the house after dark now.

I rubbed my hands over my thighs, light glinting off the clear polish. Jude despised my gel French manicures and was always pushing me to break my rut and go for more vibrant colors. Or, she'd say, flashing her own chipped dark purple nails, embrace that perimenopausal rage and paint them black.

Golems, vampires, how far had she taken her own advice? So much for my plan of a quick in and out of the magic community. I was going to throttle my best friend when I located her.

"You okay, there?" Ava crouched down next to me.

"You know, if asked, I'd have said Jude's priorities were her friends, her art, and seeing how many cups of tea she could safely ingest in a single day. Cavorting with the undead wouldn't have made the list."

"I hope it's cavorting," Ava said. "If she's gotten on the wrong side of the head vamp?" She pointed to a female patron in her early thirties with prosthetic legs, her jaw set. "Janice assisted him for years until she decided to move into the Sapien corporate world, and gave notice. Her severance package was more literal than she expected."

"And the Lonestars let this vampire get away with it?"

Janice's male companion finished his turn and Janice readied her shot. The ball hit the lane with a slam that shuddered through the room. She took no joy in her strike, returning to her seat with the same dead expression.

"She didn't report it," Ava said. "Are you kidding? She was lucky to get out alive. Her husband pays for us to fix that lane every few months."

My search for Jude had skewed dangerously out of my wheelhouse, and I couldn't do this alone. There was a reason cops worked in pairs. I smoothed out my wrinkled sundress. Huff 'n' Puff was a dick, but he had some serious skills that I now required. Even better, he wasn't a Lonestar, nor did he give a damn that I was, as he so charmingly put it, a "fucking BS."

Everyone had their price. I'd find his and hire him to help me.

"Do you know a white wolf shifter who's French, though that only explains some of his stratospheric levels of arrogance?" I said.

"Laurent Amar?" Ava massaged her lower back, and then motioned for me to scoot over so she could sit down beside me. "Overdid it at kickboxing yesterday," she said. "What do you want to be messing around with Laurent for? If this is

76

about finding Jude, you'd be better off going to the Lonestars."

I really wouldn't. "He already knows about my search so…"

Ava shot me a doubtful look but gave me an address.

"Thanks for all your help." I stood up.

"No problem. Come back any time."

"I'll do that," I lied. "It was great meeting you, Ava."

"You too. Hang on." She pulled out her phone. "Give me your number. Let's grab a coffee sometime."

She had a funky style, intelligence, and a quick wit, and in some other reality, she was the type of person I'd like to become friends with, but she was an Ohrist. Jude was too, but she didn't know I had magic. The only way for me to have entered the bowling alley was with powers, which meant I'd either have to lie to Ava about what I could do, which was a sucky way to start a friendship, or trust her with the truth.

I fiddled with my purse strap.

Ava lifted her hands up. "Hey, no worries, if you're not interested."

"I just—"

"Willie, you son of a bitch," Ava muttered. She marched over to the bowler, who'd shifted into a long cobra, and grabbed his tail. "I warned you."

The snake spasmed and morphed back into a now-naked trembling human, eyes wide, who took one look at Ava and fainted on top of his sweats.

I frowned. Ava was angry, but fainting was a bit much.

His buddy sighed. "Ava."

She wagged a finger at him. "Don't you 'Ava' me. It's not like I made him shit his pants in fear. Though if he shifts again here, all bets are off. Got it?"

Ah. She'd manipulated Willie's emotions, making him

terrified of her. Note to self: don't shake hands on the way out.

"Got it." The friend prodded Willie with his foot to wake him up.

Ava headed back to me.

A crescent of light blazed up out of nowhere, and without thinking, I threw my cloaking mesh over Ava, enveloping her a fraction of a second before she was engulfed in a blinding light, which winked out as quickly as it came.

The bowling alley went dead silent, every single patron staring our way.

And why wouldn't they be? A blindspot, a flash of light that killed Ohrists, had just flared up. Ohrists played Russian roulette every time they used their powers, because the same wellspring of magic that they tapped into could rise up at any time to devour them instead, thus replenishing the magical power supply. Even the tiniest action could trigger a blindspot, which was why some Ohrists never used their talents at all.

And here I was, the schmuck who'd called upon her powers to save one of them from it.

Willie fainted again.

"Lucky it missed you," I said, too loudly. As a Banim Shovavim, I didn't have to worry about blindspots. Our magic was bestowed by Lilith and therefore not subject to the same rules.

Ava's hands were over her mouth. "You saved me."

I mentally cursed myself. Revealing my fancy shadow magic to the wolf had been bad enough, but here I was flashing it to all and sundry. "Nonsense," I said, lying through my teeth. "If Ohrists could save each other, we'd have figured out a buddy system a long time ago."

"You're Banim Shovavim."

I stumbled back a few steps, my skin clammy, and my heartbeat thundering in my ears. "I—" I spun around and ran for the exit, but I was grabbed from behind. I struggled, but—

"Thank you! You saved my life!" Ava bear-hugged me. "Hey. You're shaking."

I braced my hands on my thighs and bent over, taking deep breaths, but it didn't help. I'd publicly outed myself. "They'll find me."

"Miri." Ava placed a hand on my shoulder. "No one has cared about your kind in decades. Well, maybe that kind of fear is still warranted in some backwoods areas, but not a city like Vancouver." She waved a hand at the other patrons. "Look. They've all gone back to their games. No one gives a damn."

Willie, his sweat pants back on, glowered at us, but that was probably for Ava's benefit.

"You don't understand," I said. "It's not our history of being hunted."

"Then what are you scared of?" she said.

I paused, and took a breath, forcing myself to say the words out loud. "The people who murdered my family."

8

Ava handed me an open can of Coke and made me comfortable in her desk chair in the back office. "Drink this. The sugar will help."

I leaned back, staring at the calendar above her desk with its painted vintage scene of a pin-up girl bowling, and took a sip. The soda was so cold, it burned my throat going down.

Ava pushed aside a bunch of papers to sit on her desk. "You want to talk about it?"

I traced my finger through the condensation on the can's seam. "I haven't in years. Not since it first happened."

Even Eli didn't know. I'd told him my parents had died in a house fire and that's why Goldie Feldman, my mom's cousin, had raised me. Goldie was unaware of the real facts, as well. She wasn't magic so how could I tell her? And besides, she'd easily accepted the story that my dad's best friend spun about the fire. He was the only one who knew the truth.

Hell, after all these years of repeating it, I'd almost convinced myself of the lie.

Almost.

"It might help," Ava said gently.

I snorted. Sure, what was one more promise to myself broken? I'd set my shadow free again. It was only a matter of time before I broke this resolution to not talk about my parents' deaths either.

"I don't even know that much about it, but I suspect it involved a business deal gone wrong." I laughed bitterly. "I was woefully ignorant of what business my parents were in, but let's just say that my mom didn't tell me bedtime stories of thieves and spies who had our magic for no reason."

"Probably not."

I'd been hiding since I was fifteen, keeping this secret and my magic locked down tight. I took another sip. Well, I'd blown that up spectacularly today, but as scared as I was, I couldn't regret saving a life.

Had enough time passed that I was truly safe? Their killers had never come after me, but Ava had seen my magic. She didn't seem like the type to sell me out, but more importantly, I needed someone else to share the truth with, if only so I wouldn't be the only one who guarded it anymore.

I had another drink, then cast my mind back to that fateful day.

Dad jerked awkwardly after the dish glove hit him, his neck jolting to one side. At first I thought he was kidding, pretending that Mom had wounded him, but he crumpled to the ground, all the vitality sucked from his expression, his eyes wide and lifeless.

I clamped my lips together, staring through the archway to the living room at his body as Sinatra sang about worship and adoration to a bouncy swing tempo.

Mom yanked me out of the kitchen chair and shoved me toward the back hallway. "Hide," she whispered.

I cloaked myself, expecting her to do the same, but she didn't. She called her shadow up around her like knives of darkness, sweeping towards the assassin who charged into the kitchen. It was lethal and elegant and reckless.

"She gave you the chance to escape," Ava said, when I paused the story.

"Yeah. For years I felt so guilty about it, but then I had my daughter and…" I shrugged, calming my bouncing leg. "I'd have done exactly the same."

I'd frozen in the backyard, crying, and watching the fight play out through the kitchen window. Mom had the upper hand, but when the assassin got the jump on her and snapped her neck with their magic, I ran without a second look back.

"What happened when you left?" Ava said.

"We had a creek out back and I'd seen some movie where they crossed water to throw off any tracking, so I did that." I took a long drink of the soda and the sugary bite made my teeth hurt. Still, it bought me time, and the pain grounded me in the present moment, not in the inertia of that memory, with the adrenaline and the endless loop of questions I'd had.

Cold, wet, scared, running on fumes and fear—the enormity of it defied retelling. "It was a long night," I finally said.

"I bet. Did you ever find out who did it?"

"No. Who would I have asked to investigate?"

"Weren't there Lonestars where you lived? This was still a double murder. The regular cops would be called in and—"

"The Lonestars burned down the house with my parents' bodies in it that same night. They destroyed the crime scene. Faulty wiring, tragic accident strikes family, I'm sure you know their process. Magic must remain hidden after all," I intoned, unable to keep the bitterness from my voice.

"That is so shitty. I'm really sorry." She rubbed her thumb across her other palm. "I really do try not to use my magic and influence other people's emotions, but if you want me to temporarily make you feel better?"

"I appreciate it, but no."

The Lonestars' actions that night were made worse by the

speed at which they'd responded. Our house was too far from any neighbor to see or hear the struggle and I didn't tell anyone about the murders until I got to Uncle Jake, Dad's best friend, around dawn at the local lumber mill where he worked the graveyard shift. The Lonestars must have known ahead of time that this hit was planned and they either didn't care enough to protect us, were paid to look the other way, or were part of it.

I never found out, and I'd never trust any of them for that reason.

Jake hid me until he was convinced that no one was after me, at which point he'd reached out to Goldie on my behalf. He'd cut off all contact at that point so that I'd appear to be another Sapien kid, but birthday cards with money in them had shown up with no return address every year until I turned forty. I'd found his obituary in my old hometown's paper. Jake had passed away after a long bout with cancer, leaving me alone with the secret.

Even though we hadn't spoken in years, it reassured me that someone else out there had the real facts, because retelling the house fire story hurt. It made me dissociate. I wanted to scream that it wasn't a tragic accident, even as I sadly told the lie to my daughter. Without anyone to back me up, I sometimes questioned my own memories—and sanity. Remembering that Jake was aware of the truth had helped me cope, and his loss had hit me hard, my grief yet another secret to hide.

Ava put her hand on my arm. "You okay?"

I shook off my reverie. "Yeah."

"You know the chances of your parents' killers finding you are tiny," she said.

"Intellectually, sure, but it's hard to overcome a lifetime of conditioning. My magic is really rare and now everyone out there has seen it."

"True." She nudged my leg. "You're the first Banim

Shovavim I've ever met. Though, technically, calling yourself that is wrong on a couple levels."

"How come?"

"First of all, that's the plural form." She picked up my empty soda can and shook it in question. I shook my head that I didn't want another one. "You're a single person," Ava said. She tossed the can in a recycling bin. "Then there's the issue that Hebrew is a gendered language. The phrase translates as rebellious or wayward children but by children they meant sons. So you'd need to use both the singular and the feminine, which would be an entirely different term."

"And you gave me grief for my weird bowling fact? Why do you know this? Are you Jewish?"

She raised an eyebrow. "Is that impossible because I'm Black?"

"No. It simply means that we have to now perform the mandatory ritual of figuring out every single Jew that we have in common and how our grandparents may have been related."

Ava laughed. "My parents do that with Jamaicans. Nah, I followed a boy to a kibbutz many years ago."

"How'd that work out?"

She flashed me a thumbs-up. "I met a really great Israeli girl who's now my wife, so pretty good."

"Hey, mazel tov."

"You married?"

"I was," I said, "until my husband admitted he preferred men."

Ava winced. "That had to do a number on your self-esteem."

"I'm not sure it's entirely past tense, but I'm also glad he's being true to himself." I swiveled from side to side in the desk chair, nervous about crossing this one last rule I'd made for myself, but wanting a friend who knew about all this stuff. Who knew about me. "I should get going, but uh... if you're still up for a coffee sometime?"

"Definitely."

We exchanged contact info and Ava walked me to the front door. None of the patrons gave us a second glance, easing a knot of tension inside me.

"Hey, that wolf shifter—Laurent—watch yourself with him, okay?" she said. "He's an alpha."

"I got that impression," I said dryly.

"No, I mean he literally is an alpha. Or was. I don't know what happened, but it was bad enough for him to walk away from it. I've heard everything from he slaughtered his pack himself to he murdered an entire community of Ohrists who killed the pack."

My slim understanding of wolf shifters was that some chose not to live in packs, but you didn't become an alpha and then leave. "Is this a 'friend of a friend of a cousin said' kind of thing?"

She shrugged. "Whatever went down, it was bad enough that he now voluntarily kills people on a regular basis."

"The dybbuk-possessed? I thought they weren't human anymore," I said.

"They still look human," she said. "And he's executing them on the regular. What kind of person would willingly choose to do that?"

I didn't know much about dybbuks, but it seemed to me that Laurent was dealing with the shit no one else wanted to handle, and all for the greater good. Still, I wasn't about to get into it with Ava, so I kept my opinions to myself.

"Thanks for your concern," I said, "but I only want to hire him to help me find Jude."

"Well," she opened the door for me, "you could do worse than scoping out that eye candy on the regular."

"True," I said. "In short dosages anyway."

A car horn blared at another vehicle taking forever to

parallel park and a cyclist whizzed by, no one taking notice of a door that had opened out of nowhere.

I waved at my new friend and stepped outside.

The address that she'd given me took me to Railtown, which had been the epicenter of Japanese-Canadian culture in Vancouver before the population was forced into Internment Camps after the attack on Pearl Harbor. The old warehouses and factories in this tiny neighborhood wedged between Gastown and Chinatown were slowly being converted into edgy microbreweries and office spaces for creative professionals.

I parked across the street from a small three-story hotel, its sleek sharp edges tempered by rusted wrought-iron balcony railings and a faded chevron pattern in black running horizontally between each floor. Dirt streaked the stone exterior and there were bars over the frosted windows on the ground level.

Over top of the boarded-up front entrance was a sign with flaked-off letters reading "Hotel Terminus." Had Ava played me or was this dump really where the shifter lived? I wrinkled my nose, questioning the wisdom of aligning myself with someone who chose to live in a place like this.

A man squatted down in front of the hotel with his back to me, but I couldn't tell if it was Laurent, because he had a slouchy black knit cap covering his hair. The build was right, as was the tight denim-covered ass, so I eased out of the car, my purse slung across my chest.

He held out his hand, making kissing noises at a tiny gray kitten crouched in the grass. "Minou, minou," he crooned.

Aw. I leaned against my car, watching them.

"I'm planning on eating it," Laurent said, without turning around.

The kitten warily sidled closer.

"Please," I said. "That's not even an appetizer size for

you. It's not worth skinning." I beeped my fob to lock the car. "How did you know it was me?"

"I smelled you." With his French accent, his lyrical cadence when he spoke turned his words into poetry. Everything sounded charming. How irritating.

I crossed the street, checking my pits, but only smelled deodorant.

As soon as the kitten sniffed his fingers, Laurent scooped up the tiny ball of fluff and cradled the animal against his chest. After he admonished it in French, it was my turn. "You here to insult me again?"

"Depends." I stepped onto the sidewalk. "Care to comment on my advanced age once more?"

"Fait chier. I didn't say you were old. I said you were too old to not know about dybbuks." He winced and unhooked the kitten's claw from his green T-shirt.

I twisted my hair up and, not finding the elastic that I was positive was in my purse, speared the 'do with a pen to secure it. Time to see if the old adage "you can catch more flies with honey" applied to cranky wolves. I pasted on a bright smile.

"We got off on the wrong foot. I'm Miriam. My friends call me Miri." I stuck out my hand to shake.

He scratched the cat's ear. "And?"

I dropped my hand, only the joyous memory of punching him in the face allowing me to keep my smile. "I'd like to hire you to help me find my friend."

"Not interested." He walked around the corner.

I followed him. Okay, time for bluntness and the truth. "Look, I wouldn't be here if I wasn't desperate. You're the only person I can turn—"

A short bald man who resembled a boiled egg in owlish glasses appeared out of nowhere.

I jumped back, clutching my heart. "Holy fuck."

"Neat, right?" the bald man said, in a mild voice. "Light

refraction. I practiced for years to nail it. What's your speciality?"

I floundered. What, was this like zodiac signs to Ohrists, comparing magic abilities? "I—uh—well—"

Laurent shook his head. "Why are you here, Rupert? Is there a problem with my tax return?"

"I—" Rupert blinked, his brows drawn together. "*Is* there a problem with your tax return?"

Laurent sighed and thrust the kitten at me. "Hold her."

The cat hissed at me and I wagged a finger at her. "Stop it," I said sternly. "Listen," I said to Laurent, "if I could just have a minute—"

Laurent shifted one hand into wolf claws and slashed Rupert's arm.

"Are you insane?" I said, and tried to muscle between them.

But instead of freaking out or yelling or doing literally anything that a normal person would do when some rando sliced them like Kobe beef on *Top Chef*, Rupert smiled slyly. "I'm going to kill you."

Two balls of light appeared in his palm.

"Never mind," I said, backing up with the kitten still in hand. Was this some kind of feud? What had I even walked in on?

Rupert flung the light orbs like a pitcher on steroids, his focus scarily intent.

Laurent flipped sideways, his knit cap falling into the grass, and messy chocolate brown curls flopping into the shifter's face.

The light magic crashed into the side of the hotel, sizzling into the stone.

I flinched and shielded the kitten, so she wouldn't be hit by a stray shard.

Rupert's shadow looked normal, but he whipped off his glasses with a cackle worthy of a villain tying some helpless victim to the railroad tracks, and screamed in a deep rumble, "I shall destroy you!" before renewing his magic attack.

A little surprising, given my first impression of him.

Come to think of it, Alex had switched into a different personality that first night. I'd chalked it up to him dispensing with the game of seducing me into doing his bidding, but what if there was more to it than that? Focusing in on Rupert's shadow, I felt that same abomination that I had inside Alex. While it was fainter in this man, I still itched to destroy it.

I could sense dybbuks.

I paced to the sidewalk and back, rubbing my cheek against the kitten's silky fur. It was fine. This new skill set changed nothing about my plan and Laurent had this under control. It was his job. He'd dealt with the dybbuk inside Alex efficiently and this would all be over momentarily.

The shifter swept his hair out of his eyes and *tsk*ed Rupert. "That all you got?"

Huh?

Rupert pitched balls of light at him like the World Series was at stake, but Laurent danced backward on the balls of his feet, elegantly dodging the attacks. It would have been breathtaking if the dumbass hadn't had a sneer on his face.

"Come on, do it," he crowed at Rupert, then smacked his own chest. "Center mass, baby. Can't miss."

Why was Laurent baiting him?

This was ridiculous. I had laundry to get to, plus Jude was missing, and I had to hire him already, so I picked up a twig and lobbed it between them. It hit one of the flying orbs of light and disintegrated into a pile of ash and I placed my hand protectively over the kitten. "Could you shift and finish the dybbuk off already? I really need to speak with you and time is of the essence."

Laurent shot me a "what the fuck" look.

Rupert toed at the ash. "I'm not a dybbuk." There was a

plaintive note in his voice, almost like he was hoping to be told otherwise.

Sorry, dude. Facts were facts.

I waved a hand at him. "Specter inhabited. Phantomly challenged. Plasma blaster. Your pick."

Laurent barked a rusty laugh that was bright and pure in its delight, his eyes sparkling with a warm mirth, and my heart twisted. Didn't he have much hilarity in his life?

No feeling sorry for the wolf.

"I don't care what you call yourself," I said, "so long as we get on with this so I can talk to Laurent."

"He's still human," Laurent said, with a thoughtful expression. His behavior made even less sense if Rupert was still human, though if thinking I could sense dybbuks was a glitch on my part, that was fine by me.

Rupert let out a huge breath. "Told you."

"Shut up," Laurent and I said in unison.

Rupert looked down at his hands, then took a couple of steps closer, a belligerence to his strides. "Why, when I can use my mouth for better things?" He waggled his tongue.

I planted the kitten-free hand on my hip. "You use that mouth to talk to your mother?"

A look of confusion flashed over Rupert's face and then he swore softly and pinched the bridge of his nose. "Sorry. You're right, that was really rude of me."

I pointed at him. "Wild personality swings. Classic dybbuk behavior." Based on my sample group of two possessed Ohrists, this was empirical fact, not because of some magic Spidey-sense.

"Enough talking," Laurent said. "If you're going to finish me, then finish me." He chest bumped Rupert to add injury to insult.

Rupert clenched his fists, his eyes screwed tight. Light swarmed up from his feet through his legs and torso, but it wasn't nearly as bright or as powerful-feeling as when

Laurent had channelled light over his fur while fighting the dybbuk inside Alex.

Laurent threw his arms wide, but the fervent gleam in his eyes undermined the cocky pop of his hip and his chin notched up in dare. This wasn't a game of chicken, it was a man so desperate to feel alive that he welcomed death.

Did he hear a constant thud of bodies hitting the ground and feel flesh yielding to his claws? Did he wake in the night haunted by all the faces he'd committed to memory? Had he numbed himself to survive?

I lay my hand over my heart, but sharply dropped it.

I'd come here to rescue my friend. Laurent was the only person I'd met so far who seemed to have any chance of accomplishing that for me, and right now we were wasting time.

"Men," I said to the kitten, who meowed in agreement. As it was a sunny day, casting lovely shadows, I kicked Delilah into motion.

Before the light fully engulfed Rupert and he shot lasers or detonated or whatever the hell he planned to do, Delilah hooked an arm around his neck from behind and choked him out.

The light disappeared and Rupert went limp in her arms. Delilah dropped him.

"As I was saying." Still cradling the cat, I awkwardly rolled Rupert onto his back with my foot. No point in him suffocating. "Time is of the essence."

Laurent's eyes snapped open. They glowed brilliant emerald. "What. Did. You. Do?" He growled and advanced on me, both his hands shifted to deadly sharp claws.

Jude was still missing, I now had to worry about the undead snacking on my child, and I'd missed lunch. I'd been pushed to my limit and I was not going to be bullied by an overgrown dog with a death wish.

I scratched the kitten's ears. "It's like your own personal Vorpal Blade."

Laurent stopped dead and blinked. "Quoi?"

"Your claws." I made slashing motions with my free hand. "Jabberwocky? 'One, two! One, two! And through and through. The Vorpal Blade went snicker-snack.'" I batted my lashes at him. "You going to snicker-snack me, Huff 'n' Puff?"

Laurent glared at me, a muscle in his jaw ticking.

I notched my chin up, the air between us growing charged. Static energy shivered into the marrow of my bones but I didn't give an inch. I'd birthed a seven-pound human without anaesthetic, my poor vag expanding like a python muscling down a cow. Try me.

His hands returned to normal. "Give me my damn cat." He grabbed the kitten, set her on his shoulder, and jerked a finger at the still-unconscious Rupert. "Grab his legs."

"Why?"

"He needs to be chained up inside."

"So shift and take him yourself."

His growl this time made me take a step back. "You knocked him unconscious before he short-circuited himself with his magic. I was testing something."

"How to be turned into pink mist?"

The cat kneaded Laurent's shoulder and he tapped her head in admonishment. "Rupert isn't powerful or talented enough for that."

Had I mistaken Laurent's death wish for him pushing Rupert to a calculated limit? Had he wanted to achieve this all along? Maybe, but it hadn't seemed that way in the moment. "You're still strong enough to carry Rupert into the hotel on your own."

"Don't push me, BS. You want something, then help."

"My name is Miriam. Or Miri. I do not answer to that other term." I picked up Rupert's legs. "Lead on, Macduff."

"It's 'Lay on, Macduff.'" Laurent stuffed his fallen knit cap in his back pocket and lifted Rupert up under the arms. "Look at that," he said wryly at my surprise, "the wolf is book-learned and everything."

"Bully for you. It doesn't make you less of an asshole. Do you practice in the mirror or is it a natural talent?"

"Most wouldn't dare mouth off to me like you do," he said, walking backwards down the sidewalk, the two of us adjusting our holds to balance Rupert's weight.

I smiled tightly. "Don't forget about socking you in the nose. I certainly remember it fondly."

"About that. You got your one free shot. Hit me again and this time, I'll hit back. Capisce?"

My magic swam up my body to form two dark horns on my head. "'Beware the Jabberwock, my son!'"

Laurent gave me a snarky look. "Snicker-snack."

9

LAURENT PRESSED HIS HAND AGAINST A REBAR X that was propping up a sagging side entrance, with a sheet of plywood instead of a door. It disappeared, revealing an intact frosted glass door.

"Neat trick," I said.

He shifted Rupert into a one-handed hold, and grabbed the handle. "I traded a demon his life for this illusion on my place."

"Who got the better end of the deal?" I winced as the door clipped my shoulder.

"I did." He shot me a very wolfish grin, his white teeth flashing against his olive skin. "He got the business end of my claws after he finished the enchantment. You came here to talk about your friend, so talk."

We stepped into the former lobby and I came to a halt, shamelessly rubbernecking.

Above the polished expanse of checkerboard parquet was a gently arched ceiling painted a pale yellow with warm lighting that made the deep red walls glow. There was no television in sight, but a 1940's radio softly playing Dean Martin sat on the mahogany dining room hutch next to the enormous sofa in the seating area by the fireplace. On the other side of the room, an old upright piano hugged up next to a couple of black floor lamps that reminded me of the classic London streetlights.

You wily wolf, using that ramshackle exterior to make people underestimate you and keep them at bay. His thinking was calculated, ruthless, and designed to give him the advantage—exactly who I wanted in my corner.

The kitten jumped off Laurent's shoulder and scampered away.

I whistled softly. The piano wall was lined with framed prints of vintage alcohol ads, but bookshelves ran the length of the opposite one, from the fireplace to a curved staircase that led to a boarded-off second floor. Every shelf was packed with neatly organized titles and I longed to trail my fingers over the spines and smell the pages, letting the choice of books reveal the man.

"Is this another illusion?" I picked up Rupert's legs again, whispering a silent apology to the man for the indignity of hauling him around this way.

"No. I restored this place. This floor anyway."

For all of Eli's many good qualities, handyman was not among them. Our first home, a fixer-upper, had tradesmen traipsing in and out for years. My brand-new townhouse had been a relief, but being in this hidden gem, each bookshelf hand-finished, carefully polished and sealed, the floors stable and not-creaky—had me close my eyes for a moment and inhale the smell of wood stain, this sanctuary working its spell on me.

This was someone deeply loving a place enough to sweat over it and callus their fingers trying to save it from oblivion. It was a home restored by someone who would never call in professionals, because that person savored every second and last ounce of energy poured into its bones. No one else would see the dream of being stretched out languid on that sofa with a good book on a cloudy day in this room, and how lovely that could be.

I forced myself out of my reverie, because I was here on business.

"I'm impressed," I said in a mostly steady voice. "Which way? Rupert's heavy."

As we continued across the floor, I told Laurent all about Jude, from my initial suspicions about Alex to the break-in at her studio and missing brunch, to the golem—minus the domino stuff—and Blood Alley.

We stopped in front of a large elevator with old-fashioned copper doors carved with diamonds and swirls, which was situated to the right of the staircase. There was a matching pattern on the plate with the call button.

"Put him down," Laurent said, fishing a key out of his pocket.

I dropped Rupert's legs a bit harder than I intended. "Whoops."

He groggily raised his head. "Wha—"

Laurent cold-cocked him and the other man's eyes rolled back into his head.

"Look, I really need your help. I think my friend was involved with the head vampire and—"

"You want, what? To rescue her from his draconian undead clutches?" Laurent sniffed and his fingers drifted to his left side, where that nasty scar I'd seen before lay. "Then I suggest getting yourself a flamethrower and a small tank."

I counted to ten. We all had baggage, but I also had a ticking clock here. "Will you help me out or not?"

Laurent flicked on a light switch next to the call button panel and unlocked the elevator door, revealing a cage gate across it. "Depends." He named a fee that made me wince.

"What happened to"—I dropped my voice into a blustery imitation of his from the other night—"I'll do whatever the fuck is necessary?"

"Did I say I'd do it for free?" Laurent pushed the gate open. On the large side for an elevator, the space had been renovated into a bunker-like room lined in iron.

I ran a finger over the wall. "Does the dungeon suite come with turndown service?"

"Yeah. I turn down their skin off their bodies and then leave a small chocolate next to their glistening intestines," he said.

"Are you joking?" I said, uncertainly.

Laurent grinned evilly and dragged Rupert into the elevator. "There's no chocolate."

Refusing to smile, I ran a finger over the wall and fired off a price that was forty percent of the original.

Our haggling grew fierce, until we arrived at a number that was doable with some creative budgeting on my part.

"I can live with that," I said. "Do we have a deal?"

"D'accord. I'll do it. And you're right that time is of the essence."

"So, do you know where Jude is?"

"No, but I've got a reasonably good guess who took her. Successful golem making is a lost art." He propped Rupert against the wall. "This may be the break I've been looking for on a different case."

I crossed my arms. "You're using my problem to solve something else you're investigating and you have the gall to charge me? Mercenary jerk."

A muscle ticked in his jaw, then he shrugged. "You're not the first person to think that. You won't be the last."

I rubbed my hand over the back of my neck, wondering if I should apologize. Why shouldn't he get paid for what he did? I opened my mouth but he met my eyes for a brief second and then turned abruptly away.

Was this moody wolf really my best bet? I cleared my throat. "Why is golem-making a lost art? Can't anyone with animator abilities make one?"

"Anyone with animator ability can make clay move," he corrected, "but giving them sentience is a lot harder. That makes Jude a valuable commodity."

"Not just sentience," I said. "Emmett prophesized something."

Laurent shot me a grim look. "You sure?"

"Positive. Why?"

Rupert plopped over sideways, and I knelt down to prop him up.

"You know the old myth about the Philosopher's Stone?" Laurent said. "Turning metal into gold?"

"Sure, alchemists were determined to find a way."

"There's a similar desire around creating the perfect golem. Since they are alive and yet not born, some believe it's possible to create one who isn't locked into seeing only the present and past like we are, but the future as well." He shook his head. "It's foolish and dangerous."

I shared that belief, but felt compelled to defend my best friend out of loyalty. No one got to dis her but me. "I'm sure she didn't intend any harm."

Laurent snorted and manacled Rupert's wrists to cuffs that were attached to the wall by thick chains, long enough to allow someone imprisoned to pace inside the elevator car.

"Don't do that. It's barbaric."

Laurent tugged on the chains. "There's a dybbuk inside him."

"I knew it!"

"But he's not fully possessed yet." Laurent sat down with his back against the wall and his legs outstretched. "Get it out."

"How?"

He looked at me incredulously. "Work your magic."

I shook my head, walking backwards out of the elevator. "This is ridiculous. I don't know anything about dybbuks.

Stop fucking around, help this poor man, and let's make a plan for finding Jude."

"I can't help him," Laurent said. "And if you don't, then in a matter of days, the dybbuk will take over his body entirely, and infuse itself into every part of him. Rupert's essence or soul or consciousness, whatever you want to call it, will cease to exist. This evil entity will have free reign to live in Rupert's body with access to magic. He'll prey on others, his rage and malevolence causing pain and destruction." Laurent spread his hands wide. "Unless you save him."

I stopped. "What makes you think I can?"

"Last night. You didn't know what a dybbuk was, but you understood there was something wrong with the man, right?"

"Only because Alex's shadow was fucked up. Rupert's isn't."

"And yet you still sensed the dybbuk inside him." Laurent ran a hand through his curls. "Banim Shovavim can kill dybbuks."

"So do you, and you're an Ohrist."

"I'm the only Ohrist who can, and I had to..." Laurent stared off distantly, fur bursting out on his arms and shoulders before he blinked it away. "Train specifically to detect and dispatch them. And I don't see anything different with their shadows. I can only scent that they're possessed once the host spirit has died."

"What about other Banim Shovavim? Don't you know any?"

"Not anymore," Laurent said. Well, that wasn't ominous or anything.

I already had finding Jude on my plate. This wasn't my problem, but there was a poor man in chains with his life on the line. I knelt down next to Rupert, but even with that same deep sense of wrongness, no solution instinctively presented itself.

"I'm sorry to disappoint you, but I don't know how to kill dybbuks and I definitely don't know how to help Rupert." I softened my tone. "You're not giving yourself enough credit. The takeover isn't complete yet, and you knew there was one inside him. Extrapolate from your training."

Laurent rubbed his jaw. "This isn't my first rodeo. Other enthralleds have shown up to take me out. And there's nothing to extrapolate. The only method open to me kills the host immediately."

"You kill them anyway," I said. "In the end."

"After the dybbuk has. I'm not murdering a human." There was a story behind his vehemence.

"Is this what you were testing with Rupert? Whether him short-circuiting could expel the dybbuk?"

Laurent rubbed his forehead. "I'll try anything."

"This matters a lot to you, doesn't it?" I said gently, wishing I could take back my cruel earlier comment.

"Of course it does. If I could get enthralleds out, I'd be rolling in cash." His stare was a hard challenge.

Sadie had given me that look before, all fierce and puffed out. I didn't push it those times and I wasn't going to now. Instead, I examined Rupert.

After several tense minutes, Laurent spoke again. "Look, I'm certain that you can do this. It makes sense. Why would you be able to detect dybbuks at the enthralled stage if you couldn't help the host?"

The weight of his expectation was crushing me. I jerked on the chains. "Let him out, all right? He should spend whatever time he has left with his friends and family." It wasn't much, but it was something.

"It's not a sudden takeover, you know," Laurent said. "The second a dybbuk inhabits a human host, a tug of war for possession begins. We call it the enthrallment period to differentiate it from being fully possessed. Ultimately, the human always loses, dying at some point between the following Friday and Saturday sunsets, but during that week of enthrallment, there are times the dybbuk momentarily gets the upper hand."

That explained Rupert's abrupt changes in personality. And Alex? Were his sexual predator tendencies due to the dybbuk? His nerdy tie flashed in my head but I shoved the pang away. I'd never know and it hardly mattered anymore.

"Still, if it's just momentarily—" I said.

"One moment is all it takes to blow up someone's life."

"I get that, but if he only has days left to live, isn't there some way to safely release him into the custody of people who could care for him?"

"People are fallible. But have it your way." Laurent yanked a set of keys out of his back pocket. "Have you ever seen a baby's neck torn out?"

I flinched, the memory of my parents' deaths hitting me like a punch to my solar plexus, and slapped his hand away before he could unlock Rupert. I pressed my hand against my stomach, fighting the nausea down.

"Stop it. You've made your point." I lay a hand on Rupert's chest. He remained unconscious but his breathing was steady.

The kitten poked her head in the door and Laurent held out his hand. She bounded toward him, purring loudly as he scratched the base of her tail.

"Minou is an unusual name," I said.

He arched an eyebrow in question.

"I heard you call her that when I first got here."

"That means kitty in French. This is Boo." He put the gray kitten in his lap. "I didn't name her. Quit stalling."

"I'm not." I felt Rupert's pulse, which was strong and steady. "But I have no clue what to do."

"Then Rupert will die."

I straightened Rupert's glasses. Did he have a wife who laughingly pointed out that the glasses were on his head when he went through his house looking for them? Did he have a child who'd drawn him as an owl in bright crayon? Would Rupert spend his last days mired in regret or angry at all the milestones he'd miss? "That's not fair."

"Life isn't fair," Laurent said in a harsh voice. "If you can innately sense dybbuks while in the enthrallment stage, then you have the ability to do something about them. You can save people before it's too late."

Rupert's shadow hadn't turned sickly and crimson yet, the way that Alex's had, but my instincts said that the shadow was key.

Rupert blinked, his eyes woozy, and tried to get up, rattling the chains. "Oh," he said in a small voice.

Laurent squeezed his shoulder. "We'll fix this."

"I got a promotion, that's why." Rupert's lower lip trembled. "I mean, I'd been so careful my whole life, and what were the odds that the one time..." He drew his knees into his chest. "Pretty good, I guess."

I didn't fully understand what Rupert was talking about, but he was aware of his condition, and his quiet resignation broke my heart. "Let me try something."

He glanced up at me, his face alight. "Yes. Okay."

I stroked my chin. I hadn't been able to catch hold of Laurent's wolf shadow, but I had with Alex once the dybbuk had taken over his body.

Was that because Alex's human essence was dead by that point and my magic was rooted in the ability to manipulate death and darkness?

If that was true, then what did it mean when a dybbuk had enthralled someone, introducing an element of death, but that person still lived?

I placed my hand on top of Rupert's shadow, which looked completely normal. It was trickier to catch a hold of, but after a couple of attempts, I succeeded, and crumpled it in my fist like a balled-up napkin. Once again, darkness oozed through my fingers, but it was only lukewarm to the touch. The dybbuk's cry of rage and need pounded in my head, albeit at a lesser volume.

I fumbled it, but stayed the course, swallowing against the nausea that speared through me. "You good?"

Rupert's lips were pinched tight, but he nodded.

Laurent leaned forward, rapt, the kitten forgotten. When was the last time anyone had looked at me with that glint of fascination? I'd held a lot of identities in my adult life: wife, mother, librarian, friend. And while I'd gotten varying degrees of respect and, yes, love for them, how long had it been since someone was excited about me for my own sake versus what I could do for them?

How long was it since I'd seen myself that way?

I was Banim Shovavim. I'd sensed there was something wrong with Rupert and seen Alex's sickly shadow. The solution was in me somewhere, hard-wired into the very DNA of my magic. I closed my eyes, taking a few steady breaths. Just pull it out of him. How difficult could it be?

I yanked hard on the shadow.

10

Rupert screamed, all color draining from his face.

The kitten turned tail and ran.

"I'm sorry!" I dropped my magic and sprinted blindly from the elevator back to the side exit. I tugged on the handle, but when it didn't budge, I rested my head on the door.

Magic equalled death. Wasn't that the rule I'd lived by all these years? Why did I keep on testing the boundaries of this power when I'd have to put it back in its box after all this got resolved?

If Jude was involved with vampires—or worse—what exactly did I think I could do about that? Damn her for whatever she'd gotten into. She'd chosen this trouble, but I could still get out before I crossed a line that I couldn't undo. *You've already changed your mazel*, a voice in my head said. *It's too late for second thoughts.*

A snifter of dark amber liquid was pressed into my hand.

"Scotch," Laurent said. I hadn't heard him cross the main room over to the door. He stood there with the drink held out, his eyes kind, and I wanted to accept this sympathetic gift.

But that would lead to him asking me for things I couldn't deliver. "Please let me out."

"Come sit down for a minute, okay?" He touched my elbow and I allowed myself to be led to the wing-back chair closest to the fireplace.

"I can't do this." I handed him the snifter, and brushed a strand of hair out of my eyes, having lost the pen that held it back. "I'm sorry that I wasted your time."

"You're Jewish, yes?" he said.

I nodded, my hands relaxing on the arms of the chair.

"As am I."

"You're Sephardic, aren't you?" I said.

"My parents are Moroccan Jews who moved to Paris after they got married." He drank some scotch, then balanced the glass on his thigh, as light from a copper sconce played along his cheekbones. Plastic sheeting from one corner of the ceiling crinkled as the ventilation kicked in, and he sighed. "What do you know of the Jewish concept of Gehenna?"

It rang a bell. I sorted through the random facts I'd accrued over the years. "It's some kind of underworld."

"Exactement. While it isn't mentioned in the Torah, some rabbinic texts believe God made it on the second day of Creation. Specifically, it's the place where wicked souls go after death to be punished."

"The wicked souls are dybbuks?" I leaned forward.

"Yeah. The word is a Yiddish derivative of the Hebrew phrase dibbuk me-ru'ah ra'ah or 'the spirit who cleaves.'"

"Really?" I sat up, practically salivating over this cool fact. "Unfortunately, whoever is in charge of Gehenna isn't doing a very good job if these spirits keep breaking loose and coming to earth."

"Well, to be more precise," Laurent said, offhandedly sipping his alcohol, "they let them out."

I nearly dropped my purse. "What?"

He nodded, his expression somber. "Both the wicked and those that torture them get the Sabbath off. The dybbuks are free to come and wreak havoc, which they can only do if they possess a body."

I buried my head in my hands, wishing we'd quit this conversation back at "cool fact." We had an underworld and fugitive spirits on the lam from torture? "Is that what I saw when you opened that portal? Gehenna?"

He nodded, totally chill, when I wanted to flip his ottoman over and freak the fuck out.

"I'll take that drink now."

Laurent chuckled and brought me a finger of scotch, which I slugged back.

Knowledge was power, sure, but returning to my nice little bubble of safety by never using my powers again was very tempting. I put the empty glass down. Could I even do that anymore? I may have been a grown woman with a child, but times like this, I wished my own mother was still around to counsel me.

"What about Sapiens?" I said.

"They're safe. Dybbuks only possess those with magic. If a dybbuk has not found a host body to inhabit and enthrall when the angel Dumah blows his trumpet at sunset on Saturday, they must return to Gehenna and their torture begins anew."

I shivered. "I heard it. The trumpet."

Laurent stilled, the glass halfway to his mouth, knocking the ice cubes together. "You did? I can't." He stared into the amber liquid. "Seems wolf hearing isn't good for everything."

I ran the knuckle of my thumb over my teeth. I'd never heard it before either, but I'd never been in the presence of a dybbuk at sunset either, so I couldn't say if the ability was new. I tamped down my unease. "Don't get excited. I still don't know how to help Rupert."

Laurent swirled the scotch in his glass, his voice as hypnotic as the motion of the dark liquid. "Dybbuks aren't like other ghosts who are fairly benign. They're pure rage, needing extremes to feel alive. Some lash out, others engage in vices, glutting themselves to death. They have friends, family, and those people must watch as one with the face of their beloved engages in destructive behavior." He abruptly set the snifter down on the over-sized ottoman that served as a coffee table. "It causes unimaginable suffering."

Was that why Laurent did this? Did he know first-hand whereof he spoke?

"But if they could be saved before the dybbuk kills them?" He braced his elbows on his hands, that brilliant green gaze trained on me.

I wasn't some bastion of hope. I was an ordinary woman doing her best to get through every day, same as most people. Laurent was assuming I could save Rupert based on some pretty slim evidence. If he hadn't found a way when his entire job was dealing with dybbuks, it was unfair to believe I could waltz in and get it done.

Looking away, I dug my buzzing phone out of my purse. Sadie was texting, wondering where I was and if her red sweater could go in the dryer? Shit. The laundry had been sitting wet all day. I texted back that I'd be there in twenty minutes and yes, it was fine.

"I have to go," I said.

"What about Jude?" he said.

How awful a person would I be if I let this play out and stayed to the safety of the sidelines? If vampires were involved and Sadie was at risk of getting drawn in, then maybe I was better off letting Jude sleep in the bed she made. My stomach felt sick and heavy, but just as with Rupert, what could I possibly do about the situation?

"I... don't know."

Laurent's grip tightened on the glass. He took a sip of

scotch, then he nodded. "Your call. But if you change your mind?" He gave me his number.

Sadie was sitting at the kitchen table eating ice cream out of a mug when I got home. She sucked the chocolate off the spoon in the exact same way that she had when she was little, her face scrunched up against the cold, and my heart contracted.

The night she was born, I paced with her through silent hospital corridors, marveling that here was a total stranger whom I would already lay down my life for. After sixteen years of this smart, mouthy, stubborn, amazing kid, that desire had only intensified. As a single mom, I'd had to temper my tendency to helicopter parent with the reality of Sadie taking on a fair amount of independence as she navigated between two loving households.

I'd vowed that magic would never impact her life as it had mine, and yet, this weekend it had been hammered home to me that it lurked around every corner. So how did I go on from here? And what should I do about Jude?

Sadie held out her spoon to me.

"Ice cream isn't dinner." I dug out a clump and swallowed a mouthful of coconut chocolate chip. "Damn. This is good."

"Right? What's dinner anyway but a construct? I say we reject Big Food's notion of serving sizes and types. Forge our own path." She snatched the spoon back. "Starting with ice cream."

I dumped my purse on the counter. "Does that mean I don't have to feed you anymore? Because I'm down with that."

"Let's not get crazy."

"No. This is good." I opened the freezer door and pulled out a jar of pesto and a container of raw turkey meatballs, both of which I put in the microwave on defrost. "I support you being an individual and foraging your own path."

Sadie gave me puppy dog eyes. "I could eat that."

"Make the salad and I'll consider it."

She slid off the stool and grabbed the ingredients, snagging the cutting board from the top of the fridge while she was there. Putting her phone in the stereo dock, she turned on her current favorite playlist of Broadway musicals.

For a while we prepped dinner, singing along to *Chicago*. I pulled the items out of the microwave, testing both to check if they were defrosted and ignored the chiming work alerts coming in on my phone, until Sadie rolled her eyes.

"Answer them already," she said. "You'd think the world was going to end if they didn't get their dumb law stuff first thing in the morning."

"It matters to their clients." I wiped my hands off on a dish towel and replied to the various lawyers that I would be sure to check their emails first thing tomorrow and get on their requests.

"I could never be a lawyer. I'd stab myself out of boredom. Give me passion. Drama. Theatah." She drawled the last word out, striking a dramatic pose.

"I'd never have guessed, stabbing oneself out of boredom being such a conservative response to any situation."

"You're not funny. Speaking of drama, do you have my library card? That teen King Henry the Eighth retelling finally came in."

"He should have had pre-nups. Less drama. And check your rain jacket. That's where it was last time." Chuckling, I flicked on the burner, the gas hissing to life, and heated up the oil in the pan. "Can you imagine if kids' books were written with legal contracts? Well, Aiden, the reason that Susan, Edmund, Lucy, and Peter had to sign a release of liability form before going through the wardrobe was to keep the White Witch from being sued. No, Rachel, Frodo was right to explain to Gollum that his best course of action regarding the ring was to prove providence."

"You'd be a great children's librarian," Sadie said, softly

as she washed lettuce leaves. "I know that's why you got your Masters in Library Sciences. I wish you hadn't given up on that dream."

I slid the meatballs into the sizzling oil.

"It's not that easy." I adjusted the heat. "Dreams are great, but they don't always pay the mortgage or grocery bills. Also, children's librarian positions are highly coveted— whenever I applied, I never seemed to make it. But come on, it's not as if I'm on my feet eight hours a day gutting fish. I work in a law firm with a fancy schmancy ergonomic spinny chair. That's pretty good, all things considered."

"But it's not what you want," she said, then sighed.

I let it go. She was passionate, and I loved that about her, but in a family full of people chasing their dreams, some-times you needed a realist. "Hey, why didn't you call me before you left Nessa's?"

"Aunt Genevieve gave me a lift."

Great, now she'd bitch to her brother about me. Genevieve had pretty much cut me out of her life after the divorce, which suited me fine. She'd never believed I was worthy of her baby brother, but she was close to Sadie, which was all I cared about.

"Where were you all day?" Sadie chopped cucumber into thin slices. "I was doing homework and kept expecting you to come home. Were you day drinking with Jude?"

"Day drinking while on vacation is a perfectly respectable tradition."

"You guys did it last weekend."

"What did the labour movement fight for, if not for week-ends to be times of rest? To be, in effect, vacations?" The lid on the boiling water rattled, steam pouring out. I dumped in the rotini and set the timer.

Sadie snorted. "And you wonder where I get it from? Seri-ously, were you with her?"

"No. I had stuff to do."

She slid the cukes into the salad bowl, before pointing at me with the knife. "Is something wrong with her?"

Hot oil splattered onto my wrist and I winced. "Why?"

"Uh, hello. You know how competitive Jude is. I was winning our Scrabble game. She'd want to catch up." Sadie looked at me, totally guileless and trusting, and I couldn't do it. I couldn't tell her that her aunt was missing. She waved the knife. "I knew it. What's wrong?"

"Nothing. She had a family emergency and had to take off for a couple days. I'm sure she'll play as soon as everything is clear."

"Okay." Sadie finished up the salad, but she stopped singing along.

Dinner was a subdued affair, with both of us pushing our food around our plates but not really eating. My daughter was upset, and I felt sick with guilt for lying, for abandoning Jude, and for not helping Rupert.

Sadie got up to clear the table but I stopped her.

"We can do that later. Let's watch *Buffy*." Sunday nights were sacrosanct TV date nights. Even if Sadie was at Eli's that week, she came home on Sunday after dinner so the two of us could watch our current pick.

We settled in to watch the episode in season five where Dawn runs away after finding out she's the Key. I was glad we'd both seen the series before, because I was finding it hard to concentrate, and given Sades' restlessness, she had the same difficulty.

She finally curled up on the sofa with her feet in my lap. "Spike's right," she said, after the scene where the vampire and the Slayer fought over keeping Dawn's origins a secret. "Buffy should have told her sister the truth."

"How do you break something like that to a person?" I picked at a loose thread on my beige couch. I'd drooled over this crazy amazing orange velvet couch in the showroom, but it was too showy, so I'd settled for sensible stain-resistant furniture.

Sadie shrugged. "You just tell them. It's always better to know because the truth is still out there whether you want to admit it or not. All we can do is choose how to handle it. Besides, being the Key is cool. Dawn would see that if she hadn't been treated like a dirty secret."

Schooled by a sixteen-year-old.

As my wise child said, the truth was out there—Jude was out there—and the only choice I had was in how I handled it.

I sent a text to Laurent. *I'm game if you are.*

11

MONDAY MORNING WAS THE SAME MAD RUSH AS always when Sadie was switching over to her dad's place for the week. A multitasking marvel, she took a bite of her bagel while pulling on her red sweater. Her head got caught and she swore, jamming her arms into the sleeves and then fixing her ponytail.

I sipped my coffee, shaking my head as she dumped the contents of her backpack onto the table and frantically pawed through everything.

"I need my calculator for my final." She sniffed the left-over sandwich in her lunch bag, shuddered, and dumped it in the trash.

"You don't have math until tomorrow. Look for it after school."

"That means I have to come all the way back here." She frowned at a sheet of paper and then slid it over to me. "Sign."

I motioned for her to get me a pen. "All the way back from next door? How lazy are you?"

She unzipped her pencil case and tossed me one. "I have stuff to do. Like study?"

"Tone the attitude down a notch." I read the form she'd given me. "You probably left it at your dad's in the first place. Check there and then if you don't find it, take ten minutes to conduct a calm search of your room here."

"Fine," she muttered. "Jeez. Do you have to read everything? It's not a contract signing my soul away to the devil."

"Which I would do with no hesitation." I tapped the field trip permission form. "This is due this afternoon."

"Yeah, I—" She waved her hands around, her leg jiggling.

"Breathe, honey." We'd gone through counseling with Sadie for the perfectionist pressure she put on herself. When things spiralled out of her control, her throat would close up and she couldn't form coherent sentences. Her leg bouncing was another sign I'd learned to recognize that she was agitated and heading for the breaking point.

She took a few slow breaths.

"Better?" I signed the form, my stomach in my toes.

She nodded. "Yes."

"Come here." I held out my arms and she hugged me, her head resting on my shoulder. "Worst case scenario and you can't find it, ask your dad to go on a Staples run tonight."

"Okay. Thanks, Mom."

I kissed her cheek. "Anytime. Love you, Sades."

"You too. Oh, man. The time." She tore through the kitchen like a tornado, stuffing school supplies and lunch items into her backpack, remembering the form at the last second, then ran out the back door. "Bye!"

It slammed shut behind her and now I was the one who breathed deeply, taking in one moment of perfect silence. The kitchen was a shambles from breakfast, but I didn't have the time or inclination to deal with it. Today was my performance review and I was going to nail a much-needed raise. Then tonight, I'd meet Laurent and we'd find Jude.

I headed out the back door, preceded by Delilah who

tossed her hair and sashayed to the car. Hell, yeah. I had this in the bag.

Shirley, the firm's HR manager, closed my file, setting it atop a listing pile on her desk. "You're always one of my easiest staff to review. As usual, we're delighted with your work and we hope you'll be happy with your cost of living increase."

My chair was upholstered in a color only found in nature as the result of a digestive disorder. Its nubby fabric didn't help with the impression that I sat in the contents of a blown-out colon.

"Thank you," I said. Mortgage rates, utilities, food, all of them had risen across the board, not to mention that Sadie had been accepted into a youth theater troupe for next year that was going to cost money, and my car was almost twenty years old. "It's definitely appreciated."

Shirley steepled her fingers together. "I have something else that I think you'll be excited about."

Increased benefits? Extra vacation days? "What is it?"

"As you know," Shirley said, "we've taken over another floor because we're adding immigration law to our services. That means the library will be expanding. You'll have a larger budget to work with for purchases."

I matched her bright smile. "I'll also have a further fleshed-out job description and more work on my plate."

"Not at all." She opened another file and handed me a resume. "We're hiring you an assistant. Isn't that wonderful? He comes highly recommended and I'm sure you'll enjoy working with him. Congratulations."

The new hire did have an impressive curriculum vitae, but I'd never had any desire to supervise someone else. I'd sat in on management training that the firm provided for its lawyers. Effective delegation was one thing, but I'd be expected to be a mentor, keep my assistant motivated, and be an effective communicator.

Then again, I could off-load a lot of smaller, more tedious tasks and keep the best parts of the job.

"He seems extremely competent," I said, and placed the resume on the desk.

"You'll have a chance to welcome him yourself soon. He starts in two weeks." Shirley stood up and walked me to the door.

"I'm looking forward to it." I'd gotten my raise, and if I had to manage an assistant, so be it. But I remembered my conversation with Sadie and paused in the doorway. What would it be like to follow my dream?

Shaking it off, I headed back to the library to get my things, grateful this appointment had been at the end of the day, because I was exhausted from worrying about whether or not I was getting my raise this year.

Blake waited at the elevator for a car. He barely acknowledged me, busily chatting Addison up. Her eyes were fixed firmly on the floor numbers and she wasn't responding other than to shift over when he got particularly excitable telling her how skilled he was as an amateur race car driver.

An empty elevator arrived and Addison hurried on to it, positioning herself in the corner.

Blake got on next, crowding her and continuing his monologue of the Blake Show. Addison was lower than Blake in the pecking order, not to mention she was a young woman, new to our firm. She'd put up with his behavior because it didn't actually constitute sexual harassment, and that tiny ball of rage inside her would grow a bit larger.

I kept quiet for all of two floors until Addison pressed herself so deep into the corner that one millimeter more and she'd be in the elevator shaft.

"Blake, I'm sure Addison has had a long and busy day and

simply wants some peace and quiet as she goes home. Yes?" I said.

She nodded. "Yes, please."

"We're just talking," Blake said.

The young woman sighed.

"You have a law degree so you must have a brain." I smiled sweetly. "I encourage you to use it and read people better, especially women. She's not interested."

"Butt out, *Mara*," he sneered.

The elevator slowed to a stop and the doors opened.

"You're right. It's none of my business."

"Damn straight," he said.

His position as big man firmly established, Blake strutted out and immediately tripped over Delilah's outstretched leg. He spilled out onto the marble lobby floor, disheveled but unhurt, attracting the attention of everyone there. Including two of our senior partners, who didn't appreciate the spectacle.

"Have a nice night, Addison," I said, stepping out.

At the sight of Blake splayed on the ground, his bluster gone, the tension in her shoulders relaxed. "You too."

Petty? You bet. But intensely satisfying. Maybe there were a few perks to having magic in a world where most people couldn't see it.

I was still smiling when I got home to change. Sadly, the kitchen hadn't miraculously cleaned itself. I tidied up, then headed upstairs to my bedroom, pulling my dress off along the way to expedite getting my bra off. Unclasping it, I sighed in delight, rubbing the red marks across my chest, then grabbed at my stockings as the little bastards made a dash for my thighs, rolling down into a lumpy line. Shuffling knock-kneed into my room, I flopped on the mattress to pull them off, followed quickly by my Spanx.

My belly fat splayed sideways, matching my boobs who

were trying to acquaint themselves with my armpits. I didn't care. The cool air on my freed body was delicious.

I opened iTunes on my phone and cranked the volume to the opening notes of Thelma Houston's "Don't Leave Me This Way," bumping and grinding around the room.

Wriggling into jeans, I struck a sassy pose and belted out the chorus, flinging lingerie out of my drawer until I found a clean sports bra. I added my favorite blue sweater, tied my hair back with an elastic I found in Sadie's room, and crammed some leftover pesto pasta into my mouth.

Fortified as I was going to get, I drove over to Laurent's, munching on a couple of breath mints, and texted him that I was outside. Having been cooped up indoors all day, I sat on my hood, enjoying the mild weather.

He came outside, saw my sedan, and crossed his arms. "I'm not riding in your Give-Up-Mobile."

"Sorry, my Romulan Warbird is in the shop. You'll have to make do."

Another rusty laugh burst out of him, surprising even himself, before he glared at me, as though I'd destroyed his carefully curated balance of curmudgeon and asshole.

Then he marched back inside.

What the heck? "Hey!" I called. "I'm paying you to solve my problems, not walk away because you have issues with my jokes."

"Wait," he called out.

I played Tetris until he returned and shoved a motorcycle helmet and black leather jacket at me, his own helmet looped over one arm. "No way," I said. "Those things are death traps."

"Says the woman paying a visit to vampires."

"That's where you come in, Huff 'n' Puff. You're the red shirt." I patted him under his brown leather jacket. "You're already in the right color."

Muttering under his breath in French, he stalked off down

the block to a big-ass motorcycle, the kind that the Four Horsemen would ride into the apocalypse. "Coming?" he said, impatiently.

Grabbing my sunglasses, I locked my purse in my trunk and followed, circling the bike warily. "I've never ridden one."

"Imagine my great surprise," he said dryly, swinging a leg over. "Put on the jacket and helmet. I'll adjust the fit for you."

The jacket smelled like him, faintly of cedar, but also with a trace of a musky cologne. I zipped it up, rolled up the sleeves, and put on the helmet.

Laurent secured the straps under my chin. His calloused fingers brushed the underside of my throat and I squirmed.

"That tickles."

He tugged on the helmet and, nodding, kicked up the side stand. "Get on and wrap your arms around me."

I'd seen enough movies to know how this worked. I'd have to sit flush up against him, gripping his chest in a tight hold.

"How's Rupert?" I blurted out, buying time to psych myself up for the ride.

"How do you think?" Laurent shook his head, his lips in a thin line. "He knows he has only days to live."

I winced. "That's awful. I didn't know enthralleds were aware of their predicament."

He didn't answer and somehow that made the thought of being pressed up behind him even more awkward. How did you even begin to unpack something like that?

How did Laurent deal with that when he confronted a dybbuk?

"I'm sorry," I said at last. "It's not fair that this happens or that you're left to deal with the aftermath."

His brows drew together, his glance at me almost startled, then he jerked a thumb at the motorcycle. "Get on."

Our positions were exactly as expected, with me plastered against him, holding on for dear life, my cheek pressed against his back, and the heat of his body thrumming through me—and that was before he'd turned on the engine.

I tried to match his even breathing, but a paper bag to hyperventilate into would not have been remiss right now.

"Bien," he said. "Watch your feet and don't move around." He started the bike and the ensuing roar danced up from my feet to the crown of my head.

I screwed my eyes shut. For the first few minutes of the ride, I was unable to do more than sing "I Will Survive" in my head. I was sitting atop this raw power, holding on to a werewolf, but as tense I was, Laurent was relaxed, driving slowly and leaning us into the turns more gently than I'd anticipated.

Small details filtered through my terrified haze: muffled radios in cars next to us at a red light, the wind kissing my face, the smell of grilled meat. I opened my eyes. We'd passed a BBQ joint.

Laurent sped up, the entire world kicking into fast forward. The hum of the tires took over the melody in my head, while the vibrations did saucy things to my nether bits. I flushed, my eyes practically rolling back into my head, and Laurent's laughter floated back to me.

He couldn't know what I was feeling, could he? I winced. Werewolf. Heightened sense of smell. I hunched into my shoulders wishing the ground would swallow me whole, but embarrassment trumped fear and I started enjoying the ride. I wasn't locked behind glass and steel, like in a car. I prowled through the world in full contact, my senses almost overloaded.

I was on a mission with some sexy wildcard to see vampires and rescue my friend. I'd let magic back into my life and as terrifying and overwhelming as it all was, I hadn't felt this rejuvenated in years.

We overtook a bus, zipping into the lane in front of it, and I laughed.

All too soon, it was over. Laurent darted into a parking garage downtown and cut the engine.

The silence was almost shocking.

"Pit stop," he said, helping me off.

"For what?" My legs were shaky and he gave me a knowing smirk.

"Information." He took my helmet and locked it to the motorcycle with his own. "It's freeing, isn't it? Riding?"

I was ready with a quip about being glad I'd survived, but I paused, choosing a more honest answer. "Yeah. It's scary, but it's exhilarating, too."

"That's why it's exhilarating." He looked fondly at his bike, then his eyes met mine, and his smile lit up his entire face. For a moment, there was only the two of us, sharing our excitement like a giddy secret.

"The rush is out of my normal comfort zone." I pressed the backs of my hands to my cheeks because I was blushing. "But I liked it."

"I'm glad." His smile widened for a second and then dropped abruptly. "Stay here."

I blinked. Really? After having an honest-to-goodness bonding session, I got dumped outside like baggage? I jammed my sunglasses on my head. Thanks for the emotional whiplash, dude. "Oh, absolutely. Would you like something to eat while I wait? Should I wash your bike?"

"Don't touch the bike," he said, and I was pleased that there was a dash of uncertainty in there, like he wasn't sure how dangerous I was or not.

Maybe the extra teeth in my smile gave it away.

I rattled the handlebars. I kind of had to at that point.

Like I was a toddler who had beeped the horn one too many times, he lifted me up and away from the motorcycle. "Stay."

"I'm not waiting out here," I said. "I'm paying you, remember? That means I call the shots."

Laurent snorted and rubbed a spot on his handlebars, like I'd sullied them.

I clenched my hands into fists. "I'm coming with you."

"Then don't speak once we get inside," he said. "It's dangerous."

"I'm dangerous." I wasn't, but he didn't have to be a jerk.

"You're a sitting duck."

"Yeah? Well, you're being a dick. How's that for four-letter d-words?"

"Sometimes I am a dick." He gave a very Gallic shrug and walked to the elevator. "I'm French."

I let him pass me, mouth agape. Could I use that in my homicide trial? In my defense, Your Honor, he was French.

"What floor?" I said, once we were inside.

"Basement."

I shook my head. "There's no button for that."

He tapped his foot impatiently. "Yeah, there is."

Groaning, I focused on the panel. I stepped forward, I stepped back, all to no avail. The button didn't reveal itself.

"Any lifetime now," Laurent groused.

"Shut up." I relaxed my eyes, trying to see through the panel, and there it was: a black button marked with a white B. "Aha!" I pushed it and we descended into the bowels of the garage.

When the elevator opened, Laurent stepped out into a tiny concrete foyer and lifted the broken handle of the ancient payphone bolted to the wall. Twice, he clicked the part that hangs up the call.

"That's a switch hook," I said.

Frowning, he looked at the black handset in his grip. "It is?"

"No, that's the handset with the transmitter and receiver. I mean the part you depressed." I mimed the motion with my index finger. "It's where the saying 'my phone was ringing off the hook' came from."

He considered the receiver for a moment. "Did it ever really fall off the hook?"

"Maybe?"

"English has ridiculous expressions," he proclaimed.

"Yeah, but you were still curious."

"Others won't be," he said. "Not in here." He hung up the phone and an entire section of wall, including the pay phone, swung open.

I gasped. "Did it send some kind of signal? Did hanging up the phone make it do that or did someone buzz us in from the other side?"

"It's—" He shook his head. "No more questions. No more trivia." He stepped through the wall. "If you want to get out of here unnoticed, then stick close." I opened my mouth but he cut me off with a slash of his hand. "And no talking."

12

LAURENT STOPPED SO SUDDENLY INSIDE THE threshold that I smacked into his back.

"Out," a massive Indo-Canadian man said, blocking our way.

I peeked past him and my mouth fell open.

We were in a speakeasy with gleaming burnished tables and curved leather banquettes. Sconce lamps hung in regular intervals on the gold brocade wallpaper, bouncing their light off the pressed tin tiles on the ceiling, while a chandelier made of dizzying twists of black metal hung over the bar at the far end of the room. A jazz band on a small stage played a raucous tune with whooping clarinets and a rumbling bass that would be a great soundtrack to make bathtub gin to.

"Now, now, mon ami," Laurent said, really slathering on the French charm, "we agreed to let bygones be bygones."

The other man shook his fist. "You killed my mother-in-law."

"I killed a dybbuk, Vikram," Laurent said, all pretense of good cheer gone. "Your mother-in-law didn't exist by that point and you know it."

"Tell that to my wife. She hasn't stopped crying in a

month." Short brown fur broke out over the man's skin. His ears turned stubby and round, and a snout protruded from his nose.

"Grizzly," I squeaked. Growing up in northern British Columbia, we hadn't been warned about stranger danger as much as we'd been warned about bears. Every kid knew the story of the boy who'd gotten his scalp ripped off in his own backyard and had to be flown to Vancouver for reconstructive surgery. I'd seen bears in our back garden. They were scary enough through a window, so being this close to one, even one that was still mostly human, caused the lizard part of my brain to scream "Run!"

Laurent briefly touched my shoulder, then got up in the other man's face. "Step down, Bear. Kaia got drunk during the Danger Zone. On your watch."

Vikram hung his head. The innately human movement alleviated some of my fear, and besides, now I was curious.

"Danger Zone?" I said. "What's that?"

"Who are you?" Vikram said.

"No one," Laurent said, miming for me to zip it.

Vikram shifted back. "Who have you dragged into your shit now, Wolf?" He turned to me. "The Danger Zone is what we call that time from sundown Friday to sundown Saturday. Dybbuks require lowered inhibitions to inhabit a body, so we're not supposed to drink or get high during that time." He scratched his chin. "I've heard other people call it the Dead Day, maybe that's what you're more familiar with."

"That's why Jude didn't drink on Fridays when we went out," I said. "She said it was because she had to wake up early and get to the studio." She never drank, but I did, unwittingly putting myself in harm's way. Innocence was bliss, but it also could have gotten me possessed, even if I'd never used my powers again.

I worried at my bottom lip. What other things was I missing out on knowing that could keep me safe?

"How did you not know this?" Vikram said. "Are you a Sap?"

Laurent glared at me, but not answering Vikram would be more suspicious.

"The more important question is why you allowed your mother-in-law to get drunk, knowing full well what could happen." I wagged a finger at Vikram. "Shame on you."

He threw his hands up. "Believe me, I tried. There was no arguing with the woman." His expression turned sly. "Much like someone else I know."

Laurent briefly closed his eyes. "Merde."

"Want me to announce your presence?" Vikram bounced gleefully on his toes.

"Do it and I'll gut you," Laurent said. "Is she in the gallery?"

Vikram nodded, just as shouts came from the left side of the establishment.

I tried to see what was happening but Vikram was in my way.

"Let me talk to Harry and we'll be gone," Laurent said.

Vikram shrugged. "You know the way."

Laurent strode off and I half-jogged to keep up.

A server created tiny balls of light that she dropped into glass jars and placed on tables, while another woman danced the Charleston on the parquet dance floor by herself, hovering a couple of feet above the ground. Two businessmen in a nearby banquette under one of the many crystal chandeliers shared a charcuterie. One of the men popped a cracker with salami in his mouth and his furry ears perked up, while the other pawed through a bowl of olives with a wolf-like growl of pleasure.

They saw Laurent and both turned away. My companion tensed up.

"Speakeasies got their name because people used to speak quietly about them in public so as not to alert police or nosy neighbors," I said. Laurent had taken on the unpleasant tasks that no one else wanted. Like moms did all the time. I felt oddly protective of him, and glared at the men who'd dissed him. "They were also called Blind Tigers."

Laurent frowned, but his tension dissipated. "What does a tiger have to do with drinking?"

"Some speakeasys would put a tiger statue in the window and if there was a blindfold on it, it meant the cops weren't watching and it was safe to enter."

"That's stupid. Then the police would know where it was."

I scratched the back of my head. "That's why they were constantly shutting down and springing up somewhere else. Who's in the gallery?"

"No one."

"Your forthcoming nature is so endearing." I glanced over at the art-house crowd on the other side of the shared space, half of whom wore colorful funky clothing and radiated excitement, with the rest in black, made darker by their ennui-laden expressions.

Wondering what they were all so engrossed in, I wandered over.

The white walls of the small art gallery attached to the speakeasy were bare, but a contest of some sort was taking place. Two massive slabs of wood were propped on bases. A bare-chested man faced off against this old lady, in her eighties if she was a day, with a silver pixie cut. She sported oversized, red-framed glasses and a 1960's style A-line white minidress with lime-green polka dots. Her stick-thin legs were encased in white tights, the entire ensemble topped off with chunky red heels.

One of the spectators yelled, "Go!"

The man splayed his hands against the wood and cracks spiderwebbed through the grain. My eyes widened as the slab twisted, pieces dropping off, and the smell of sawdust tickling my nose. Sweat dripped off the man, his chest glistening as his creation took the shape of an eagle, its wings outstretched.

The other artist's slab was steadily shrinking, but not into any recognizable form.

I let out a breathy sigh as the eagle took flight, soaring around the art gallery.

The male artist let out a raucous whoop, his face red with exertion. "Top that," he cried.

The crowd cheered him on.

I rose on tiptoe.

The old lady held up what looked like a tiny nut made of wood, then she dropped it to the ground and stepped on it.

Confused murmurs ran through the crowd and then there was a gasp from the front.

I pressed forward for a better look.

She'd reduced her slab of wood to a single seed from which a slender trunk now grew. It lengthened and thickened, its bark growing rough, and slender branches sprouted.

The woman who'd said "go" held up a hand. "Clap for the winner."

Artist dude got a smug look on his face and his eagle circled the room one more time.

The old woman smiled indulgently, and the tree bloomed into hundreds of paper-thin wooden blossoms. There was a collective "oooh" and then the gallery exploded in cheers.

Even the male artist acknowledged her victory, holding her arm up in triumph.

Someone grabbed my elbow.

"What part of 'stay close' did you not understand?" Laurent hissed, keeping his back to the spectators. He dragged me over to the speakeasy side.

"It was harmless. I was standing in a crowd watching a performance for two minutes, not giving lap dances."

"You hired me for my expertise, so take it."

"Fine." I had no desire to be singled out anyway.

We reached the bar and Laurent rapped the top twice. "Eh, conard. You here?"

"Oi," a male voice with an English accent boomed. "Go bugger yourself."

The bartender emerged from under the bar and I broke into a sputtering cough.

Broad-shouldered but stocky, he wore a long silver necklace that came almost halfway down the fitted blue shirt that clung to his bulging biceps. Tattoos covered both arms, including a scorpion about to strike and the phrase "no regrets."

Two words came to mind: fuckboy and... I laughed delightedly, eyeing his rock-hard skin. Not rock-hard abs—skin made of gray stone, along with a wide face, large ears and stubby horns.

Laurent and he exchanged man-bro slaps on the back.

I cleared my throat. "You're a—"

"Brit?" the gargoyle said. "Yeah. Been here since the nineties."

"The eighteen nineties?"

He snorted, wiping down the bar top with a rag. "Cheeky, ain'tcha? Nah, shit went pear-shaped on a job and I had to leg it across the pond. Decided I liked it here." His massive biceps cracked faintly as he moved.

"Are there a lot like you?" My head swam with visions of dark forms swooping in the night sky that might not have been birds.

His expression darkened. "You got a problem with my kind?"

I clapped my hands. "Are you kidding me? I spent an entire summer during university finding gargoyles in Europe."

"Here we go," Laurent muttered, but he didn't even glare at me. I was totally growing on him.

The gargoyle rolled his black eyes and I swear I heard the sound of marbles. "Notre Dame. Them boys get all the credit."

"Sure, but also the ones on the Milan Cathedral and Il Boccalone." I ticked off items on my fingers. "Cologne Cathedral and Holy Cross Church in Great Ponton."

The gargoyle's face lit up. "No way. My cousins live there."

"And you're all sentient?"

"Nah. Only some of us were hit with animator magic way back when, and of those, even fewer evolved to have intelligence. Most of my kind are a pretty face on a water spout." He held out his hand. "Harry."

"Miri."

His fingers enveloped mine, but his grip was gentle, and his skin was as smooth as silk. "What's your poison?"

"This isn't a social call," Laurent said.

"Soda and cranberry, please." I surveyed the club in the mirrors behind Harry. "I can't believe all this exists."

Harry filled a tall glass with ice and sprayed soda from the dispenser into it. "How's that, luv? New to town?"

I'd found the wardrobe, fallen down the rabbit hole, survived the tornado, and entered a world rife with possibility and reinvention. "Something like that."

On the bar was a small bowl of matchbooks with "Bear's Den" written on them. I helped myself, intending to have them on hand when someone made a hate crime in my bathroom.

Harry added cranberry juice, the red liquid swirling through the glass until it all turned a rosé color. "Here you go."

I tried to pay him but he waved me off.

Harry jerked a thumb at Laurent. "This one can owe me."

"Merci," Laurent said, sarcastically. "Can we dispense with the niceties and get what I came here for?"

"Bloody ray of sunshine, 'e is."

"Tell me about it," I said.

"We'll be back in a few minutes," Laurent said. "Stay out of trouble."

"Not in the agreed-upon rules," I said, and swung the bar stool around.

The two wolfy businessmen eating charcuterie were speaking quickly and throwing not-so-covert glances at Laurent.

I sipped my drink, curious to know what they were saying. No one was looking, so I surreptitiously deployed my magic, carefully sliding Delilah from shadow to shadow on the ground. She blended in perfectly; no one would notice anything amiss.

I bent my head over my drink, because this required all my concentration, and I'd gone slack-jawed. Having a set of eyes crawling along the floor looking up in night vision was weird beyond belief and unfortunately the angle wasn't ideal to hear anything. Sound wasn't as sharp when I was in Delilah, and even with *my* hearing the club's noise had narrowed down to a buzzy din. I was about to abort the endeavor when someone said, "Didn't your mother teach you that eavesdropping was rude?" clear as a bell and I jumped.

Garbed in an old-fashioned tuxedo, the most notable part of their androgynous features was their beaky nose and spill of long hair that was the same dark blue as a pool at night.

"I don't know what you're talking about," I said.

The person took the bar stool next to mine, settling their tuxedo tails as they sat. A deck of cards with the same inky iridescent sheen of a raven's wing appeared in their gnarled hands.

"Let's play a game." Their voice made my throat tickle, like I'd swallowed a feather.

There were a series of answering "caws," and the hair on

the back of my neck stood up because there were no birds in here.

I stood up. "I'd rather not."

A hand clamped down on my wrist and two beady black eyes homed in on me. They nodded towards the wolves' table. "Some would be displeased at being spied upon. We shouldn't like that to occur."

An argument broke out between the two businessmen shifters. One of them clawed at the other's throat, but their paw was grabbed in Vikram's huge hand before they could slice the flesh open.

Menace rolled off the grizzly as he spoke quietly to the two.

"Do your worst," I said. "Those wolves have more pressing matters than me to worry about."

The games master smiled thinly, jutting their chin at Vikram. "I did not mean the wolves. There are rules you are unfamiliar with here, and you are perilously close to breaking one. Please, let's be civilized about this."

Vikram grabbed each of the men by their collar as if they were pups and dragged them, struggling, off to a back-room door that was so nondescript in this character-laden space that it was ominous. He glanced our way and I shrunk back.

My neighbor cleared their throat. "Well?"

"You're blackmailing me," I said.

"Quid pro quo," they said. "Play this game and we shall endeavor to assist you with the answers you seek."

Anything that spoke about themselves in the third person was bad news. Still, I wasn't going through that back-room door and they might have information about Jude.

"How do I know you can help me?"

The bird person shrugged. "You don't. Life, sometimes, is a gamble. But if you win, you'll find out."

"And if I lose?" I leaned in. "What happens?"

They tapped the deck of cards against the bar. "All will be as it was."

There had to be a trap but I couldn't find it and I was backed into a corner. I twisted my engagement ring. "What's the game?"

"Memory." They shuffled in a blur, cards flying from hand to hand, before laying them face down on the bar. "Pick two."

"I know how to play." Sadie and I had engaged in endless rounds when she was little.

The first card I flipped over showed a diploma. The next was a painting of a blue house. I'd always liked blue houses. Still, this was the oddest card deck I'd ever seen. I reset them. "Your turn."

They shook their head. "Again."

Feathers tickled my throat more strongly. I sipped my cranberry and soda to clear the sensation. "Whatever you want."

I flipped over two different cards. One showed a woman, her dark hair falling forward to hide her face as she looked down at the sleeping baby in her arms, and the other depicted the same woman in a wedding dress. She was only seen from the back, revealing a distinctive lace back that plunged low, with three chains of pearls strung across it.

Exactly like mine had been.

I snatched my hand away.

The dealer rubbed their hands together. "Again."

Was this game of memory testing mine? Stealing them? Feathers choked me.

"No," I coughed out.

"Again." Their voice was a harsh caw.

Coughing, my hand shaking from trying to resist, I flipped over a card showing stars tumbling from the sky.

Mazel.

The bird shifter leaned over the card humming. "One more," they said, greedily.

Icy tendrils hooked into me and I fought my turn, but it was hopeless. Other than my left arm, I was paralyzed, my vision narrowed down to the cards.

I turned over the final card.

A blond man resembling Alex stood over the bloodied body of the dark-haired woman.

I gasped. That hadn't happened. Was it supposed to?

The card rippled and went blank.

The shifter grabbed my hand and slapped it down on the card. The instant I made contact, a cold wind blew under my palm, and I snatched my fingers away.

Darkness gusted across the card, portent with an ancient evil, and screams filled my ears. I clapped my hands over them but I couldn't shut out the cries.

The card went blank again before cycling back to the Alex image, and then displaying the darkness, which encompassed more and more of the card.

My scalp prickled.

The deck exploded into motion. Random cards flipped over, each revealing either a blank face, my corpse, or the darkness, while the last card that I'd played remained face up, cycling through all three images.

I froze at the chaos before me, my brain scrambling to make sense of it all.

The dealer shook themself and translucent feathers ruffled off their body in agitation, breaking my trance.

I snatched a paring knife from behind the bar and stabbed the card face.

The deck fell still and the darkness on the card faces blew away to reveal a summer's day. Songbirds chirped.

"We need more information. Another." They grabbed my hand.

"No." I wrestled to get free.

The shifter's nose transformed into a beak that they jabbed forward toward my eyes. I wrenched sideways, their beak scraping against my temple, and slammed my glass into the side of their head.

They screeched, glass and cranberry fizz dripping down.

"Oy vey. Such mishegoss." The elderly artist had gone behind the bar and was examining gin bottles. Her voice was the dulcet tones of the New York Jew, braised in Manischewitz and Marlboros, just like my great-aunt Adele's had been.

First the Big Bad Wolf, now Grandma. Note to self: stay out of the woods and avoid the color red.

13

"YOU." THE OLD WOMAN POKED THE BIRD SHIFTER, who wiped themself off with a stack of napkins. "Pick up your cards and move it along, you little pisher."

"I'm calling Vikram," the shifter said.

My shoulders tensed up around my ears, my heart sped up, and I darted a glance to the doors that the wolves had been dragged through. "Do it," I fronted. "Since our only witness caught you forcibly restraining me."

The elderly artist sloshed gin into a martini glass. "She's got you there, Poe. You do get a bit overwrought with your game playing. Vikram would be very upset to hear that you'd injured some poor patron."

Poe's hands morphed into talons. Their gaze clashed with the woman's for a loaded moment. The elderly artist looked like she could easily be snapped in half, and Poe had some damn sharp body parts.

I looked around for help, because this was about to go sideways fast.

Poe broke first. They shifted back, and inclined their head.

My eyebrows shot up. Who was this woman?

"Not so fast," I said to Poe. "You said you could give me answers." I showed them a photo of Jude. "Do you know her?"

Poe glanced at the artist, who motioned for them to pick up their deck faster.

"Hey," I protested, wiping up the spill on the bar and placing the larger shards of glass in a pile. "Birdie and I had a deal."

"Calm your tits," the elderly woman said. "I'm doing you a favor. Don't play games with Poe."

The shifter cawed. "You overstep, Tatiana."

"Pshaw." She added some vermouth and a couple of olives to her drink.

Having collected their cards, Poe left without answering my questions.

I shivered against the sensation of a single feather being trailed down my spine, but I quickly brushed it off, grabbing another bunch of napkins and wiping down the bar top. "Thanks for the intervention."

The woman added a couple of olives and took a sip, nodding in satisfaction. "Laurent doesn't bring friends around. I'd hate for him to lose one of the few he has."

I tensed. "We're not friends."

"Really?" She tapped the sleeve of Laurent's leather jacket that I was still wearing. "In my day, boys gave us letter sweaters." She slid an olive into her mouth with a smirk. In that lime-green mini and those crazy glasses, she was five feet eight inches of giving zero fucks.

I decided then and there she was my new role model.

She was also an artist, which teased out a thought. "You're Tatiana Cassin. The world-renowned painter. I saw your Barbie in the Big Bad World exhibit a few years ago. The juxtaposition of this all-American female gaze in those traditionally masculine spaces was jarring and brilliantly cheeky."

"You grasped my intention. Good girl. I like the sharp ones." Tatiana made me another soda and cranberry.

"Do you use magic in your art?"

"That would be cheating. I get far more pleasure from using my talent and years of hard work in developing my craft. I only used it today because I was tired of that mumser Adrien going on about his brilliant sculptures. He's so derivative." She waved a dismissive hand. "And sculpture isn't my genre."

"You still kicked his ass."

She handed me the glass. "This old dog still has some tricks up her sleeve."

"How do you know Laurent?" I grabbed a lemon wedge from a bowl on the bar and squeezed it into my drink.

"My late husband and I lived in Paris for decades and the boy's grandparents were our dear friends. I've known him since he was born. Consider me his aunt." She scooped up her martini. "Ten minutes on those stools and I get a pain in the tuchus like you wouldn't believe. Get us a table."

I grabbed my drink. "They're all full."

Tatiana shot me a *So?* look and marched out from behind the bar to a banquette. She swatted at the other patrons as if they were mosquitos. "Move."

A sharp-featured woman glared at Tatiana. "Really, and who are you? The Queen of England?" Her mousier friend whispered in her ear, and the first woman paled. "Apologies," she said, not making eye contact, and they scattered.

Vikram intercepted them with soothing words, finding them new seating.

Tatiana slid into the padded booth with a grunt. "Sit."

The leather cracked under my butt. "I get the feeling there's more to your friendliness than my knowing Laurent. Are you my fairy godmother?" I joked.

"Bubeleh, please." Tatiana downed half her martini. "I'm not big on the whole God thing."

"Do you not believe at all?"

She wrinkled her nose. "It's less a question of belief and more that the entire Jewish patriarchy labelled Lilith a demon because she wouldn't do missionary with Adam. I always thought that was so unfair. As should you, being one of her descendants."

Had my jaw been able to unhinge, it would have hit the floor. I slid over, ready to make a break, but Tatiana raised an eyebrow, and I stayed put, resolved to brazen it out. "How did you know?"

"I'm the city's leading bonne vivant and a very famous artiste. People love to tell me the latest on dit," Tatiana said in a snooty tone, and then cackled. "I'm delighted one of you finally showed up here. Ohrists get so boring. There's such a wide range of ways we can manipulate light and life energy, thanks to ohr, and we end up with so many shifters. Oy vey." She drank some more of her dirty martini. "The men are the worst. Wolves, bears, blah blah blah. They all have the exact same equipment and insist on showing it off like we're going to be dazzled. Fangs, claws, you've seen one, you've seen them all."

I traced a finger through the condensation of my latest cranberry and soda. I really had to pee but I clenched my bladder until we finished our conversation. "Shifting seems pretty exciting."

Tatiana ate the other olive from her martini glass. "Anything seems exciting at first. That's how they suck you in. Then thirty years have gone by and your arms are tired from the same old flagellation games and there's no passion anymore."

"Okaaay." I remembered the basics of what my parents had taught me, but I had questions and no one to ask. Hiding my head in the sand and not using my powers wouldn't keep me safe. "How much do you know about Banim Shovavim?"

"Live as long as I have and you pick up just enough about too much," she said. For a moment, her wrinkles grew more pronounced, her eyes rheumy with age, but maybe it was the light, because they quickly resumed their clear sparkle. "What do you want to know?"

I crunched on a piece of ice. "We're descended from Lilith and Adam, but there's a whole story about how three angels killed all her kids, so where did we come from?"

"They killed the first passel." She snapped her fingers and a passing server handed her a pencil. Tatiana unfolded a paper napkin and began to sketch.

"After Adam and Eve got kicked out of the Garden of Eden, Adam went looking for Lilith, because he couldn't resist the bad girls." Her simple line drawing took form, the minimalist illustration imbued with a kinetic energy.

Two naked bodies coupled on a hilltop with a vigorous athleticism bordering on downright contortionist when Tatiana drew the woman bracing her arms on a pillow with her ass in the air in a wheelbarrow position. Her partner held her legs and impaled her from behind.

"According to the oral tradition that I learned," Tatiana said, "Lilith had a thing for day drinking and bad decisions, and long story short, Lilith and Adam schtupped like bunnies."

"You did not learn that story at Hebrew school," I said, crowding her to get a better view, as under Tatiana's playful skill, the bodies gleamed with sweat.

Tatiana snickered. "It was a decidedly more ribald retelling." She erased the woman and redrew her, still impaled but in plank position in mid-air.

"No amount of crunches would get me that core strength." I patted my much softer belly. "Actually, that doesn't even look enjoyable."

Tatiana added lines to indicate the jiggle of the young woman's boobs. "Don't knock it till you try it," she said in her New York accent and turned the woman's face into her own.

"Fuck me." I pressed my cool drink against my forehead.

"Don't be a prude, Miriam." Tatiana tapped her finger against her martini glass and Vikram lumbered over with a new drink for her. The fact that she knew my name was hardly surprising.

"I am sex positive." I weakly raised a fist. "Sisters are doing it for themselves. Ladies of all ages have needs." Don't make me see the grandma sex again. "How about you give me the synopsis?"

The gist of it was that Lilith and Adam produced a bunch of new kids known as Banim Shovavim, the rebellious or wayward children, who had their own type of magic. This time, Lilith hid her offspring so the angels couldn't find them.

"Adam had magic?" I said. "I kind of assumed it was all from Lilith."

"Try living nine hundred years without it," Tatiana said, dryly. "So, what are your specific powers?"

After Eli came out of the closet, I'd spent a lot of time in therapy unpacking my complicated emotions around secrets. Both our romantic and sex life had been good, hadn't it? What I'd come to realize was that the truth had masked the secret that Eli was bisexual, but preferred men. His love and attraction to me had been real, just not the full truth. Eventually, therapy allowed me to be honest that I'd willfully blinded myself to certain things because I'd so desperately craved the normalcy of a loving nuclear family.

I listened to my instincts telling me that Tatiana's friendly interest was only a partial truth. She hadn't shown up because of Laurent, but because she was interested in knowing more about me. Why? What did I know about Tatiana, other than she was powerful, well-versed in my magic, and acquainted with Laurent? Hell, he might have been the one to tell her about me. Who was this woman if I stripped away the eccentric artist veneer, and was it safer to lie to her or be honest? If I lied about my abilities, what would I even say?

Some of my kind were necromancers, able to commune with the dead, and there were tales of the ones whose touch was instantly fatal, though my parents had never met any of those people. I didn't know what else Banim Shovavim were capable of, because my parents had the same abilities as me of invisible cloaking and an animated shadow.

A tightness surged through my ribcage. For the first time in my life, I hated them for whatever shady business had gotten them killed. They should have stuck around long enough to guide me safely to adulthood with all the tools and information I'd need to survive.

No, to thrive.

"Animating my shadow," I said.

Tatiana got a shrewd look in her eyes and a chill swept through me. "That's it?"

One of the clarinetists onstage launched into a mournful tune, which I took as an omen to hold back about my cloaking.

"Pretty much."

"Hmm." Tatiana reached for her glass. "Always hydrate." She jerked her chin at me to drink up. "Anyways," she said brightly, squeezing my hand, "I'm glad you have magic. Life is so much more exciting with it."

"Absolutely. Excuse me a moment."

I hurried to the restrooms, done in stark black-and-white tiles, my eyes watering in sweet relief as I voided my bladder. Someone had written "When will the devil come for you?" on the wooden stall door. The way my magic encounters had been going, this wasn't so much an existential question as one of scheduling.

Washing my hands, I stared at my reflection, unnerved by

that game of Memory and Tatiana's revelations. Ravens in mythology were tied to prophecy and as such, considered bad omens. First Emmett, now Poe.

That card with Alex on it. If I hadn't snapped and unleashed my magic, would I be alive now? What about that darkness? Was that on me, or did I stop whatever that was and bring sunshine into the world? Was I an agent of good or evil—or neither and there was some other meaning entirely to these cards?

I blotted my face with a damp paper towel, feeling like I was falling further and further down a slippery slope. Had I really been destined to die and, having now cheated death, my future was blank with infinite possibilities?

If that was true what did I want my future to look like? For the year or so from when my powers kicked in until I'd cut them off, Delilah was the best non-imaginary friend ever. She'd been my accomplice and confidante, and shutting her down had caused an ache like a phantom limb that I'd forced myself to ignore until it had finally faded—but I had faded, too.

With my parents' murder, life turned into an endless series of me ceding tiny pieces of my identity, which was accelerated when my marriage broke up. Determined to prevent Sadie from seeing me curled into a tiny ball, crying my way through the night, I'd overcompensated, making certain that her life stayed as positive and as free from pain as I could make it.

Sadly, I'd been so busy hiding and "being normal" that I'd forgotten the joy my powers gave me. My magic was no longer a secret. Why live as though it still was? I didn't have to be reckless about it. It's not like I was going to trash all my responsibilities and blow up my life like Jude had suggested, I'd just let some magic back in.

My power allowed me to be invisible, but shadows were nothing without light. Plenty of women were magnificent in middle age and older and from now on, I would be one of them.

Hi, my name is Miriam Feldman and I'm a Banim Shovavim. Fuck you, haters.

I flashed my reflection a thumbs-up.

But in the interests of playing it smart, how should I deal with the woman waiting for me? I re-applied my lipstick. Tatiana was playing games as much as Poe had. Let her think she'd won this round. Maybe my years of suppressing my true nature and being invisible could be weaponized. After all, being underestimated had its uses, and as my parents always said, "the best thing about Banim Shovavim magic was that no one saw you coming."

Tossing the paper in the trash, I high-fived Delilah.

I got back to the banquette moments before my partner-in-crime returned.

"Laurent!" Tatiana beamed, turning her face up to him.

He kissed her on both cheeks, wrinkling his nose when she brushed a curl out of his eyes, but the smile he gave her was genuinely fond. "Ma chère tante. Are you corrupting Feldman here?" He slid in next to me and draped an arm over the back of the banquette.

I stared at him, suspicious of his jovial tone.

Tatiana spread her thumb and index finger apart, then she laughed. "Kidding. I'm a paragon of perfect behaviour, Lolo."

Lolo? I stifled a snort.

"You, on the other hand, are very rude." Tatiana gestured at me. "You should have introduced this delightful woman to me the moment you'd arrived."

"You're right," he said. "Am I forgiven?"

She tapped her lips. "Only if you come see me as I requested."

If Laurent's thigh hadn't been right up against mine, I'd never have noticed his sudden tension, because his smile didn't slip. "Another time."

"He wants to see you. He's pack."

My ears pricked up but I pretended to check my phone for a text so I wasn't staring avidly at the two of them.

Laurent crossed his arms. "I have no pack, remember? I'm the crazy loner who kills humans for money."

I touched his shoulder. "I shouldn't have made that mercenary crack."

He stiffened, then tapped a teaspoon against the tablecloth, not looking at either of us. "Forget it."

Tatiana sniffed. "I won't mix in."

His expression softened. "I know you mean well, but some things can't be fixed."

She patted his hand. "I wish it were otherwise."

Laurent caught my confused stare and pulled away. "We've got to go. We have shit to do."

Tatiana shot us a knowing look. "Miriam, it was a pleasure."

"Same." Agreeing was smarter than saying, "Not really, because I think you are dangerous and if I see you coming, I'm running the other way." My mother didn't birth a fool.

Laurent stood and abruptly strode off, ever the gentleman.

I bade Tatiana goodbye and hurried after him. Did he think she was harmless or did their connection blind him to her game playing?

"What the fuck?" he hissed. "I told you repeatedly not to speak to anyone."

"But—"

"Allow me to escort you out." Vikram had joined us and it wasn't a request.

The shifters had never emerged from the back room. I didn't ask.

Ignoring Laurent, who still shot me daggers, I said, "Is this a 'Thank you for coming to my lovely speakeasy' seeing us out, or a 'Darken my doorway again and I'll kill you'?"

"Any friend of Tatiana's gets special treatment," Vikram replied.

"Since when?" Laurent said.

Vikram smiled enigmatically.

I dodged a server carrying a full tray of cocktails. "Can I come back? And if I do, is there some code of conduct I should follow?"

"Yes and yes."

"Care to enlighten me?"

"Where's the fun in that?" Vikram held the front door open.

"So this place is some kind of Darwin 'survival of the fittest' test?" I said.

"Or the Darwin Awards. Guess you'll find out which way you land."

"That's cold, man." I nodded. "I think I'm going to like you."

Vikram's face contorted. "I don't do friends."

"Challenge accepted." Throwing a finger wave over my shoulder, I stepped out into the foyer of the carpark.

Laurent jabbed the call button.

"Should I take your thunderous disposition to mean that you don't take your aunt at face value?" I said carefully.

"Yeah, because I'm not a fucking idiot. I told you not to speak to anyone. I said it was dangerous. You don't listen."

I got into the elevator. "Perhaps if you had thoroughly explained who I was not to speak to and the reason for it, I would have conducted myself differently. I have no idea what the stakes are if I mess up! And you let me walk into that blind."

Laurent frowned and shifted his weight from one foot to the other. "You're right. I should have been clear." He said it stiffly, but I'd take the apology.

I smoothed down my sweater, my chin notched up. "Thank you. And it's not like I was randomly chatting people up. I was trying to get information about Jude. Besides, if anyone was in danger from those encounters, it was me, not you."

"Those?" He punched the button to shut the doors, his eyes emerald green lasers. "Who else was there other than Tatiana?"

I waved a hand. Details. "What does she want with me?"

"It depends on what she thinks our relationship is."

"The world doesn't revolve around you. Newsflash: plenty of people are interested in me for me."

"Not Tatiana."

"Why?" I poked him. "Answer me."

"Let's just say she doesn't like what I do for a living." He strode out of the elevator, back into the carpark.

I dropped it, for now. "Did you get your information?"

The sun had set and, outside the garage, street lamps glowed cheerily along the boulevard.

"Yeah."

"Do people often punch you in the throat? Because seriously."

He fished his keys out of his pocket. "You asked me a yes or no question and I answered it."

"You know I wanted you to elaborate."

Laurent's footsteps rang out in the parkade. "Heh. Yes, but you're easy to rile."

Delilah grabbed his ear and twisted.

"Merde." Laurent narrowed his eyes. "I warned you about hitting me."

"That wasn't a hit. That was a side effect of being peri-menopausal. Hormone fluctuations. So sorry. Now speak. You're on the clock."

Laurent circled his motorcycle, inspecting it for dings or scratches.

"The nearest car is parked three spaces over. Your

precious bike is fine." I twirled my finger in a *get on with it* motion.

He nudged me out of his way and unlocked the helmets. "There's this dybbuk that leads a gang of Ohrists. Last time I closed in on them, they'd already relocated."

"You want the dybbuk in charge? Who is it? Someone you know?" My curiosity resulted in a helmet being shoved at me but zero answers. "Your conversation skills are so consistent," I marveled. "Some people might even call them predictable."

He bared his teeth at me. "Some people can bite me."

"As you advertised on your shirt, the first time we met." I batted my lashes at him. "Got a particular kink, do you?"

"Remember when you didn't speak for an entire minute? A precious memory."

"Ha. Ha." I busied myself putting on the helmet, then stopped, turning stricken eyes to his. "Do you think Jude was taken because she pulled off divination and these dybbuks want a golem like Emmett or because they intend to stop her?"

"Probably the former, and it's dybbuk singular. Only the leader is possessed. The others are regular criminals with magic. The dybbuk-possessed don't play well together."

"So where is this gang now?"

"Harry didn't know, which means a visit to the bloodsuckers, which I was hoping to avoid."

"Maybe Jude's vampire employers have rescued her already," I said.

He strapped on his helmet. "They can't. Harry heard the dybbuk outfitted the new place with a bunker running off its own generator, and every inch is lit with full spectrum bulbs."

"Sunlight bulbs." I clicked the helmet straps into place. "Kind of genius. Good thing we won't have that problem." I inadvertently glanced at where Laurent's scar was. He'd survived at least one encounter with the head vamp, but at what cost? Would this push Laurent to more of a breaking point? He was already someone anxious to be broken, but voicing my concern might accelerate his actions, so I forced a note of bravado into my voice. "Blood Alley, here we come."

14

"Tomorrow night," Laurent said.

"What? No. Jude's been missing since Friday. It's Monday. We can't wait any longer to find her."

"We have to." Laurent disengaged the kickstand.

"Why?"

His hands paused on the ignition, and his cheeks flushed briefly, but when he spoke, his eyes had regained their usual acerbic distance. "Harry has to verify that the bloodsucker we need to speak to is in town. No point surprising someone with a confrontation who isn't there to receive it."

"Maybe, but that's not all. Tell me or I'll apologize profusely for any and all previous verbal slights, which you seem to dislike."

"Merde, you're annoying."

"Wait till I really get going. Well?"

"Tonight is the last night of the full moon."

"Don't you shift at will?" I said.

"Yeah, but there's still a pull. I'm not as in control during a full moon."

I tensed and stepped back.

Laurent rolled his eyes. "It's not sunset for another half hour. 9:21PM. You're fine."

"As were you on Saturday when you fought Alex."

"Because the sun hadn't fully set. You getting on or what?"

He wouldn't risk riding if a shift was imminent, and I had my cloaking to fall back on. I got on the back of the seat. "Is this why you've been so grumpy the entire time I've known you? It's that time of the month?"

"It's not a period," he snapped.

"Sure it is. The word period comes from the Greek, but transitioned into the Latin, 'periodus,' means recurring cycle."

He looked down at me haughtily. "Did I look curious for further details?"

"You hide it well, but all is revealed under my keen observations. You're welcome."

He snorted but one side of his mouth quirked up in a half-grin.

I patted his shoulder. "Try a nice bath. Or chocolate. They usually chase away my crankiness."

"There is nothing to chase away," he said through gritted teeth and swung his leg over the bike.

"Whatever you say, buddy." I smirked at his back.

The motorcycle started up with a loud rumble and I tightened my hold on Laurent's waist.

The adrenaline of the ride blew away my edginess from the Bear's Den, if not my worry for my friend, though the world of everyday people going about their business had a surreal edge to it. Did that dad with the baby carrier outside the fruit market have magic? Was the asshole cyclist riding on the sidewalk actually a shifter?

Laurent leaned in to a right turn, the motorcycle dipping low to the ground, and I pressed my cheek against his back.

His traps bunched and flexed under his leather jacket, and when I felt his soft laugh rumble through him, I whooped.

It had rained lightly while we were inside and the wet concrete smelled sweet and musty.

I was giddy, colors whizzing by tweaked and sharpened, like the metallic purple of the Corvette next to us or the sunflower yellow on a restaurant awning. We hurtled through the city in a cloud of freedom.

Also in a cloud of exhaust from the dickwad with the deafening muffler in front of us. I gagged on the thick, acrid smoke, the back of my throat burning.

All too soon, Laurent pulled up in front of Hotel Terminus. I dismounted with the same high as when I rode the wooden coaster at the amusement park—and the same desire for another go-around.

He reached out to touch my face, then dropped his hand just shy of making contact. "You're all flushed."

"This reminded me of how much I love trampolines."

He frowned. "You're comparing my motorcycle to a children's toy?"

"Oh no, your bike is for big boys." I grinned at his scowl. "See, when I was in elementary school," I said, "my best friend had a trampoline. It wasn't like nowadays with netting and parental supervision. The two of us spent hours in the summer doing flips and trying to make each other touch the sky. It was that same scary rush." I was babbling quickly by the end, because his frown had deepened. "That freedom."

"You're not bouncing around. It's a dance with a lover." He got off the bike and engaged the kick stand.

"Because you ride her?" I said sarcastically.

"Because two become one." His rumbled words grazed my skin. "You have to learn what she likes, how she wants to be handled. How deep you can go in a turn, the perfect tempo to coax her into opening up, and when to pull back on going full throttle to make her purr." He stroked the curved seat with a firm hand.

I wet my lips, a flutter behind my breastbone. "That's uh, a more poetic way to describe it."

"As you know, I *am* French." His eyes sparkled.

He was also a subcontractor that I'd hired because my friend was in danger. I shook myself out of my daze and handed him the helmet and jacket. "I'll see you tomorrow."

He took the change in topic in stride. "Be here at ten. We'll hit the vamps when they first wake up and are preoccupied with opening Blood Alley."

I groaned. By ten I was in my pajamas. Why couldn't Jude have gone missing in January when sundown was at five?

"Problem?" Laurent said.

"Nope."

Helmets tucked under his arms, he strode off without a goodbye.

I started up my car, my adrenaline leaving me in a sudden rush, and rested my head back against the seat. Being locked behind glass felt stifling, so I rolled the window down, letting the cool breeze wash over me.

Tonight had been, dare I say it, fun—Poe, Tatiana, and all —thanks to crankypants. Hearing his rusty laugh in my head, I cruised through the east side, watching people spill out of restaurants. I yearned for a romantic partner with whom I could go home and share my very strange day, but I was going back to an empty duplex, without even Sadie's bright chatter to liven it up.

The end of the day when Eli and I could take a moment to slow down and connect had always been my favorite part, especially since I spent a lot of time by myself at work. I honked at a car swerving into my lane. Well, I didn't need a romantic partner to connect. As soon as I found Jude, I'd come clean about my magic.

I turned south on Main Street, driving past the many

cafés, vintage clothing stores, local boutiques, and yet more restaurants that made up my neighborhood, wishing I was inside one of them eating and chatting with friends.

When I pulled up to the curb outside the duplex, I considered going next door to Eli's, but he'd be zoned out watching a movie, half-asleep already, and if Sadie was awake, she'd be online chatting with friends around the world from some of her fandom groups.

Sighing, I let myself into the dark house, and turned on every light. By the time I'd taken a quick shower and gotten into pj's, I'd convinced myself that my place didn't need to be lit up like a city skyline, but I'd just clicked off the living room lights when the motion sensor went on.

Putting my cloaking in place, I tiptoed into the kitchen, slid a knife out of the block on the counter, and peered out the door. There was no one there.

I tested every window and door twice to ensure it was locked, and still couldn't convince myself to turn out my bedroom light. Sliding the knife under my pillow, I prepared to lay awake all night, but all the emotional drain of the past few hours kicked in, and I fell asleep.

Tuesday morning began with me being jolted awake by the slam of my front door and Sadie yelling, "I know where I left my calculator," followed by her thudding up the stairs.

I let go of the weapon under my pillow.

"Okay, water buffalo," I said, blinking blearily at my alarm clock. I had ten minutes until it was set to go off, so I pulled the pillow over my head.

More thudding and the slam of the door again kiboshed those last precious moments of sleep. I zombie-walked downstairs and peeped through my front door, but there was no sign that anyone had visited last night. Crossing through the house, I cautiously cracked the back door.

There weren't any tracks and none of the patio furniture had been disturbed. Shaking my head at my lingering paranoia, I locked the back door. It had probably been that damn raccoon who roamed the neighborhood like a Mafia don.

Feeling slightly foolish, I hurried through my morning routine so I could stop for a large mocha with two shots of espresso and extra whip to get my day back on track.

Nice idea. Between document management, fixing order requests, and tracking down periodicals that had gone astray, work was crazy. I got a much-needed break late in the afternoon at a retirement party for one of the paralegals, where I chatted with colleagues while eating a delicious chocolate ganache cake, absolutely not thinking about other French delights. The partners told me how pleased they were with my work, and when I thanked them and said I was looking forward to the library expansion, I meant it.

Beyond raises and new challenges, my job was good for another thing. I called Daisy Alverez, the private investigator whom the firm kept on retainer and asked her to look into Tatiana Cassin. Even though Tatiana's magic wouldn't be unearthed by a Sapien investigation, she'd been a success in the Sapien art world for decades, and as such, Daisy would have no trouble amassing the basics of her personal and professional life. From there, I'd use my magic knowledge to assess the information for any red flags. Tatiana might be like some of my cousin Goldie's friends and simply relish the power that being in the know gave them, but if there was more to her than that, this was a good start.

Daisy gave me the friends and family discount provided I threw in my secret raspberry shortbread recipe that she'd tasted on several occasions at my holiday open house parties. She'd gotten guilted into being on the bake sale committee for her kids' school and meant to show up the mommy mafia with her show-stopping baking.

My agreement was a no-brainer—what was tougher was when she asked me if she should only put together a profile for one person, or if there was someone else I had in mind too. Curiosity warred with ethics. Unlike Tatiana, Laurent hadn't shown any interest in my personal business, and it felt unscrupulous to dig into his background, especially since we'd only be working together until Jude was found, but damn was I tempted. The man was an enigma, and he intrigued me like no one had in a very long time.

Ignoring my voice of temptation, I signed off on solely Tatiana.

There was only one way to get into the right head-space for tonight's vamp visit. I hit a local fast-food chain for a bacon cheeseburger and extra-large fries, then put on my stretchiest Lululemon knock-offs back home and ate my body weight in salt and grease. Fuck table manners, I went to town on that beef like it was the lead singer of that shitty alternative band I'd been so eager to impress as a gamine youth. I even made the same noises and followed it up with the same generous pour of white wine to cleanse my shame-filled palate.

Forty really was the new twenty.

Afterwards, I lay bloated on the sofa, scrolling endlessly through Netflix without watching an actual program, only the short previews that came up for each show. It was binge-watching for those of us without the energy to pare down the glut of choices and commit.

It drove Sadie crazy when I did that, but she wasn't here.

At 9:30PM, I hopped into a pair of jeans, and proceeded to spend the next couple minutes re-arranging my belly in order to get the zipper up after that grease extravaganza. It was a vigorous process involving the loss of my dignity but I found an earring under my bed that I'd misplaced, so it wasn't a total wash. Sadly, all my sports bras were dirty, so a regular torture chamber it was.

I emerged from the experience clad in denim and deter-mination, shoved my phone, a credit card, and driver's license in my pockets so I wouldn't be hampered down with a purse, and got into my car. As I reversed down the driveway, a pale-skinned young woman with a crop top and frosted pink lips leaned out from the shadows of my back seat.

I screamed and hit the brakes.

"Keep driving." The scent of the watermelon gum filled the car. "Do as I say and there won't be a problem." She blew a bubble and popped it. With her fangs. "Understand?"

My shoulders notched up an inch. This was what was waiting for me outside last night. "Got it. Where am I going?"

"Blood Alley."

On my own, without any wolf back-up. Had Harry given the vampires a heads-up about our plans? I hit the gas too hard and the car jerked forward.

"You made me swallow my gum," she growled. Her eyes glowed red.

My stomach knotted up, my hands slick on the wheel. "Sorry."

"Ooh, is that the Weekly Top 40?" She pointed at the radio. "Turn it up."

I jacked up the volume with a trembling hand, glancing in the rearview mirror every couple of seconds as we drove closer to our destination.

I couldn't unbuckle my seat belt and get out of the car before she attacked me. Nor could I go on the offense, strapped in as I was. Admittedly, the only vampires I'd ever fought were back during my videogame days, in pixel form, but I'd kicked ass. Surely some of the mechanics were the same.

Switching lanes, I scoffed at my delusions, recalling when a seven-year-old Sadie had insisted on joining Little League because she was so good at videogame baseball. It was debatable whether the ensuing season had been more Greek tragedy or farce.

Bring it. I was a woman of a certain age, a mother, and extremely pissed off. The vamps didn't stand a chance.

The bloodsucker sang along to some love ballad, her dramatic flair failing to compensate for her utter lack of musical ability.

"I'm Miri." Television was a veritable treasure trove for survival skills: in the event of a zombie apocalypse team up with a slower person, in quicksand stay calm and slowly pull each leg to the surface, and when kidnapped, establish a rapport with your captors so they see you as a real person. "What's your name?"

A car cut in front of me and I hit the brakes, braced for the vamp to retaliate, but she threw back her head and belted out the chorus about being her own woman and not needing a man.

I lowered the volume on the radio. I wasn't making any connections here and I was already halfway to Blood Alley. Time was slipping through my fingers.

Then it hit me. "I guess being a female vamp is the ultimate in girl power, huh?"

The vamp sucked in a breath and I tensed, worried that I'd offended her somehow, but she screeched delightedly and clapped her hands. "It totally is. Those stupid boy vamps think they're the shit, but everything about vampires is female positive. Like take my name, Lindsey BatKian."

"Yes?"

"I used to be boring old Lindsey Douglas, but then I got made and I took on the name of the estrie who'd founded our line."

"What's an estrie?"

"Estries are the female demons that turn Ohrists into vampires. Duh." Lindsey punched my shoulder, sending us over the yellow line.

I jerked the wheel sharply back. "Cool. So an estrie made you?"

That earned me a huff. "I said they only *start* the line. No one's seen an estrie in like a few hundred years. Ohrists hunted them all down." She rolled her eyes. "They hate anyone different."

"Weren't you an Ohrist before you became a vampire?"

"Nope. Vampires haven't turned Ohrists in ages because the Lonestars got all pissy." She flapped a hand. "We have to stick to Sapiens."

My stomach twisted. Could I lock Sadie in her room? She was safe from dybbuks who needed a magic host but not vamps.

"Sapiens bond better once we're turned anyways," Lindsey said. "Like me and my bestie. He's a newbie, but it's like we've known each other forever." She snickered. "Guess we will. Anyway, estries start a line but after that vamps continue it. Still, we all take the name of the founding estrie as ours."

"And your estrie's name is BatKian?" Weird name.

"Her name is Kian. That becomes our last name with 'Bat,' which is Hebrew for 'daughter of,' because to estries, all their children are daughters. Now that's girl power."

I nodded, driving smoothly through a green light. The world was a lot scarier than I'd previously realized, sure, but so was studying deep sea creatures. Demons and estries, female lineage, I wanted to read a book on this. "That's actually really amazing."

"Right?" She patted my shoulder.

"How do vampires feel about others with magic?" I asked. Now that we had some common ground, maybe I could turn this to my advantage. Or at the very least, walk into Blood Alley with a little more knowledge of where Jude, Laurent, and I stood.

Lindsey shrugged. "We don't really care about anyone until they get in our way. It's Ohrists that have a stick up their ass about who should or should not have magic." She snickered. "Doesn't matter how much they hate us, under the cover of night, they crave what only we can give them."

I listened to her with only one ear. Even if Harry had told the vamps we were coming, why would they be upset about that? I planned to rescue Jude so she could go back to work for them.

My hands tightened on the steering wheel. "What's this about?"

"Pizza!"

"Huh?" I glanced in the rearview mirror.

"Pull over. I love trying new places. Hurry up." The vamp reached forward and yanked the wheel to the right, almost colliding with another vehicle that was pulling out of a spot. She rolled down the window and gave the driver the finger.

I jerked the car out of the way, thankful for my quick reflexes honed while accompanying Sadie on her practice drives. Even when we were parallel-parked safely, I sat there gripping the wheel, breathing heavily and trying to calm my fast-beating heart. Did Lindsey really want pizza, or did she just want to frighten her prey before eating me?

"Yo!" Lindsey rapped on my window and I jumped. "Get out. Can't have you taking off."

I stepped onto the sidewalk. "I think they're closing up."

"No time to lose." She hauled me off, practically lifting me off my feet, and dragged me into the alley.

Nothing good ever happened in an alley. I sighed, but couldn't break her grip.

A pimply-faced employee stepped out of the pizzeria's back door with a bulging green garbage bag, headed for the dumpster, an unlit cigarette hanging out of the corner of his mouth.

Delilah rose up to grab Lindsey, but my shadow's fingers closed on thin air as the bloodsucker blurred forward in a burst of speed and seized the hapless young man.

The vamp pressed him up against the brick wall, leaning into his pelvis, and bit his neck.

He sagged in her hold, the trash and cigarette falling to the ground. In a state of bleary response, he looked much younger, maybe only as old as Sadie.

I was on Lindsey in a moment before I could think better of it, trying to pry her off. But I wasn't strong enough, would never be strong enough, and she threw me one-handed across the alley into a building. My tailbone blazed with needle-hot pain and I slid down the wall onto my ass with a groan.

The vamp dropped her victim, daintily licked a smear of blood off the corner of her mouth, then belched. "'Kay, let's go."

He was pale, but still breathing. Good.

I stood up, one hand on my throbbing lower back. "We can't leave him there."

She turned a puzzled look on the man. "Why not?"

"He needs medical attention or something."

"Oh. In that case..." She walked over and snapped his neck.

I stifled my scream with my fist. What had I done? Would he have lived if I'd said nothing?

The psycho looped her arm through mine. "Come on. We don't want to be late."

If Lindsey got me to our destination, it was game over. I slid my other hand behind me, grabbed the wooden stake stashed against the small of my back that I'd stolen from one of Sadie's cosplay outfits before I'd left the house, and stabbed Lindsey.

New fact: stakes don't slide into vampires like knives through butter. I tore through the skin and muscular tissue, but the stake got lodged ineffectively between her ribs.

We both looked down at it then Lindsey ripped it out of her chest.

The wood hit the ground with a clatter, right as I hid beneath my invisibility cloaking.

The vamp turned in a circle. "Where'd you go?"

She couldn't smell me under my magic, and given she was peering in the opposite direction from where I stood, she couldn't hear my heartbeat either. Perfect.

I let out a quiet sigh and snuck over to the dumpster, easing it away from the wall far enough to worm behind it. Dropping my cloaking, Delilah and I shoved the dumpster at the vampire.

Lindsey's eyes widened comically as the dumpster ran her over. Only the vamp's pink sparkly heels stuck out.

Ding dong, the bitch is dead. I did a quick Moonwalk, a highly underrated gesture in the triumph pantheon.

Lindsey screamed and cursed me out, very much not dead.

I kicked a pop can into the wall. I couldn't exactly leave her here, nor did I want to reverse the dumpster over her a few times. I'd done that once accidentally with a raccoon, but I'd never managed to actually kill it and put it out of its misery. It just got mushier with the occasional crunchy texture under my tires, its cries growing more piteous, while I stuttered out "sorries" before fleeing like a criminal. To this day I couldn't go over a speed bump without flinching.

The dumpster rose an inch off the ground and collapsed back down with a shuddering thud.

I ran for the mouth of the alley, but there was a savage cry and the trash bin flew over my head, crashing down and rolling over to totally block my exit. Garbage exploded like nasty-ass stink bombs and my stomach lurched.

The vamp blurred toward me... and came to a standstill an inch out of arm's reach. She glanced back at Delilah, illuminated by the light blazing out from the open pizzeria door. My shadow had grabbed hold of Lindsey's and crumpled it, immobilizing the vamp.

Wow. Farming that out to Delilah actually worked.

Lindsey looked me in the eyes, her irises darkening. "Release me."

There was the slightest desire to accede to her wishes, about on par with when Sadie begged me for a puppy. For a moment I entertained the notion, wanting to make her happy, then I gave the vamp the same answer I'd give my daughter. "Not in this lifetime."

She rolled her eyes. "Whatever. You'll get tired and release me soon enough. And then you're dead meat."

"That is a problem." Now what? Using the stake was a no-go. I'd already proven that I wouldn't be quitting my day job to become a Slayer, given how I'd botched the first attempt.

I circled the vamp. Everything except her facial expressions were frozen. I tapped my lip, my eyes narrowed on my shadow. Whatever injury Delilah sustained, I experienced. It was the way that our magic, rooted in death and darkness worked. The undead were creatures of the night, so how much harm could I do to Lindsey's physical body if I inflicted damage on her shadow?

A loose plan came together. I knelt down and closed the eyes of the murdered pizza employee. His mother was going to face her worst nightmare because children weren't supposed to die before their parents. After taking a moment to remember the deceased's face, I found his lighter, walked over to Delilah, and took the vamp's shadow from her.

Lindsey tried to pull free, but couldn't.

The darkness that oozed through my fingers was ice cold, turning the tips white.

"What are you doing?" Lindsey said.

I hesitated. Our rapport, thin as it was, cut both ways. Once upon a time, Lindsey had been someone's daughter, too. I shook my head. It was too late for her, but I could prevent any other parents from losing their children to this fiend.

"I'm sorry." I flicked the lighter and dropped her shadow into it.

The vampire burst into flames, both of us equally astonished. For one brief second, her eyes met mine, and she looked so heartbreakingly young that I dropped the lighter.

But it was too late. She disintegrated into a pile of ash.

I bowed my head for a moment, mourning both her and the poor employee, then I used the phone in the pizzeria to call the cops about a fight in the alley, hanging up when they asked for my name.

There'd been too much death in my life. A ticking clock hung over Rupert unless I miraculously pulled a way to save him out of my ass. And Jude...

She had to be alive. Any other option wasn't a possibility. We'd made a pact that when one of us died, the other would pluck our chin hairs before anyone else saw the body. Being two years older than her, I fully expected her to be the one to keep up that deal.

I drove to Laurent's house in a numb haze. My car still smelled of watermelon bubble gum, but I snapped off the radio so I wouldn't hear any more pop songs.

Even though the streets were awash with light that slid over my face, I couldn't shake off feeling like I was blanketed in darkness. Maybe this was the price to pay for my magic, but I clung to my belief that I'd stopped a killer from taking another life. That mattered a lot more than ordering this year's edition of the *Annual Review of Law & Practice*.

I parked alongside the Hotel Terminus and ran to the side entrance to tell Laurent that the vamps were on to us.

The door was ajar.

The hair lifted on the nape of my neck. I slammed my magic over me, seeing the world through the black mesh, crept inside and smothered a gasp.

Books had been knocked off the shelves, the piano bench was smashed, the radio broken and scattered in a jumble of parts. The vintage ads were knocked off their nails, jagged shards of glass glittering on the floor planks.

There was even a footprint marring the piano keys. I frowned. This wasn't a coldly methodical job, it was vicious. Personal. Someone had taken great joy in this carnage.

I swallowed the lump in my throat, my shock giving way to a burning rage climbing in my chest at the long, wet crimson smear painting a swathe along the parquet floor.

Laurent was my team member, for now at least, and I took care of my own. He might not be in a position to hit back, but one way or another, I'd make the perpetrator pay.

15

GIVING THE BLOOD A WIDE BERTH, I TIPTOED
through the hotel, hoping I'd find Laurent alive.

I checked on Rupert first. The elevator door was still
locked, but the hole where something had bashed through
the drywall rendered that kind of moot. I flicked on the light
and stuck my head through.

He sat on the ground with his legs hugged up to his chest
and his head resting on his knees.

"Rupert? Are you hurt?"

He raised his head, revealing the two puncture marks in
his neck. His eyes were glazed and he wore a dopey smile.

The hairs on the back of my neck rose. I looked around
but I was alone. However, my sense of dread grew stronger,
so I checked the walls and floor for blood. There wasn't any.

The problem was Rupert's shadow, which was a sickly-
gray and flecked with crimson. Exactly like Alex's had been.

No, no, no. My hands balled into fists. I hadn't known
this guy, not at all, really, but he was supposed to have more
time than this.

The dybbuk had fully possessed the host and Rupert as
I'd known him was dead. I still didn't understand how.

Dybbuks inhabited a body during the Danger Zone between sunsets on Friday and Saturday night, and according to Laurent, remained in the enthrallment period until a week later.

It was only Monday. Could a vampire bite speed up the effects?

Rupert rattled his chains. "Where'd the other one go? I liked her."

Another female vampire. Had there been more than one? "Did she have any friends? Did they take Laurent?"

"She and cauliflower boy grabbed him." Rupert lunged at me, rattling his chains, his face a mottled red. "I hope the shifter's dead."

I flinched at his viciousness. That was the dybbuk talking, not Rupert… because Rupert was gone. I'd failed him. "I'm sorry."

He tilted his head, considering me with narrowed eyes. "For what? That you didn't save that poor miserable wretch?" He drew out his words mockingly. "Make it up to me and let me out."

"I can't."

He rattled the handcuffs. "Let me out, you bitch!"

I fled, his curses ringing in my ears. Ignoring him as best I could, I searched the rest of the floor, since the top two stories were boarded up.

At the back of the main space was a hallway that ran the width of the building. To the right was a spacious, airy kitchen. A lovingly-crafted room, it boasted weathered gray cabinets, oil-rubbed bronze hardware, granite counters, and —I frowned—a cheap laminate table with one chair.

The dybbuk inside Rupert had run out of steam and fallen silent. The iron band around my ribcage fell away and I took a deep breath, heading into the narrow bathroom on the opposite side of the corridor.

It was completely utilitarian with a basic white toilet,

nondescript shower stall, and box store cabinets, with the peculiar addition of a frosted sliding door at the back. I slid it open and stepped through, my eyes lighting up at the patio area, its high walls covered in greenery. Moss peeked through the crooked flagstones and smooth river rocks created a path between the sliding doors and the showpiece of the space: a massive copper soaking tub under a roof woven from thin strips of criss-crossed cedar.

The space was imbued with a reverence and I wondered if Laurent ever brought a lover or partner here, or if this was for him alone. I caught myself trailing my hand over the tub and hurried back inside, feeling like I'd transgressed.

There was one room left to check: the bedroom. I stepped through the door connecting it with the bathroom, expecting some ode to masculinity with a huge wood bed, though I wryly conceded that might be wishful thinking. Instead, the room was spartan with a basic queen-sized bed, a chest of drawers, and a lamp on a bedside table, the scent of cedar wafting out from the partially ajar closet door.

It was as if Laurent allowed himself to be surrounded by beauty, but only up to a certain point. He hadn't simply lost interest, something else was at play—like penance, because there also wasn't a single photo of any friends or family, whereas Sadie and I had them stuck to the fridge and lining shelves and windowsills.

My curiosity about the man deepened, but it paled next to my concern. The vamps had gotten him and it was my fault. I'd have to play spy in their territory and locate him. Besides, I was paying him to work and find Jude, and he'd probably demand hazard pay for being chained up, which was a big no-can-do.

I parked my car at the edge of Blood Alley and stood on the sidewalk, fists clenched, spiraling in frustration, because it remained the same two-block long stretch that it always was.

A couple strolled past me and turned into the closest restaurant.

I couldn't continue standing here. For one thing, I was too exposed. Just because I couldn't see into the vamp version of Blood Alley, didn't mean they couldn't see out here, or worse, didn't have sentries posted to await my arrival. If there were, I refused to risk any innocents getting caught in the crossfire.

The pizza employee's face flashed into my head. Any *more* innocents getting caught.

The moment my cloaking took effect, the wide, cobble-stoned alley vanished, replaced by spiky gates with a large metal sign reading "Blood Alley" spanning them. Gargoyle statues crouched on each corner of the sign.

Immediately inside the gates, four narrow crooked lanes branched off, each one running uphill.

I pumped the air in victory. No more standing and squinting to reveal hidden spaces. Simply deploy my cloaking and bam!

The bumpy cobblestones of the real Blood Alley gave way to smooth pavement as I threaded my way past the Ohrists milling about. One French-speaking group in brightly-colored dashikis huddled around someone's phone, glancing every now and again at the door they stood in front of, while two girls with thick Scottish brogues flew past, one of them complaining that they'd already been up this street.

If I reached out my arms, my fingers would almost brush against the black lacquered doors lining either side. There were no identifying signs, only red lightbulbs above each entrance, washing the entire street in a bloody haze. Some doors had one bulb, others two or three.

Most of the lights were on, but the ones that weren't were accompanied by open doors, so I peeked into one of the three-bulbed rooms.

Two bare-chested male vampires with tight six-packs and

hair to their shoulders, their eyes ringed with kohl, lounged sensuously on velvet divans. The wide floor planks were stained the same black lacquer as the door, while a black wrought-iron chandelier completed the goth vibe, turning their pale skin almost luminescent.

It was so over the top that I almost snorted, resisting the urge to ask if they'd like some wine with their cheese.

"It's getting out of hand." The blond vampire lifted a silver chalice with an ennui-heavy sigh. "Zev expects us to be his cash cows."

"What do you expect?" the raven-haired one answered. "Blood Alley was voted the number-one attraction on Ohrists Abroad for six years running. The free market wants what the free market wants." He licked his lips, his fangs descending. "There are perks."

Despite knowing that no one could see me under my cloaking, it still felt horribly inadequate. A flamethrower and a small tank might have been a good idea.

"Excuse me?" a woman said from behind me to the bloodsuckers.

I veered around the timid woman and her equally shy friend unnoticed, thanks to the black invisibility mesh. Was Zev the head vamp? I bit off a ragged cuticle, Janice's prosthetics and Laurent's scar looming large in my mind.

"Ladies." The blond vampire held out a hand, his dark eyes heavy with promise. "Come inside."

The other vamp hit a button on a small sleek remote control and a dark, melancholic tune accompanied by a sonorous male singer played over a fast-paced drum beat.

The women tittered nervously, one of them touching her neck.

This was madness. I wanted to grab them and shake some sense into them. For centuries, humans had armed themselves against the evil creatures, staying out of forests and barring their doors at night, but our pleasure-seeking culture had turned these encounters into some kind of titillating amusement park. I guaranteed that even if it was forbidden to go as far as turning Ohrists, what happened in Blood Alley did not stay in Blood Alley, although Lindsey's words about Ohrists craving what only vampires could give them made a lot more sense now.

The women accepted the vampire's invitation, shutting the door behind them, and the bulbs glowed red.

I stomped up the lane, the pressure of the dark clouds overhead causing a throbbing ache in my head.

"Always room for more." A Black female vamp in a beaded cocktail dress beckoned the crowd, waving a cocktail shaker. There was only one red bulb over her door.

A large blue lava lamp spilled its shadows over the walls of the well-stocked bar, giving the feeling of being underwater. The hypnotic feel was amplified by the languid electronica flowing through speakers.

A party of Japanese men with Beatles haircuts and skinny suits hurried to join her.

An Ohrist exited a different watering hole, a two-bulb establishment, where people drank to the blast of industrial music at a bar built from scrap metal, projections of a post-apocalyptic city swirling over the walls and floor, with Mad Max vampires of indeterminate genders head-butting patrons in a small mosh pit.

In another three-bulb door farther down, a vampire with the build of a small mountain range took off his shirt to face off against a man missing three teeth who looked like he threw logs for fun. The vampire cracked his knuckles and threw the first punch, and the man staggered back against the door, slamming it shut.

In the final room I spied on, again two-bulb, a jewel-toned stained-glass lampshade hung over a poker table with a beautifully carved base and a leather bumper running its circumference for players to rest their cards on. An Asian vamp croupier shuffled with impressive speed while he waited for his patrons to get settled.

There were dozens of doors over the four streets and Laurent could be behind any one of them, but if I had to guess? I stopped at the top of the hill where all the roads converged.

A round windowless limestone building loomed over Blood Alley, its dark purple lights spelling out "Rome." Hilarious.

Gargoyles crouched unevenly on the expanse of unkempt lawn between myself and my destination. I hurried past the first one, my stomach knotted, assuring myself that these were statues. Movement out of the corner of my eye made me jump, yelping, but it was a raven landing on the head of one particularly hideous gargoyle.

"Poe?"

The bird shook out its wings, turning fathomless black eyes on me.

I held that staring contest longer than any sane person should before power-walking through the rest of that unsettling sculpture garden and around the club, which occupied roughly a city block.

When the front door slid soundlessly open to admit me, the bouncer inside got up off his stool and walked to the entrance, frowning. He couldn't see me, but the motion sensor had detected my presence. I added that fact to my mental indexing. Did they detect vampires or had someone else checked out my property the other night? Someone with cloaking abilities—did Ohrists even have those?

I glided past the bouncer, out of the foyer where bass and drum rumbled up from the black tiles, and into the packed club. My mouth fell open.

The outside walls curved into a mural on the ceiling of the night sky, its inky darkness revealing itself as nuanced smudges of indigo and midnight blue like a kiss of silk from the heavens.

Cozy seating areas were grouped in the shadows outside the flickering glow cast by lit torches mounted on the glossy stone walls. The firelight softened the cavernous space and created a false intimacy that beckoned and seduced as much as the vampires prowling the room and flirting with patrons.

Ohrists worked here along with the undead. The human staff wore shirts with "Rome" embroidered in black over their hearts. The play of torchlight on the red fabric cast a bloody wash over the employees, which I had no doubt was intentional.

Some Ohrists took drink orders, others bartended or bussed tables. Two men worked to restore a stone gargoyle water feature set within a tiny oasis of greenery. While each and every human employee was ridiculously attractive, they didn't compare to the otherworldly beauty of the vampires of all different ethnicities. Even the occasional ugly vamp had an incredible sexual allure.

The faintest hint of some exotic musky spice wafted out from air vents, and my nipples tingled. The vampires outside had leashed their full potency, but in here, even I wasn't immune to the intoxicating presence of the fiends.

Rome sold the not-so-thinly veiled promise of sex and beauty set against a dangerous edge. This entire territory was a theme park allowing Ohrists to flirt with the dark—

I knocked into a table.

A male vampire was feeding off a young man in a shadowy corner, their bodies writhing together. Even fully dressed, it was provocative and carnal, especially when the human shuddered and cried out.

I snapped my mouth shut, and spun away, my cheeks flushed, and came up against another human/vampire pair leaning against the wall. Humans didn't have fangs so why was he sucking on her—oh, that's how that worked.

173

There was a fine line between playing a game of seduction and crossing the line into something more hardcore. Not everyone indulged to that extent, but there were enough couplings that I tried to keep from peering into the darker recesses of the room as I cleared each level.

I came out of one stairwell and almost tripped over this young woman who lay spread eagle on a sofa, her dress pushed up and a vamp sucking on her inner thigh. Her eyes were unfocused and her hips arched. Was this part of the allure for Jude? Were all these people willing participants?

Had Laurent been seduced or coerced into a similar act, his lithe body rolling in a slow groove and a dreamy cast to his expression?

My fingers drifted to my lips and I shifted to ease the restlessness inside me.

The vampire raised her head and wiped a trickle of blood off the corner of her mouth, wiping it on the sofa.

Now all I could think about were cleaning supplies and how often this place was disinfected.

When I didn't find anywhere this "Zev" the vamp had mentioned might be stationed, I made my way downstairs to the dance floor mostly convinced that I'd leave here safe and sound with Laurent. After all, every vampire was dangerous, as were Ohrists for that matter, and not one of them had noticed me here. My cloaking magic would get me out of anything.

A vampire violinist in a semi-translucent floor-length gown stood on a high platform at the far end. Two torches burned on either side of the mad fiddler, her body weaving in wild abandon.

Lush, throbbing music grabbed me in my gut and hips. I hadn't gone dancing in years, but I wished that I could lose myself in the press of bodies on the dance floor who were so tightly packed together that they sinuated as one.

The sprung dance floor was bouncy under my feet and the

air was as hot and muggy as a tropical forest, condensation running down the walls. Keeping my cloaking up was exhausting and I was way over-dressed for this place. Wiping off the sweat trickling down the side of my neck, I snaked along the edges of the crowd, following in the footsteps of the large vamp ahead of me pushing through the mass of people. He held a cocktail glass in each hand in which a dark jade liquid rolled from side to side like angry waves crashing on the shore.

The beat grew faster, the dancers writhing with their arms flung high.

My skin prickled in awareness and I broke through the crowd right as a familiar figure disappeared through a nearby door.

I'd found my missing golem, and this time, I wasn't leaving without answers.

16

I BARRELED FORWARD THROUGH THE DOOR MARKED "Employees Only" to catch up, but there was no sign of Emmett in the cool cement stairwell.

A door clattered from below. Taking the stairs two at a time, I jumped down and burst through into the subterranean level.

It was a totally different vibe down here. The long wide corridor was made of cement, not stone, and there were no torches, just regular overhead lights, along with staff changing rooms, a laundry room and a kitchen with Ohrists washing down trays and pulling glasses from dishwashers in billowing clouds of steam. The normalcy of it was jarring and almost creepy.

At the end of the hallway was a red door that Emmett must have gone through.

I made it halfway there.

Someone grabbed me by the collar and shook me gently, dislodging my magic invisibility cloak. Their touch was light, as if it was nothing that they'd plucked me out of thin air.

"Banim Shovavim. How delightful." The smooth cultured

voice poured gasoline on the spark of fear fluttering in my belly. "Ms. Feldman. Welcome."

Chin up, I turned around. It was almost laughable that I'd questioned if any other vampire was the boss. While not as bulked up as the vampire I'd followed on the dance floor, Zev BatKian was a core of steel draped in fine fabrics, his navy pinstripe suit and silk tie straight off Saville Row and his brown eyes suffused with a piercing intelligence. He appeared to be around my age, with short mahogany hair, and a trim goatee.

"Mr. BatKian." I nodded at him.

"I expected you earlier." He looked around. "Where might Lindsey be?"

I clocked the distance to the red door. I'd never make it, and who's to say it was even an exit? "She's going to be a little late. She ate something that didn't agree with her."

His lips quirked up in a smile. "Proper diet is so important." He waved a hand. "Ah well. Perhaps it's better that she's indisposed and I needn't chasten her for allowing you to deliver yourself here unescorted. Terrible breach of protocol."

Had Laurent been chastened for some breach?

"My apologies." The words came out croaked and I cleared my throat. "I'll be sure to follow proper procedure next time."

"That is much appreciated. Please." He extended an arm to the red door.

"Don't mind if I do." I showed myself in.

His office included an art gallery that ran under half of the club, though the soundproofing was top notch. Nary a rumble disturbed the hushed silence.

A Persian rug in deep reds and blues covered one small section of the floor, the furniture on top of it tending to sleek lines and unusual wood grains. All the surfaces were bare, save for a silver laptop on his desk. Beyond the office area, art hung on white walls, each one bathed in its own spotlight.

"Allow me to give you a tour." Zev spoke passionately about each piece.

Chagall paintings told stories steeped in Ashkenazi folk tales, while the play of light and shadow in the Rembrandts was almost ethereal, and marble sculptures depicted humanity in both the throes of ecstasy and despair's lament.

They weren't reproductions.

Secrets hidden in truths. A monster. An educated man. A level of civility and culture that was aspirational. Humanity's worst nightmare.

"Impressive," I said.

Zev led me over to a narrow cardboard box on a wooden pallet in the middle of the room, cut open the top flaps with an X-Acto knife, and peeled the cardboard away. The sculpture inside depicted a young boy writing in a book that was perched on his bent knee.

"What do you think?" Zev circled the piece.

It was exquisite. I crouched down, half-expecting the boy to notice me and look up from his scribblings. I reached out to touch it, then quickly reconsidered, curling my fingers into my palms.

"The artist perfectly captures the boy's look of pensive concentration, but there's this air that suggests he's not writing down facts but dreams." I straightened. "It's incredible, especially given the cold hard nature of marble."

"Mmm." He traced his finger over the boy's chipped elbow, then in a blur of motion, slammed his fist down on the top of the sculpture, pulverizing it.

I threw up a hand against a stray shard, unable to stifle my cry. The vampire could rip my throat open and drain the blood from my veins, but it was his expression of utter indifference to this violent act that sent a chill running down my spine. "Wh-why would you do that?"

"It was blemished." He dusted off his hands. "I don't tolerate imperfections."

He made his desires sound almost reasonable. After all, everyone wanted their money's worth, but most of us would utilize the refund option rather than remove the offending item from the face of the earth. My jaw grew tighter and tighter. He could clothe himself in the finest outfits and surround himself with renowned art, and it didn't change his utter inhumanity.

I took a deep breath to calm my galloping heart. The strain of not blurting out my true assessment of his character was exhausting. "This has been a wonderful tour and all, but—"

Emmett entered the gallery from the opposite end to the office and pulled up short at the sight of me. If it was possible for golems to look wan, then he rocked that pallor. He wore a pair of drab sweats belonging to Jude that she wore to clean her apartment, the top stretched tight across his shoulders.

Zev glanced over. "Do you two know each other?"

"Something like that. If I may?" It was not better to ask for forgiveness than permission with this vampire.

"By all means."

Zev's acquiescence was like a starter gun going off. I stormed over to the golem and shoved him up against a large bronze frieze of cavorting gods and goddesses. "Saving your ass instead of saving Jude?"

Emmett twisted his clay fingers, smoothing out a callus. "Golems aren't heroes, we're servants," he said. "If I can't do that, then I have no purpose."

Zev coughed politely.

Cold rushed down my back as it dawned on me that I'd turned my back on the vampire, which might be yet another breach of protocol. I released Emmett and turned around, giving a small bow.

"Sorry for the outburst," I said.

"Did you mark my frieze?" Zev said in a bland voice.

I shoved Emmett out of the way to check the artwork, my head bunched into my shoulders. Thankfully, it was blemish-free. "No."

"Hmm." He turned his attention to a text that had come in. It was hard to tell if he was pleased or disappointed.

My nerves were ground down to raw nubs. "Did you sic him on me?" I hissed at Emmett.

"You don't get it, do you?" The golem whispered back and waved an arm. "This is the safest place for me to be." Especially if the rival gang planned to have the only golem in town.

The vampire slid his phone into his pocket.

Emmett spoke louder now. "You should thank me. You're only here because you're Jude's friend and Mr. BatKian looks after his people."

"I endeavor to protect my family." Zev clasped his hands behind his back.

He couched his psychopathic narcissism in fancy words that I longed to throw back in his face. How'd you misplace Jude then, hot shot?

"We share a common goal," I said. "Where is Jude and what have you done with Laurent?"

"Let's discuss this like civilized people, shall we?" Zev said.

I wagged a finger. "That would be a challenge as you are neither civilized nor people."

With a gasp, I clapped my hand over my mouth. Oh, fuck. I'd said that out loud, hadn't I? My life flashed before my eyes, but there was an odd sort of relief to having committed to a suicide mission and I took the first full breath since I'd encountered the vampire.

Zev's brows drew together, but there was a faint smile on

his face, like he was curious to see how committed to this path I was.

"He's totally civilized," Emmett said hotly. "He doesn't even drink human blood."

"True." Zev wiped some dust off an ornate frame. "Developments in synthetic blood have made it possible to live without the real thing."

"Yeah," Emmett said. "Mr. BatKian's been funding research into plant-based heme. The stuff in those veggie burgers that bleed."

The vampire tilted his head. "I was lucky that the University of British Columbia is one of the pioneers in this area. It was one of the reasons that I relocated here."

"A true visionary," I said. In for a penny...

"I do like pushing boundaries. Conquering new frontiers, so to speak."

I threw my hands up. "Your vamps in Blood Alley haven't gone vegan. Their snack of choice is still GMO-fed human." I flashed back to the fight room. "Some of them even tenderize their food first."

"A very human impulse to beat their meat." Zev removed a pocket watch from his pocket, turning it absently over and over.

Emmett snort-laughed and I glared at him. The golem stepped sideways to stand next to the vampire.

Okay, that was a good one, but BatKian didn't get to joke. He was a monster and I resented his sense of humor. Stick to menacing.

"Every visitor to Blood Alley is a willing participant," Zev said.

I notched my chin up. "The man Lindsey killed tonight wasn't."

Zev wound the watch. "You assume our humanity died with our bodies, but that's not the case. We were teachers, fathers, doctors, carpenters. I, myself, was a rabbi. In fact, the Jewish prohibition on drinking blood fueled my funding in heme and alternate protein sources, which helps the entire planet. Vampires aren't wiped clean upon our rebirth. Our past experiences stay with us."

I crossed my arms. "Teasing that argument to its logical end, then you were all immoral murderers comfortable with taking a life when you were human, which proves my point that you're still a monster in death. Your acquired hungers have only exacerbated that."

Zev's hand tightened on the watch and his eyes darkened. "Do take care, Ms. Feldman. You are a guest here and as such, I've permitted you a certain leeway, but I find my patience growing thin. Speak your piece regarding Judith."

I moderated my tone to be more deferential. "These are the facts as I understand them, and please correct me if I'm wrong. Jude has been abducted by a rival gang run by a dybbuk. You can't get her because of the sunlight bulbs they've strung up in their bunker. Give me the location, return Laurent, and I'll get her back for you."

"That's one version," he said. "A more likely one is that Jude defected. Betrayed me. You will fetch her and bring her here."

"Betrayed? No way," Emmett said. "I'd have divined it."

"A fair point," the vampire said, "which begs the question of why you didn't? Is your magic failing, rendering you of no use to me, or did you deliberately withhold this information?"

"Neither," Emmett sputtered. He grabbed me and shoved me in front of him.

"Where are they holding her?" I said.

"The old Kemp substation off Highway One," Zev said.

I curbed my impulse to fist pump. We had the location! Everything I'd gone through tonight had been worth it. It wouldn't be a walk in the park, but I could take things from here. The hard part was done. Jude could be saved—provided

I convinced the vampire that keeping her around was in his best interest.

"Did you have an exclusive contract with her, specifically stating that she was not to contract her services to anyone else?" I said.

Zev laughed. "More of a handshake deal. Do you think I should sue?"

My heart leapt into my throat. Was that a throwaway or did he know where I worked? I pointed to his desk. "Have you got proof of this betrayal?"

"One of my vampires alerted me to the situation and the golem confirmed it. Judith went of her own free will to those people."

Emmett shifted uneasily.

The vampire put the pocket watch away. "What's it to be, Ms. Feldman? Will you bring my escapee back for me to dispose of, or will you insist on making this messy for the both of us? Is it to be your life or Jude's?"

Would my death be instantaneous or would the vampire wield pain like a conductor with a baton, breaking me under a symphony of torture, until all that was left was my discordant begging to end it?

Or would the true torture lay in leaving my daughter without a mother and dooming her to relive every day that moment when she first woke up, happy, only to remember I was gone? She was only a year older than I'd been when I lost my parents. Would the scent of my favorite perfume catch her unawares in the middle of a department store one day and send her searching for my face, even knowing that was impossible?

Would my loss turn her into a shadow of all she could have been? I wouldn't do that to Sadie.

But I couldn't live with Jude's death on my conscience either.

"No deal," I said.

"Very well," Zev said, clapping his hands together. "Do remember in your death throes that I gave you a choice."

There was a slight tug in my brain.

"Nice try, but your compulsions don't work on me," I said.

The vampire stroked his goatee. "That would be unfortunate, were it not for one thing." Zev opened the door that Emmett had originally come through.

There was a low growl and my pulse kicked into overdrive.

A larger than normal white wolf stepped into the doorway. There was no sense of recognition in those feral green eyes.

Zev tugged on his cuffs. "The compulsion wasn't for you."

17

"LAURENT." I HELD UP MY HANDS. "IT'S ME. Miriam."

The wolf barked and lunged. I jumped behind a marble statue, narrowly missing having a chunk taken out of my thigh.

Zev caught hold of Laurent's ruff, and all the fur on the wolf's body stood on end. He strained in the vampire's hold, white flecks of foam on his muzzle.

I pressed farther back behind the sculpture. My cloaking didn't do squat in Zev's presence, I couldn't outrun or outfight a wolf, and Delilah couldn't best the vampire with physical strength.

From his magic to psychological warfare tactics, Zev was more powerful than me. I'd assumed that Laurent and I would meet these vampires on our terms, and between his abilities and mine, persuade them to either hand Jude over, or assist with finding her.

I rested my head against the cool marble, the wolf's growls obscuring all other sounds, damning myself for my cockiness, then slapped myself lightly on one cheek. I had all the time in the world to berate myself, provided I got out of here.

Since Delilah had a hard outline where I stood, I animated her and sent her up the wall behind me, careful to keep her out of any spotlights, while I kept Zev talking to distract him. "What if Jude swears she'll never make another golem for anyone?"

"Her record is already blemished," the vampire said.

"Then let her unblemish it," I said tightly.

While I couldn't see the others from my hiding spot behind the statue, Delilah's vantage point on the ceiling noted them clearly. It was getting easier to stay in both my vision and hers at the same time.

Zev still restrained Laurent. "Some tarnishes cannot be shined away."

"Come on. It's never too late to give someone a second chance," I said.

Just a little closer...

"How human," Zev scoffed. "You speak of morality on one hand and then argue that lies and broken promises should go unpunished when it impacts you."

"How easily you distanced yourself from my kind," I said. "You drape yourself in humanity like it's a tailored suit to put on, but it's no longer an essential part of you."

Delilah dropped to the ground in the same pool of light in which the others stood and kicked Emmett in the ass.

He flew into the wolf, knocking the animal free. Laurent yipped, startled, and Emmett sprinted across the room, the wolf hot on his trail.

Zev tried to follow, but couldn't move, because I'd crept up behind him and seized his shadow.

Emmett wrestled with the wolf, who bit him, then sneezed and spat out a mouthful of clay. The golem's pompadour went skidding across his floor, his bald head nicely proportioned.

Zev stepped to the side, not immobilized one iota by my magic. "What outcome were you expecting?" he said. "Do you really think that someone like you can kill me as you did my young associate?"

Still gripping the vampire's shadow, I gaped at it with a sinking feeling. Like Titanic-level sinking. Desperate, I crumpled it as hard as I could, but instead of icy darkness curling through my fingers, the shadow turned to fog, reforming on the ground several feet away.

I swallowed. How could I kill the vampire with the lighter if I couldn't paralyze his shadow?

Would that tactic even work on him at all?

The wolf circled me and I held my hands up like I was some exotic animal tamer. Who knew that would have been the most relevant career choice in my life? I fought back a lump in my throat. How was I supposed to reason with a wolf driven mad by compulsion? We were supposed to keep giving each other grief until we found Jude together, not until he ripped my throat out.

I backed up involuntarily.

Zev smirked. "How sweet. I see you two are having a heartfelt reunion, so I shan't intrude further. Though, it's a pity his joy in seeing you again will probably tear you apart." He strode out the door, locking it behind him.

Emmett ran past me and the wolf pounced, knocking the golem to the ground. The wolf snarled, Emmett screamed, and a clay leg clad in shredded green cotton flew across the room.

I snapped my fingers. "Yo! Huff 'n' Puff!"

Laurent jumped off the golem and came at me, but his shadow wasn't moving correctly. It jerked along in starts and stops, with a limping wounded quality to what should have been a fluid gait. Okay, I saw dybbuks in shadows—could it also be that I saw vampire compulsions?

The shifter leapt and I dropped to the floor, rolling out of his way, my cloaking in place. He landed, spun, and pawed at the ground, swinging his muzzle from side to side.

The tension in my shoulders eased. He couldn't scent me or hear my heartbeat under my magic either. Only Zev had the ability to pierce my magic invisibility.

The golem belly-crawled toward his severed leg. "Don't leave me with him!"

I remained silent and hidden, my mind working feverishly. A compulsion wasn't a dybbuk possession. It wasn't something physical to pull out of a person, and yet it did have to be removed. Was it akin to being drunk? Could I sober Laurent up, so to speak? Snap him out of it? Since once again, the issue was an abnormal shadow, there was probably some magic fix to it, but as with Rupert, I had no idea what that might be, and I didn't have time to trial-and-error my way to success.

Plan B it was.

Six feet of corded muscle sheathed in white fur put his nose to the ground and hunted me. There wasn't even the illusion of human skin to let me believe I was anything other than prey to him. Stress ground down my nerves, but this was all on me. I'd gone into that forest, and partnered up with the wolf, fooled by his human face.

There was nothing human behind those eyes now.

But I wasn't Red, waiting for the hunter to save her. I was the Jabberwocky and Laurent was the vorpal blade in my employ, so he could damn well stop trying to kill me.

I ran over and snatched Emmett's leg away. Nice and solid, a good heft to it. Jude did exceptional work.

Emmett screeched and pounded the floor in frustration.

"Shut up," I hissed. "You'll get it back."

The golem looked around confused, since he couldn't see me, then sighed and rolled onto his back.

Clutching the limb to my chest so it stayed hidden, I snuck up on Laurent, got into the stance that Sadie's Little

League coach had made me practice in order to help her at home, and swung.

Home run! I cracked the wolf across the head so hard that the clay leg snapped, the shin hitting the ceiling like a champagne cork and knocking out one of the lights. Glass tinkled to the ground.

"Fuck my life," Emmett moaned.

The wolf skidded across the floor, his limbs flailing like a cartoon character. He crashed into the wall head first, then stumbled backward, shaking himself dazedly.

I peered at his shadow, but it blended into others on the ground, and I couldn't tell if it was normal again. "Laurent?"

His gaze was muddled by anger and an unquestionable hunger. A wolf's hungry expression was not a cue to put on some Barry White for a little bow chicka wow wow. It was a time of deep regret that I hadn't gone to the gym more because I was the equivalent of a grass-fed cow.

"Are you still under BatKian's influence, or just mad?" I said at his growl. "Look, I had to hit you to break the compulsion." I peered closer. "I did break it, right?"

He loped towards me, his lips bared in a feral grin.

Uncertain of whether he was compulsion-free, I waved the stumpy leg frantically. "Wanna play fetch?"

"Don't you dare," Emmett growled. He wobbled up to standing on his one leg and motioned for his errant limb. "Give it back."

"Go get it boy." I flung the leg back at Emmett. It hit him in the stomach, knocking him over. "Wow. Your balance is shit. Try yoga."

At Emmett's loud thud, Laurent stopped and looked back at the golem. That's when the crescent of light flared up next to the wolf.

"Laurent!" I flung my shadow at him, but didn't reach him in time.

The blindspot engulfed him. I threw my hands up against

the dazzling light with a cry, but when it winked out, the wolf stood there, unconsumed by the ohr, that supernatural life force that fueled their magic.

"Tha—that's impossible," I stammered.

The wolf flashed me a very familiar look of impatience, flicking his tail at me, his shadow echoing the gesture with its normal fluidity. He threw back his head and howled a torrent of rage, pain, and frustration that echoed off the walls. At least the compulsion was gone.

That didn't mean he wasn't going to kill me all on his own initiative for clubbing him.

"Feel free to thank me for returning you to your right mind." I backed away in quick jerky steps that turned into a sprint as the predator charged me in a cloud of explosive violence. I tensed for the bite of his jaws tearing through bone, but the wolf raced past me, ramming the door until it splintered open and he escaped.

I gusted out a breath and dropped my magic.

"How the hell am I supposed to walk now?" Emmett flung his broken shin at the wall.

"Stick it back on."

"I'm not Play-Doh. My bits have to be cast and fired. Help meeee," he whined.

"You sold me out."

"I had to. The vamps got me and I had to prove my worth."

"Didn't you? You told them about the dybbuk."

"I confirmed the dybbuk's involvement. It wasn't new information and I couldn't answer other questions because I can't control when my magic works. I'm defective, and BatKian knows it." Emmett rubbed his hands over his face. "They're going to destroy me."

This was not my problem. I had to find the wolf and get us both out of here before Zev came back and finished us off himself.

"I'll try to return for you, okay?" I gestured at the door. "But I have to go."

"Fine," Emmett said, in an Eeyore voice. "Go. Abandon me, like Jude did. I'll just lay down and wait to die. Maybe you could roll me over to that smashed sculpture before you go, so they don't have to clean up two messes?"

His divination might be defective, but his guilt-tripping was top notch.

"I liked you better drunk." I did a quick sweep of the room and ran over to the office area.

Emmett theatrically flung an arm over his eyes. "Me too."

I wheeled the rolling desk chair over and helped him into it. Awesome, now I was committing grand theft desk chair. To make matters worse, it had a wonky wheel that pointed in a different direction from the other three. I had to lean into the back of the chair to make it move, but I bumped us out the door.

"Could you push it more smoothly?" Emmett said.

"No, but I could break off your other leg and shove it down your throat so I don't have to listen to any more complaints."

"Touchy. Did the wolf even go this way?"

We turned a corner and I stopped so abruptly that Emmett almost fell out of the chair.

Laurent had made short work of the two vamps he'd encountered here. And by short work, I mean that I slid in their blood as I stopped the chair, booting the half-mangled torso of one vamp into the wall.

"I'm going to go with yes," I said in a warbly voice.

The other bloodsucker lay on his back, his fingers twitching just out of reach of his torn-off face that looked like an undead pancake.

Why couldn't they all turn to nice piles of ash?

Gagging, I drove the chair over the corpse blocking our way. It took a few tries because office chairs aren't ATVs, but we resumed our journey, following the wolf's trail of bloody pawprints and adding our own tracks to the mix. The sound of the squeaking wheel pinched the muscles from my butt to the top of my neck, at which point it burrowed into my brain.

The trail of destruction turned grislier—and gristlier—the farther along we got.

Wet smacking sounds trailed over to us from a hallway branching off to the left, where Laurent gnawed on a vamp's arm like a chew toy.

I looked him up and down and sighed. "Normally, when it's my time of the month, I want chocolate and salty snacks, but you do you."

The fiend's other arm had been so thoroughly shredded I could have stuffed it in a sausage casing and served it up at the International Hellhouse of Pancakes with the creature's severed head as a garnish.

If this was the "in-control" version of the wolf, I never wanted to encounter him during a full moon.

"Laurent." I crouched down with my hand outstretched. Blood matted his fur, not all of it from the vamps, and some of his gashes were still bleeding. "We've got to get out of here."

The wolf looked at us, his nostrils flaring. He pulled his lips back, baring his incisors, then he dropped his toy and jumped over the dead vamp.

Emmett tried to spin himself around, but the wolf nosed up to the chair and backed us into the wall.

"Quit it, you bully." My black mesh swam up from the ground to knee height and flickered out.

I swear the wolf smirked.

"Wow, nice gratitude when I came here to save you." I pulled out the lighter and jabbed it at the shifter, but shockingly it wasn't as effective a deterrent as a flaming branch. "Back up."

Laurent head-butted me towards a door marked "boiler room," growling when I stopped. Questions and arguments were poised on the tip of my tongue, but one look at the untamed light in his eyes and I sighed, continuing to our destination.

"Is he going to cook you before he eats you?" Emmett said. "Aren't wolves supposed to like raw meat?"

I tilted the chair and dumped Emmett on his ass.

"Kidding." He hoisted himself back into the chair.

Laurent pawed at me until I opened the door.

I clung to the doorframe with all my strength, but he nipped me in the ass, and then knocked Emmett and me into the room, growling some more.

"I don't know what you want. Shift and talk to me." Unless he couldn't. Unless he was stuck in wolf mode? Was this why Laurent hadn't wanted to come here on the night of a full moon? Was its hold on him still too powerful, even now in the waxing gibbous phase? Holding the top of the chair, I ducked under pipes, the wolf steadily herding us backward until I tripped over a heavy metal ring.

"A trapdoor?" I hoisted it up, peering into the darkness. Delilah's vision might have had the same green tinge as night vision goggles, but I couldn't actually see in the dark, even with that magic. "I'm not going down into God knows whaaaaaaa—"

He'd pushed me, sending Emmett and the chair over the edge as well.

Emmett hit something with a grunt, while I cracked my funny bone on the metal arm of the chair. "Fuuuck!" I waved my arm, trying to shake off the pain.

It wasn't much of a fall and I wasn't injured, but it was very, very dark. Something ran over my back and I screamed.

"A little help," Emmett said.

I groped around until I found him and assisted him back into his makeshift wheelchair.

Green eyes glowed from next to me in the darkness and the wolf huffed.

"Now what, asshole?" I said. "I can't see anything."

Laurent had yet to hurt me in wolf form and I was so tired that it was easier to assume that if he hadn't torn out my throat yet, it wasn't going to happen and I could trust him.

"Where to?" I said.

His tail brushed my hand. I flinched and it flicked my skin once more.

"This better not be the wolf equivalent of pull my finger," I muttered, and gently caught hold of the tail.

The wolf led us through what I presumed was a tunnel, hewn from rough rock, that scraped my fingers when I accidentally bumped into it. The path sloped downward for quite some time, but the universe cut us a break, and we didn't encounter anyone—or anything else.

We hit a dead end and the wolf rammed against it until something gave way and moonlight streamed in. We exited through a hole in a wall into in a boarded-up storefront. Dirt, used condoms, and cigarette butts littered the floor.

Emmett had his leg draped over the arm of the chair, and was snoring away.

The wolf shoved the decrepit wall paneling back against the tunnel's entrance.

"Wait here and I'll get my car," I said. It was only a couple blocks away.

He tossed his head and snarled.

"Have whatever pissy fit you want. You aren't walking home like that, and I assume if you were capable of shifting, you'd have done so already."

He roared his fearsome roar and gnashed his fearsome teeth. And then his legs buckled from exhaustion and he crashed onto his belly.

"Uh-huh," I said, and left.

18

THE CITY HAD FALLEN INTO A 3AM DREAM-LIKE hush. This stretch of the downtown east side was deserted, save for a couple of downtrodden men trudging wearily to one of the single room–occupancy hotels nearby. Vancouver was full of contradictions: gentrification butted up against one of the poorest neighborhoods in Canada down here, a mandate to be green and bike-friendly warred with luxury gas-guzzling vehicles, and attempts to situate it as a world-class destination contradicted its local nickname of No Fun City.

The marginalization in this predominantly Sapien neighborhood was hard to reconcile with the lush seductiveness experienced in Blood Alley.

I jumped at every little sound while I hurried to my sedan, dropping into a crouch with my keys thrust outward between my fingers when a car backfired. I peered into my back seat for any more vamps trying to get the jump on me, and only once I'd made absolutely certain it was safe did I get in my car.

The vampire had been a rabbi, so the myths of holy water

and crosses were out. Could he enter my home without an invitation? Lindsey had broken into my car. Was that the same thing?

I actually took a moment when I was locked in my vehicle to search online for industrial flashlights that took full spectrum bulbs, but didn't find any useful options.

When I got back to the storefront, the wolf was prowling back and forth inside the door, his tail stiff, and the golem was still asleep. I motioned to the open back door on my car. "I'm tired, so skip past your temper tantrum and get in."

Laurent's compliance was less obedience, more sheer exhaustion, because the second he scrambled onto the spacious seat, he lay his head down on his paws and closed his eyes. I covered him with an old blanket that I kept in the trunk, mostly so that anyone who looked in the car wouldn't see a giant wolf, but also in case he shifted.

"Hey, Sleeping Beauty, wake up." I touched Emmett's shoulder.

He jerked awake and karate chopped my forearm, ducking his head when I glared at him. "Sorry."

I wheeled him to my open trunk. "Get in."

"Oh sure." He stabbed a finger at Laurent. "Pretty boy gets to ride in the chariot, but I have to role play an Amber Alert victim."

"Red clay isn't a normal skin tone and I have nothing else to hide you with." I crouched down so I was eye level with him. "I am going to count to three and if you're not in that trunk, then I will leave without you. One…"

He notched his chin up at me.

"Two…" I slammed the trunk shut.

"You said I had until three."

"I lied. Bye now."

"Okay, okay, I'll be good."

I unlocked the trunk again.

He climbed in unsteadily, his broken leg left behind in

Zev's office, and curled into a ball, resting his head on my emergency kit. "See? A perfect angel."

"Uh-huh." I slammed the trunk shut again.

A werewolf and a golem walk into a bar... damn, a drink sounded good.

I drove with the windows down to stay awake. A few blocks before we reached our destination, there was the sound of skin tearing.

All I could see in the rearview mirror was a rolling, bumpy movement under the blanket. Ripping skin sounded remarkably like roughly crinkling a paper bag, which wasn't so hard to listen to, but I flinched at the ongoing percussion of breaking bones. Laurent's guttural groans and heavy breathing reminded me of being in labor. If that was the level of pain he had to go through every time he shifted and he didn't have a cute baby at the end of it, I didn't see how it was worth it.

After a few minutes, I heard a deep sigh and the final pop of a joint falling into place.

It had taken me years to let my guard down around Goldie, and a lot of that growth had regressed when my marriage fell apart. Everyone was shaped by negative experiences, but there was a wariness with those of us who'd lived through deep trauma. I recognized them by certain smiles that never quite reached their eyes—which matched the ones I'd practiced in the mirror when I was younger—and the way they angled their bodies slightly away from others.

Laurent fought hard for people, but who did he let into his corner? The first time I'd been around him when he shifted, he'd chased me off. Had he done it with me here out of necessity, or was this, even as much as he'd hidden under the blanket, a sign of trust?

The battered front illusion of Hotel Terminus came into view.

Pulling up to the curb with a lightness in my chest, I put the car in park. "You okay?"

Laurent sat up, once more human, the blanket draped over his head and held tightly together in the front. Good. I didn't want him flashing his tight abs or powerful thighs or...

I cleared my throat and disengaged the child locks.

With his bleary eyes and curls falling into his face, he looked like a little kid. I smiled at the image of a smaller, curly-haired version of him grubby and happy, tramping through the woods, catching frogs and climbing trees.

"That bastard compelled me." His voice was raspy, his accent thicker, but the hate was crystal-clear. "You know the dybbuk's HQ?"

"Why?" I said, unlatching my seatbelt and twisting around to face him. "So you can storm the castle without me?"

"I want to go in now before they get a heads-up, and you look like the walking dead."

"You're one to talk. You are literally covered in blood. You have eaten undead people. And let's take a moment here to recognize that I'm the one who got the address. The Kemp substation off Highway One. You're welcome."

Laurent shrugged. "I got it too."

"From who? The vamp whose face you'd Hannibal Lecter'd or the one with his rib sticking out of his eye? Besides, there's no way you're some ball of energy, post shift, post compulsion, and post fighting off five vamps." I shook a finger at him. "Don't be an idiot."

"Six. Heh." He laughed, reliving the good times. "And I'm fine."

"Yeah?" I jabbed his shoulder and he winced. "The blood on you isn't all vamp. If you go, I go."

"You gonna take me on, Mitzi?"

I refused to smile at his diminutive of my name, even if it was cute. "Miri. And yeah. I killed a vampire tonight. You're not half as scary, Huff 'n' Puff."

"You didn't kill Zev."

"I didn't mean Zev."

His eyes narrowed and he pursed his lips. "We might be up against more than magic with these Ohrists. Some could have guns."

I scraped at a small stain on the hem of my sweater, trying not to think about what had caused it. "I can cloak us so we walk in, grab Jude, and leave. The only one who's been able to sense me under my magic was Zev, and this dybbuk isn't as powerful as he is, right?"

Laurent closed his eyes with a sigh. He was silent so long that I leaned over to wake him up when he spoke. "Okay, but we can't stay here until I've fixed things. It's not safe."

"Did you invite a vampire into your house?" I crossed my fingers that he'd answer in the affirmative because at least then my house would be off-limits.

He opened his eyes to roll them at me. "No, but I screwed myself over with that demon illusion on my door. It was a loophole that allowed the vamps to walk right in."

I nodded in relief. "How many did they send?"

"Two," he said.

"Did they compel you to go with them?"

"They tried but they weren't skilled enough." He gave me an address and settled back against the seat, the slash of a streetlight illuminating his fatigued expression. "They were stronger than me," he said grudgingly.

I headed east to the Capitol Hill area of Burnaby, about ten minutes away. "Where are we going?"

"A friend's house."

"You have friends?" I gasped in an exaggerated fashion.

He slid the blanket off his head and settled it around his

shoulders. "The ones I haven't eaten because they pissed me off."

"So this is your only one?"

"Ha. Ha."

The house I pulled up to was a lovely Arts and Crafts bungalow with low-pitched eaves, a welcoming front porch, and narrow stained-glass windows on either side of the front door.

"We'll take an hour to rest," he said, "and when we go to the substation, you do as I say and don't fight me."

"No problem."

He shot me one last searching look, but I kept my most pleasant and innocent expression on my face and finally got a tight nod.

Even with a ratty blanket wrapped around him that hit mid-thigh, Laurent didn't walk; he prowled. He stalked. Dress him up in a suit and he still wouldn't lose all vestiges of his predatory nature. And yet, this beast of a man chose to surround himself with books and music, and made his home into a work of art.

There was still so much I didn't know about him.

We made our way up the front sidewalk and he rang the bell.

A man in his late thirties with platinum blond bedhead that popped against his brown skin opened the door, tying the sash of a silk robe closed over his boxers and T-shirt. He raked a lazy glance over Laurent, but there was a piercing gleam behind the insouciance. This guy didn't miss a trick.

"Let me guess? Date night?" The blond spoke with a posh British accent. "You all right, poppet?" he said to me. "Smack Laurent in the head once for yes and twice for no."

"There's no way you're friends with Huff 'n' Puff," I said. "You're far too delightful."

The man stuck out his hand. "Naveen. My friends call me

Nav, and you just earned your way into that highly sought-after circle. Treasure your position."

I laughed. "Miriam. My friends call me Miri, and likewise."

"I need a shower." Laurent pushed past Nav into a warmly painted foyer. "Do you still have my spare clothes here?"

"Well, Goodwill didn't want them," Nav said, leading us into the living room.

It was a cozy room with inviting furniture in plush fabrics and a large honey oak coffee table, all buried under an explosion of toys.

I slugged Laurent. "You brought us to a house with a child? There are vamps after us. Are you crazy?"

"We'll handle anything that shows up," he said, rubbing his arm. "If they manage to get past all the wards."

"Uncle Woooollllf!" A toddler with ringlets and the same warm brown eyes as Naveen ran in on chubby legs, her green nightgown billowing around her. She held a stuffed bunny out to Laurent. "Arrrr."

"Arrrr," he growled back.

She squealed in delight, hopping up and down in place. Seeing a blood-streaked Laurent wearing nothing but a blanket didn't even faze her. She was either going to spend a fortune in therapy when she grew up or become a real-life Buffy.

"You know," Nav said, "Uncle Wolf isn't anything special. Uncle Nav's secret weapon, on the other hand, is a marvel of length and…" He shook his head. "Let's abandon that sentence right there, shall we?"

"Did we wake her?" Laurent said. "Sorry."

"No." Nav sighed, and picked the girl up. "Evani woke up an hour ago."

"I'm waiting for Mommy," she said, and sucked one of the bunny's ears into her mouth.

"Daya had a delivery?" Laurent asked.

"Twins." Nav motioned down a hall. "You know where the towels are. I'll clean off the sofa for you, Miri."

"No problem. I can do it." I moved cups from a plastic tea set onto the coffee table. "Wait, Daya as in Dr. Kumar?"

"Yes. My sister."

"No way! She delivered my daughter."

Laurent frowned. "You have a kid? Why didn't you mention it?"

"When should I have brought out the photos?" I said. "When we were fighting the dybbuk-possessed dude, the dybbuk-enthralled other dude, or escaping from the vampires?"

"Definitely the vampires. They do love a good slideshow," Nav said. "Show me."

I pulled up one of the latest snaps. "That's my Sadie."

"Beautiful girl," he said.

Laurent looked at the photo, grunted, and walked away. "One hour, Mitzi," he called back, "then we ride."

"How do you know Laurent?" I said, tossing wooden blocks into a Rubbermaid.

Nav threw the lid on the container. "We've worked together. The more interesting question is how do you? The Lone Wolf doesn't randomly bring people over, *Mitzi*."

"He's helping me find a friend." I gathered up a trail of colorful elastics, leading to a doll with hair styled to look like a unicorn. "Pretty."

Evani held out her hand for the doll, dropping her bunny.

"Because charity is a virtue he holds dear." Nav rolled his eyes at his niece's prodding. "Do you need both of them?"

She nodded and, sighing, he picked up the stuffed animal.

"There's a dybbuk involved," I said, "so our interests align. Also, I'm paying him."

"Uh-huh." Nav pointed to the blanket draped over the sofa. "Feel free."

"Thanks, but we're only going to be here an hour."

"Regardless." He tickled Evani. "Say goodnight, monster."

"Goodnight, monster." She made her bunny wave at me.

Smiling, I waved back. Damn, I missed cuddling a warm sleeping Sadie at that age, her head buried in my neck and her silky strands tickling my cheek.

I curled up on Nav's sofa, which was really comfortable, and undid my jeans with a deep sigh. My belly exploded out like an air bag. It was glorious. Next I took off my bra, tears of joy streaming down my face as I rubbed all the red lines on my body. Between the pants and the underwire, I looked like a slab of beef that had been marked into cuts for butchering.

The timer on my phone seemed to go off seconds later, not an hour. Yawning, I pushed through my fatigue and forced myself to open my eyes and sit up. It was just after 6AM and there was no way I'd be going in to work.

I had heaps of sick days, another perk, so I left a message for Shirley cashing one in. The stomach flu was a lie, but I didn't fake how miserable I sounded. If I'd earned anything in my forty-two years, it was the right to a full night's sleep, and I was running on fumes. I'd used more magic tonight than I had in decades and I'd come face to face with death. Putting in a full day of work was totally out of the question; still, the sheer relief I felt at not going in was odd for me.

Somewhat jokingly, I googled job openings in Spain, but without any knowledge of the language, I'd be stuck serving swill at some beach resort catering to English-speaking tourists. Visions of lobster-boiled, handsy old letches spun out before me, followed by the worse image of being the resident mom at a backpacker hangout and listening to tales of love lost and STIs gained during full-moon parties. Hard pass.

So my job wasn't the most exciting? Lots of people found

fulfillment with hobbies outside their work and I had my magic. Putting my bra reluctantly back on, I focused on our victory: we had the dybbuk's location and could rescue Jude.

How naïve I was.

19

Once Laurent and I settled our differences on which vehicle to take (mine—unless he planned to double Jude on his handlebars), the first part of the operation went off without a hitch.

Laurent had showered off the blood and lost that *Lord of the Flies* vibe, but he was still moving stiffly when he came into the kitchen.

His chocolate brown curls were damp. Regardless of whatever bathroom set-up Nav had, I pictured Laurent soaking in his outdoor copper tub, his head tipped back in relief, the hot water easing his tight muscles and steam curling up against the cool night, while the scent of cedar from the patio roof provided a relaxing balm.

His wash and nap hadn't been that refreshing, because there was an exhaustion in his pinched features that looked like it ran bone-deep.

"Good morning, sunshine. Food's up." Nav placed a plate in front of Laurent, then returned to frying bacon.

The coffeemaker burbled loudly, the smell of the roasted beans perking me up.

"Good." Laurent grabbed the plate, hovering impatiently beside Nav while he finished cooking.

I put down my toast and pretended to hold up a microphone. "And now we have Huff 'n' Puff modeling from the fall collection of the House of Big Bad. The practical blood-hiding nature of the all-black ensemble receives a touch of whimsy with mismatched socks."

Laurent finished loading up on pork products, glanced down at his one brown and one black foot and scowled. "Must you bust my balls?"

If I ate that much at a single sitting, my legs would no longer support me. Besides, I was too nervous to do more than nibble at a couple strips of bacon and a piece of toast.

"Yes, actually, I must bust them. I am contractually bound to do so. You should have read the fine—oh, shit!" Dropping the bacon, I ran outside and opened the trunk of my car. "Heeeeyy, buddy."

"Really?" Emmett glared balefully up at me, a stalk of grass stuck to his ear and sand on his sweats. Guess I hadn't vacuumed my trunk since last summer.

Laurent joined us, peering down at the golem. "Sorry about the leg, man."

Emmett shrugged. "Shit happens. I'm Emmett."

"Laurent." They exchanged chin nods and Laurent got into the car.

What a relief that the bro club was cool with each other.

I rapped on the passenger window until Laurent rolled it down. "We can't take him with us," I said.

"Nav won't care. Leave him here."

"You could help, you know."

Laurent doubled over. "Period cramps. Oooowwwww."

"I hope you get fleas."

Since I had to go to the trunk for Emmett, I also grabbed my gym bag. Might as well change into more comfortable clothes.

Nav was a sweetheart about taking in a one-legged golem. His only comment was, "Interesting choice of chaperone, Miri."

"You're sure this won't scar Evani?"

"Nah. I'll tell her he's a robot." Because that passed for normal around here?

Emmett shrugged and kept flipping through TV channels.

I examined my reflection in Nav's bathroom mirror, relieved that the bruises on my neck had finally faded. Raking wet fingers through my hair, I secured it in a ponytail before putting on some deodorant and a swipe of lip gloss that was tossed in the bottom of my bag. After a moment's consideration, I checked my ass in my yoga pants and my boobs in the green tank with a built-in bra worn under a cute V-neck hoodie. All in all, I looked hot enough to work out at the snooty gym that our firm paid for memberships at.

Good to go, I bade the guys farewell and got back into the car.

Laurent bitched about our first stop—a drive-through run —though that didn't stop him from putting in an order for a mocha with a double shot of espresso and extra whip.

"What? No plain coffee that's as black and bitter as your general view of humanity?" I plugged the address for the substation into my phone, which was an hour's drive outside town.

"Cynicism, like salt, is not a flavoring to be applied every-where." Laurent removed the lid of his piping hot cup and licked some whipped cream, his eyes warming in a pleasure that looked so carnal I burned my mouth on my own London Fog. He hadn't lost that gleam when he looked at me and said, "Sometimes I crave a little sugar."

I bit into the chocolate biscotti I'd ordered, licking a crumb off my lip. "Don't we all?"

He snorted and drank some more coffee.

This was the first time that Laurent had ridden in the

passenger seat and he took up a lot of room. Not physically, because his build was lean and rangy like a soccer player's rather than a linebacker, but presence-wise. Now that he wasn't asleep in the back, blanketed in shadow, he was this mini-testosterone factory, adding this element of overt masculinity into my practical family sedan that felt decadent. Dangerous.

I braked at a red light, sliding my gaze sideways to the shift of his biceps as he did an arm stretch.

The advance left turn light went green and the cars in the lane next to mine moved forward.

Laurent flexed his fingers, momentarily changing them to claws.

My light turned green as well and I crossed the intersection, merging into the lane to get on the highway heading east. "What does it feel like to shift?"

"Like I'm being torn apart and put back together." There was none of the predator lurking behind his eyes, just a soft vulnerability, there and gone in a blink. "I dread every second of it."

I shook my head. "That sounds awful. Why do it?"

"Because every time I survive, the world is sharper and sweeter, and I feel like I can do anything. Those first moments are like the opening notes of a symphony." He gave a self-deprecating snort.

"I felt that way after I gave birth."

He nodded. "Then you understand what I mean."

We drove in companionable silence for a while. Outside this car was an angry vampire to survive, a missing friend to rescue, and a dybbuk to best. The stakes were deadlier than the items on my usual to-do list, but every day came with challenges that had to be met. As a mother and a working woman, I'd learned to find micro-moments of self-care and push everything else aside.

I drank some more London Fog, savoring the honey-sweetened Earl Grey. It was warm and gentle and made me feel like I was heading to the library for some books to read by a fire.

"Have you ever gotten stuck in wolf form?" I said. "Is that what happened last night?"

Laurent's back stiffened, almost imperceptibly, then he turned the radio on, scrolling through stations until he found a piano solo.

Maybe I'd overstepped with that question.

"This is beautiful," I said. "The music sounds like a waterfall."

"It's Chopin's 'Fantaisie-Impromptu in C-sharp minor.'" He played along one-handed with it. "Chopin never intended to publish it."

"But it's gorgeous."

Laurent grabbed his coffee cup. "He was worried that it sounded too close to Beethoven's 'Moonlight Sonata' and asked a friend to burn it after his death. The friend wrestled with the decision for six years, then published it. And now it's a doorway to somewhere else. You can listen to it and not have to be where you are for a little while. But it doesn't last forever. Eventually, we have to come back to reality."

If this were a date instead of a dangerous mission to rescue my best friend, his illumination on Chopin would be the closest thing to foreplay I'd had in years. Who was I kidding? It still was. New to-do list item: buy batteries.

"How long did it take you to come back to reality?" I said softly.

He swallowed the remainder of his coffee. "Some would say I still haven't."

Every new fact I unearthed about this man made the big picture swim farther out of reach.

Highway traffic was relatively light this early in the morning, and I settled into a comfortable speed without any asshole on my bumper urging me to go faster.

"So, is shifting a choice or a compulsion?" I said.

"Both. It's addictive. I was too young to remember the first time it happened. The shift took a long time and my parents were terrified." He looked out the window at the sun peeking up over the horizon streaking the indigo sky with gold, and his voice was quieter when he spoke. "And disappointed."

I offered him some biscotti, but when he refused, I popped the piece into my mouth. "They don't shift?"

"No. They don't possess such common powers." His lips twisted wryly. "They have different talents, but they rarely use them. My father takes great pride in the fact that all his achievements have been done with intellect, not magic."

"What does he do?"

"He founded a financial management firm that's now the second largest in France. What is it you really want to ask me?" I glanced at him, startled, and he pointed to my chest. "I can hear your heart racing."

"Could you hear it when I'm cloaked?" Because if so, that was a huge problem.

"No. The magic must prevent it."

Nodding, I pulled down the visor to block the sun from my eyes. "How do I keep myself and my family safe from Zev? No, wait. First tell me how you survived a blindspot."

"It's complicated." He rested his head against the seat. "I told you I trained to scent dybbuks. It's tied to that. As for Zev, I suspect you turned down the same offer he gave me? To hand Jude over?"

"Yeah. I don't get it. Emmett ratted me out, but why did Zev come for you that way? Emmett didn't know we were working together. Would Harry have—"

"Never." Laurent shook his head so firmly it was clear that he believed on pain of death in the gargoyle's loyalty. He frowned, though, as he spoke again. "But BatKian knows about my interest in this particular dybbuk. I failed to stop Mei Lin once before, but she won't get away again."

"A woman is the head of this gang?" I said.

"Hashtag feminism," Laurent said acerbically. "At the time, I was warned to drop my hunt. Mei Lin and Zev already had agreements in place regarding territory, and it was impressed upon me by the Lonestars that if I disturbed that by killing her, the vamps would not be happy."

"But bringing Jude in to make a golem was seen as an act of aggression and Zev changed his mind."

"Yeah. He dragged me down for our little chat and gave me the conditions under which I could go after Mei Lin. When I refused to give him Jude, he compelled me to do it anyway, after I'd dealt with Emmett."

I sighed. The golem wasn't being paranoid about the vampires intending to destroy him. "And me."

"A last-minute addition," Laurent said.

"Aren't I special? Well, we've both pissed him off now, so how do we stay safe?"

"Either offer him something he wants more, or find someone who can protect you."

"Do you know what he wants?" I drove onto the Port Mann Bridge, which crossed the Fraser River, the fan-like pattern of the cables supporting the bridge deck soaring like sails overhead.

"Other than your friend's return? No idea."

"Even if the Lonestars didn't want you going after Mei Lin, why don't they do something about Zev?" I said. "All that traffic in and out of Blood Alley is a good way to blow the secret of magic."

"And yet, it hasn't. The vamps have dealt with that problem through illusion or compulsion, and like Ohrists, they police their own. Also, Blood Alley is one of the few places where Ohrists can work without fear of revealing their magic. It's a necessary evil."

Laurent turned the volume up slightly and I let the classical music wash over me, coming to terms with being a tiny insignificant speck in this vast supernatural universe. To comfort myself, I mentally categorized everyone. At the bottom of the pecking order were Sapiens. They had the greatest numbers, but unless they learned of our existence and acted, they weren't a threat.

Who would I put next? I drummed my fingers on the wheel, running through the various strengths of the rest of the supernatural world.

Probably golems and gargoyles were the next step up on the food chain. Laurent had mentioned a demon, but estries at least hadn't been seen in ages, and demons hadn't come up in conversation with anyone else. I would have asked my passenger about it, but he was relaxed against the seat, his eyes closed and his breathing slow, and I couldn't bring myself to wake him. Maybe that put demons on the rarer side? I set them aside for the time being as an unknown.

Above golems and gargoyles, I'd list dybbuks. No one wanted to tangle with these dangerous spirits, but they tended to be loners, which was for the best, because the idea of roving dybbuk gangs causing mayhem was unsettling.

If a dybbuk did inhabit a host, then there was a week of enthrallment, where they battled for possession of our body, but only I could sense them at that point, and the person's shadow still looked normal.

Once the dybbuk fully possessed the host and that person's spirit or essence was no longer alive, Laurent could scent them, but he was unable to see that their shadow had changed to that sickly gray streaked with crimson flecks.

I chewed thoughtfully on the rest of my biscotti.

Maybe other Banim Shovavim were out there doing something to combat that problem, but there weren't many of us worldwide and the Ohrists here weren't inclined to do more than bitch and leave it to Laurent. To be fair, they weren't able to unearth dybbuks naturally, but I didn't think the training to scent them could be that bad—until the obvious torment that Laurent had suffered while destroying the dybbuk came to mind.

I licked a smear of chocolate off my lip. If widespread Ohrist help was off the table, then it was a relief that we couldn't be inhabited, provided those of us with magic were smart during the Danger Zone.

Sapiens at the bottom, then golems and gargoyles, then dybbuks. Much as I hated to admit it, Banim Shovavim were less powerful than vampires, so I listed us next. We were few and far between, and given the centuries of Ohrists hating and hunting us, we remained in an extremely vulnerable position.

That brought me to the vamps whose powers grew stronger over time.

Speaking of bloodsuckers, what did Zev want? He had money and power. Was there a piece of unblemished art he desired that I could bribe him with to leave me alone? I shook my head. As if I could afford anything he collected. Maybe Jude would have some insights, if she was willing to share personal information about him. My magic was going to be a huge shock, plus she'd be dealing with the trauma of her abduction. She might not be willing to add to Zev's wrath by sharing secrets, if she knew any, but it was the only straw I had to grasp at.

The only reason I placed Ohrists at the top of the food chain above vampires was that there were more of them. I snorted. Ohrists certainly acted like they were above everyone else, equating their light and life magic with some bullshit nobility.

In terms of a magic community, they had the highest numbers and an incredible range of powers, even if most of them were limited to one type of talent.

I slid my gaze sideways to my companion. What *exactly* had he undergone to sniff out dybbuks?

The maps app announced our destination on the right and Laurent and I exchanged glances. We were out on a backwoods road in the middle of nowhere with the dybbuk's HQ down some dirt driveway that curved off into the trees.

Laurent instructed me to park on the side of the road and leave my hazard lights on. That way it would seem as if we'd had car trouble and gone for help.

"Stick close," I said, getting out of the car. "I've never actually tried cloaking another person."

"You don't have to now, either." He pulled off his shirt and tossed it on the seat, his back muscles flexing. "I'm going to shift."

"That's not the plan." I put my keys in the pocket of my hoodie, having left my purse in the car.

"If we want to escape quickly and unharmed, we use all the tools in our toolbox." He toed out of his shoes. "You get your friend and I'll find you when I've taken care of Mei Lin. This is my best shot at stopping her from flooding the city with more drugs. Or worse." Pulling off his socks, he threw them in the car. "The longer a dybbuk possession lasts, the more unstable the host becomes, and Mei Lin is at the one-year mark. That's close to a record."

I really wanted to see him shift, but it seemed like too personal an ask for our casual acquaintance. "Lock the door before you go furry."

Even with the black mesh hiding me, I walked along the grass so my footsteps wouldn't give me away on the gravel in case there were guards posted in the forest. My magic prevented my breathing and heartbeat from being detected, but if I spoke or stepped on a twig, those sounds were heard loud and clear.

Rain drizzled down on this gray and depressing day. Birds barely sang and the heavy dew soaked into my runners.

Sadly, my cloaking didn't have useful umbrella properties and I got damper and damper.

There was no sight or sound of Laurent.

The trees ended in a scraggly clump, revealing the abandoned substation. Situated next to a weed-choked, rusted-out rail line, the squat building had blown-out windows and front stairs that had disintegrated into rubble. There was no sign of working electricity, never mind the place being lit with full-spectrum bulbs. Was this the correct location?

On the side was a partially rotted-through door, but the grass was trampled and the mud in front of the door was smoothed down, so I eased it open, rubbing my hands in anticipation of this high-stealth mission. I had mom hearing and shadow magic: call me Feldman. Miriam Feldman.

So much for my high hopes. My face fell because the substation was a gutted mess. Pitted walls were covered in graffiti running the gamut from cartoon characters to the grim reaper to names tagged in bold graphic letters, but the iron girders bracing the ceiling seemed intact, so I walked through the wide open space. I threw an arm over my face at the stench of urine wafting out from the corners, making my way past piles of rubble, some of them soot-streaked from vandals attempting to start fires.

Avoiding bits of broken pipe and holes in the floor, I passed a broken wall and arrived at a metal door guarded by a short man smoking a cigarette. I pressed behind a concrete post and sent Delilah slithering on the ground back the way we'd come.

She picked up a chunk of fallen concrete and threw it in the opposite direction from the guard, then jumped high to catch hold of one of the iron roof girders.

The guard raced down the hall to investigate. Once he'd passed her, she dropped silently to the ground.

I powered her down, calling up the black mesh again, and slipped inside the metal door, immediately screwing my eyes shut. The light blinded me—they weren't kidding about the full-spectrum bulbs. It was like stepping out into the bright noon of a summer's day from a dark room. Shielding my face with one hand, I half-closed my lids until I'd acclimated to the brightness and headed down the narrow staircase.

The basement, as brightly lit as the stairwell, was a rabbit warren of hallways, but it was oddly quiet. One room had packages of cocaine left unattended, while in another, stacks of bills and a money counter sat on a table, ripe for the stealing, but there were no people.

The deeper into this maze that I got, the stronger the feeling of eerie nothingness grew. Convinced I was being set up for the jump scare of all time, I started flinching in anticipation. Several times I hit dead ends and had to turn around, but after a long slow sweep, I entered a corridor that I had yet to clear. Honestly, by this point, I was wrung-out, and ready to call the mission a bust.

A man sat propped against the wall next to a closed door at the end of the hallway, his head lolled to one side and his eyes closed. Sleeping on the job. I tsked. Good minions were so hard to find.

Regardless of where everyone else had gone, he'd been left here to guard that door, meaning that something important was behind it.

A sickly-sweet charred meat smell grew stronger the closer I got to the guard, dread deepening with each step, until I reached for the man with a shaking hand.

He fell over, and I screamed, losing my cloaking in shock.

His spine was burned out.

A two-hundred-pound blur of white slammed into me, knocking me onto my stomach. A rush of adrenaline flooded me, my mouth dry. I processed it was Laurent as his claws flexed against my spine, and I mewled, anticipating the same end as the guard.

The door bashed open off its hinges, whizzing so close

overhead that it ruffled my hair as it passed. It shattered against the concrete wall, one edge of it blackened and smoking.

"Oh God, Jude!" I gasped, trying to get out from under the wolf, and save my friend from whatever *had* killed the guard and blown the door off.

A shadow fell over us and Laurent leapt off me, his ears forward and his fur bristled. Growling, he pushed his snout up, exposing his gums and front teeth.

A woman in a blood-spattered tennis outfit wrapped a strand of hair around her finger, her crimson-flecked sickly shadow really bringing out her highlights.

"Welcome to the party," Mei Lin said, and fired two hard light beams from her eyes.

20

LAURENT POUNCED AND KNOCKED HER OVER, sending Mei Lin's magic wild. It scorched the ceiling, raining plaster down on us. For an encore, his claws transformed as if they were made of light and he ripped out her heart.

Her body hit the ground with a wet thunk and the dybbuk burst out of her in a seething mass of crimson and gray.

Oh, okay. The heart was the release button, so to speak. Facts were good. I swallowed and turned away from Mei Lin's vacant gaze, waiting for Laurent to spear the ghostly fucker before sending it back to Gehenna where it belonged, but no.

The wolf batted the entity at me.

I dodged and screamed as it swarmed me, singeing my skin with its touch. There was no relief from the enraged spirit, its howls echoing in my head.

"I don't know how to kill these... motherfucker!" I curled into myself, my shoulders hunched, the dybbuk assuming a triangle shape and stabbing at me like a homicidal humming-bird. It didn't hurt like a knife wound, but every hit it landed filled me with a revulsion that made me want to tear my skin off.

Laurent sat down, his tongue lolling out, and cocked his head to the side.

"This is not a teachable moment and you are not Mr. Miyagi." I tried to snare the dybbuk in a shadowy net, but it slipped through, continuing its assault on me.

Laurent calmly licked blood off a paw. At least it didn't pool under the corpse, his magic having cauterized the worst of it.

Weaving and bobbing to keep the dybbuk at bay, I almost tripped over Mei Lin's corpse. Wait. The word dybbuk meant "one who cleaves." As in cleaves to, clings to. But what if the other meaning was also true?

I fixed a handy cutting weapon in my mind.

My shadow snaked up my body and flowed down my left arm to become a sword. Okay, I lie. It was more of a dagger with gout, and when I slashed it through the seething crimson mass, the blade fell sideways like a flaccid penis.

I shook it. "What do you need? Mood music? Foreplay? Work already!"

My stupid team member snorted.

I narrowed my eyes at the useless magic weapon. Not a sword, then. How about a buzz saw blade? Nice simple shape, jagged edges.

The dybbuk redoubled its efforts, hammering at me.

In theory, a buzz saw was a great idea. In practice, it looked more like one of Dali's melting clocks.

The wolf yawned.

Keep it up, Huff 'n' Puff. You'd be next on my death list. I tilted my head. Death and darkness… could it be that obvious?

I reshaped my shadow into a scythe. Slaying vamps might not have been my forté, but I swung that curved blade with all the panache of Inigo and the Dread Pirate Roberts dueling in *The Princess Bride* and sliced through the dybbuk.

The weapon's form held and the dybbuk jolted backwards, but I hadn't destroyed it.

I blew my hair out of my eyes, readjusting my grip on the long handle. "Die, you fucker! Die!"

Mut, a voice in my head whispered.

"Mut, you fucker!" Hebrew letters appeared on the blade, and this time when I slashed the dybbuk in half, all color leached out of both parts. The spirit imploded with a sucking noise and winked out of existence.

The wolf made a strangled sound. His eyes were wide and his snout kind of wrinkled up, as if dumbfounded. What was his problem? I'd killed the malevolent spirit as directed.

I tossed my shadow scythe into my right hand, the letters on the blade fading away. "I'm not even left-handed." The scythe vanished. "Actually, I totally am. I just love that movie too much not to quote it."

My smirking triumph was short-lived.

"Jude!" I ran into the room, but the only thing in there was a discarded tennis racquet and a couple of blood-stained green balls, with corresponding marks on the wall Mei Lin had served them against.

"Where is she?" Shaking, I whirled on Laurent. "You killed Mei Lin before we could find Jude."

The dybbuk had burned that guard's spine away with her light magic. What had she done to my best friend?

The wolf caught hold of my sleeve and herded me through the corridors. The stench of human BBQ had me gagging long before we reached the kitchen, where burned bodies littered the ground, some still smoldering.

"No," I said softly.

The wolf head-butted me forward. Wolves' fur might look silky, but it was like being propelled by a bristly kettlebell.

I dug my heels into the ground. "I don't want to see her."

He trotted over to the first pile and knocked corpses aside.

I shuddered. He wasn't going to eat them, was he?

When he was done, he looked back at me expectantly. I stared blankly at him, and he pawed at one of the men.

Oh! Was that why he'd touched dead people with his muzzle? To show me there were no women?

I hopscotched my way from pile to pile, confirming that every single one of them was male, while Laurent cleaned himself, then I sagged against the stainless-steel counters. "Jude is still alive. Thank you."

He thumped his tail.

"Zev was convinced Jude would be here," I said, "and even Emmett confirmed it. So where…?"

The golem. If I could figure out how to use my magic, he could do the same and divine where Jude was.

"To the car," I said, striding past the wolf. "We're not out of leads yet."

We took the stairwell back upstairs to the ground level of the substation. Blood droplets ran from a discarded cigarette all the way to the rotted outside door. I decided not to ask what had become of the guard, choosing to believe that Laurent had merely ripped off his arm.

I shook my head, mentally chiding myself. How had that become my most palatable scenario?

Back at the vehicle, I opened the door for the wolf but he didn't get in the car. "Do you want to shift?"

He nudged me aside, snatched his jeans off the seat, and loped into the woods.

I sat in the driver's seat, my leg jiggling, trying to distract myself with music and not go after him and spy on his transformation.

Did he burst out of his skin or fur all at once like the Hulk? Did his hair and teeth fall out? Wincing, I leaned into the back to check, but happily that wasn't the case. I drummed my fingers on the wheel. Did Laurent know he was shifting? Was there a switch when his thinking became more human than animal and vice versa? He understood me in wolf form, but he also had no problem tearing his enemies apart. Did he always possess the same level of sentience and those were both aspects of who he truly was?

I got a crick in my neck trying to peer into the trees and satisfy my purely academic curiosity, but I couldn't see anything.

Laurent finally emerged, barefoot, popping a shoulder into place, and I winced. Maybe I didn't want to see a shift.

He shrugged into his Henley, shoved his socks in his pocket, and got into the car. When I started the engine but didn't go anywhere, he glanced up from pulling on his boots. "What are you waiting for?"

"You to finish and put on your seatbelt."

"You're kidding, right?"

I half-turned to face him. "Do I look like I'm kidding?"

He yanked on his other boot and clicked the seatbelt in. "Happy?"

"Delirious." I started the engine.

He pulled out his phone and made a call. "Get your asses out to the old Kemp substation. Mei Lin's dead and you need to clean up her mess." His eyes narrowed as he listened. "Yeah, well, it was a surprise to me too when I found she took out her own crew. Dybbuks, man. Maybe next time, believe me when I say I know what I'm talking about, and back me up against the vamps."

Disgusted, he hung up.

After Laurent made me stop so he could scarf down a couple of subs, because shifting used up a lot of calories, he rubbed his perfectly flat stomach, then reclined his seat.

I ate a single wrap and a cookie and looked five months pregnant. I seriously got the short stick on magic metabolism.

The closer we got back to Vancouver, the more the clouds rolled in, dark and heavy, but they had nothing on Laurent's mood.

I turned down the music. "Does it bother you? Killing dybbuks?"

"No."

"But they're in human bodies."

"They're not human." He looked out the passenger window.

I'd felt buoyed by our success and our bond, especially after Laurent's compassion in showing me that Jude wasn't among the dead.

My mistake.

I changed radio stations from classical music to one playing hits of the 60's and 70's. I'd killed my first dybbuk, and he didn't get to sulk and ruin that victory for me.

"Care to comment on how kickass I was?" I said.

He finally looked at me, and I wished he hadn't because his green eyes had darkened to the color of a stormy tropical sea. "You killed it," he said, accusingly.

"You're the one who told me that Banim Shovavim could do that in the first place. So what's the problem?"

"I send them back to Gehenna through a portal. They can always break out again the next time they're free." He tapped his fist lightly against the window. "I'm putting a Band-Aid on a bleeding artery. But you didn't send the dybbuk away, you ended it. Forever. The spirit imploded and disappeared. I'd never actually seen a Banim Shovavim kill one and I didn't realize. . ." He pressed his lips into a tight line.

I laughed. "Are you jealous?"

He crossed his arms. "No."

"Liar."

He glared at me a moment before giving in to his curiosity. "How'd you finally figure out what to do?"

"I extrapolated from its meaning of 'one who cleaves' to

223

get the scythe, and then when I went berserker on it, I heard this voice in my head say 'mut.'"

"That's Hebrew for 'die,'" he said.

"I figured, though I only know a few words of Hebrew."

He was silent for a minute, a thoughtful expression on his face. "That was really clever of you. How did it feel when you succeeded?"

I curled my fingers around the wheel as if I could physically grasp hold of his compliment before the words blew away. Even when sulky, he saw my worth in a way no one else had, and had no problem telling me. In my head, a cog in the machine representing our partnership fell into place with a well-oiled click.

I grinned. "Great. I mean, I literally vanquished evil. Hey, maybe I'm the vorpal blade."

Laurent chuckled. "Snicker-snack." He paused. "Don't you want to keep feeling that way? You solved how to deal with the fully possessed, you can save the enthralled."

My mental image of our partnership broke a timing belt, shuddering and grinding as it fell into discord. Had he only complimented me because he wanted something?

"Please don't start that again," I said. "Not now."

Laurent didn't speak until we'd pulled into Nav's carport out back. Since it was daylight, it would be better to smuggle Emmett out through the yard. "Figure out your magic, Mitzi."

"Why?" I cut the engine.

Rain pattered down on the carport roof.

"Because you'll be unstoppable."

My face heated, my brown eyes meeting his gleaming green ones across a crackling in the air, and I unbuckled my seat belt to better draw in a breath. It was as if I was back on his motorcycle in that moment when through my tunnel of fear I felt that first inkling of exhilaration.

Static skittered over my skin and I cleared my throat. "Uh... thanks."

I longed to live up to his image of me, but I couldn't. Alex had been dealt with, and we'd rescue Jude soon, but there was a difference between keeping my magic and being drawn deeper into this world as an active force. This may have been Laurent's calling, but it wasn't mine.

However, I couldn't bear to think about how different my life might have been had this rock solid belief in my magic been present twenty years ago.

Laurent regarded me for a moment longer, then glanced at the house.

There was a twitch of a curtain.

"Better get the golem," he said, and got out of the car.

I pressed my hands to my flushed cheeks, feeling like I'd lost something precious.

The rain pelting down quickly cooled me off, and I hurried after Laurent, splashing through a rainbow iridescence in an oily puddle.

Nav flung the back door open before we could knock. "You're Banim Shovavim?"

I took a step back under the ferocity of his glower. "Is that a problem?"

Laurent cut Nav a hard look. "It's not a problem at all, is it, Naveen?"

"Get your golem and go," he said in a tight voice.

I opened my mouth to apologize, then shut it. I wasn't at fault for the type of magic I'd been born with. His prejudices were his problem, not mine. "Done," I said in a cool voice. "Emmett." I walked into the airy kitchen. "Time to leave."

The golem was squished into a tiny white plastic chair having a tea party with Evani. Green eyeshadow was applied from his lids over his eyebrows and onto his forehead and his lipstick was a clownish smear around his lips. The toddler, in contrast, wore a pirate costume.

"Fancy," I said.

"Get me out of here," Emmett muttered.

Evani pounded the table with her chubby fist. "Bad robot. Drink your grog."

Emmett sighed. "Aye aye, Captain." He took a delicate sip and she snatched it out of his hand.

"You're doing it wrong. I'll teach you. Like this." She shot the imaginary drink back like she was at a kegger.

I choked on a laugh. This was entertaining as all get-out, but I didn't want to spend a second longer when I clearly wasn't wanted, and besides, I'd had years of practice extricating Sadie from playdates.

Toddlers were much like vampires. Offer them something else they craved more and all would be well.

"Evani." I crouched down. "Emmett has to go home and have his nap now."

"No." Her lip trembled.

"How old are you?"

She sucked her lip into her mouth, watching me warily, then held up three fingers.

"See, that's pretty old," I said. "But Emmett isn't a big girl like you."

She nodded. "The robot is a baby."

Emmett opened his mouth to protest and I smacked his shin.

"That's right," I said. "If you let him go home now, then next time you and he can visit Boo and you can show him how to play with the cat. Would you like that?"

She nodded and toddled over to Emmett, trying to push him onto the floor. "Get off my chair, baby. Go to sleep."

Emmett heaved a world-weary sigh.

Laurent deigned to lend a hand this time, helping the golem up.

"Bye, Evani," Laurent said.

She wrinkled her nose at him. "I want crackers." She

opened a tall cupboard and pulled out a rolling shelf with snacks on it.

Nav remained by the open back door.

"Thank you for helping us," I said.

He looked away.

I scrubbed a hand over my face, suppressing a sigh, and stepped onto the porch.

Laurent shook his head at his friend. "I'll call you later."

Nav didn't thaw out to Laurent, but Emmett got a genuine smile. "You were very patient with Evani. I appreciate it."

"She's a good kid," Emmett said gruffly, and hopped his way to the car. He wasn't thrilled to go back into the trunk, but one look at my face and he climbed in without further protest. Smart golem.

21

"I APOLOGIZE FOR NAV'S BEHAVIOR," LAURENT said, once we were on our way.

"Forget it. I'm only surprised I hadn't encountered that attitude sooner. So, Evani named Boo?"

"Yeah. It was supposed to be her pet but Daya is allergic."

"And you take care of the kitten for the little girl?" I chuckled.

He shifted uncomfortably. "It's not a big deal. I barely keep it alive."

"Again you lie," I said. "You're like that big dog Marc Antony in those old Warner Brothers cartoons where he has that tiny kitty he loves so much and he's scared that Mom has baked it into a cookie."

"I have no idea what you are talking about." His accent grew more pronounced when he added huffily, "But I am not a dog."

"No, you're not," I said, tamping down my mirth.

We helped Emmett into the hotel and my heart sank. I'd forgotten about the break-in and how Laurent's sanctuary had been violated.

Emmett whistled. "Dude, get a housekeeper."

I elbowed the golem, but Laurent didn't seem to hear him.

Laurent's stare went from the wreckage to the blood on the floor. He rubbed a red gash running up from his collarbone and the fight drained out of him. His expression was so blank he'd either dissociated or retreated into some faraway memory.

Boo scampered in and rubbed herself against his bare shin.

Laurent blinked slowly at her and then at me, his brows faintly creased, like he'd forgotten I was there.

"I can help clean up." I winced, remembering the extent of the damage, both collateral and not. "Can vampire bites speed up the timeline for possession?" I said gently.

He swung his head in the direction of the elevator and scrubbed a hand over his face with a soft "merde."

"I'm sorry." I placed my hand on his shoulder to help steady him against the shock of this news. "Can I do anything to help?"

The offer was barely out of my mouth before he'd turned a mocking gaze on me.

I dropped my hand.

"It's fine," he said sharply and picked up the kitten. "Leave the mess alone. I'll deal with Rupert and lose the demon illusion so no vamps can get in." He placed Boo on his shoulder, one hand on her back like she was a talisman, and headed for Rupert, but his steps were heavy and slow, unlike his usual confident stride.

I'd assumed Laurent would be able to save Rupert, because that was what he did. He solved problems. But beyond my initial lame attempt, I'd done nothing to help. Laurent rarely requested assistance, and I hadn't appreciated how much saving enthralleds had to matter for him to push himself out of his comfort zone and ask me.

I picked up a book, dusted it off, and set it on a shelf.

The elevator door closed from further back in the room.

"Wow, this place is a real sty, huh? I know the dude's an animal, but it's hard to believe that anyone could live like this." The golem stuffed a cushion under his stump of a leg, and kicked aside a broken frame. "What a mess."

"He was literally attacked by vampires right here, Emmett." I pointed to the blood on the floor, resisting the urge to scream. "Do you have to judge everything all the time?"

Emmett sunk into himself. "Sorry."

I took a breath, trying not to think about what Laurent was doing. "Look, I wanted to ask about Jude." I sat down next to him. "When you told Zev about the dybbuk, had he already mentioned it to you?"

"No. He asked me where she was."

"You didn't know the answer when I asked."

Emmett picked up a fallen book and half-heartedly flipped through it. "Like I said. I can't control my magic. He asked. This time I had an answer."

"Did Jude create you to work for the vamps?"

"I was her special project." The golem sneered. "A legacy art piece for a private collector."

"For Zev?" I shook my head. "I still don't understand. Jude has animator magic, that's how she brought you to life. How did you get that other power? What was the secret ingredient?"

"Laurent, spare me," Rupert's voice cried out plaintively. The closed door muted his plea somewhat but not nearly enough.

The wolf's eerie howl vibrated through the room.

"What the fuck is that?" Emmett said.

"Unchain me first, you coward!" The thing wearing Rupert's body screamed obscenities.

I'd take it over the agonizing sounds of Laurent's shift.

The golem got up, but I tugged him back onto the sofa.

"Laurent won't want an audience," I said.

Emmett gave one more wide-eyed glance over to the elevators, then plucked at the sweats he still wore. "I don't remember what we were talking about."

"Your divination powers."

"Mr. BatKian had a Banim Shovavim with necromancer magic. They thought since necromancers speak to spirits and spirits can predict the future, that this was the missing piece."

Laurent growled and Rupert's cursing cut off mid-word. The wolf must have killed the host, the dybbuk itself now free.

Emmett and I exchanged uneasy glances.

I gripped the arm of the sofa, hoping the closed elevator contained the spirit, and tried to focus on this talk. "The vamps have one of my kind?" I had to rescue this person. They'd have valuable answers about who I was and what I could do.

"Had." Emmett looked down. "He didn't survive making me."

I flinched.

"Sorry," he mumbled.

"It's not your fault." It was Jude's and the vampire's. I didn't expect BatKian to have a conscience when it came to murder, but Jude? It didn't matter that she didn't know what I was, she'd been reckless with a person's life. Or was that man not a person to her because of his magic?

How many shadow freaks will you smite?

The humming-vibrating noise kicked in. Laurent had opened the portal to Gehenna.

I sucked in a deep breath, but the air around me had the consistency of mud, and there was a hollow spot in the pit of my stomach at the idea of facing my best friend.

"Why create you?" My voice was hoarse. "What was the point?"

Emmett looked at me like I was an idiot. "Power."

The humming sound cut out and a moment later, the elevator door opened.

I glanced over but couldn't see the wolf.

"Wouldn't you want to know the future?" Emmett said. "Know how any decision would play out?"

Not really, because I'd become mired in indecision. Even if one action had a favorable outcome, what if that led to something bad afterwards? And what if knowing the outcome beforehand led to me doing something I might not have done otherwise that I should have?

Knowing I'd had mazel, destiny, was bad enough, but to know the future? There was too great a chance of it shaping my life, and not for the better. How easy would it be to become obsessed with knowing what would happen, rather than fully living?

"It was all for nothing anyway." Emmett tossed the book on the floor. "I'm not the perfect golem and the BatKian wants me destroyed."

"I'm not going to let that happen," I said, squeezing his shoulder.

He jerked away. "Right."

I let the sting wash over me. For all of the golem's raunchy comments, he had the emotional maturity of a young child, and it wasn't fair to expect more grown-up behavior from him, even if his actions hurt.

"Just a few more questions," I said. "Was Jude being with a dybbuk the entirety of your answer or was there more to it?"

"That was it."

"And then Zev said what?"

"He was with this other vamp, who said, 'I told you.' Ugly fucker."

"When was this?" I said.

"Right before sunrise yesterday."

"Can you use your magic again? If we don't find her—"

"I won't get my leg fixed. Yeah, I know." He looked around. "Can I get a drink?"

This was about more than his leg, but once again, he didn't have the capacity to confront the hard stuff.

"Later. Where's Jude? Is there a second dybbuk that we have to find?" The faster we found her, the faster I could look her in the eyes and see if my best friend was a stranger.

Emmett made a face like he was taking a shit, then threw his hands up. "Nothing. See?"

I got up, putting books back on the shelves so I didn't smack the intractable jerk. This entire section contained non-fiction titles. I reshelved a hardcover book about Einstein and quantum physics, deciding to change the topic and circle back.

"So what was that whole mazel business?" I said. "What did you mean that I was the first domino?"

Emmett scrubbed a hand over his face, smearing his makeup even more. "I'm not trained to decipher what I say." Sadly, neither was I. "Can we stop with the catalog of my failures?"

"You answered Zev's question, so you aren't a failure." I smoothed out a couple bent pages in a book about wealth and income disparity.

The golem rubbed the stump of his leg. "BatKian had asked me about forty others first that I couldn't answer, so draw your own conclusions."

"That must have been scary."

"No shit."

Emmett's magic had worked with me when he was drunk and with the vampire when he was scared. Both were instances when he wasn't stuck in his head about how badly he sucked.

"You know what?" I said. "A drink sounds good. Let me see what I can rustle up." I left the room, catching up with

Laurent in the kitchen, who was filling a bucket with water, staring hollowly at the billowing steam. His feet were bare and he'd put his shirt on inside out.

I shut off the tap, because the bucket was overflowing. "Did you... is Rupert...?"

Laurent blinked dazedly, then poured some of the water out. "The Lonestars are coming later to retrieve the body."

I placed my hand on his sleeve. "It doesn't get easier, does it?"

"No." He picked up the bucket and a mop that leaned against the counter. "How's it going with the golem?"

"Not great." I sighed and went through my hypothesis of Emmett needing to be drunk or angry or scared to be able to tap into his divination powers.

Laurent listened thoughtfully, then left as I rummaged through the fridge.

A few minutes later, I returned with a cold beer.

The golem was pressed up against the wall with Laurent's claws at his throat.

"Did you tell Naveen that Miriam was Banim Shovavim?" Laurent's eyes were wild.

I'd told Laurent to snap Emmett out of overthinking, not terrify him—and I wasn't entirely sure this was an act. The only thing I had the bandwidth to deal with right now was finding Jude. I'd trust Laurent not to take it too far.

Emmett cowered. "I didn't think it would matter."

"You were wrong," Laurent growled.

Emmett's breathing was raspy. Perfect.

"Where's Jude?" I said.

Emmett swung his head at me, but his eyes were replaced by cosmic swirls of stardust. "With the dybbuk." His voice took on a languid cast.

"Mei Lin is—"

I shook my head at Laurent to stay quiet. "Where did the dybbuk take her?"

"Not take," Emmett said.

"So Jude went willingly?"

"No."

I tapped my foot. Not taken. Not gone willingly. This was the freaking riddle of the Sphynx. "What is Jude doing?"

The golem patted his chest, then his hands dropped to his sides.

"You mean literally making another like you? With fucking divination powers?" I white-knuckled the beer bottle. Had creating this perfect golem become an obsession where murder was justifiable? Pain shot up the side of my head and I relaxed my tightly clenched jaw. "Did she get hold of another Banim Shovavim?"

Emmett stared ahead for a moment before shaking himself out of his stupor, edging away from me with wide eyes. "I don't know."

Laurent mopped up the bloody smear. "There a problem?"

I swallowed hard. "Jude and Zev used a Banim Shovavim with necromancy magic to give Emmett his divination magic. The man didn't survive."

Laurent paused, leaning on the mop. "But you're not a necromancer."

"I'm not worried for myself. They killed someone. Or doesn't that matter because he was a BS?"

"You're very loud," Emmett whispered and slid down the wall, hunched into himself.

Laurent scrubbed at a stubborn patch of congealed blood. "When it comes to magic and power, none of us matter. The bloodsucker would have done the same to anyone."

"How could Jude cross that line? Is she doing it again?" She was one of the people I trusted most in this world. An aunt to my kid. How could I have misjudged her character so badly? Sighing, I handed Emmett the beer. "Here. I'm sorry. I'm really not mad at you."

Emmett took the bottle, then jerked a finger at Laurent. "Was all that bullying just to scare me?"

"Yeah. Needs must." Laurent wrung out the mop, then did another pass over the floor.

"Did I help at all?" Emmett said.

I shrugged helplessly, wishing I could discern how far my friend was willing to go. "We always suspected Jude was with a dybbuk and making a golem. It's the exact same scenario Zev was told to begin with, but Jude wasn't at the substation. Unless Mei Lin stashed her somewhere else?" I rubbed my eyes. "I'm missing something. How many other golems has Jude made? There were other body parts at her studio."

"Those were test runs for yours truly," Emmett said.

"Do you know how she made you? Was there anything special about it?"

Emmett ran a finger around the rim of the bottle. "Other than the…" He looked at me guiltily and then quickly away. "I don't know. With clay and sculpting tools and shit."

"Ordinary clay?"

"Nothing about me is ordinary," he leered.

"You want to keep your other leg?" Laurent said mildly. He dumped the mop in the bucket, the floor once again clean, and wiped his hands off on his jeans, before reordering the books I'd shelved.

"Sculpting clay." Emmett drank some beer.

"She'd need a workspace and tools to do that. Mei Lin might well have set her up somewhere else." I stacked more books on the table for Laurent to categorize according to whatever system he used. "Factoring in extra clay for mistakes and excess pieces," I said, "that's a few hundred pounds. You wouldn't buy it online because shipping costs would cripple you, if they'd even do it. And you can't walk in to the store and buy that large an amount. Though you could have it delivered once you special ordered it."

If I got an address, I could stop Jude and prevent anyone else from being harmed.

Laurent sat down on the floor to organize the bottom shelf. "There's probably only a few places that sell it, but none of them are going to release customer information."

I smiled. "Maybe not to me."

22

My new friend, Ava, leaned on the counter of the arts supply store. "How would a lady go about ordering a lot of sculpting clay?"

I crossed my fingers that we'd hit the jackpot, because there weren't any other stores in town left to check out.

The employee cut open a box with a picture of paint tubes on it. "Depends on how much is a lot."

"Say for a huge sculpture," she said. "A few hundred pounds?"

"Well, we could order it for you, but it would take a couple weeks." He checked one of the tubes against the packing slip.

Ava brushed her arm against his. "Do orders that large happen often?"

The man smiled. "Not really."

She shifted so that her hand touched his wrist. "Has it happened recently? Could you check?"

He dropped the packing slip, his eyes glowing. "I'd be happy to."

"You're so kind." The bling on her cat-eye glasses flashed when she winked at me.

All Ava did was gradually amp up a feeling of joy in the man and his natural desire to continue experiencing that emotion had him going above and beyond in customer service.

He typed on the keyboard and then spun the monitor around. "Here we go. Last month."

I noted the address. The name on the order was Smith, so probably a fake.

"You've been a peach," Ava said.

"No trouble," he assured her. "Would you like to put in the clay order now?"

"Maybe another time. I need to double-check the amounts again." Ava straightened up, smoothing out her cute yellow blouse with ruffled sleeves.

"Well, you have yourself a nice day."

"You too," she said, and we left.

She'd assured me that the feelings would gradually wear off to a minor glow that he'd experience for a few more hours.

"I really appreciate this," I said. "Thank you."

"It's for a good cause, so you're welcome."

I jammed my hands into my armpits, my bedrock solid belief in my best friend turned to silt. If Jude was in danger, then I'd rescue her, no question, but even if she hadn't intended to kill the necromancer, he'd died because of her pursuits. She could have stopped in time to save him, couldn't she, or had the vampire threatened her if she didn't complete Emmett?

Ava nudged me. "You okay?"

"Yeah."

There was an envelope tucked under my windshield wiper. I ripped it open to find a Polaroid of Sadie coming out of Eli's place, backpack on, headed for school, with "Jude. Tomorrow. Sunset." written on the back.

I dropped it, my hand slamming down on my hood for balance, because my knees had buckled.

"What is it?" Ava picked up the photo.

"Vamps can go out in daylight?"

"No, but they have human employees." Ava frowned at the message on the photo. "Is this your daughter?"

I nodded, black spots dancing in my vision. My chest was too tight to take a breath and answer.

Ava took my keys and bundled me into the car. "We'll figure this out."

Delilah rose up with a furious whoosh, blocking out the dashboard. The pounding in my head urged me to go to Blood Alley and end BatKian for daring to threaten my baby girl. It would be reckless and I not only didn't care, I relished the idea of spilling his blood.

Ava stood at the driver's side door, watching me warily.

I exhaled sharply, uncurled my fists, and shut my magic down, my skin hot and tight. "Nothing is more important than Sadie's well-being."

"We'll call in the Lonestars." Ava slid into the driver's seat and started the car.

"We can't." I shook my head.

Ava drove back to Stay in Your Lane like this was the qualifying round for the NASCAR finals. She took her hand off the wheel to gesture expressively while she drove. "They're threatening a kid."

"A Sapien kid and the Lonestars already sided with the vamps once." The first time that Laurent wanted to go after Mei Lin.

Little by little, I locked down my emotions into a tight box before they swept me under, all to the upbeat disco classics CD that I kept in my car. I had to be smart, not emotional, because power-wise I was no match for BatKian. No matter how I decided to proceed with my friendship with

Jude, everyone in my current inner circle was coming out alive and unharmed.

"Ooh, Kool & The Gang." Ava sang the first verse of "Ladies Night," then nudged me. "You need a plan."

I opened the app on my phone. "A new to-do list."

"To-do lists are the bomb."

We exchanged a look of perfect agreement.

I typed as I spoke. "I need proof that Jude didn't betray the vampires." Proof that she hadn't gotten some God-like taste of power and decided she craved more.

"Are you sure she didn't?" Ava said kindly.

"Mostly? Jude is impulsive but willingly fucking over deadly supernatural beings seems extreme, even for her. Then there was the fact that her studio was trashed." I sighed. "Unless the vamps did that."

"You have the name and address of the person who ordered that shipment of clay. If Jude was forced, hand that person over instead. The vampires will get the truth out of them."

"That's condoning murder," I said. Did all supernaturals operate on an entirely different moral scale, only following Sapien laws for the sake of keeping magic hidden? How was I supposed to live in a world like that?

Ava braked at a red light. "There's no good solution here. Only what you can live with."

"And if I can't live with any of these choices?"

Ava grabbed Sadie's photo off the dashboard and handed it to me. "Then you'll lose everything anyway."

I hadn't reconciled myself to any particular plan by the time we'd reached the bowling alley.

"Come inside for a while," Ava said.

"Thanks, but I'd better not."

We got out of the car to switch places.

"When all this is over," I said, "you and your wife should come for dinner. Meet Sadie."

"Okay, but I'll bring dessert. I make a mean chocolate mousse."

"To-do lists, disco, chocolate, where were you when I wanted to get married?"

Ava blew on her fisted nails and rubbed them against her sweater. "I'm a catch."

We hugged and I drove home to take a cold shower and change. I couldn't stop yawning, and even with all the windows down and the A/C blasting at my face, my lids were so heavy it was like there were lead weights on them.

I had to get some sleep or I'd be in no condition to do anything, but I ran into Eli as I was going inside.

"Hey, Mir." He shifted his gym bag to his other hand and kissed my cheek. "How come you're home early? It's only four."

"Not feeling great." One of the things that had come out of all our therapy was the importance of being honest with each other. Good thing I really did feel like crap.

He frowned and motioned at my outfit. "You wore yoga pants to work? And how come you didn't call Sades last night to ask about her final? She said she didn't care, but she kept looking out the window for your car. What's going on?"

I blinked blearily at him, wishing I'd married an accountant instead of a cop. My brain was stuffed with cotton and I blurted out the first thing that came to mind. "I bled through my work clothes."

"Oh."

Eli wasn't squeamish about buying tampons when we'd been married, but he hadn't been enthusiastic to swim in the Red Sea either. Happily, my vibrator, Lady Catnip, had been there for me in rain, sleet, and uterus cleansing, because damn, I got horny at that time of the month. Batteries, right.

"Yeah," I said, getting a burst of creativity. For lying. Like a criminal. "Bad time of the month. I parked in the garage last night because I felt like shit and I skipped book club."

Another lie, since we didn't meet until Thursday. "Marsha has been known to check people's houses for absentee members for public shaming and I wasn't up to dealing with that, but I'll apologize to Sadie."

My small garage had turned into something of a storage unit and until I cleaned it out, it was a real pain to navigate my car into the tight space left for parking, so I generally left it out front.

Eli chuckled. "Yeah, Military Marsha is a piece of work. Call me if you need anything." He hoisted his gym bag on his shoulder and walked out to his car.

Sitting down on my stoop, I wrote Laurent a long-winded text about everything that had happened and that if he was game, I'd pick him up at midnight.

Sadie arrived as I hit send. She pulled out her earbuds and sat down next to me, but didn't say anything.

"How was your final, Sadie Mayhem?" Sadie May had been named after my mom Sarah, and Eli's mother Mae. After sixteen years, my ex mother-in-law hadn't forgiven the slight of her name going second.

My daughter rolled her eyes at her nickname. "I came over when Dad was watching the game last night and you weren't here. You never go out in the middle of the week."

And wasn't that pathetic? These were some of my best years and I was spending them on a job that was less exciting than watching concrete harden and a limited social life.

I tapped a finger over my lip. "Maybe it's time for some changes in my life."

"Are you having a midlife crisis?"

"More like a midlife reclamation. Would that bother you?"

She shrugged. "You mean like you want to date?"

"Maybe. Though that's not the be all and end all." I could just have sex. Feel a hard body on mine as he—child-appro-

243

priate thoughts, Mom. "I might want to take some courses, or make new friends and go out."

"Does that mean I can have a later curfew?" she said.

"Not even remotely."

She made a face at me. "Fine. And it's all good. Dad shouldn't be the only one who gets to have a job he likes and a social life."

My phone buzzed with Laurent's confirmation that he'd be ready.

Sadie poked me. "What's that smile for? You *are* dating."

"I'm really not."

I was under the gun to rescue Jude and extricate all of us from Zev's deadline. Thinking about the consequences if I failed felt like there was a boulder pressing on my chest that could shift and crush me at any second. Yet the fear that my friendship with Jude might not survive even if I was successful was worse. Was our mazel to part ways? In creating Emmett, had Jude fulfilled her destiny or changed it? Even if Emmett and the necromancer's loss of life were written in the stars, that didn't absolve her of guilt. It couldn't.

Despite all these concerns, I longed to throw on my playlist with the disco classic "Born to Be Alive," crank the volume, and dance around.

I wrapped my arms around my daughter. When Sadie was little and had been afraid of monsters, I'd given her Monster-Be-Gone—water and peppermint oil in a spray bottle glued with clumps of gold glitter because Sadie decided monsters were allergic to all things sparkly. Every night we'd sprayed that mixture under her bed and in her closet. She'd gone to sleep secure in the knowledge that her mom was keeping her safe. Monsters had turned out to be real, but I'd still keep her safe, no matter what.

I breathed in the familiar scent of her coconut oil conditioner. My journey towards empowerment wasn't simply about having magic back in my life. Magic was important because it was a part of me that I'd denied, but ultimately, I wanted to be a positive role model for my daughter, and show her how a woman of any age could live life on her own terms. It wasn't about power per se, it was about powerful choices.

"I'm sorry I didn't ask about your final," I said. "How'd it go?"

"Aced it." She twisted away and grabbed her backpack. "You don't need to keep asking me about every little thing, you know."

I reluctantly let her go. "I'm not ready for you to stop being my baby girl yet."

"Oh, Mother. You do need a life." Sadie grinned at me and let herself into her dad's place.

Stifling another yawn, I dusted myself off and went inside. I'd given my daughter all the love and confidence for her to become an incredible young woman. Time to take care of myself as well.

I snuggled into my soft sofa under a fleece blanket and fell into a deep stupor.

23

THE DEMON ILLUSION ON HOTEL TERMINUS WAS
gone and the side door looked normal, but Huff 'n' Puff was
crankier than usual when he got into my car.

"The golem used my best towels to wipe off his makeup,"
he said. "Then he tried to wash the dirt and clay off them
and broke my washing machine. Get him out of my place or I
won't be responsible for my actions."

"Okay, Martha Stewart. I wouldn't want your domestic
routine upended in any way. Besides, this should all be over
tonight."

He grunted, found a classical music station, and closed
his eyes.

The address Ava had gotten from the arts supply store
didn't seem promising. It took us over the Oak Street Bridge
and out to Richmond, a city to the south of Vancouver, which
used to be mostly farmland and now included tons of condos
and really great Asian restaurants.

This particular property had a sign out front advertising
fresh strawberries, though as it was the dead of night, it was
closed. Too bad. Sadie and I would have to come to a farm
soon and get a bunch to freeze for winter.

I parked on the street and Laurent opted not to shift this time as Mei Lin was dead and he still wasn't recharged from all the magic he'd expended lately. I didn't use my powers either, since the darkness provided plenty of cover to stealthily check out the grounds.

In front of the trim clapboard house was a small parking lot for customers. To the left stood a shuttered farm stand with a sign proclaiming fresh strawberry ice cream and a painted metal strawberry sculpture that was about five feet high next to a picnic table.

We skirted the house into the fields out back, headed for the small red barn, where I tugged on the locked door. Laurent offered to hoist me up to look through the window, but I refused. I was a healthy size twelve and while I really did like my body for the most part, I had a flash of me crushing him. I hadn't even liked Eli to dip me when we were dancing, because I was convinced he'd drop me.

Everyone had their irrational issues.

I fished inside the small purse slung across my chest for the penlight I'd tossed in, and turned it on. "Hold this on me." There wasn't enough light to get a hard shadow otherwise.

Delilah slithered up the wall and in through a gap in the shutters.

"Whoa," Laurent said.

It was really dark in the barn and all I could make out in her green vision were a lot of large bulky shapes that seemed to be farming equipment.

"Jude's not here." I snapped Delilah back to me and Laurent flicked off the penlight. "Makes sense if she's in the house. It would have been the easiest place to bring the clay in."

Laurent picked the lock on the back door, which was a handy little skill, and I stepped inside and grimaced.

The kitchen was an ode to the humble strawberry. A tea

towel printed with strawberries was folded on the counter, matching the round table cloth. Framed strawberry paintings hung on the wall, and salt and pepper strawberry-shaped shakers sat along the back of the stove. However, the pièce de résistance were the row of small gnome figurines on the picture rail running along one wall, all of whom had knitted strawberry hats.

A tiny yippy dog ran into the room, and Laurent growled softly at it, causing the animal to stop so abruptly that it skidded across the linoleum and bumped its nose on a chair. The dog lay down, lowering its gaze, its ears flattened back.

Laurent petted the animal on the head. "There's no one up here."

We made a quick tour of the ground floor, because if Jude had made a golem, I didn't want it coming out of some hiding spot to surprise us. What wasn't a surprise were the strawberry-printed bed linens and strawberry-shaped soaps in the bathroom that were so strong my eyes watered. Laurent refused to get anywhere close to them, claiming he could smell them from the kitchen and that was bad enough. Other than an overabundance of folksy fruit décor, however, nothing jumped out at us.

Laurent scoffed in disgust at the living room shelf that held zero books but a whole slew of sports awards. All of them were wrestling trophies for one Kirk Holdencott. This was making less and less sense. Had we broken in to some innocent person's house?

"Book snob," I whispered.

"Damn right."

I entered the TV room and was greeted by a wall of photos, mostly snapshots of a sandy-haired young man whose ears became more mashed-up over the years, but there were also more formal ones, such as at his high school graduation with a petite woman who had to be his mom. On the sofa was a knitting basket with a half-finished man's sweater. A piece of paper had Kirk's name scrawled on the top along with some chest, arm, and neck measurements. I ran my hand over the wool, wistfully. My mom had been a knitter but I'd never picked it up.

On a side table were a couple of issues of *The Progressive Farmer*, addressed to Mrs. Diane Holdencott.

Laurent came into the room. "There's a car coming."

I moved the curtain aside a fraction of an inch. I didn't hear anything, but sure enough, a few moments later, headlights swept into the parking lot. Diane and Kirk, the mother and son from the photos, got out of the car.

I grabbed Laurent, placing my cloaking over both of us.

The front door opened, the man cutting himself off in mid-sentence, and Laurent and I tiptoed into the front hall. Well, I tiptoed. Laurent did his stealthy wolf walk.

"What is it?" Diane looked more haggard than she had in the photos, with gray in her hair and worry creases on her forehead.

Kirk sniffed the air. Lumpy and misshapen human ears protruded out under his buzz cut, and his nose was squashed with a decidedly sideways angle to it. The hazards of wrestling. "People have been here. Let me check it out, Ma."

"Shifter?" I mouthed.

Laurent shrugged, his cedar scent easing some of my tension. He stood partially behind me, his chest pressed into my back, loosely gripping my bicep. His warm breath stirred the fine hairs on the back of my neck, and I found myself falling into rhythm with his calm inhales and exhales.

He steadied his other hand on my tailbone and I bit my lip, my head bowed. There was something oddly transgressive about being hidden in plain sight together, more so than if we'd been in a closet blanketed in darkness, because standing here together in full light under mesh felt like being intimate in front of curtains that weren't fully drawn shut.

I kept my eyes on Diane straightening coats in the packed

hall closet with quick anxious movements, constantly craning her neck to check for her son's return. But I was aware of the tiniest shift in pressure of Laurent's splayed fingers against my body and how when he made a faint sound at the back of his throat, his whispered "sorry" against my ear was a hot sweet rush of air.

Kirk returned, snapping me out of my daze, and declared that there wasn't anyone else here.

"Peter came over earlier discussing some inventory concerns," Diane said. "That's who you must have smelled. You've been jumpy lately."

"Can't imagine why," he snarked, giving her a pointed look.

Laurent's grip on my bicep tightened.

"Kirk William Holdencott, don't you take that tone with me. Especially not when I'm going through all this trouble trying to help you." She tugged on her son's sleeve, pulling him into the kitchen. "Come on. I'll make you soup."

We followed the family drama into the next room.

"Ma, I'm not hungry for soup." Kirk tossed his jacket over a chair. "We talked about this."

She lay her hand on her son's cheek. "Whatever you need, I'll help you get it."

Kirk shifted his weight from one foot to the other, looking uncomfortable, and took her hand. "You can't. Let me grab my stuff from the bedroom and then you can drive me back, okay?" His fangs flashed when he spoke and I tensed but his mother merely smiled.

"It'll be like old times when I took you to all your wrestling competitions."

"Yeah, sure, Ma," he said gently. "Back in a sec."

Diane kept her smile up until he'd gone, and then her lips trembled and she pressed her fist into her mouth to stifle her sob. She picked up his jacket and held it to her face, her body silently shaking.

I swiped the side of my hand against my damp eyes, my heart breaking for the impossibility of her situation. I'd love Sadie if she was turned, but the grief would be unbearable. Not simply because her being undead negated any vision I'd had for her future happiness, but because I'd have to watch my daughter lose her humanity.

How many times would Diane relive this loss until Kirk either cut ties or, worse, saw her as a threat or an unwanted reminder of a life that was no longer his?

"Grab the mother before the vamp gets back," Laurent whispered, releasing me and shifting his weight to move away. "I'll take care of him."

I shook my head, clamping onto his wrist so he wouldn't go anywhere.

Kirk's footsteps grew closer and his mother hastily dropped his jacket over the chair again, pasting a bright smile on her face as he entered carrying a duffel bag.

"Got everything you need?" she said.

"I think so." He hefted the bag onto his shoulder and grabbed his jacket. "Come on. I'll tell you all about my new job in Blood Alley."

"It's going well?"

He paused, then decided against whatever he was going to say with a shake of his head. "Yeah. Great."

"I can't wait to hear about it," she said.

They left the kitchen but I didn't recall my cloaking until the car pulled away.

"You're a soft-hearted fool," Laurent said, sounding half exasperated and half bemused. He pivoted and marched into the basement.

There was just enough light coming in through the window to safely creep down the darkened stairs behind him.

"Her son is a vampire," I said. "Don't you think she's suffered enough?"

"Have you forgotten why we're here? Your friend is

missing and a large shipment of clay was delivered to this address."

"Of course, I haven't forgotten," I snapped. "But our odds of rescuing Jude are a lot better without a vamp hanging around."

Laurent shot me a disdainful look over his shoulder. "Keep telling yourself that's the reason."

The basement held a laundry room, furnace room, storage room, a pantry with rows of strawberry jam in neat glass jars, and a locked door.

Laurent rapped on the wall. "Concrete, not drywall. Could be a cellar of some sort." He sniffed and winced. "Something stinks in there. Not like dead," he said at my flinch. "More like really dirty. You want your shadow to check it out first?"

"Her name is Delilah."

He snorted. "Is my strength in peril?"

"Like I'd give you a heads up. We don't need to check the room out. Jude is in there, I'm sure of it." She had to be, because I had less than a day to keep Zev from going after my baby girl.

Laurent made quick work of the lock and I stepped inside and flicked on the light, revealing a makeshift potter's studio.

There was a pyramid of sculpting clay on an industrial metal table, a kiln the size of a fridge in one corner, and Jude, blood caking one nostril on her battered face, handcuffed to a radiator.

Jude's lips were cracked and when she said my name, it was more of a croaked whisper. Three fingers on her right hand were taped to a small ruler as a stopgap splint.

She was alive. That was all that mattered right now. I let out a deep breath.

"Don't speak." Pulling out my phone, I snapped a photo, making sure to get both Jude and the unused clay.

"Souvenir pix, Mitzi?" Laurent said. "That's dark."

"Proof," I said. "That Jude didn't come here willingly. Nor did she make a golem." Maybe Jude *had* been coerced by Zev into making Emmett and I'd misjudged my friend. "Can you pick the lock on these?"

"No need." He tossed me a small key on a ring. "Universal handcuff key."

"Aren't you the Boy Scout?" I uncuffed Jude, giving Laurent my car keys when I returned his key ring. "Could you please drive the car up?"

"No problem." He took off at a trot.

Jude grabbed my sleeve, her eyes slightly unfocused. "Are you really here?"

"Yeah," I said, helping her up. "And I gotta say, your choice of getaway leaves a lot to be desired. I know you always meant to visit Sweden, but this budget Stockholm Syndrome vibe isn't quite the same thing."

She gave a broken laugh then winced, cradling her injured hand to her chest. Her face drained of color. "That woman—"

"Isn't here," I said. "I'm busting you out."

Much as I wanted to hurry the fuck out of there, convinced her abductor would show up like Annie Wilkes in *Misery* to thwart our escape and break our legs, our progress was slow going, especially since every tiny noise made Jude flinch.

I kept one arm around her shoulders, encouraging her in a gentle voice to keep going.

Jude couldn't see out of her swollen eye, and she was dehydrated, making her dizzy. We rested for a moment in the kitchen, until she said it had passed.

Miraculously, we made it out and around the front of the house without further trouble.

Laurent pushed away from my car, coming over to help.

I motioned to the sedan. "Okay, Jude get—"

Jude stiffened. "You."

My pulse spiked but there was no one else here. "Who...?"

Jude levitated the human-sized metal strawberry sculpture with her animator magic and hurled it at Laurent.

It ploughed into him, pitching him halfway across the parking lot.

My fingers tingled with icy pinpricks and I got a sour taste in my mouth. Jude's shadow looked normal, and more than anything, I longed to take it at face value, but I couldn't. Cursing softly, I sent my awareness into it.

I jerked back at the faint feeling of a seething violent cry, and buried my face in my hands. My worst-case scenario of a reckoning with my friend over what she'd done to the Banim Shovavim with necromancer magic hit a new rock bottom.

Jude was enthralled.

I took a deep breath. She was still alive, but if I didn't figure out how to get the dybbuk out of her, it was a death sentence nonetheless. The entity would take over and then Laurent would kill the dybbuk left in her body.

Laurent. I gasped and snapped my head up.

He hadn't moved, his body immobile in a crumpled heap on the concrete. I rubbed my hand over the pinch in my chest, pulled apart by this succession of disasters falling like dominos, and silently screaming at him to move, because I couldn't get the words out.

A hand landed on my shoulder and I jumped, whirling around with my fists up.

Jude looked at me with the same confusion that Rupert had before he'd turned violent. She scrunched up her dirty red curls, swaying slightly. "I don't feel so great. Can I sit down?"

I nodded, unable to answer her, and dug my fingers into my palm, wishing I could wake up from this horrible dream. See, I had trouble running in dreams. My feet were always weighted down and I could only lift them with an enormous effort. I had the same problem now, except this wasn't a dream. It was a horrific reality where time dragged while I pushed past my friend and crossed the parking lot to where Laurent lay, glancing back at Jude stumbling to the car.

Where did I get to vent my anger? On Laurent for getting hurt?

On myself for not protecting him?

On my best friend, the root cause of all this, even as she faced death?

Give me a target, universe, because my skin felt like it was splintering.

I dropped to Laurent's side and pressed my fingers to his neck.

His pulse was thready, but there, and his neck didn't appear to be broken. I was about to call 911 when a ripple ran up his right side, ending in a punch outwards from his bicep.

I dropped the phone. He was shifting from an injured, unresponsive state. Would he be aware of who I was when the transformation was complete, or would I be fodder to be taken out before he killed Jude?

Laurent's ears shrank to nubs that crawled up the side of his head and grew into furry triangles. He let out a pained cry, his bones visibly rearranging themselves in his torso with a grinding noise.

Headlights swept into the parking lot and over my car and I moved protectively in front of Laurent, like anyone pulling in could miss the sight of a man transforming into a wolf, even if they were a Sapien, but the car backed out, having used the driveway to turn around and go the way it had come.

My sigh turned into a yelp as Laurent's shirt tore off him, then he screamed, and I pressed a hand against my mouth, scrambling back on my ass because his knees were reversing direction to the steady beat of snapping bones and ripping denim. He shook his shoes off, freeing his hindlegs with their sharp claws.

His face bulged and contorted, his muzzle popping out with a crunch. His eyes snapped open, a green supernova of fury, and he threw back his head and howled.

It was grotesque and oddly beautiful and mesmerizing, especially when white fur blossomed over his body like a snowfall.

Laurent pushed up onto all fours, his arms turning to forelegs. His muscles readjusted themselves and he shook off the tattered remnants of his clothing.

"Miri!" Jude was half out of the car.

"Shut the door!" I yelled.

The car door slammed and the wolf bared his lips at me.

"Laurent." A swirl of sickening fear rolled through my veins, my gaze lowered like the yippy dog's had been, but I held myself steady on the cold concrete, my knees drawn into my chest and my hand outstretched. "You can trust me. I won't hurt you."

He stopped, warily assessing me, which I took as a good sign.

Some of my anxiety receded. "That's right. Let me help you."

He prowled closer and I screwed my eyes shut. Running would definitely paint me as prey, so I stayed still, trusting in the bond we'd formed working together.

His cold wet nose brushed against the underside of my jaw and I swallowed, pressing my hands against the concrete so hard that tiny pebbles stuck to my skin. His hot breath gusted over my skin, his teeth scraping against my fluttering pulse, and my heart skipped a beat. He smelled musty, but not in a bad way, kind of like an old forest, and when his fur tickled my neck, the faintest trace of cedar kissed my skin.

Two hundred pounds of muscle leaned into me.

I cracked an eye open, his gaze hitting me like two flares.

He stayed that way for two slow blinks, then he gave a dangerous growl that shivered down to the tips of my fingers, tore himself away, and sprinted behind the house.

Cold sweat had plastered the sides of my shirt to my body. I sat there, trembling, colors heightened into a sharpness that was almost painful.

"Hurry!" Jude cried, her head sticking out of the window.

The dybbuk. I stood up on rubbery legs and got into the car.

"You good?" she said, her eyes clouded with worry.

"Yeah. You?"

She dropped her gaze, twisting her hands in her lap. "As well as can be expected."

Laurent had left the keys in the ignition so I started the engine, fiddling with the heat and staring into the night. If only I could turn back time and take back my words about him being a mercenary, because even with payment, a true mercenary would have cut and run a long time ago. But this lone wolf had stuck by my side through vampires, his best friend's anger, and making sure that Jude was safely found. Once more, he'd been hurt because of this job, and yet, even wounded and in wolf form, he hadn't attacked me.

I couldn't repay him with callous abandonment.

Jude started with a sharp intake of breath, before scrubbing a hand over her face.

"Jude—"

"Oh fuck," she said, and dropped her head between her knees.

I rubbed her back, feeling tangled up in a ball of yarn, unending, unyielding, growing ever more knotted and trapping me in place.

A desolate yowl pierced the night and Jude flinched, her eyes wide.

Did she know she was enthralled? Rupert had, but my

friend didn't give any indication of being aware she'd hurt Laurent.

My shoulders slumped. It was a long way back and I couldn't risk having the wolf in the car with us.

"Sorry," I whispered, and peeled out of the lot.

24

I SPED THROUGH THE DARKNESS, MY MIND GOING almost as fast as the car, super attuned to every little motion Jude made. It was early Thursday morning and the dybbuk would kill her and take over her body at some point between Friday and Saturday sunsets.

Laurent believed I could save enthralleds, but how? Who would I ask, and where the hell could I stash Jude in the meantime? Even if I hadn't abandoned Laurent, I couldn't lock my friend up in his hotel elevator. Sadly, I couldn't let her remain free either.

I pulled into a convenience store. "Back in a sec."

Jude gnawed on her thumbnail, staring numbly out the window.

My resolve to question her about being enthralled lasted until I returned to find her in the same position, her face pale. I pulled a bottle of Gatorade out of the bag and cracked the cap with a sharp snap. Seeing my wisecracking friend beaten down like this killed me, but a dull voice in my head chanted that she'd brought this on herself. The desire to rail at her for her stupidity in going down this road burned its way up my sternum and I shoved the bottle at her.

"Here. Sip it slowly," I said brusquely. "If you drink too fast, you'll get sick." I placed the bag on the floor at her feet. "There's also water in there."

She took the bottle though her stare remained vacant.

I headed for the highway, hoping a destination would come to me, and darting glances at Jude every few seconds.

"Drink some already," I said.

She nodded absently, but had some of the Gatorade.

I played out variations of possible conversations until we were crossing the Knight Street Bridge back into Vancouver and I had an opening statement that was reasonable, rather than accusatory. "Sadie was waiting for you to play your Scrabble word. I'm guessing your kidnapper took your phone or you would have sent me cryptic clues like help and golem," I said. "You know, like the one you sacrificed a Banim Shovavim to make, the one named Emmett?"

So much for my good intentions.

Jude turned stricken eyes to me. "How do you know about him? You're just a Sapien."

I white-knuckled the steering wheel. The Ohrist superiority complex at its finest. Any hope that Jude had been coerced by Zev and, thus, not responsible for the Banim Shovavim's death, vanished. "You think a Sapien could have saved you?"

Jude spat out a sliver of nail. "Have you been keeping secrets, Feldman?" She'd injected a cruel note into her voice. "How naughty. I wouldn't have thought you capable. You do love to share."

A muscle ticked in my jaw.

"Aw, kitten," Jude said. "Did I hurt your feelings?"

This was the dybbuk talking, not the friend who'd sat on my sunny back porch a couple weeks ago, the two of us crying with laughter watching a comedy skit on my laptop about a woman trying to take a nude selfie. Or the aunt who later that night helped Sadie paint flames onto a pair of old roller boots that Jude had unearthed for her. Though how much of that person was even real?

I was bone tired, and her jibe lodged under my skin like a splinter. I didn't want gratitude for saving her, but I hadn't expected viciousness.

"What's your magic?" Jude twirled a curl around her finger. "Wait. Let me guess. Healer. Always fixing people."

Nav's disdain had stung, but seeing as I'd known him for all of five minutes, I'd shrugged it off. Seeing that smirk on my best friend, however, I itched to slap it off her face.

Checking over my shoulder for oncoming traffic, I merged into the turnoff lane for East Vancouver, timing my answer to our car passing under a streetlamp. I deployed Delilah, who jumped onto the dashboard, her hands on Jude's shoulders pressing her back against the seat.

Jude yelped, one arm thrown up over her face.

"Guess again," I said, recalling my magic.

The silence stretched and thickened.

"Don't go speechless on me now," I said.

"Sorry. That wasn't me. It was..." She shook her head with a helpless shrug. "Dybbuk."

I waited for the rush of relief that I wouldn't have to tell her or a welling of compassion for her situation, but my chest tightened and tightened until suddenly it was like a dam broke inside me.

"Tell me, Judith, was it worth it to kill that Banim Shovavim? Did you feel powerful, kitten?" I sneered. "That's your thing, right? Power?" I pushed my hair off my shoulder, hating myself for this vitriol, but I couldn't stop the toxicity spewing out of me. I was scared that if I did, it would eat me up from the inside. "Except you're a successful woman who's living life on her own terms, so explain to me how creating Emmett was a good idea?"

"It was art," she said.

"It was ego," I shot back.

She screwed the cap back on the bottle and placed it in the cup holder. "It was supposed to be my legacy. Something wondrous to outlive me. Isn't that why people have kids?"

"Debatable, but having a child doesn't generally involve murder."

"I didn't intend for him to die."

"Manslaughter, then, not culpable homicide."

"Could you—" She swore and briefly pressed the heels of her palms against her eyes, then she jutted up her chin. "Do I get a trial, Counselor, or are you judge, jury, and executioner?"

I waved a hand at her, my shoulders tense. "Knock yourself out."

"First of all, the man was paid to donate some of his magic. It had taken us months to find a Banim Shovavim, so when I had a willing participant, yeah, I took the opportunity to have him infuse his necromancy into the golem and see if it took. The test was successful, and the man was fine. Initially. But a couple hours later, he dropped dead of a massive heart attack. It might not have had anything to do with me."

I shot her a skeptical look. "You can't really believe that."

"No." She sighed. "I know I'm responsible and I have to live with it, but it was never my intention to callously disregard someone's life."

"Even if he was a BS?"

She crossed her arms. "Yes, Miriam."

"Don't get snotty. Five minutes ago you said I was 'just a Sapien.'" I made the air quotes.

Her eyes flashed. "Are you mad because you think I look down on non-Ohrists or because the person who died was a Banim Shovavim like you? Would you be this angry if the victim was a vampire?"

I flinched, Lindsey's final expression of heartbreak flashing in my mind's eye. "Vampires aren't human."

"They still have sentience and reason and emotion."

I smacked the wheel. "They're monsters who prey on humanity. I watched one kill a perfectly innocent person the other night. Hell, Zev was ready to kill me because I refused to hand you over to him for your perceived betrayal."

But Kirk had checked out the house first in case anyone was there to hurt his mom, and he'd been kind to her. My head pounded.

"Humans make perfectly good monsters all on their own." Jude ran a hand over her broken fingers. "I never expected that I'd spend days in the dark in a semi-drugged haze, listening for every creak overhead that meant the psycho was coming back for another one of her 'persuasive chats.' And she's a Sapien. So don't for a second think that I underestimate them," she said fiercely.

I'd put Sapiens at the bottom of the food chain, but even with magic, Jude had been at Diane's mercy and I'd killed Lindsey, who was arguably stronger. I lived my life according to a black-and-white morality based on a legal ethical frame and a rigid viewpoint of human versus inhuman, but I was swimming in a sea of gray.

"I don't know what to think or what to believe anymore," I said.

Jude paused, fiddling with her splint. "Are we still friends?" she said in a quiet voice.

We crested a hill on Clark Drive, the downtown skyline a twinkling distant jewel. While so much in my life was murky, this choice, at least, was easy.

"Yes, dummy. We're friends."

Jude smiled and stuck out her uninjured hand. "Hi. I'm Jude. Long-time Ohrist, first-time dybbuk-enthralled."

I took a hand off of the wheel and shook. "Miriam. My parents didn't die in a car accident, they were murdered."

Jude gasped and pressed my hand against her heart.

I gave her a watery smile and put my hand back on the wheel. "I've also hidden my magic ever since. I win."

She paused, then shook her head. "That's honorable mention at best."

We looked at each other and burst out laughing.

Jude's shoulders shook, but her laughter caught and turned into a half-sob. "I don't want to die."

I squeezed her shoulder. "Listen up. That is not going to happen. Laurent thinks my magic can save you. Admittedly, we're working on a bit of a tight deadline, but I'm not going to lose you, got it? I could not afford the therapy for my child if that happened."

"Plus, there's the whole chin hair pact." Jude ran a finger over her jawline with a wince. "You better keep your end of that deal."

"You'll be plucking mine, but whatever."

My low fuel light came on. Sure, the owner's manual said I could drive seventeen kilometers before I ran out, but I refused to test that theory. I pulled into the closest gas station and up to an available pump.

Jude twisted in her seat so she could see me with her non-swollen eye. "Will the wolf be okay?"

I shrugged, turning off the engine. "Laurent is tough. I hope so."

"Laurent, huh?"

"Yes. The person I paid to help find you when I learned you'd lost your mind and gotten involved with vampires." I popped the gas tank open.

"On the midlife crisis scale from stalking my high school crush on social media to going full *Thelma & Louise* off a cliff, vampires seemed pretty middle-of-the road." She paused. "Zev really thinks I betrayed him?"

"He does."

"Shit." Jude got out of the car with me.

"Tell me everything about Kirk and Diane Holdencott to

264

convince him otherwise," I said, punching in my payment information at the pump.

"Who's Kirk? My kidnapper was this woman maybe ten years older than me. I guess, this Diane person, petite, dark-hair?" she said. I nodded, one eye on how much gas I was pumping and she continued. "She caught me at the studio Friday night pretending to be an interested client, and when my back was turned, she injected something into me." Jude rubbed her neck with her good hand.

"Lowered inhibitions during the Danger Zone. That's how you were enthralled." The pump hit the limit I'd pre-programmed and shut off. "Fuck."

"I have a hazy memory of her helping me to her car and then I woke up chained in her basement and she was demanding I make her a golem. It's not like I advertise that service. In fact Zev had approached me with the idea, because I'd never made one before. I certainly wasn't going to screw him over by making one for this psycho, even a golem without divination powers."

Replacing the nozzle, I grabbed my receipt and screwed the gas cap back on. "Good thing I have photographic proof of your condition and the untouched clay."

"I was wondering why you took a photo of me like that, you weirdo." She adjusted the splint where the tape was coming loose. "Thanks for covering my ass."

"Okay, new to-do plan."

"May it save us all," Jude said, pressing her hands together in prayer formation.

We got back in the car and were shortly on our way.

"I'll meet with Zev and get him off our back, then I'll pay a visit to Tatiana Cassin. If anyone knows where to find a Banim Shovavim who can teach me how to help you, it's her."

Jude shook her head in disbelief. "I'm gone four days and

suddenly you're hanging with the movers and shakers of the Ohrist community?"

"Long story," I said.

"One that involves the French hottie?"

"Tangentially." I made another aimless turn, hoping that inspiration about a safe place to stash Jude lay around the corner. "Want to go sit on the beach? We could talk until the sun comes up like we used to."

Jude gave me a sad smile. "You're stalling, Feldman."

"Big time." I shook my head. "I can't let you remain free. I'm sorry."

"You and me both." She spread her hands wide. "If my time on earth is limited, I want to go out with a clean conscience. So, where are we going?"

"To Laurent's place."

"Tangentially." Jude elbowed me. "You are so full of shit."

We parked outside Hotel Terminus. Laurent hadn't returned yet—not that I'd expected him to beat us here—so Jude and I had a very long–overdue conversation about our magic, and everything that had happened since Friday night.

She listened to the events with Emmett and Poe with a serious expression. "When I made Emmett, I assumed Zev would ask him business-related questions, not existential ones. I didn't realize at first that his magic was wobbly and these prophecies randomly came out. The question is, now that you know this, can you unknow it? Won't everything be colored by his pronouncement?"

"That's exactly what I'm afraid of."

Jude took my hand. "I really fucked up. I'm sorry."

"I tried to show Eli my magic and he couldn't see it," I said. "If the first domino was the reclamation of my powers, what if the darkness is my inability to share this part of my life with him and Sadie? I don't want to hide who I am from them. Or worse, what if I convince them and they're horrified?"

"Then you find a good Ohrist therapist and do family counseling, but I guarantee those two won't be horrified. They aren't uptight Ohrists bottle-fed on stupid prejudices."

"Well, even if Sades does think her mom is a freak, if Aunt Jude gives it the seal of approval and shares her own magic, she'll come around."

"The girl has good taste in role models. Don't worry, I'll be next to you the whole time." Her voice wobbled a bit when she said that and I squeezed her hand.

"You bet you will be," I said.

Jude paused. "So, not a house fire, huh? Does Eli know your parents were murdered?"

"Not even Goldie knows. And there was a house fire." I shot her a pointed look.

"Lonestars. Shit."

"Yeah. When it was all over, I was so scared that someone would come after me that it was safer to let it be a tragic accident than figure out how to spin the truth without including magic."

Headlights swept up behind us. Laurent, once more human and dressed in different clothes, got out of a pick-up and spoke to the driver.

I scrunched down in my seat until the truck was gone, both because the driver was Nav and, if I was being honest, because I'd abandoned Laurent.

"If I can face the wolf," Jude said, "you can too. Besides, after everything I just went through, I could use a little fun."

I slid farther down in my seat. Shoot me now.

25

SHE STRODE UP TO LAURENT AND GAVE A SMALL wave. "Hi. I'm Jude and I'm really sorry that I hurled that godawful sculpture at you. Next time, I'll throw a car."

I smirked, eavesdropping through my partially rolled-down window.

Laurent swung his key chain around his finger. "You and Mitzi share an overinflated sense of your comedic abilities."

Jude cackled, and I winced, cringing with a specific embarrassment I hadn't felt since I was a teenager, and that I'd been happy to never experience again. "I can't speak for *Mitzi*, but I'm the life of the party, darling." She held out her wrists. "Now, I guess you'd better lock me up." She shot me a sly grin. "Unless you'd like to do the honors, Feldman, seeing how versatile you are with cuffs? Hug that strapping cop ex of yours for me when you see him, will you?"

I thunked my head against the wheel because my forty-year-old artistically successful friend was acting like she was fourteen, and enjoying herself far too much. I was also never telling her anything again.

Thankfully, Laurent merely looked perplexed.

"I'm not coming in," I said.

"However will I survive?" he said, dryly. "Oh wait. I'll comfort myself with the warmth of your departing headlights like I did at the farm."

I swallowed and mustered up a weak smile. "Great." Even if Jude had accepted being temporarily imprisoned again, I couldn't watch her be chained up. "Well, I have some things to do."

Laurent narrowed his eyes and walked toward me. "Where exactly are you going at this time of night?"

"Later!" I hit the gas before he could stop me. Just because I had almost a full day before Zev's deadline was no reason not to get the jump on him. Laurent was too much of a risk to bring since BatKian could compel him.

It was time for my second visit to Blood Alley.

I only used my cloaking to reveal the hidden space, dropping my magic the second I stepped inside vamp territory. I expected to be approached or, more likely, apprehended by a vampire sooner rather than later, but I wasn't prepared for Zev to fall into step with me partway up the outside right lane.

"Ms. Feldman. You came alone and you didn't bring me a new desk chair. How disappointing on both counts." The vampire wore another bespoke suit.

"On the plus side, I didn't sneak in. Look at me following proper protocol." I drew in a deep breath. "I wanted to discuss some incorrect assumptions you made."

He cocked an eyebrow, dubious, but his polite manner could have been lifted from the fussiest etiquette book when he invited me to have a drink with him.

We walked a short distance through the patrons, passing a young woman using her magic to change her hairstyle from a long braid to an explosion of tight curls.

A crescent of light flared up next to her.

I stepped forward to throw my shadow over her, but Zev clasped my arm with a curt shake of his head.

The young woman's mouth fell open in an "oh," and she was consumed by the blindspot, which flashed and vanished in an instant.

Everyone else had given her a wide berth, their eyes averted from the tragedy as they continued to their destinations.

It was all so senseless.

"Ohrists understand the risks inherent to their magic," Zev said, and rapped briskly on the only door that didn't have any red lightbulbs above it.

"Humans understand the risks inherent to getting on a boat and we still throw people a ring and a lifeline if they go overboard."

"You may well be the sole Banim Shovavim in this city. Do you plan to save everyone? For the ohr to be replenished, people must die." There was a crisp click of the door being unlocked. "Learn from the wolf's experiences, Ms. Feldman," Zev said. "You will not be heralded for your good deeds. Quite the opposite."

The truth of his words grated on me, both for myself and Laurent. However, he was correct that I couldn't save everyone, nor did I desire to play knight in shining armor for that community. It was a losing battle anyway: a life jacket against a tsunami of magic.

A vamp of Japanese descent welcomed us. "Zev. Perfect timing. I just chilled the sake."

The vampire leader clasped his shoulder. "Thank you, Yoshi."

Yoshi looked about twenty, but given how fast and gracefully he moved, like a fast-running stream, I'd bet he was quite old. There was also an ease between the two vampires that suggested a very long friendship.

The door closed silently. There were no tables and no other patrons. I could disappear without a trace and no one would be the wiser.

I took the stool closest to the door, gambling on the fact that Zev had a moral code. A psychopathic one, involving a strict adherence to procedures of his devising and an almost fanatic loyalty to him, but that was exactly what might save us all now.

Behind the polished length of the bar top were dozens of bottles with Japanese labels, each one spotlit in its own display.

Yoshi presented us with a delicate earthenware carafe and two small glass cups, then withdrew to the end of the bar where he watched a baseball game on his phone.

Zev poured my sake and then explained that I should do the same for him.

I held up my cup in cheers. "Kanpai."

"Kanpai," he said. "Do you often drink sake?"

"No. I've only ever had it a couple of times, but I was taught that kanpai means 'dry cup' and that struck me as more poetic than bottoms up." I sipped the cool liquid, pleasantly surprised by how light and fruity it tasted.

Once we'd both sampled our beverages, Zev set his glass down with a businesslike air. "I take it you found the photo of your lovely daughter."

My hands tightened on my glass, but I forced myself to put it down gently. "Let me be clear about one thing. If any harm ever comes to anyone I love, I will rain hell down upon you and whoever touches them. I don't care if magic is outed, or who I upset. My only loyalties are to my family and friends. Banim Shovavim were hunted for eons, and I have absolutely no compunction about letting all the rest of you have a taste of that from humanity at large." I opened the photo of Jude on my phone.

Zev looked at it without comment.

"Jude didn't go willingly and she didn't betray you," I said. "There was no golem made."

"Props and makeup can tell any story you want. Photos

271

are easily manipulated and mean nothing. My vampire confirmed she was with Mei Lin, as did the golem."

"Actually, Emmett didn't." I took another sip for fortification. It wasn't a great idea to hand Zev a weakness, but I had no choice. "He said she was with the dybbuk, and she is," I said, "but not Mei Lin. Jude is enthralled. It happened sometime during the Danger Zone when Jude's kidnapper drugged her. And yes, this person wanted her to make a golem but Jude didn't. In fact, she doesn't even know—"

A cheer went up from the baseball fans. Funny how crowds at sporting matches all sounded the same.

I stilled, the pieces of this puzzle falling into place.

Kirk's wrestling, a vampire described as having cauliflower ears who had been part of the attack on Laurent, it all fit. He'd probably told his mother about Jude a few weeks back, likely an offhand comment since he'd sounded like he enjoyed being a vampire. When he learned what his mother had set in motion, and knowing Zev's stance on betrayals, Kirk had realized Zev would retaliate.

I bet he'd broken in to Jude's studio and cleaned up all signs of the struggle, and he'd used Emmett's prophecy to convince Zev that Jude had betrayed him. I set down my cup.

Would I give up a vampire to keep my daughter safe? In a heartbeat, but it had been bad enough *imagining* Lindsey as someone's daughter. I'd seen firsthand how much Diane loved her son.

Zev leaned forward. "Care to fill me in, Ms. Feldman?"

Kirk wasn't a monster or a lost cause to his mother. How could I condemn him to die, when I'd do anything to protect my own child?

"The vampire who told you that Jude was with the dybbuk," I said. "Is his name Kirk?"

Zev narrowed his eyes. "It is."

"Whose idea was it to threaten me with my daughter's photo?"

272

"Kirk's. He was very upset after Lindsey's death. I often assign a vampire to mentor a newer addition, and she was his."

Her newbie best friend. I released my death grip on the sake cup. Things had escalated after I'd killed her with the threat on Sadie. Well, Kirk should have come after me directly. There was no choice I could live with here, but only one I could make.

"How recently was he turned?" I said.

"Yoshi?" The vampire glanced over his shoulder. "When did Kirk join us?"

"About six months ago," the other vampire said.

"Join?" I said. "Did he have a choice?"

"Of course," Zev said. "Informed consent, Ms. Feldman."

"First of all, there's no way it was informed. There is nothing in the human experience to compare it to, and second, even if he consented, well, drug addicts consent to their next hit. It doesn't mean their families are happy about it."

Everything went deathly still, the world sharpened to a tipping point. I braced myself for a violent outburst, but Zev's expression remained eerily dispassionate. His fingers tightened on his glass, crushing it into tiny shards that fell to the bar top like diamonds. The vampire paid no attention to the blood dotting his skin, the cuts already healing.

"A member of Kirk's family kidnapped Jude to make a golem? What did they hope to divine?" he said, in an exceedingly polite voice that made me want to put a continent between us. He wiped himself off with a napkin.

"A perfect golem may divine, the rest stick with a task until it's done," I said. "They were going to send it after you for turning Kirk. Mei Lin was a red herring to throw you off the real culprit."

Zev's eyes darkened. "Yoshi."

"On it. I'll find him." The vampire slid his phone into his pocket and left.

I wouldn't have to kill Kirk now, but his blood was on my hands all the same.

"You will tell me who abducted Judith," Zev said.

"You aren't going to touch this person." But was it mercy damning Diane to a lifetime of suffering knowing she'd cost her son his life?

Zev's fangs descended and the air chilled.

Goosebumps dotted my skin but I refused to wrap my arms around myself. I toyed with the zipper of my purse, but even if I could get the lighter out, I couldn't pin the vampire in place to set him on fire. However, I wasn't backing down. I wouldn't send Kirk's mother to the slaughter.

"Mei Lin went over the line and took out her entire crew," I said. "You prevented Laurent from dealing with her months ago and now the Lonestars have a hell of a mess on their hands. How much goodwill do you have left with them? They won't interfere with Kirk, but his mother, a Sapien farm-owner with roots in her local community?" I sipped some sake for show, because it tasted like sour fear. "You think the Sapien press and police won't get involved if she disappears, or worse? Jude didn't betray you. Let this go."

Zev ran his thumbnail over his lip, then he slid off his stool. "It appears our business is concluded. You get to walk away from me for a second time. Not many can say that."

"And my other people whom you've threatened? Including the golem."

"I'll restrict my attentions to my vampire. But Ms. Feldman?" His smile coated my glass in a thin layer of ice. "Do stay out of Blood Alley. Third time is not always the charm."

I nodded, not moving until he'd slipped soundlessly away.

The faintest traces of dawn smudged the sky when I left the bar. Tourists and vampires alike had retired for the night and the lane was empty. I ran out of Blood Alley and back into Gastown, my breath coming out in white puffs.

"Happy now?"

I screamed, pressing a hand to my beating heart. "Wear a bell. I'll get you one to match Boo."

"I'm not a cat," Laurent said, falling into step with me.

No, he was a wolf. That had been made clear when he'd pressed up against me in the parking lot, his feral gaze homed in on mine, and yet it was even more evident now in his loose-limbed walk. Tangentially. Right.

I crossed my arms so he didn't see my hard nipples poking through my shirt. "How did you find me?"

"The bloodsucker threatened your daughter. You wouldn't have waited to confront him." Laurent stuffed his hands in his pockets. "You didn't want me to come."

He didn't sound like he cared, but you didn't drop a statement like that if you were indifferent.

"It was more expedient this way," I said. "You're compellable. I'm not. I also took care of our problem with Kirk. How's Jude?"

"She attacked me again when I was chaining her up, but no cars were harmed."

We reached my car. "I'm sorry I left you at the farm."

He shrugged. "I had to shift to heal and I had a phone to call Nav."

I sat on the hood, typing a quick text to Officer Terence to tell him that Jude was safe and she'd had a family emergency. I sent the same text to Eli. He'd let Sadie know.

Laurent hopped up next to me. "Did you square things with BatKian?"

"As much as one can." I started a long note on my phone, working on a Sapien-friendly story that Jude could give to Eli.

Laurent placed his hand over mine. His calluses rasped

my skin, but his touch sent a comforting warmth through me. "Do you ever stop?"

The two of us had gone through a number of high adrenaline situations together in a short period of time, but it would be foolish to mistake that shared experience for something else. I pulled my hand away. "Are you kidding? My life is an endless run of things to check off and none of this has lightened my load. Doesn't matter though. It's all fine." I resumed typing. "I want things the way I want them and that means that people I love are safe and life is running smoothly."

"Safety is a fool's illusion," he said in a gruff voice.

I deleted a nonsensical autocorrect. "Then why do you bother helping people? Why were you so insistent that I figure out how to remove the dybbuk from Rupert if not to keep him safe?"

"I didn't say it wasn't worth trying, just that you can't write down 'find a happy ending to this mess' like it's any other task."

"Being an optimist is not the same as being an idiot," I scoffed, to take away the sting of his scorn. "I'd rather not share your cynical outlook when my friend's life is on the line, thanks so much."

"No, you're not a cynic. You're a thrill junkie."

I put my phone down and planted a hand on my hip. "What the fuck is that supposed to mean?"

"How many years had it been since you used your magic, and then one taste of it again and you were running headlong off a cliff?" He crossed his arms.

"I didn't have a choice," I said. "Jude was taken."

"How convenient."

"Nothing about this has been convenient. Trust me." It would be easier to brush his comments off. The world was so much kinder to women of a certain age if we smiled and played nicely.

What had nice ever gotten me? A lifetime of hiding and fear and denying a vital part of myself. I wasn't doing this for the rush, but because my friend's life was on the line. If women were slotted into caretaker roles, then who was Laurent to condemn me for doing whatever I had do to take care of Jude? Men got to live on that adrenaline curl where facing one's own mortality heightened the sensation of living, and they were hailed as heroes, but how dare I experience that for myself?

Something dark rushed through my veins, heady and powerful.

"What if I am enjoying myself?" I said. "I'm not reckless. The opposite in fact. I'm taking great pains to be responsible and make sure that when all this is over, me and everyone important to me is still standing, unlike the way you approach life."

"Do explain," he said with a tight jaw. "I live for your pearls of wisdom."

Truth masking secrets. I white-knuckled the phone. It was more like people fooling themselves: Zev that he still possessed some degree of humanity, Jude that her choices were about being a powerful woman when they'd been about ego, Laurent about being in control.

"You didn't simply wound those vampires the other night," I said, "you didn't even just kill them. You eviscerated them. And with Rupert when he first showed up at Hotel Terminus? You can say you were testing a theory to see if you could get that dybbuk out, but I saw you." I punctuated the air with angry jabs, my cheeks flushed. "You want to talk about running off a cliff? You strap on dynamite before you launch yourself and I can't tell if it's because that's the only way you feel alive or because you want to die. Either way, I'm nothing like you."

His anger crashed over me like waves on a stormy sea, and then he went still, all his energy sucked inward. Even when he'd been lying on the ground after Jude's attack, his presence had been palpable. This was such a total withdrawal that there might as well have been a chasm between us.

I shivered, the air noticeably cooler.

Laurent slid off the car. "Let me know if you figure out how to save Jude."

"Yup." I returned my gaze to my phone so I didn't have to watch him leave.

26

I DRAGGED MY BUTT INTO THE HOUSE, MY HEAD drooping and my eyelids heavy. I intended to wake myself up with a cold shower but when I tripped twice on my way upstairs, I veered into my bedroom and collapsed on my mattress. I stayed awake long enough to type an email to Shirley, saying that I'd developed a fever and would be off until Monday, but I hesitated before sending it, because I'd never played hooky before, not even from school, since that would have meant drawing unwanted attention to me.

Work could wait. Jude couldn't. I hit send.

Comforting myself that Kirk couldn't get into my house without an invitation and Sadie was safe during the day, I was asleep in seconds and didn't wake up until late afternoon. Between the sleep and a long shower, I felt vaguely human again. I wrapped my hair in a bright orange towel, slipped on a fuzzy bathrobe and my favorite slippers, made myself a hair-raisingly strong coffee and a toasted sesame seed bagel, and phoned Daisy, our firm's private investigator.

Tatiana remained my best shot at quickly finding another Banim Shovavim to tell me how to get the dybbuk out of

Jude, but forewarned was forearmed. She'd gotten the jump on me at our first meeting, and that wouldn't happen again.

According to Daisy's intel, the eighty-year-old had lived a colorful life. Born in New York to Jewish immigrants who'd fled the Nazis, her parents found slow but steady success in the diamond district. Their increasing wealth went hand-in-hand with more extreme religious views until the family was firmly ensconced in the Hasidic community.

Tatiana rejected an arranged marriage and fled to Paris to pursue her art. Eventually she met Samuel Cassin, originally from Vancouver, who was working in one of the banks there. They lived in Paris for decades as Tatiana's art career took off, globe-trotting all over the world to her openings, before they moved back to Vancouver about fifteen years ago. Samuel passed away several years later, but Tatiana stayed.

This woman had defied religious and societal expectation to make a name and a space for herself. She was an inspiration and yet I couldn't shake the feeling that she was dangerous to me. Even Laurent didn't trust her.

I topped up my coffee. Not that he was the best judge of character.

Daisy offered to send me the large document of all Tatiana's professional achievements. It was incredible that the artist was such a public persona and yet even as skilled an investigator as Daisy hadn't unearthed her being an Ohrist.

Unless Daisy was one herself and didn't think I'd believe her.

"Was there anything else? No matter how unbelievable?" I said, stirring sugar into my mug. "I can handle it. I'm no Sap."

Daisy laughed. "You sound like you're hoping for something specific."

"I guess not." I thanked her and said I'd send the cookie

recipe she'd asked for as soon as we hung up. I even included the special tip about freezing the dough and then grating it into the greased pan, snickering at the memory of my ex-sister-in-law Genevieve making this recipe without it, and the resulting bricks that her guests had tried to gnaw their way through.

Tempting as it was to throw on yet another pair of sweats, I went for a more polished look with tailored pants that made my ass look amazing and a sleek black wrap top with white French cuffs. I twisted my hair into a chignon and put on a light coat of foundation, a swipe of pale shadow, and a thick coat of mascara, finishing it up with my favorite red lipstick.

Tatiana might want to meet and I was determined to present myself as professional and capable. If for some reason I ran into Laurent when I checked on Jude later, he could damn well see me the same way.

Daisy had provided me with Tatiana's contact information, and while the artist was surprised to hear from me, she greeted me warmly.

"To what do I owe the pleasure of your call, bubeleh?" Her cigarette-infused, New Yorker accent rasped the sentence, turning the word "call" into "cawl."

"I've got a family emergency and I need to speak with an experienced Banim Shovavim."

"And you came to me. I'm flattered." She sounded much like the devil would if I'd been looking to trade away my soul. Like we both knew there was no real other option, but we could be civilized and pretend otherwise.

I had another sip of coffee, but even with all the sugar, it tasted bitter. I got up and dumped the contents down the drain. "You're well connected and this really is urgent."

"Don't be coy. What are your specific requirements?"

My stomach rumbled and I opened the fridge looking for something healthy to eat. "It's kind of personal."

"I'd hate to steer you wrong," she said. "Given the urgency."

Sighing, I grabbed some mocha-flavored yogurt and dumped it in a bowl. I'd hoped to avoid the particulars, but the one unsuccessful attempt I'd made with Rupert had hurt him, and this time I needed a home run. I required guidance and if letting Tatiana in on the particulars was a necessary evil to achieve that, so be it. "I need to get a dybbuk out of someone who's enthralled."

There was a pause. "Did Laurent put you up to this?"

"He has no idea I'm calling you."

Tatiana laughed throatily. "Oh, to be a fly on the wall when you tell him."

I sucked some yogurt off the spoon. What was the deal between the two of them? I'd swear they really liked each other, but why did she disapprove of his livelihood so much? She didn't strike me as a traditionalist who'd push for him to follow in his father's footsteps.

"Can you help me?" I said. "Or do you know how to do it?"

"Not remotely. I'll connect you with my friend Max. Cantankerous bastard, but if anyone can help, it's him, even though he's an Ohrist."

"I appreciate it."

"My pleasure. After all, it would be a shame to lose such a talented artist as Judith."

I dropped my spoon, splattering yogurt onto the table. "How did you know it's her?"

"People like to tell me things," Tatiana said.

Had Laurent filled her in? Was meeting Tatiana some con? I ripped off a handful of paper towels and mopped up the spill. No, I was being ridiculous. Laurent had warned me away from her. And what could either of them possibly want from me anyway, other than my ability to save the enthralled, which Laurent had been pretty upfront about?

I tossed the paper towel in the trash and exhaled. Perhaps I was getting paranoid, but why did Tatiana feign ignorance when she was plugged in to the precise situation?

"Miriam," Tatiana said. "Should I connect you with Max?"

Was this my out? My last chance to walk away and not get caught up in whatever game she was playing? I rubbed a hand over my neck. "Please."

"He's working now, but I'll arrange a time for you to meet later today."

"Wait. Do you know if Mr. BatKian found Kirk yet?"

"My understanding is they are on top of the situation." Tatiana disconnected.

"Goodbye to you, too."

There was a knock on the kitchen door and I jumped.

Eli waved at me through the glass.

I unlocked the door and moved aside so he could enter. "Coffee?"

"No, thanks." He loosened his tie with a happy sigh. "You must be relieved."

I stared at him blankly.

"Jude's back."

"Right. Yes." I tapped my head. "Super fuzzy. Didn't sleep well last night."

"Come for dinner tonight with the spawn and me," he said. "Chris will be there and he said he'd swing by the cheesecake place and get the one with extra strawberries."

My smile was more of a grimace, the memory of strawberry-capped gnomes and Laurent's inert body flashing up. "I'd love to, but I can't. I'm going to spend time with Jude. Rain check?"

Good. Sadie and Eli would be together at home.

Eli grimaced. "Wellll…"

I smacked him. "Another one? You have the attention span of a gnat."

"I tried, Mir, but the man hates hockey. Considering his stick handling skills, you think he'd be a fan."

"And yet I wasn't either. You sad, sweet optimist." I got the vacuum cleaner out of the broom cupboard next to the fridge.

"I'm a true romantic," Eli said. Off my snort, he shot me a superior look. "What? I'll feed Chris first and our uncoupling will be done with such charm that he'll leave happier for having lost me than if he'd never had me at all. As you did."

"Dream on. Also, you didn't make me bring you dessert when you broke up with me."

"Had I known that was an option, I would have," he said, closing the cupboard door. "Sadie didn't like him anyway."

"She never mentioned that to me. Why not?"

"He called her cosplaying 'dress up.'"

I jerked a thumb to the back door. "Terf the bum."

"Exactly." Eli smiled, but although he was within arm's reach, if I tried to touch him, I expected to only encounter thin air. I didn't want a schism in my life, but I wasn't sure how to bridge it and get him and Sadie over to where I was standing.

I hugged him. "I love you, Eli."

We might not be married anymore, but we'd created a kid and had built a life together. No one could ever take his place.

Eli squeezed me tight. "I'll save you a piece of cheesecake."

"You'll intend to."

"It's the thought that counts, right?"

"Not even a little bit, Detective Chu."

Laughing, he left.

To pass the time until Tatiana called back, I vacuumed, vanquishing a horde of dust buffalos that swarmed me from behind the couch. For an honor roll student, my kid couldn't grasp the basic concept that some furniture was moveable and you didn't have to bash vacuum cleaners up against things.

Tatiana finally sent a text with an address and the word "Midnight."

I had hours to kill, but if I stayed home, I'd obsess about the overwhelming odds that were not in my favor.

After a quick stop at Jude's favorite bakery, I drove over to Hotel Terminus, then sat outside for a good ten minutes playing out both sides of different arguments with Laurent. With each new iteration, my retorts grew progressively less angry until I was composed enough to walk in and behave like a reasonable human being.

Discussions always went better when I'd spent my anger on imaginary fights than if I confronted the person with the first draft of my argument.

I rapped on the door.

Laurent opened it and crossed his arms. He was in jeans and a fitted navy button-down shirt with the cuffs rolled up over the corded muscle on his forearms. The top two buttons were undone, exposing a triangle of olive skin. "You here to see Jude?"

"I am."

He moved aside. "You know where she is," he said coolly.

So be it. I handed him a cheque. "The agreed-upon fee. Thank you, Laurent."

He shoved it in his pocket without looking at it, his eyes narrowed. "Why did you call me that?"

I stepped inside the hotel. There was no longer any sign of the vandalism. Even the radio had been replaced with a similarly art deco-styled one that played a Louis Armstrong and Ella Fitzgerald duet. "Why did I call you by your name? Are you serious?"

"You never have. It's always that ridiculous nickname."

"You're insane. I've used your name a bunch of times."

"Vraiment? Name once that wasn't when I was in wolf form."

I shook my head, crossing the floor. "Have it your way. I didn't come here to—"

The opening strains of Sinatra's "Come Fly With Me" came on the radio and I froze, my hand pressed to my stammering heart. "Can you turn this off?" I whispered.

"Quoi?" Laurent came over and did a double take at my expression.

The song crescendoed, the room replaced by my dad's body falling to the ground in time to the blast of trumpets.

"Please turn it off."

He hurried across the room. The silence was almost worse because with it would come questions I didn't want to answer.

I blotted my forehead. "Thanks."

"Want to tell me what that was about?"

"I should go see how Jude is doing." With that, I bolted for the elevator, Laurent sighing behind me.

The hole in the drywall had been repaired, but the door and gate were open, and the lights were on.

Emmett, still missing a leg, but resplendent in one of Jude's silk kaftans, sat on the ground playing cards with my best friend. He slapped down his final three cards and threw up his arms. "Gin Rummy, bitches!"

I sat down cross-legged next to them, setting the box between Jude and me.

"Is that what I think it is?" She squinted at the box, one eye still puffy and swollen.

"You bet."

"Yum. The perfect bondage food." Jude tugged on her cuffs, rattling the long chains attaching them to the iron wall. "They're VIP level. Very baller." She opened the box and took out one of the treats with her good hand. Her broken fingers had been wrapped in fresh tape and gauze, and she'd showered, but the bruises on her face were even more ghastly purple and yellow.

"Emmett," I said.

"Yeah?" The golem picked up the cards.

"I spoke with Zev. He's not going to come after you. You're safe."

"The first day of the rest of my life. The magic of new beginnings." He jammed the cards into the deck hard enough to bend one.

Jude leaned over and squeezed his arm. "We'll be okay. I won't desert you."

Emmett rolled his eyes but he uncrumpled the card.

Jude sat back with a shaky smile. They'd have to find their way through this.

"You're safe too," I told my best friend.

"Phew. The downside of vampire employers." Jude bit into the dessert bar. "The termination sucks."

I barked a laugh. "How'd you get clean clothes?"

Jude rolled up the cuffs of her sweater. "Laurent went to my place and picked them up."

"What a prince," I muttered.

Jude frowned. "What crawled up your ass?"

"Nothing." I bit savagely into a bar. Laurent wanted to be Mr. Nice Guy with Jude when with me it was sarcasm and bullshit psychoanalysis? Fuck him.

Emmett sniffed the treats. "What are these?"

"Nanaimo bars." I licked custard off my lip. "Invented in Nanaimo on Vancouver Island. They have a coconut graham cracker base, a custard filling, and a layer of hard chocolate on top. You want one?"

"I don't eat." Emmett shuffled the cards. "Should I deal you in for the next round?"

"Sure," I said.

"Any luck with my predicament?" Jude said.

"Yes. I'm meeting someone who should be able to help me. This will all be over soon, I swear."

The cards fell to the ground.

"It's only just begun." Emmett spoke in his dreamy voice, his eyes replaced by the swirls of the cosmos and starlight.

"What has?" I said.

"The game."

Jude leaned in close to his face. "Strong showing of magic in both eyes, no stuttering in his pronouncements," she murmured. "I don't understand why it isn't consistent."

I smacked her leg, because now was not the time for a tech survey. "This better not be more domino bullshit." Or about Tatiana. Were my fears valid that she was playing me? "What game, Emmett?"

His gaze went distant, then he blinked and shook off his trance. "Game? Gin Rummy." He picked up the cards and shuffled again.

I ate another bite, the sugar mixing uneasily with the dread in my stomach. What was the point of free will and changing my mazel if there was always some other prediction? How escapable was fate? Had I merely altered certain events, but my larger destiny was still in play? Were we born into a kind of cosmic stream that swept us along some grand path, where we could choose whether we used a front crawl or a backstroke or floated along hanging on to a piece of driftwood, but that current was ultimately a one-way predetermined trip?

Or was everything up to chance and personal skill, in which case our mazel was changed with every decision we made? Maybe destiny was no more than a set of birth conditions, encompassing everything from genetics to the kinds of parents we had and the environment we were born into, and then it was up to us to take those and make something of our lives.

I rejected any notion that my life had been mapped out. If

mazel was anything, it was a wake-up call that I'd gotten complacent. That's it.

"Shake it off, or it'll do your head in," Jude said.

I rearranged my cards. "Don't worry. Nothing will distract me from helping you."

We played a few super competitive rounds, replete with a lot of accusations and laughter. If it had a manic tinge to it, well, we could be forgiven for trying too hard to forget that the sands of the hourglass of Jude's life expectancy were slipping away.

Jude nudged the bakery box at me. "You going to offer one to the wolf?"

I laid down a run of four diamonds. "He knows where we are."

Emmett picked up a card. "He's a grumpy asshole."

"Thank you," I said.

"I like him," he added.

"And I've attacked him twice and he hasn't retaliated," Jude said, peering at her cards with her one non-swollen eye. "He's even fed me, watered me, and given me bathroom breaks." She pointed at the folded blanket and pillow in the corner. "Brought me those."

"That's basic jailhouse conditions. Gin Rummy." I lay down the rest of my cards.

Emmett declared he'd had enough and hopped his way back into the main room, taking the cards with him.

I lay my head on Jude's shoulder. "Did you sleep at all?

"I hyperventilated into a brief fainting spell."

"A disco nap. Nice." I stood up, one hand on my lower creaky back.

Jude sat with her legs in a V-formation, stretching over to touch one foot, then the other. "Take him the last bar, Mir."

Pacing around the elevator, I ticked items off on my fingers. "He got to kill a dybbuk thanks to me, I undid Zev's compulsion on him, and he's been paid in full. Our business dealings are squared away. No pastry necessary."

"He's really gotten under your skin, huh?" Jude brought her legs together and leaned forward, touching both toes. "Good. You need someone to challenge you."

I tried to mirror that while standing but my fingertips dangled uselessly at mid-calf, and my legs burned. "Annoy and challenge are not the same thing."

Jude pushed the bakery box at me. "Give the nice man who brought me clean clothes the damn pastry, Miriam."

I straightened up with a huff. "Fine. I will."

She grabbed the pillow and stuffed it under her head.

"I *will* be back tonight to take you home." I rolled my hips in circles, hoping my spine would loosen up already.

Jude rolled onto her back, staring up at the elevator car's ceiling. "You know the funny thing about all this? I was so certain that I was going into it with my eyes open, and that so long as I didn't break my contract with the vampires, I wouldn't get hurt. Excitement with minimal risk—other than possibly being consumed by a blindspot because I used my magic."

"You wanted to touch the sky," I murmured.

"I didn't stop to consider what it would be like for Emmett or that the necromancer…" She shook her head with a sigh and held up her injured hand. "I never saw this coming."

The trouble with trying to touch the sky was that you eventually fell to earth, and gravity was a hard-assed bitch. The summer before my best friend moved away, we were horsing around on her trampoline as usual, and she ran inside for a minute, but I decided to keep doing flips. I'd done them a million times, what did it matter if she was around to spot me or not?

It all happened so fast that I didn't have time to worry. One second I was tumbling in mid-air, the next, I'd landed funny, the air violently knocked from my lungs, unable to move. I was positive that I'd broken my neck. I lay there, trying to breathe, staring up at the sky that was still so blue and clear.

The sun's warmth didn't penetrate the blanket of pain in my chest and neck, and time spun out into a meaningless eternity. Eventually, I felt well enough to get up and keep jumping, but I never did flips again. Physically I was fine, but my sense of invulnerability had cracked.

I never told anyone. Maybe that's why it had never healed, but it didn't have to be that way for Jude.

"That's part of why I came over here," I said, reversing the direction of my hip movements. "Do you want to make a statement to the cops? I could get Eli to take it for you once you're back home. Leave out all talk of golems and say this was a straight-up kidnapping."

"I've already spoken to the Lonestars." Jude rested her hands on her stomach.

"They can't touch Diane. She's a Sapien."

"Who kidnapped an Ohrist and tried to force me to use magic. She poses a risk to us and they needed to know that."

"She did it because her son was turned into a vampire."

"That was his choice."

"Are you fucking kidding me? He's undead, Jude. He didn't drop out of school to smoke weed and play video games."

She shrugged.

I smacked the wall. "God damn it. I kept Zev from getting his hands on this woman so she could face proper justice on a kidnapping charge, but if the Lonestars get her—"

"They'll do what's necessary to ensure she never does this again and no word of magic gets out. That's how it works."

"It doesn't have to be."

Jude's answering look was filled with pity. "Of course it

does. If you leave out all mention of magic, there is no case. No motive. Nothing. This is the compact we all agree to in exchange for magic."

"She didn't know that."

Jude adjusted her handcuffs, massaging her skin. "She wanted to make a golem to go after vampires. I'm betting she had at least an inkling of how this might go down."

"Sure, with regard to the vamps, not the Lonestars. Take me, I'm magic and I didn't agree to shit."

"Your parents should have taught you otherwise."

I picked up the bakery box, my jaw set. "I'm going to take that as the dybbuk talking."

"I love you, Mir, but you're being naive. Magic isn't Narnia. Different isn't good. Were Saps to know of our existence, they'd hunt us."

"Like Ohrists hunted Banim Shovavim?"

Jude flinched. "Yeah. So you of all people should understand why this is the way it has to be."

"Then I don't want to be part of it."

"You really think you can go back now?"

"I stopped once."

"Because your mom and dad were killed. You were a kid and you were scared. You won't stop now. It's who you are." Jude faced the wall. "I'm tired."

Summarily dismissed, I walked out and dropped the bakery box on the coffee table. Emmett was playing Solitaire and Laurent was nowhere to be seen.

"Tell Laurent the last bar is his," I said, and left.

27

It was pedal to the metal all the way back out to Diane's farm. If I could get to her before the Lonestars did, then I'd convince her to turn herself in to the Sapien cops, and if the magic police were already there, well, I'd figure it out when I arrived.

The concession stand was closed, but the door was open and inside, a man was restocking jam on shelves.

I waved at him until he saw me and took out one of his earbuds.

"Hi," I said. "I'm looking for Diane."

"Now's not a good time," he said. "She just got word that her son was killed in a car accident."

The vamps had already taken out Kirk? My relief felt wrong in light of his mother's grief. Was the car accident a story that Diane had come up with or were the Lonestars behind this? If they were here already, I was probably too late to save her, but I had to try. How exactly remained to be seen, dependent on the circumstances when I found her.

"It's actually in regards to Kirk. Is there a way I can reach Diane?"

He studied me for a moment and then nodded. "She's in the house."

I marched briskly up the stairs, took a deep breath, and knocked.

Diane opened the door, her eyes red. "Yes?"

"I'm here about your former guest."

She frowned and shook her head. "Who?"

I chose my words carefully in case there was anyone inside who shouldn't hear what I was saying. "The red-haired woman you had over to deal with the people from Blood Alley?"

"I have no idea who you're talking about and now's not a good time. My son..." She took a wavery breath. "I'm sorry. You must be mistaken."

I didn't think she was lying. She genuinely had no idea what I was talking about. "No, I'm sorry to have troubled you."

Back in my car, I sat there for a moment, then fired off a text to Ava, asking if Lonestars could erase people's memories.

She replied that it was one of the tools in their toolbox. Diane had no memory of what she'd done, no memory of magic, and no idea that her son had been a vampire. As much as it protected the magic community, the Lonestars had done a mitzvah by not making Kirk's mother live with the guilt that her actions had brought about her son's death. I hadn't expected that from them.

Were the Lonestars involved in covering up my parents' murder the exception or the rule? There sure hadn't been any compassion shown there.

I didn't intend to get on their radar and find out. Putting this entire mess behind me as best I could, I went to see Tatiana's friend.

Max lived in a ramshackle bungalow in need of a good pressure washing. The flagstones were choked with moss, and the railing on one side of the front stairs listed precariously, but streetlights made the spiderweb at the front window shimmer prettily.

When I knocked on the door, it was opened only as far as the chain went. An eyeball pressed up against the crack.

"What's the password?" a man said.

"Uh, Tatiana sent me."

The door slammed shut.

I texted Tatiana. *Do I need a password?*

A phone rang inside the house.

"You never let me have any fun," the man said on the other side of the door.

The chain rattled and then the door opened again, all the way this time.

A short man with bushy hair that had never met a comb it couldn't defeat and a hideous tattoo of what was either an alien uterus or an extremely maladjusted butterfly on his forearm motioned me inside. "Mi casa es su casa. I'm kidding. I'm not even going to offer you a drink." He grabbed my arm with fleshy fingers. "Hurry up already. I'm not heating the neighborhood."

I stumbled over the threshold, my eyes watering at the reek of lavender.

"Leave your sandals on," he said, heading down the hallway. "I don't like feet."

Tatiana had sent me to a madman.

Dumbfounded, I followed Max to a living room at the back of the house and my mouth fell open. Everything was covered in plastic. Not just the sofa, or even the coffee table, which was weird enough, but even the old television and the clock on the wall.

When I sat down, the plastic creaked.

He dropped into his old recliner, taking his time to settle in, like he had to warm up the plastic to mold it to his body. "Dybbuks, huh? Bad business. You want my advice? That was my advice. Bad business. You don't listen too well, do you?"

I leaned forward, my ass sliding on the plastic. "I don't have the luxury of avoiding them. Do you know how to get one out of an enthralled person?"

He groaned. "If I say yes, are you going to make me show you?"

"That's the general idea."

"Do I have to show you how to kill one that's already possessed a host, too?"

"Got that covered."

"That's something at least," Max said. "Dazzle me with your knowledge."

"I say the word 'mut,' tear out the possessed host's heart, and cleave the dybbuk in half with my shadow scythe," I said. "Is it a similar technique for someone who's enthralled?"

"Ha. Try it." Max waved his arms like a magician doing a trick. "And be amaaaazed when the person punches you in the face for trying to rip their chest open. But hey, if you do, I suggest faking your death and finding a country without an extradition treaty."

"Obviously, I didn't mean tearing their heart out," I said. "Just using the scythe and the die command."

"Why would you actually tear out their heart to release the dybbuk anyway? So much mess." He grimaced.

"That's what someone I know does."

Max stared at me for a beat and then made a raspberry noise. "You mean the wolf? Don't model him. You're Banim Shovavim." Max's gruff admiration made me think he saw my magic as superior to his own Ohrist powers. "Your magic is entirely different. Have some pride."

I pressed my palms flat against the yellowed plastic. "Then how do I kill a dybbuk when the host is fully possessed?"

He pulled the handle on the recliner and the footstool popped out. "Stabbing them in the heart with your scythe is enough because of your magic. The dybbuk will leave the corpse for you to kill it."

"And with someone who's only enthralled?"

"It's similar, but with an important caveat."

"Will this work for Laurent as well?" If I could teach him how to save the enthralled, I wouldn't feel so guilty about not doing it myself.

"Did I or did I not just tell you that you're Banim Shovavim with different magic? That jumped up do-gooder is lucky he can kill the possessed. This is beyond his abilities."

My heart sank. "Is there anything he can do for enthralleds?"

"Not that I know of."

I nodded. "Okay. What do I do?"

He shifted to one side and let out a fart. Then he grabbed a can of odor eliminator and blasted it.

I coughed at the lavender spray that hit me in the face.

"Stand up," Max said. "Let me run you through some things with your magic."

I did, clenching my hands into fists so I wouldn't fan the air in front of my face and insult the man who was going to help me save Jude.

"The first thing you need to know about dealing with the enthralled," he said, "is—"

A car alarm blared outside.

Max snapped the footstool down and went to the window. "Damnation." Muttering angrily, he stormed out of the room.

I followed, gulping down fresh air. Lavender and ass were not a winning combo.

He marched down the stairs of his back porch and across his yard to his carport, where he beeped a fob at his car to shut off the alarm. "Stupid thing is so sensitive," he said. "Goes off if you look at it the wrong—"

Someone picked Max up and pitched him to one side like garbage.

Kirk sneered at me. "Payback is a bitch."

So much for dead. However, I didn't have time to have some villainous showdown because the clock was ticking to save Jude.

I widened my eyes. "Are you Kirk Holdencott, the wrestling star? No way."

He blinked, taken aback, then grinned and puffed out his chest. "Yeah, actually. You a fan?"

There were no lights in the carport, and thus no way to animate Delilah or grab the vamp's shadow, since it didn't have a hard outline.

"Oh," I said, calling up my invisibility cloaking, "you have no idea." I ran over to Max, who massaged his shoulder, and shielded him as well.

"We don't hide from vampires." Max shoved me off of him.

I cloaked him again. "We do when they're bent on vengeance and we have a magic lesson to finish."

"You ruined my life." Kirk's razor-sharp fangs descended. "Get out here."

"Hang on, the grown-ups are talking," I said. So much for hoping Yoshi would be Zev's well-oiled death machine hench-vamp. What happened to being on top of the situation? "Listen up, Max, I don't have time for either of us to get injured or worse. My friend's life is on the line."

Max cracked his knuckles. "I can take him with one hand tied behind my back."

"I threw you into a wall," Kirk said.

"Big deal," Max said. "You tiddled me with a bit of fore-play, but can you hammer it home?"

Kirk looked scandalized. "Gross, you pedo."

I grimaced. "There will be no hammering of any sort."

Kirk chucked a metal trash can at Max's car, shattering the driver's side window and bashing in the door. "Let's finish this!"

Max roared and barrelled toward the vampire, head butting him in the stomach. "I just paid that off!"

The two of them hit the ground in a tangle. Kirk went to bite Max, but his face swelled up, his eyes all but disappearing and his fangs swallowed by his fat lips.

I dropped my cloaking. "Is that all out of your system now? Can we get back to the lesson?"

"He. Wrecked. My. Car," Max said. Each word was accompanied by another body part of Kirk's swelling up, until the vampire looked like a Thanksgiving Day parade float.

The vampire lurched to his feet, and Max snickered. It was hard to take the bloodsucker seriously when his hands looked like tiny T-Rex hands in comparison to his bloated limbs and body. I didn't feel like laughing, but I was glad Max had diffused the threat.

Kirk snarled something at us that was totally unintelligible.

"Yes, you're very scary," I said. "Payback will have to wait, however, because I'm busy tonight." Diane had been told Kirk was dead, so Zev wouldn't draw this out. What had gone wrong? Or had this been the plan all along, to tell everyone that Kirk was dead and then quietly shuffle him off overseas?

Max flicked the light on to better inspect the damage to his car, bathing us in a cold bluish glow.

"Max," I said impatiently. "The car isn't going anywhere. Come on."

He stood up with a huff and jabbed two fingers from his eyes to Kirk's. The vampire's eyeballs started to bleed. "Let's go."

"Finally," I said, but as I turned around, there was a meaty thud.

Kirk had tripped Max. The vampire belly-flopped on top of the Ohrist and tore out his throat.

Max gurgled, his eyes wide under deeply creased brows. He reached for his neck, but with a raspy wet breath, his arm fell limply down, and his head lolled sideways, blood staining the concrete like a Rorschach test.

"You killed him." I pressed my hand against my breastbone.

What kind of bullshit magic world was this anyway, and how did I seem to keep triumphing over immediate danger, trying to navigate doing as little harm as possible, only to be blindsided by something so much worse?

How would I save my best friend? Was this the start of me losing everyone who mattered?

A hot rush of rage danced through my veins and Delilah jumped into a combat-ready stance behind me thanks to the overhead bulb.

"Did that hurt? Good." The vampire rushed me, but he wasn't as fast as Lindsey. Right, Kirk had only been turned six months ago. However, with Max dead, the vampire's body had returned to normal.

Ducking low, I spun away, grabbed his shadow and crumpled it. Cold darkness glooped over my left hand.

Kirk struggled to move, calling me every name in the book. Unlike Lindsey who still had very expressive facial movements even if her body was immobilized, Kirk was so paralyzed by my hold that he could barely speak.

"Shut up, you murdering piece-of-shit." I visualized my shadow scythe but nothing happened. "Mut." I shook out my hands, my teeth grinding from the efforts of my concentration. "Come on. Mut."

Nada. Stupid dybbuk-specific weapon.

"I'm going to kill you, you cunt," the vampire said.

"Language," I tsked, and circled him. "You came to my house in the middle of the night, didn't you? To scope things out."

He hawked a glob of spit at my feet.

I tightened my hold on his shadows, my knuckles turning white, and the vampire gasped. "Allow me to share a hard truth with you," I said. "I didn't ruin your life, you did. You lied to Zev about Jude's betrayal, and you told your mother about the golem. I could have forgiven all that but you cost me—" My voice caught. "You cost me answers and took an innocent man's life."

"So you're going to kill me now?" he said. "An eye for an eye crap?"

"Isn't that why you came for me?" I pulled out the lighter that was in my pocket and flicked it, bringing the flame closer and closer to his shadow.

His breathing turned fast and shallow.

I'd flamed Lindsey as some form of justice for killing that pizza employee, but I didn't want to take a life tonight.

I just wanted to save one.

Maybe I was a fool.

The flame went out and I dropped his shadow. "I'm not going to kill you."

Kirk shot me a triumphant smirk, like I'd signed my own death warrant, then his body curled around a stake that was stabbed into his heart. He looked down at it. "Shit," he said, and dissolved into a pile of ash.

I kicked his remains. "I didn't say you weren't going to die."

Yoshi picked up the stake, inclined his head at me, and disappeared into the night. I'd seen him right before I extinguished the lighter, but there's no way he'd just arrived. If he'd acted a few minutes earlier, he would have saved Max.

What a good little minion following his boss's directives to the letter. Spare me, kill Kirk, Max's life was irrelevant.

My belief that all vamps were monsters to be stopped cemented into place.

I knelt down beside Max and gripped his hand, holding it so tightly I was convinced his pulse raced up through my skin, even as his lifeless eyes and glistening flesh from the tear in his neck told a different story. It was a tale nested in the copper tang of old pennies and set to the tune of "I Can't Get No Satisfaction," playing out a nearby open window and the erratic beating of my heart, while I hovered on a shaky precipice with no idea how to find my way back to solid ground.

Eventually, I pulled myself together enough to call Tatiana.

"The artiste is not receiving. Leave a message and when I am so inclined, I'll return it." There was a beep.

Fuck. I hung up. My finger hovered over Laurent's number.

It was one thing to hire him to help me find Jude, but he'd played his part. I had no problem asking for help, but especially after our fight, this was sickeningly like a damsel in distress sending up a flare.

I looked from Max to my phone, made a face and dialed Laurent.

"What?" he said.

"It's Miri, and—"

"Why are you bothering me?" He dripped French arrogance. "I'm certain I have no desire to speak to you. If you think otherwise, leave a message and try your luck." Beep.

"Are you kidding me right now?" I jammed my phone in my pocket.

Fine. I closed Max's eyes, then grabbed him under his armpits and dragged him back into the house. Things got a bit dicey on the stairs, but it's not like the bumps to the back of his head worsened the situation, and he wasn't bleeding anymore so I only tracked dirt across his floor.

The plastic creaked and groaned when I hauled Max onto the sofa. I put a pillow under his head, readjusting his limbs until I settled on his legs stretched straight out and his arms folded across his chest.

"You didn't deserve this and I'm so sorry. Please don't come back as a dybbuk and haunt me. Okay. Well, I'll make sure someone comes for you soon." There was no way I was sitting in a strange house with a corpse, but it was wrong to leave him this way.

After a moment's consideration, I grabbed the can of odor eliminator and sprayed Max from head to toe. There. I think he would have been pleased with that final touch. I bobbed an awkward bow at his body, then headed out into the night.

28

As I drove, I wrote a new to-do plan in my head. The first item was easy. Tell Tatiana about Max. The second—figure out how to unenthrall Jude—was where I got stuck. As in quicksand stuck. Assuming cleaving the dybbuk with my scythe was the same, how did I get it out of Jude to dispense with it?

I had to assume the worst-case scenario that the dybbuk would kill her at sundown on Friday, not Saturday. That gave me less than twenty-four hours to figure this out.

I pulled up in front of my house and cut the engine, resting my head back against the seat. Max was dead because I'd brought trouble to his door. I held my head in my hands, a hard lump gnawing in the pit of my stomach, then I steeled myself and dialed Tatiana's number.

"Miriam," she said. "Was Max able to help you?"

"He's… a vampire got him. I'm sorry."

"Zev already called to apologize that they hadn't gotten their rogue vamp in time." Bullshit. But I put it in my back pocket for another day. Tatiana sighed. "If I know Max, he couldn't wait to get into it with the bloodsucker."

Zev and Tatiana had enough of a connection that he

304

informed her when one of his vamps killed a friend of hers? More than that, he knew who was in her circle? My blood chilled and I rubbed my hands briskly over my arms. If I pissed Tatiana off, would she send the vamps after me? I'd assumed that as Zev was able to keep Lonestars at bay, see past my cloaking, and maintain such a tight hold on his vampires that news of their existence didn't leak out to the Sapien world, he was the most dangerous figure in the city.

I wasn't so certain anymore.

"Did Max have any family?" I said.

"No," Tatiana said. "I'll take care of things. Did he at least teach you how to deal with your problem?"

"Unfortunately not."

"Oh, bubeleh." Her remorse sounded genuine. "You've got a Yiddisher kop. You'll figure it out."

Goldie always said I was smart, too. I spared a wistful smile for my cousin. She lived in Florida most of the time now, married to a great guy, and only came back a few months out of the year.

"Thanks, Tatiana."

I was about to get out of my car when Eli's door opened, and he and Chris stepped out. Chris was a nice enough guy, if somewhat blond and bland. I slid down in my seat, not wanting them to catch me spying, but totally needing to see this for myself so I could call Eli on his crap that he'd leave Chris happier for their time together.

After the shit show of tonight, I was taking a moment of gleeful pettiness. It beat drinking.

Eli clasped Chris' shoulder and Chris tensed. Yes. This was it. Let the fight begin. Eli jogged back inside, while Chris waited with crossed arms. My ex returned with the remaining cheesecake and handed it to Chris.

Chris smiled and made some joke that Eli laughed at.

Son. Of. A. Bitch.

Chris waved and got into his car.

I stared at his departing headlights, shaking my head, jealous of the blithe ease with which Eli moved through the world. Sure, he had his fair share of darkness to deal with as a homicide detective, but he had a team. I was on my own with Jude.

I bit the inside of my cheek. That wasn't exactly true. Laurent had pulled his weight, helping me even after he'd dispatched Mei Lin. I owed him an apology.

There was a rap on my window and I yelped, going for my lighter.

A woman with unnaturally defined biceps motioned for me to roll down my window. "You missed book club," Military Marsha said. "I thought you must be ill, so I brought you some of Jody's pumpkin cranberry cookies." She gave me a fake smile. "But look at you, in the pink of health."

You cow. Jody's cookies were so inedible even the garburator choked on them. I got out of the car with a determined set of my chin. Sure, I'd forgotten all about tonight's meeting, but this was my chance. I could finally break up with book club and tell Marsha my opinion of her book choices and her autocratic ways.

I braced a hand on top of the car door, reconsidering. After all I'd been through, and everything yet to come, I didn't want to be mean. I just wanted out.

"I should have called and let you know I wasn't coming," I said. "The truth is that I haven't really felt connected to our club or the books for some time now. I think it's best if I bow out."

Marsha twisted the foil packet of cookies so hard it blew chunks. "Book club is a year-long commitment. This was clearly outlined in the club rules you were first given. We can't have people flitting in and out willy-nilly mid-year. That would be highly disruptive to our congenial ambience."

"I'm still going to have to decline."

"You agreed to the rules."

"I read an email. That's hardly legally binding."

"One does not quit book club mid-year!" She took a breath and smoothed a hand over her hair. "Sharon is hosting the next one. She found a darling recipe for blinis so we're going with a Russian theme."

God, not the Russians. My shoulders slumped. Please don't be *Doctor Zhivago*. Sharon was a little too fond of her themed meetings. She'd probably cut out two thousand snowflakes and wear a fur hat. "Which book?"

Marsha gave me a vicious smile. "*War and Peace.*"

New to-do list. Fake my death and move to a country with no extradition treaty.

"You'll bring the rosé?" she said.

"Uh-huh," I said weakly.

"Excellent." She clapped her hands. Her arms were so toned that they didn't even jiggle.

If she was an Ohrist, I'd have let Delilah out to play. My fingers twitched. If only I could grab her shadow and sever it from her exceedingly fit body. Who'd be laughing then?

I stilled. Would shadow surgery work on Jude? Max had said removing a dybbuk from someone who was enthralled was similar to when they were fully possessed. What if the difference was accessing the dybbuk through their shadow as opposed to their physical body?

What was the important caveat though?

"Marsha, you might be a real lifesaver." I held up my hand for a high-five, which she hesitantly returned.

"Because of the rosé?"

"Because of the shitty wine and pretentious books and for being you."

"Oh, well. Thank you?"

"You bet." I fired finger guns at her.

She shot me a doubtful look, then thrust the wreckage of the failed baking in my hands and went back to her car.

Grinning, I drove over to Hotel Terminus. If my hypothesis was correct, I didn't want to waste a moment.

Emmett answered the door.

"Where's Huff 'n' Puff?" I said.

"Out fighting something. Like my cane?" He waved a black cane topped with a silver-plated dragon at me. "Naveen delivered it to me. I'm thinking of keeping it, even once I get my leg back."

"Very chic. Is Jude awake?"

Emmett shrugged.

"Well if she isn't, we'll wake her. It's time to get the dybbuk out." I strode confidently over to the elevator.

Laurent had left the door and gate open. He didn't extend this courtesy to others in Jude's situation. He'd done it to ease my discomfort in chaining up my best friend. This lone wolf, who was prone to violence and wielded barbed words as much as his claws, had a huge heart.

I rubbed a hand over the back of my neck, pushing aside my guilt. Apologizing to Laurent was a problem for après-dybbuk-vanquishing me.

My friend was awake, sitting with her legs hugged up to her chest and a distant expression on her face, absently scratching Boo behind her ear.

"Jude."

She gave me a wan smile. "Listen, I'm sorry for what I said earlier."

"Doesn't matter. Shut up."

"You're ruining me making amends on my deathbed."

"How about I get a dybbuk out of you instead and you buy me brunch next time?"

Jude sat up straight.

The gray kitten gave an irritated yowl and stalked off.

"If you can do that," my friend said, "then anything on the menu is on me. An entire tray of mimosas for you."

"Or," I said, a shadow flowing up my left arm to morph

into a scythe, "we'll go dry during the Danger Zone from now on."

"Heh. Yeah. You shouldn't drink then either." She jumped to her feet, rattling the chains. "Brunch on Sundays instead?"

"Hell, yes." I shook out my shoulders. "Brace yourself. This might hurt."

"Wait. Whaaaa—" Her question ended in a screech as I slammed the scythe down and severed her shadow from her body.

The tip of the curved weapon whacked into the iron floor, sending painful reverberations up my arms. "Fuuuuck!"

The dybbuk flew out of it and attacked me in a whir of crimson fury.

"That's not good," Emmett said from behind me.

"Mut!" I yelled. The letters appeared on the blade.

"Jude!" Emmett cried.

She'd collapsed, unconscious.

The dybbuk swarmed me, buzzing and stinging. I swung at it, but it veered away.

"Her shadow's disappeared." Emmett dropped to his knee, tossed his cane aside, and pressed his fingers to her throat.

My inattention cost me. I'd taken my eyes off the dybbuk and when I turned back, it was whizzing through the main room, making a break for the open side door.

"Get back here this instant!" I ran after it, my scythe aloft.

"She doesn't have a pulse," Emmett called out.

The dybbuk was too fast for me. It was going to escape.

Everything geared down into slow motion.

"Nooooooo," I cried in a distorted voice, and flung the shadow weapon.

It tumbled end over end across the room and clattered to the ground a good five feet short of its mark.

The dybbuk paused, hovering in place for a second like it

couldn't believe it was going to get away with this, then the seething mass rushed the door.

Right as Laurent returned.

It dive bombed him, blowing him toward the wall with cannon-like force. He collided with a grunt, his leg buckling as his ankle twisted.

The dybbuk snapped Laurent's head back with some kind of invisible punch and his skull cracked against the wall.

I raced for the scythe, Laurent now doubled over and brought to his knees under the pummelling. Sharp cuts rent his clothing, his blood welling up in thin lines.

"Jude isn't breathing!" Emmett screamed.

I scooped up the shadow scythe and cleaved the dybbuk in half. Leaching of all color, the spirit imploded in on itself and vanished out of existence. The second I'd dropped my magic, I spared Laurent a single glance, gauging the extent of his injuries. "You good?"

He nodded, still on his knees, his hands braced on his thighs.

I sprinted back to the elevator.

Jude lay on the ground, motionless, her eyes closed. She didn't cast a shadow.

"Don't you dare die on me." Shoving Emmett out of the way, I crouched down beside Jude and began CPR compressions.

Emmett started singing this lullaby that sounded sweet until I recognized it as a slowed down version of The Ramones' "I Wanna Be Sedated."

I shot him a *What the hell are you doing?* look between breathing into Jude's mouth and pumping her chest.

"It's what she sang to me when I was first woke up," he said. "We karaoke it together."

The healing power of punk music was no weirder than anything else at this point. I motioned for him to carry on.

The harder I forced air into her lungs, and the more forceful my compressions, the limper she became.

I sat back on my thighs, my shoulders slumped, and gave a final lame chest compression.

Jude was gone.

Emmet's final "ba ba bas" in the song were a mournful dirge.

I swiped a hand over my wet eyes. Why had I gotten so mad at her earlier? What a fool I'd been to waste our last precious hours together.

"Now you're just copping a feel," Jude said in a hoarse voice. She smacked my hand still resting on her chest away.

"Yes!" Emmett high-fived her.

I fell onto my ass with a shuddery exhale. "Holy crap. I thought you were dead."

"No, but..." She flicked her uninjured fingers at her pillow, and nothing happened. "No magic."

Was that the caveat Max had been about to explain? That saving the enthralled came at a cost?

"I'm sorry," I said.

"I'm alive." She sat up unsteadily and hugged me. "I'll deal with the rest."

Emmett scooted closer to Jude on his ass and she patted his thigh.

Laurent hobbled into the elevator, keeping his weight off his injured ankle. "Told you you could do it." He tossed me the keys to unlock Jude's cuffs.

"Impressive how you skipped the praise and went straight to know-it-all."

The cuffs fell to the ground and Jude rubbed her wrists.

"I'd hate to give you unrealistic expectations," Laurent said.

I pressed my lips together so I didn't verbally skewer him for being sharp enough to trade barbs with and for waking me up to feel incredibly alive, when the reality was I'd probably rarely ever get to use my magic or ever see him again. It wasn't fair to take that out on him.

Jude stood up. "I want to go home."

"Want me to drive you?" I said.

"No," Emmett said. "You're not stuffing me in your trunk again."

"Harley has a van," Jude said. "I'll call him."

We all walked out of the elevator. Laurent pulled the gate shut behind us, turned off the light, and hit the call button. The doors closed.

"Harley is an Ohrist?" I said.

"Yup," Jude said, pulling out her phone and dialing. "He helped me bring all the clay into the studio to make Emmett."

Harley showed up soon after to take Jude and Emmett back to her townhouse. I gave her my spare key to her place, since she'd lost her purse in the kidnapping.

"Can I come hang with you and Sadie Mayhem soon?" she said.

"Of course. I told her you'd had a family emergency and that's why you hadn't taken your Scrabble turn." I waved a hand around her face. "We'll have to make up an explanation for this, and fix the lighting so she doesn't see your lack of a… hey. Check it out." I pointed at the floor.

Where the rest of us had hard shadows, Jude had a little inky nub protruding out from her feet.

She flicked her fingers and one of the sofa cushions wobbled. "Will wonders never cease," she said.

Emmett and Laurent fist-bumped and then the golem turned to me. "You're a piece of work, lady."

"Is that a good thing?" I said.

He looked down at his stump. "I don't know." With that, he hobbled out the door using his cane.

Jude thanked Laurent, and then there were two.

He poured himself a drink. "Want one?"

"God, yes." I took a sip of the bourbon he handed me, letting its warmth roll off my tongue and through my body.

He eased himself onto the sofa. "How did you figure out what to do about the dybbuk?"

"I had some help from Tatiana's friend..." I swallowed at Laurent's stormy scowl.

"Who?"

"This guy called Max."

Laurent's eyes darkened with a turbulent cast. I didn't understand the reason for his anger so I felt compelled to add, "But he's dead now."

His hand tightened on the glass. "All this time and she could have given me a way to help them. Now I can't even talk to this guy. Fuck!"

I frowned. Help all enthralleds or was Laurent speaking about someone specific? I gestured helplessly. "It's not like that. Tatiana didn't withhold a way to save them from you."

"Semantics. Her friend knew how to help the enthralled and she didn't tell me about him."

I paused. "Did you ask?"

"I shouldn't have had to!" He kicked the ottoman, sending it flying across the room.

I balanced my glass on the arm of my chair, weighing my words. "I realize I haven't known you long, or very well, but you really do give off the impression that other people's assistance isn't required or particularly wanted."

He stared at me in stony silence, so I blathered on.

"Max only told me a bit before a vampire got him, and I had to figure out what to actually do, but he was extremely clear that only a Banim Shovavim could pull this off. I asked specifically, you see, but he didn't know of any way for you to help enthralleds, so Tatiana really wasn't holding out on you."

Something shifted in his eyes, eased, and warmed. I

folded my hands in my lap, relieved that I'd removed his anger at his aunt.

"You asked him for me? Specifically?" he said.

I gave a soft surprised laugh. "Of course."

He shook his head. "I don't know what to make of you, Mitzi."

"Anyone would have done the same, knowing how important it was to you."

He traced the rim of his highball with a finger but didn't comment.

Magenta, gold, and rose bled through the night sky, sending faint shimmering rays dancing across the floorboards. I swept my fingers through a beam, the dawn of this new day charging the air with a radiant hope, even as I wished for a few more moments of night's stillness to bask in my remaining time with this man.

Melancholy, I finished my drink. It would be weird to linger here any longer.

Laurent stretched out his hurt leg with a wince.

I stood up. "I'm going, so you can shift in private if you need to heal."

"Up to you. I'm not going to shift for this though." His clothes were torn, he had bloody gashes all over him, his jaw was starting to bruise, and he acted like it was nothing.

Laurent was dangerous, but at the end of the day, did it come down to him rattling around alone in this boarded-up hotel, with only books, music, and his inner demons for company?

"Come on, tough guy." I tugged on his sleeve.

"Where are we going?" he said, putting down his untouched drink.

"To get you cleaned up."

29

LAURENT HOPPED UP ON THE COUNTER NEXT TO the sink while I grabbed the first aid kit from the cupboard underneath.

Setting the pack on the counter, I had him track my finger with his eyes. "Any dizziness?"

"No. Are we done?" He slid forward to get down, and winced, his lips compressing.

I placed my hand on his chest to keep him from leaving. "Suck it up."

Laurent looked at my fingers splayed against his chest and his pecs under my palm tightened. "I don't need you to mother me."

I unzipped the kit with too much force, catching the fabric in the teeth of the zipper. "It's my fault that the dybbuk came after you," I said, yanking on the damn cloth until the zipper slid free. "Just let me do this. Take off your shirt."

Laurent hesitated, warily eyeing the kit clenched in my hand, but he pulled his shirt off, his biceps flexing. There was a sinuousness to his movement, his chiseled torso a testament to his strength and purpose.

I tore the package of cotton batting open, sending several puffs flying across the room, then turned on the tap, testing the water with a finger. "I'm sorry for snapping at you earlier."

"Forget it. I don't want your guilt. Or your pity." He watched me through heavy-lidded eyes, a slash of intense green clouded with wariness. "Go home, Miriam."

My jaw tensed. Laurent didn't use my proper name. I exhaled slowly. "As soon as I've seen to these cuts." Dampening the cotton, I wiped away the blood on his shoulder.

"Thank you," I said. "For helping me save Jude."

"I don't need your gratitude either."

"Then let me get a look at your jaw," I snapped, "because if it's broken we need to wire it, and wouldn't that be a damn shame not to be able to listen to you anymore."

He tensed, then slowly exposed his throat.

I fumbled tossing the cotton ball into the trash. In anyone else, his was a gesture of submission. In Laurent, the sweep of his throat to his collarbone felt like a test.

Placing one hand lightly on his stubbled jaw to tip up his head, I cleaned a cut, his pulse thrumming up through the cotton into my fingertips and his eyes never leaving mine.

What counted as a wrong move that he'd react badly to? Being too rough? Being too gentle? Having the gall to take care of him at all?

He widened his legs for me to step in closer, and when I didn't immediately, his lips curled into the faintest challenging smirk.

Heart thudding in my throat, I drew near, checking his jawline with feather-light strokes that grew firmer and slower until my palm lay against his scratchy stubble. I jerked away quickly, accidentally whacking him on the nose.

I notched my chin up to compensate for my flaming cheeks. "I've made my diagnosis."

"I'll live to snicker-snack another day?" he said wryly.

"Much to the relief of Jabberwockies everywhere."

One hand hovered over his discarded shirt and I was positive he'd reached his limit, but he pulled the handcloth from the towel holder and held it out. "Use this."

Ducking my head to hide my smile, I warmed the towel up under the water, wringing it out thoroughly before attending to a nasty gash on his left pec.

"Why did that Sinatra song spook you so badly?" he said.

I dabbed at a patch of dried blood with too much force and he winced. I gentled my movements. "It caught me off guard."

Laurent leaned in, his nose almost brushing mine. "Liar," he murmured. His French accent rolled through me, making my skin hot and cold in patches.

My belly clenched and I took a shuddery breath. "That song was playing when my parents were murdered." I braced myself for his pity.

Instead, he caught my hand, moving it and the cloth across his torso to an injury on his abdomen, his muscles tensing as the fabric brushed over them.

There were mere inches between us, the back of his hand covering mine skimming against the fabric of my clothing.

His lips parted and I tracked the movement, not daring to blink. "What a waste of a perfectly good tune," he said.

A startled laugh burst out of me and he gave this soft hum of pleasure, low in his throat, that banished any lingering self-pity.

I rinsed out the cloth and attended to the final cut on his forehead.

"How old were you?" Laurent said. He had a tiny imperfection in his left eye, a black dot that I'd never had noticed had I not been this close.

"Fifteen."

"You finished prodding me?" Laurent folded his fingers over mine, enveloping them in his warmth for a brief second.

"Yup." I zipped up the first aid kit. "Well, I should get—"

He caught hold of my wrist, stroking his thumb over the sensitive skin for the briefest instant, before releasing me. "Thank you," he said gruffly.

I stared dumbly at where he'd touched me, every nerve ending having flared to life. "It's the least I could do."

"No," he said quietly, "it was far more than most. Generally people can't wait for me to leave once I've completed a job, but you stuck around. Made sure I was okay."

I scattered facts like birdseed, but was stingy with the details about myself. Laurent was the same way with personal information and the weight of these words charged them from simple gratitude to the key to a treasure map, given while both of us tumbled mid-air.

He was cut and bruised from the dybbuk attack and he held himself tensely, cradling a shoulder. But his eyes shimmered like a verdant field on a hot summer day, mirroring my exhilaration that we might just stick our landing.

I patted his shoulder. "Get some rest."

"Come on, I'll walk you out." He escorted me to the side door in silence.

I smiled at him to cover my sudden awkwardness. "Well, thanks. It's been…" I threw my hands up. "Crazy."

"No shit." He opened the door. "I guess I'll see you around."

"Yeah." I waited a few seconds but he didn't add anything. "Take care."

I only got a handful of steps away before my phone buzzed. "It's a text from Tatiana to come see her at the Bear's Den later."

"Don't do it," Laurent said from the doorway.

"I have to. Max died. I owe her the courtesy of seeing her in person." I spared only a single glance back for the man with the frown on his face.

I left the radio on the classical music station for the drive home, humming along to the lilting piano concerto and letting the final sweeping notes fade away with a bittersweet feeling, reminiscent of the time Laurent and I had shared.

There were still decisions to be made about my magic, especially in regards to my family, as well as Jude's trauma to support her through, and I made list after list in my head, selecting and discarding ways to move forward.

I was able to get a few decent hours of sleep and another shower before I headed over to the Bear's Den on Friday afternoon, using the same parkade elevator that I'd gone through before.

This time, the basement button easily revealed itself to me. I double-clicked the switch hook on the broken payphone, hung up the receiver, and the wall swung away.

Vikram lumbered toward me.

"Hey, friend." I waved.

"Bah. Tatiana is at a banquette over by the bar."

I thanked him and made my way through the mostly empty speakeasy.

Tatiana greeted me with a smile, motioning for me to help myself to the carafe of coffee and the steaming basket of croissants. "I just woke up," she said, "and I like to start my day with breakfast, even at 2PM."

Her silver pixie cut framed her oversized red glasses, but today's outfit consisted of a one-piece purple jumpsuit with enormous white buttons. Spry and alert, she was the most youthful eighty-year-old imaginable. Despite my reservations about why she'd asked me here, there was so much to admire about her.

"It was thoughtful of you to spray Max with the odor eliminator," Tatiana said, handing me the basket of sugar packets. "He did love a good lavender shpritz."

Uh, everything in that place smelled of lavender. How did she know what I'd done?

"Shpritz, fire hose, same same." I poured some coffee,

319

adding milk and sugar, and took a sip of the rich aromatic brew. Breaking open a flaky croissant, I slathered on some raspberry jam from the small ceramic pot. "This smells incredible."

"Vikram employs a pastry chef from France."

"Is that standard speakeasy fare?"

Tatiana laughed. "Nothing about the Bear's Den is standard. But I didn't invite you here for breakfast."

"I suspected as much." The croissant was buttery and melt-in-my-mouth light.

"You're an interesting woman, Miriam. You have life experience and magic that most of us don't."

"She has a job." Laurent slid into the booth next to me. "Back off, Tatiana."

The fizzy feeling at seeing him again warred with the bristling desire to tell him that he was the one who should back off, crashing my private meeting like this, but Tatiana spoke first.

"Don't you think Miriam should decide for herself, nephew?"

"Let's just say I'm here to make sure she understands the fine print."

I looked between them, my brows creased. "Decide what? Now I feel like I'm caught in a pissing contest. Explain yourself, Tatiana. Laurent, keep quiet until I ask for your input."

Laurent crossed his arms, fur bursting out over his hands.

I rolled my eyes and the fur vanished.

"I have a side business helping Ohrists who find themselves in a bind," Tatiana said.

"She's a fixer," Laurent said sullenly.

I shot him a *Did I ask for your help?* look and he snarkily mimed zipping his lips.

"Isn't that a mafia thing?" I said to Tatiana.

Laurent took a sip of my coffee and made a face. "Consider her a mafia of one."

"You always were such a flatterer, Lolo," Tatiana said.

"So much for staying quiet." I nudged Laurent's leg with mine.

"Maybe if you'd modeled it for me, I'd be better at it," he said.

"You're impossible." I pulled my coffee away.

"If you two are finished quibbling?" Tatiana raised an eyebrow and I nodded for her to continue.

"I assist people who for one reason or another can't go to the Lonestars or the Sapien authorities," she said. "All the travel I did with my art career provided a good cover to carry out my assignments, but as I got older, I had to subcontract out."

"Tell her about your high turnover," Laurent said, pouring himself his own cup of coffee. "About how your subcontractors," he sneered the word, "are eventually killed by blindspots from all the magic they expend." He drank his java black today.

Tatiana helped herself to a croissant with the silver tongs, placing another one on my crumb-filled plate. "Eat."

"That's why you want me." I spread jam on the pastry. No point wasting these puppies because they were far superior to anything I'd ever bought. "Banim Shovavim are immune to blindspots."

"That and you brought about the death of my current subcontractor." Tatiana bit into her croissant.

A glop of jam fell off my knife onto my plate. "Max?"

Tatiana nodded, her mouth full.

Laurent opened his mouth, but I put my hand on his thigh. "One could argue," I said, "that the responsibility lies with you, seeing as you sent him to me."

Tatiana swallowed and chuckled. "Mea culpa?"

"There's also the fact that I'm not interested." I held up the croissant in cheers. "Though I do appreciate you introducing me to these amazing treats."

"I suppose if you aren't going to use your magic anymore, then it would be easy enough to put this episode behind you." Tatiana wiped her mouth with a linen napkin.

"I'm not running away and hiding again."

"Oh, nothing like that. I could ensure that the people who saw your powers don't discuss it, and convince Zev to stay mum about the Banim Shovavim in town."

"You'd do that for me?"

"Read the fine print," Laurent muttered.

Tatiana lightly smacked his hand. "I would indeed do that for you. No strings attached."

Delilah vibrated under the soles of my feet. I'd cut her away once and had withered. Now, I'd gotten a second chance to bloom. Did I really want to rip that opportunity out at the roots? Years of dull law books and silence stretched out ahead of me, the excitement and passion I'd rekindled dying away until, with a sputter, there was nothing left.

"And if I keep using my magic?" I said.

"Then you come work for me."

"Impossible. I won't engage in illegal or unethical behavior," I said, my relief at not being thrown into a moral quandary tempered by feeling I was peering through the fence at the rides at the fair, watching everyone else have fun.

"Doing what's right often involves breaking the rules," she said.

"You'd know," Laurent said.

Tatiana wagged a finger at him. "Don't be a hypocrite, Lolo. You kill people on a regular basis."

He set his cup down on the saucer hard enough to rattle it. "The host is already dead."

"You think that would matter in a Sapien court of law? All they'd see was a serial killer."

I massaged my temples. "Give me a minute."

"I'd pay you," Tatiana said. "Whatever you're making, I'll match it."

"It's not about money." It was kind of about money because I had bills to pay and a child to support.

"It's about Sadie and keeping both of you safe, am I right?" she said. "Especially since your parents' murder."

I spilled my coffee, quickly grabbing my napkin to blot up the liquid. Laurent tried to take the cloth from me, but I pushed him away and dropped the soggy fabric on the table, my fists clenched. "Did you kill my parents?"

"No." There was no guile in her expression. "You think you've been hidden all these years?" Tatiana shook her head. "I guarantee you haven't been. It didn't matter that you were raised in a Sapien household or took your cousin's last name—"

"More people telling you things?" I said, bitterly.

"Name changes are a matter of public record and I know how the dark side of the Ohrist world works. The only thing that kept you safe all these years was the fact that whomever went after your parents believed you were a blank."

Goosebumps broke out over my skin and I hugged myself. "A blank?"

"Without magic." Laurent drained his coffee. "But born to magic parents."

"That protection is gone now," Tatiana said. "You have two choices. Go back to being a blank or work for me and I'll keep you and your family safe from those people. From the vampires as well, if necessary. Zev won't make a move against you if I forbid it."

"You didn't forbid it with me," Laurent said. "It's an empty promise."

"You didn't ask," she said.

Laurent tensed, likely remembering I'd said the exact same thing to him about Max. If we'd been better friends, I would have rubbed his back to calm him down, but instead I folded my hands in my lap.

"Why can you order Zev around?" I said. "What do you have on him?"

"Zev can be made to see reason with the right incentive. The carrot is generally more effective than the stick."

My mouth twisted. "Except in my case."

"This isn't the stick," Tatiana said. "Trust me, you'd know if it was. This is the reality of your situation. If you want to use your magic, you will be in danger. I can protect you, so long as you get over your moral hang-ups. You get excitement, adventure, and the added bonus that I'll help you find your parents' killers." She smiled. "Sounds like the carrot to me. Do we have a deal?"

Was this mazel or free will? Power or empowerment? I could walk away and take my chances, never use my magic again, and bury myself in my work and my parenting like I had before, and do what was expected of me.

Or, I could blow up my life, firmly embrace my magic, and possibly trade away my morals for my family's safety and the names of those who'd destroyed my childhood.

I couldn't be a wayward child for a few hours a week with no repercussions. It either colored my entire life or I shut it down.

When Jude had quit the corporate world, it was because her Sunday night dread attacks had gotten acute. I'd never suffered from them, but now I understood. How long would it take before I lived for 5PM and that feeling of being released out of the prison gates into a fleeting freedom? Even if I miraculously landed my dream librarian job, I'd be reading about adventures instead of living them.

I turned the silver stirring spoon over in my fingers. "I—"

"She can't work for you," Laurent said, smoothly, "because we already discussed her coming to work for me saving the enthralled. She doesn't require either of your choices."

For a second, hope burst hot and bright inside me. Did the Lone Wolf really want a partner? My morals would remain intact, but given Zev's ability to compel Laurent, it wouldn't come with the same protection, nor could he pay me. Not that I was really considering his offer, because it wasn't real.

I slumped back against the banquette. I was floundering in the stormy waves and he'd simply thrown me a lifeline. Sadly, in my case, it only led to a different piece of wreckage.

There were two choices, both dangerous for different reasons, so which was the path of least regret? I glanced down at my shadow. Or the one of most possibility?

As a teen, I'd been scared and alone, and I'd hidden the secret of my magic under a shiny sheen of respectability. Nothing to see here, folks. After years of therapy with Eli, I prided myself on my self-awareness, but I'd been fooling myself as much as I'd accused the others of doing. Responsibility, invisibility, those were comforting excuses I'd used because I was scared to keep landing wrong.

"What would I tell everyone that I do?" I said.

Laurent threw up his hands.

Tatiana's expression softened, and she squeezed his arm. "It's not the same thing, Lolo, and you know it."

He shook his head and stalked off without another word.

Tatiana watched him go, her eyes clouded with worry.

"Will he be all right?" I said.

She shrugged, a weariness in her gesture. "As for you, say you've accepted a private contract from a world-famous artist to catalog years of family letters and documents to assist with her memoirs. We have a deal then?"

"I'll need to give two weeks' notice and I draw the line at hurting or killing anyone human, but yes. We have a deal."

We shook on it. Tatiana ordered another basket of croissants for me to take home.

I pulled up to my house, smiling at its neat white trim and the budding rosebush under the picture window. The sun warmed my skin and the sky was there for the taking.

Shoving my newly purchased pack of batteries in my purse, I got out of my car and flopped on my sofa, thrilled to be home with no immediate crisis looming over me.

Sadie had filled in some of the Broadway puzzle. I picked up this one piece that I'd sworn was from some other puzzle entirely, but with the new part completed, I immediately found where it slotted in. It unlocked a whole section of three other musical theater posters.

The front door opened.

"Mom?" Sadie came into the living room. "I saw your car and came to say hi."

"Hey. Help yourself." I patted the croissant box, fitting one more piece into the jigsaw.

"Did you duck out of work?" she said.

"Played hookey."

"Mother." She widened her eyes theatrically and dumped her backpack on the ground. "What a terrible influence you are." She bit into a croissant and flashed me a thumbs up.

I prayed that didn't turn out to be true. "I've got a new to-do list."

"Does it come with more of these? Because yummy." She sprayed crumbs.

"Swallow before speaking, feral child."

She grinned and swallowed. "Okay, hit me."

"Quit my job and go work as an archivist for an eccentric artist."

My daughter blinked. "I didn't see that coming."

"Go big or go home, kid."

"Evidently. Hey, Aunt Jude finally played her Scrabble word." Sadie held up her phone. "Triple word score, too."

Jude vertically laid down her tiles to fill in gaps between other words to form "renaissance."

"Impressive." I raised my eyebrows. "She kicked your butt."

"She got lucky," Sadie grumbled.

"You know, the renaissance marked the end of the Middle Ages," I said. "It was a rebirth, ushering in a different way of thinking and acting." I smiled, nodding. "It's a good word."

It could mean a lot of things, anywhere from an entirely new life slinging sangria in Spain to a new twist on an old dream. Call it a wild hunch, but I had a feeling that there would be quite a few twists in my life now that Tatiana was involved.

And almost certainly more if I crossed paths with a certain grumpy wolf.

Thank you for reading THROWING SHADE!

Join Miri in her next adventure.

MADE IN THE SHADE (MAGIC AFTER MIDLIFE #2)

Miriam Feldman's got a murder to solve, a mouthy golem to corral, and her name to clear. Quite frankly, she's swamped.

Her new gig as a fixer for the magic community is a lot like being a full-time mom to someone else's kids... they get annoying faster but don't respond to guilt trips. And sure, maybe she feels kind of grumpy and stabby about these irritating jobs, but that doesn't mean she killed her latest client!

As far as the magic police are concerned, Miri with her particular powers and her wolf shifter friend Laurent might as well have "guilty of murder" tattooed on their foreheads. If Miri and Laurent lose this fight, it'll be a one-way trip to Deadman's Island. Talk about a real buzzkill for their easy banter and deepening chemistry.

Even worse, the non-magic cops are also investigating the crime—and Miri's ex-husband is the lead detective. This wasn't how she meant to pop his cherry about the existence of magic, but the time for foreplay is over.

To unmask the real killer, Miri will have to navigate hidden agendas, lies, and the undead. But hey, she's faced worse; she used to be on the PTA.

While you're here, check out the first books in my funny sexy urban fantasy series! Both series are complete and ready to binge read.

BLOOD & ASH (THE JEZEBEL FILES #1)

Cold-blooded kidnappers. Long-lost magic. When things get serious, she goes full Sherlock.

Ashira Cohen takes pride in being the only female private investigator in Vancouver. With her skills, her missing persons case should be a piece of cake.

She wasn't counting on getting bashed in the skull, revealing a hidden tattoo and supernatural powers she shouldn't possess.

Or the bitter icing on top: a spree of abductions and terrifying ghostly creatures on a deadly bender.

And don't even get her started on the golems.

Reluctantly partnered with her long-time nemesis Levi, the infuriating leader of the magic community, Ash resolves to keep her focus on the clue trail and off their sexual tension because WTF is up with that?

But with a mastermind organization pulling strings from the shadows and Levi's arrogance driving her to pick out his body bag, can Ash rescue the captives and uncover the truth or will the next blood spilled be her own?

THE UNLIKEABLE DEMON HUNTER (NAVA KATZ #1)

The Brotherhood wants her gone. The demons want her dead. Not bad for her first day as a Chosen One.

Nava Katz cares about two things: perfecting the art of being a hot mess and her hard-working twin brother. But she accidentally torches his life-long dream when she disrupts his induction ceremony into a secret demon-hunting fraternity and steals his destiny.

Horrified she's now expected to take his place, Nava is faced with something she never wanted: a purpose.

The society isn't cool with a woman in their ranks and teams her with an ex-rock star handler to keep her in line. Too bad he's exactly what Nava's always wanted: the perfect bad boy fling with no strings attached, because a hook-up with him is as dangerous as the vengeful demon out for blood–her brother's.

And Nava's the only one who can save him.

Odds of survival: meh.

Odds of a good time before she bites it: much better.

Every time a reader leaves a review, an author gets ... a glass of wine. (You thought I was going to say "wings," didn't you? We're authors, not angels, but *you'll* get heavenly karma for your good deed.) Please leave yours on your favorite book site, especially Amazon to help other readers discover my stories.

BECOME A WILDE ONE

ACKNOWLEDGMENTS

Thank you to the wonderful best-selling authors (the Fab 13) who founded paranormal women's fiction. They didn't just sit around thinking that it would be great to write about older heroines having magic adventures, they talked to their readers and then made it a reality. I would never have known the joy of writing Miri without the work they did to get this genre off the ground.

Big hugs to my husband and daughter for listening to me for hours while I created this world. You both not only gave me great ideas, you kept me stocked in baked goods and made me go outside into the sunshine. This journey would be meaningless without you both.

Not gonna lie, it was weird writing this book during the pandemic. My online friendships became incredibly precious to me and I thank every single one of you for making me laugh and keeping me sane.

Elissa Van Struth, where would I be without you? (The answer is: filled with unvented rants and going down the path of terrible ideas.) I'm very lucky to have you as my friend.

Happily, after two complete series together, my brilliant

editor Alex Yuschik is still by my side. Their editor letters excite me, they push me to grow with every single book, and they totally get my sense of humour. I am blessed to have them in my corner.

Last, but never ever least, all of my thanks and love to my Wilde Ones, with special gratitude to Julie Watkins and Helen Wyatt for the tagline ideas. Every time I think about the fact that all of you passionate readers have chosen to spend time with the wacky voices in my head that I happened to put down on paper, I am humbled and awed. Keep the sarcasm coming.

ABOUT THE AUTHOR

A global wanderer, former screenwriter, and total cynic with a broken edit button, Deborah (pronounced deb-O-rah) writes funny urban fantasy and paranormal women's fiction.

Her stories feature sassy women who kick butt, strong female friendships, and swoony, sexy romance. She's all about the happily-ever-after, with a huge dose of hilarity along the way.

Deborah lives in Vancouver, along with her husband, daughter, and asshole cat, Abra.

"Magic, sparks, and snark! Go Wilde."

www.deborahwilde.com

Made in the USA
Middletown, DE
29 April 2021